D0119780

THIS BOOK SHOULD BE RETURNED ON OR BEFORE THE LATEST
DATE SHOWN TO THE LIBRARY FROM WHICH IT WAS BORROWED

AUTHOR	CLASS F.

TITLE

THE NIGHTINGALE SISTERS

Violet The new night sister is not all she seems. Who is she and what dark secret is she hiding? As the mystery deepens, Sister Wren is determined to find out the truth.

Dora The student nurse is struggling with her own secret, and with her heartbreak over Nick. A new arrival on the ward brings the chance to put a smile back on her face. But can she really get over Nick so easily?

Millie Dora's fellow student is also torn between two men in her life. But then an unexpected friendship with an elderly patient makes her question where her heart – and her future – really lies.

THE NIGHTINGALE SISTERS

The Nightingale Sisters

by

Donna Douglas

Magna Large Print Books
Long Preston, North Yorkshire,
BD23 4ND, England.

British Library Cataloguing in Publication Data.

Douglas, Donna
    The Nightingale sisters.

    A catalogue record of this book is
    available from the British Library

    ISBN   978-0-7505-3869-5

First published in Great Britain in 2013 by Arrow

Copyright © Donna Douglas 2013

Cover illustration © Colin Thomas

Donna Douglas has asserted her right under the Copyright, Designs
and Patents Act, 1988 to be identified as the author of this work

Published in Large Print 2014 by arrangement with
Random House Group Ltd.

Magna Large Print is an imprint of Library Magna Books Ltd.

Printed and bound in Great Britain by
T.J. (International) Ltd., Cornwall, PL28 8RW

01497724

Chapter One

It was a bitterly cold December evening in 1935 when Violet Tanner arrived at the Nightingale Hospital in Bethnal Green.

Fires were lit in every ward, as the biting snow-laden wind howled like a wild beast, flinging fistfuls of sleet at the windows. Babies cried in fear on the Children's ward, and even the patients in Male Orthopaedics, usually so full of jokes and bravado, stared fearfully at the branches swaying close to the glass and agreed they'd never known a night like it.

Outside, nurses on their way to supper clutched their thick navy cloaks around them as they hurried across the courtyard, heads bent, hands clapping on their starched caps as best they could.

Sister Wren saw her first. She usually liked to arrive early to supper, but had stopped to reprimand a student she'd found taking a shortcut down the passageway that was reserved for sisters.

The girl had complained that she couldn't go outside because she'd forgotten her cloak. But Sister Wren was having none of it.

'And whose fault is that? It doesn't give you the right to wander down the sisters' corridors, does it?' she had snapped.

'No, Sister.' The girl, a second year called Benedict, was just the kind Sister Wren most despised, with that perky blonde prettiness which drew

7

medical students like wasps around a jam jar.

'No, indeed. Now go back the way you came and cross the courtyard like all the other nurses.'

Benedict glanced apprehensively at the sleet thrashing against the window, then back at Sister Wren. Her round blue eyes were full of appeal. No doubt if Sister Wren had been a man she would be falling over herself by now, offering to carry her across the wind-swept courtyard.

'No, Sister,' she sighed.

Sister Wren watched her walk back down the passageway, head bowed in defeat. She smiled to think what a bedraggled state the girl would be in when she returned from supper. With any luck, her ward sister would be utterly furious.

She turned, saw the woman standing at the far end of the passageway, and hurried towards her.

'You there!' she called out bossily. 'What do you think you're doing?'

'I'm looking for Matron's office.' Her voice was low and husky, with the slightest trace of a country accent. Sister Wren had to draw close to hear her.

'And you are?'

'My name is Violet Tanner. I'm the new Night Sister.'

'Oh.' Sister Wren appraised the woman with a glance. In her early-thirties, very tall – although most people towered over Sister Wren, diminutive as she was – and dark. The hair that curled out from under her hat had the blue-black sheen of a magpie's wing. Sister Wren always jealously noticed hair because hers was so thin and poor, no matter how many miracle permanent waves she had. The woman's coat looked expensive, but was not the latest fashion. Sister Wren read *Vogue* and knew quality when she saw it, even if she couldn't afford it herself.

In short, someone worth knowing, she decided.

'You've taken a wrong turning, I'm afraid. I'll walk with you and show you the way,' she offered.

'There's no need. If you just tell me where to go–'

'It's no trouble. I'm going that way myself.'

She was actually heading in the opposite direction, but there was no chance she was going to miss being the first to find out everything about the new Night Sister.

'My name is Miriam Trott, and I'm Sister on Gynae,' she introduced herself as they set off. 'You'll call me Sister Wren, as that is the name of my ward.'

Violet Tanner nodded, but didn't make any further reply. In fact, she didn't offer much conversation as Sister Wren led the way through a warren of passageways back to Matron's office.

'It's rather a maze, isn't it?' she tried again. 'So easy to get lost, with all these buildings stuck together in such a higgledy-piggledy fashion. But you'll get used to it in time.' She glanced sidelong at the new sister. 'Was your last hospital a large place, too?'

'I was nursing a private patient.'

'Oh, and where was that?'

'Suffolk.' She bit out the word, as if reluctant to allow a single syllable to escape her lips.

'Really? I have family in Suffolk.' Sister Wren seized eagerly on the titbit. 'Where were you?'

'A small village. Very rural. I doubt you'd know it.'

'Well, I might–' Sister Wren took one look at Miss Tanner's forbidding expression and did not dare go on.

She tried another tack. 'I suppose you'll be moving into the sisters' block, if you haven't already? Miss Filcher – the old Night Sister, that was – had the room across the hall from mine. Not that she died in that room,' she added hastily. 'No, she dropped dead on duty. Can you imagine it? She made sure she gave her report to all the ward sisters first, though. Typical Miss Filcher, always so conscientious.' She sighed. 'Anyway, her room is very nice. It's on the corner, so it's double aspect. And it looks over the gardens...'

'I won't be living in.'

Sister Wren stared at her. 'Why not?'

'I have made other arrangements.'

'But all the sisters–'

'Ah, I see where I am now. Matron's office is at the end of this corridor, isn't it?' Miss Tanner cut her off bluntly. 'I won't keep you any longer, I'm sure you have a great deal to do.'

'But–'

'Thank you very much for your help, Sister Wren.'

'Wait...,' Sister Wren called after her. But Miss Tanner had already gone.

The fact that Miss Tanner had been so infuriatingly vague didn't stop Sister Wren being desperate to share all the gossip in the dining room.

'I've seen her,' she announced as she arrived,

10

late and breathless, at the sisters' table. Their corner of the dining room was an oasis of order and calm, their long table presided over by maids scuttling to and from the serving hatch. The rest of the vast dining room echoed to the clatter of plates, the scraping of chairs and the chatter of young women's voices.

'There you are, Miriam.' Sister Blake looked up with a smile. 'We were beginning to worry about you. We thought there might be an emergency on your ward.'

'As if that would make her miss her supper,' Sister Holmes muttered under her breath. Sister Wren glared at her as a maid quietly set a plate in front of her.

'If you must know, I was taking our new Night Sister to Matron's office.' She looked around at them all in triumph. It wasn't often she could command attention at the table. They were usually too busy discussing patients or listening to one of Sister Blake's amusing stories.

She waited for them to bombard her with eager questions. But all she got were a couple of interested nods before they went back to discussing the students' new ward allocation.

'Did you hear what I just said? I've met the new Night Sister,' she prompted them.

'And?' Sister Hyde said. 'Did she have two heads?'

Sister Wren sent her a sour look but said nothing. Not even the other sisters spoke up to the Sister in charge of Female Chronics. Sister Hyde was in her sixties, tall, gaunt-framed and utterly fearsome. Sister Wren had been afraid of her

11

since her own days as a student at the Night-ingale.

'I daresay we'll all meet her soon enough,' Sister Holmes observed, helping herself to vegetables from the serving dish.

'Really, ladies, you could show a bit more interest,' Sister Blake rebuked them mildly. 'Sister Wren is desperate to share her gossip, and no one is listening to her.' She turned to Sister Wren, her dark eyes sparkling. 'You can tell me. I'm utterly agog.'

'It's hardly gossip,' Sister Wren replied sullenly. She could never tell if Sister Blake was making fun of her or not. She always had a smile on her face, as if the whole world was some kind of private joke. 'I've just seen her, that's all.'

'And what was she like?'

'If you must know, I thought there was something rather odd about her.'

'You were right, Sister Hyde. She does have two heads!' Sister Blake laughed.

'There's something odd about all Night Sisters, if you ask me,' Sister Parry chimed in from the far end of the table. 'I've never understood what kind of nurse chooses to work a permanent night shift, prowling the corridors when everyone else is asleep.'

'Not everyone,' Sister Hyde said. 'Patients tend to be very restless at night. That's when they feel most frightened and alone. They need someone to reassure them.'

'So do the nurses,' Sister Holmes agreed. 'It's a big responsibility for a young student, finding herself in charge of a ward all night. They need

12

someone reliable they can call on if there's an emergency.'

'I used to be more afraid of the Night Sister than glad to see her when I was a pro,' Sister Blake confessed merrily. 'I was always worried she'd come across us having a midnight tea party with the medical students in the ward kitchen.'

The other sisters laughed, and even Sister Hyde looked slightly amused as she tutted and shook her head.

'It's not just that,' Sister Wren insisted over their laughter. 'There was something peculiar about Miss Tanner. Something ... mysterious.'

'Dear me, have you been reading those lurid detective magazines of yours again?' Sister Holmes said. 'You really shouldn't, you know. They only give you nightmares.'

Sister Wren felt her cheeks burn as the other sisters laughed. She thought about Miss Tanner's clipped, abrupt manner and those dark eyes that never quite met hers.

'You can laugh,' she said. 'But I'm telling you, there's something about that woman that isn't right.'

Just before midnight, Violet Tanner made another round. The howling of the wild wind seemed more menacing in the darkness of the sleeping hospital, and the swaying tree branches clawed at the windows as if they would smash the glass. With all the noise outside, Violet barely had need of the soft-soled shoes she wore to move soundlessly down the winding corridors.

The cluster of buildings, connected by a warren

13

of passageways and staircases that had been so difficult for her to navigate during the day, was already beginning to seem familiar to her, even in the darkness.

She turned a corner and found herself in an office corridor so long that the end was swallowed in impenetrable blackness. Violet held her torch higher, making the shadows leap and dance around her.

As she passed the first door, a frightened squeal made her jump.

'Who's there?' a voice squeaked. The next minute a woman's face loomed out of the shadows, eyes bulging with terror. She brandished a broom like a weapon.

Violet recognised her as one of the cleaners she had taken on earlier. As Night Sister, her first duty had been to go down to the Porters' Lodge and choose from the women who gathered there every evening, hoping for a night's work cleaning the offices. As it was so foul outside, only a few of the most desperate had come. Violet was glad she hadn't had to turn anyone away.

'Beg your pardon, Sister, I thought you was a ghost.' The woman lowered her broom, her hand moving to press against her fluttering heart. 'I got lost, and I've been wandering around here in the dark. Now I dunno where I am...' Her voice trembled. 'And the lights aren't working. I reckon there's been a power cut or summat.'

The woman's eyes were round with fear. 'On a terrible night like this and with everything so dark – well, you imagine all sorts, don't you?'

'Don't worry. You're quite safe here.'

The woman looked at her admiringly. 'I bet you're not frightened of anything, are you, Miss?'

Violet smiled to herself. If only you knew, she thought. 'Here, you'd best have this.' She handed her the torch.

'You're sure you don't need it?' the cleaner called after her as she walked away.

'Quite sure.' Darkness held no fears for Violet Tanner. She felt safer in the shadows.

The bad weather had unsettled many of the patients. On Female Chronics, the harassed young student nurses seemed close to tears as they rushed around, desperately trying to soothe the old ladies, who wailed and sobbed and rattled at the bars of their cots. It was the same on the Children's ward, where frightened babies, woken by the shrieking wind, screamed without stopping.

'Sister Parry says we're to leave them,' the young student told Violet briskly as she approached the nearest cot where a toddler was standing up, red-faced and screaming.

'Sister Parry isn't here, is she? I am.' Violet moved past her. The baby, sensing a sympathetic presence, held out his chubby arms.

'But Sister Parry says they'll get spoilt if we go to them,' the girl insisted. 'She says if we ignore them they'll exhaust themselves and go to sleep.'

'What is your name, Nurse?'

'Hollins, Sister.'

'Well, Hollins, how would you like it if everyone ignored you when you were upset and frightened?'

As the girl struggled, open-mouthed, for an answer, Violet scooped the toddler up into her

15

arms. She could feel the sobs shuddering through him as he buried his face in her neck. His warm skin smelt of baby powder.

'Shhh, sweetheart. It's all right, it's only the silly wind making a noise, that's all.' She swayed gently, rocking him in her arms as she whispered words of comfort. His soft curls tickled her cheek.

Gradually she felt the sobs subside, and his heavy weight against her shoulder told her he was asleep.

'And if he cries again, Hollins, I want you to comfort him,' Violet instructed the student as she lowered him gently back into his cot. 'The same goes for the other babies. And if Sister Parry doesn't like it, she can speak to me,' she added, as the girl opened her mouth to protest.

'Yes, Sister.' Hollins bobbed her head, but her face was pinched.

Two hours later, Violet finished her rounds and went back to the small office assigned to the Night Sister. On her way, she slipped into the kitchen to make herself a cup of tea. According to Matron, Night Sisters were allowed the luxury of a maid to bring them tea and see to their comforts, but Violet didn't want to trouble her. The fewer people who noticed her, the fewer questions they would ask. Violet didn't like questions.

But she liked the Nightingale. She hadn't been too sure about it at first, but after old Mr Mannion died she didn't have anywhere else to go. And then the advertisement for the Night Sister's job had appeared in the *Nursing Mirror*, and it seemed as if providence was pointing the way for her.

She was probably safer here, anyway. A busy hospital in the East End of London was the last place anyone would think of looking for her.

'Violet Tanner.' She said it out loud, listening as the sounds hung on the air. It was a long time since she'd called herself by that name, and she still hadn't quite got used to it again. But she generally got used to all her names, soon enough.

She stirred her tea. 'Violet Tanner, Night Sister at the Florence Nightingale Teaching Hospital,' she said again.

Yes, she decided. It suited her. For now.

Chapter Two

There was an extra place laid for Alf Doyle at the dinner table.

'Sorry, I wasn't thinking. Old habits die hard, eh?' Rose's smile was brittle as she cleared the plate away.

No one else around the table said anything, but Dora knew they were all thinking the same, thing; her mum might be putting on a brave face as usual, but she wasn't fooling anyone.

It was New Year's Eve, and round the corner at the Rose and Crown the locals were having their usual knees-up, bidding a noisy farewell to 1935. Dora could hear the sound of laughter and singing drifting down Griffin Street as she and her family gathered around the dinner table.

Any other year they would have been in the

thick of it. Nanna Winnie would be in the saloon bar with a bottle of milk stout, done up in her best dress, face heavily powdered and teeth in for the occasion, taking in all the goings on so she could gossip with her cronies later. Dora's mum Rose, flushed from too many port and lemons, would be singing along to the piano as it bashed out all the old favourites.

But not this year. The atmosphere in the kitchen at number twenty-eight Griffin Street was sombre, even though they were doing their best to pretend that everything was normal.

Except Dora's youngest sister Bea, of course. The twelve year old never bothered to hide her feelings from anyone.

'What's this?' She prodded the lump of brown meat on her plate, her freckled nose wrinkling in disgust.

'It's melt,' Dora hissed. As if Bea didn't know. The butcher sold it for threepence, and the locals called it 'poor man's joint'.

'But we always have chicken at New Year,' her sister protested.

'We had a chicken at Christmas, love. We can't run to another one.' Her mother doled a spoonful of mashed potatoes onto a plate. 'We ain't made of money, I'm afraid.'

'We always had chicken when Dad was here,' Bea said sullenly.

'Shh!' Dora, her grandmother and sister Josie hissed together.

'Yes, well, we had a lot of things when your dad was here,' Rose said briskly. 'But he ain't here now, so we've just got to make the best of things,

18

haven't we?'

She was smiling when she said it, but Dora noticed her mother's hand trembling as she passed another plate down the table.

It had been three months since Dora's stepfather Alf Doyle had disappeared. He'd just packed a bag one day and upped and gone without a word to anyone. Even his pals at the railway yard where he'd worked hadn't seen him since. Her mother and grandmother had gone to the police, but they didn't bother trying to find him. As far as they were concerned, Alf was just another bloke who'd done a flit from his family.

Dora wasn't sorry to see him go. For five years she'd suffered abuse at Alf's hands, living in fear of him creeping into her room at night, silenced by her shame. It was only when she'd found out he'd started abusing her sister Josie that she'd finally found her voice.

Not that it had done much good. The day she'd finally confronted him, Alf had laughed and given her a beating. But then, just as she thought she would never defeat him, he had vanished.

It was a shock to them all, but her mother had taken it hardest. Rose Doyle was a typical East End woman, tough and hard-working, the kind who never complained but rolled up her sleeves and got on with life, no matter what it handed out to her. She had coped eleven years ago when she'd been left widowed with five children to bring up. She had taken the blow when her daughter Maggie had died at the age of thirteen. But the disappearance of her second husband had broken her spirit, and her heart.

No one spoke while they were eating. The only sound was the crackling voice of Al Bowlly on the wireless singing 'Blue Moon', his plaintive tones deepening their gloom.

Dora stared down miserably at her plate. She had fought to get a rare sleeping-out pass from the hospital so she could spend New Year's Eve with her family. She knew her mother appreciated her being here, but Dora couldn't help thinking guiltily she might have had more fun back at the nurses' home, even under the Home Sister's watchful eye.

Nanna Winnie tried to lighten the mood. 'Why don't we all go down to the pub after tea, cheer ourselves up a bit?' she suggested.

'You go if you like.' Rose shrugged. 'I'm stopping here.'

'But it won't be the same without you, Rosie love. Come on, you could do with a night out. A good old sing-song with your pals would do you the world of good.'

'And listen to all the neighbours talking about me? No thanks.'

'No one's talking about you, love.'

'Oh, come on, Mum! You've heard them all whispering, same as I have.' Rose looked up, anger flaring in her brown eyes. 'Our family's all they talk about these days. Y'know, I heard Lettie Pike's even putting it about that I did Alf in for the insurance. As if we'd be sitting down to ox spleen for our dinner if I'd come into money!'

She laughed, but Dora could see the pain in her face. Rose Doyle was a proud woman, who liked to keep herself to herself. Knowing her family's business was the talk of Bethnal Green must be agony for her.

'Anyway,' she said, putting down her knife and fork, 'I can't go out. I've got some more mending to do.'

'You can give it a rest for one night, surely?'

'I like to keep myself busy. And we need the money, don't forget.'

'How are you managing for money, Mum?' Dora asked.

'Oh, we're all right. I've started taking in laundry, as well as mending, so that brings in a bit more. And now your brother and Lily have moved in upstairs, they're helping out with the rent. We've not got as much room to breathe, but at least it's not so much for me to clean,' she added brightly.

'We all have to share a bedroom,' Bea grumbled. 'There's no room, and we can hear Nanna snoring downstairs.'

'I do not,' her grandmother denied heatedly. 'How can I snore when my lumbago keeps me awake every hour of the night?'

Dora looked across the table at her mother. She was laughing with the others, but Dora could see the strain behind her eyes. The Doyles had been one of the few families in Griffin Street to rent their whole house by themselves, and to have to let out a room was a huge blow to Rose's pride. But at least it was only Peter and his wife who were living there. Having to live with another family, like the Pikes and the Rileys did next door, would have been much worse.

'I wish you'd let me leave school and help out,' Josie piped up. 'I told you I could get a job at

21

Gold's Garments–'

'And I told you you're not to think about it,' her mother said. 'You're staying on at school and getting your exams so you can be a teacher, and that's final. I'm proud of both my clever girls–' she beamed at Dora '–and I'm not going to let anything stand in your way. Even if I have to work all day and all night,' she added firmly.

Dora and Josie looked at each other. 'Best not to argue with her.' Dora smiled.

'Besides,' Rose went on, 'Alf will probably be back from his travels soon. Then we'll be right as rain.'

Silence fell around the table. 'For Gawd's sake, girl, do you really reckon he's coming back?' Nanna said finally, her patience giving way. 'All this time without a single word, he could be halfway to bleedin' China–'

'He'll come back,' Rose interrupted her firmly. 'My Alf wouldn't walk out on his own family.'

'He's already walked out, love. God knows why, but he's gone. Now you're not the first girl whose old man did a bunk, and I daresay you won't be the last. A man like that's not worth a spit anyway, after what he did to you–'

'Don't talk about him like that!' Rose snapped. 'He's a good man. You don't know what's happened to keep him away from us. He could have had an accident. He could be dead in the Thames.'

'I hope to God he is,' Nanna grunted, her toothless jaw set in a stubborn line. 'Because if he turns up on this doorstep after all the trouble he's caused, I'll swing for him myself!'

Never one to miss out on any drama, Bea started

snivelling. 'Mum, is that right? Is Dad dead? Has he been murdered?'

'And you can shut up an' all!' Nanna turned on her. 'People don't pack their bags if they're off to get murdered, do they? Blimey, you can see who got the brains in this family, can't you?' she muttered.

'He didn't pack everything,' Rose reminded her. 'He only took a few things with him, so that means he meant to come back.' She looked around at them all, her smile brittle. 'Now I'm sure he had his reasons for going away. But he'll be home soon, and everything will be all right again.'

'And Moby Dick will swim up the Thames!' Nanna muttered, as they cleared the plates away.

'Do you think he'll come back, Dor?' Josie asked her later as they did the washing up in the narrow scullery.

'I hope not.' Dora piled the dishes into the chipped stone sink.

'Sometimes I wish he would.'

Dora turned to face her sister in surprise. 'After what he did to us?'

'I just want to see Mum happy again.' Josie's brown eyes were solemn. Unlike Dora, Bea and their elder brother Peter, who were all ginger-haired, freckled and sturdily built like their late father Jack, the fifteen year old had inherited their mother's slim, dark-haired beauty. 'I hate him, Dora, you know I do. But I hate listening to Mum crying every night, when she thinks we're all asleep. And you know she goes out looking for him? Walks the streets for hours, she does, in the middle of the night. Or she'll go and stand at the gates of the railway yard, as if she expects him to turn up for his shift like nothing's happened. It breaks my heart.' She bit her lip. 'And she worries, too, about how we're going to manage. I know she says we'll be all right, but I can see it on her face every time the rent man knocks on the door. She's working herself into the ground.'

'I'll talk to her,' Dora said.

'It won't do any good. She'll just smile and tell you she's managing, as usual. You know what she's like.'

The rest of the evening dragged by. While revellers laughed and sang and fell over cursing in the street outside, Dora did her best to keep her family's spirits up with board games and singing along to the wireless.

Rose sat by the fire, her head down, going through the mending by the weak gaslight. No surgeon could ever stitch as beautifully as she could, Dora thought. Rose could turn a worn shirt cuff or mend a hole in a dress as if it had never been there.

She went over to her. 'I've got something for you, Mum.' She reached into her pocket, pulled out two pound notes and pressed them into her mother's hand. 'It's not much, but it should at least buy some coal or keep the rent man happy.'

'But this is a month's wages for you. I can't take all your money, love.' Rose tried to give it back to her.

'I'll be earning a bit more now I've finished my first year of training,' said Dora, hearing the desperate brightness in her own voice. 'And it's not like I've got anything to spend it on, what

24

with my board and lodgings all found at the nurses' home.'

'Well, if you're sure...?' Rose looked down at the notes in her hand. 'I can't pretend it won't come in handy.' She put down her mending and smiled up at Dora. 'What would I do without a daughter like you?'

'I wish I could do more,' Dora sighed. 'Student nurses don't earn very much, I'm afraid.'

'Yes, but one day you'll be one of them ward sisters, won't you?'

'Give us a chance! I've got to get through two more years' training first. And then, if I get through my exams, I have to be a staff nurse, and then–'

'You'll do it, love. You got this far, didn't you?'

'True.' Though there were those who still thought little Dora Doyle, the working-class girl from the back streets of Bethnal Green, had no place to be training as a nurse alongside all the respectable, middle-class students. Over the past year she'd proved most of them wrong, but it was a constant struggle.

'I'm proud of you, love. I really am. Here, give your mum a cuddle.' As Rose reached up to hug her, Dora felt her mother's bones jutting sharply under her clothes. Was she eating properly? Years ago, before Alf came along, she had known her mother go without to make sure her kids were fed.

When the old clock on the kitchen mantel struck half-past eleven, Dora slung her coat over her shoulders and went out into the backyard to listen out for the bells of St Paul's ringing in the New

Year across the rooftops of East London.

As she threw open the back door, a slice of light from the kitchen picked out a young couple standing in a passionate clinch beside the fence next door. Mortified, Dora quickly tried to retreat, but it was too late.

'All right, Dor? Happy New Year!' Her best friend Ruby Pike greeted her cheerfully as she adjusted the buttons on her blouse. Blonde curls escaped from her elaborately teased hairdo.

'Happy New Year.' She could barely bring herself to look at Ruby's boyfriend Nick Riley. It might have been Dora herself in his arms now if she hadn't been too scared to let him kiss her last year. 'I thought you'd be down the pub, seeing the New Year in?'

'My lot are all there. And Nick's mum, of course.' Ruby rolled her eyes meaningfully. Everyone knew it was a rare day that June Riley wasn't propping up a bar somewhere in Bethnal Green. 'We were supposed to be going up to St Paul's, but Nick won't leave Danny.'

Dora glanced at Nick, who was still trying to rub Ruby's smudged lipstick off his cheek.

'He gets frightened when he's on his own,' he muttered.

'He's sixteen, Nick,' Ruby sighed. 'Same age as my brothers.'

'But he's not like your brothers, is he?'

Ruby pulled an exasperated face, but Dora understood why Nick was so reluctant. He was very protective of his younger brother. A few years earlier, Danny had suffered a terrible accident which had left him brain-damaged. The rumour was that he'd been beaten by their vicious bully of a father, who was so scared of what he'd done that he'd run away afterwards. But like the lives of so many people in Griffin Street, no one ever knew the full story.

'I'll look after him, if you like?' Dora offered. 'We're not doing much, so he might as well come in and sit with us.'

'We couldn't–' Nick started to refuse, but Ruby jumped in eagerly.

'Would you? That'd be smashing, wouldn't it, Nick?' She curled her arm through his and looked up at him appealingly.

'If you're sure?' Nick met Dora's gaze properly for the first time. Even by the dim light spilling from the kitchen, he made her knees weaken. He towered over her, tall and broad-shouldered, his tousled dark hair falling into his eyes.

When had she realised she was in love with him? Dora couldn't decide, but whenever it was, it was too late. He was Ruby's now. And Ruby was never going to give him up.

Not that he'd want her to, Dora was certain. Ruby was everything she wasn't – blonde, buxom, and as glamorous as a Hollywood movie star. Just the type of girl someone like Nick Riley would want on his arm.

He probably broke out in a cold sweat every time he remembered how close he'd come to settling for a homely girl with frizzy ginger hair, Dora thought.

'He'll be fine with us,' she said. 'Anyway, it doesn't look like we've got much choice, does it?' she added wryly, as Ruby darted inside to call

Danny before anyone changed their mind.

'You could come with us?' Nick offered.

Dora smiled. She could just imagine Ruby's face if she tagged along. 'What do they say? Three's a crowd.'

Before he could reply Ruby came back out of the house, ushering Danny in front of her. He emerged shyly, his head bent and shoulders hunched. But his worried expression cleared when he saw Dora.

'Y'see? I told you,' Ruby said. 'You should have seen his face when I said you were here. If you ask me, our Danny's got a bit of a soft spot for you, Dor. Ain't that right, Danny boy?'

She flung her arm around his skinny shoulders in a rough hug and ruffled his pale hair, making him squirm and flinch.

'Leave him be. You know he doesn't like anyone touching him,' Nick said gruffly.

'Not like his brother, eh?' Ruby winked at him.

Nick ignored her as he helped Danny through the narrow gap in the fence where the slats had broken and weeds had grown up in their place. It was a gap Dora and Ruby had regularly used over the years as they went between their houses.

'All right, Danny?' Dora greeted him with a smile. He nodded and ducked his head shyly. It was the same every time they met, as if she had to win his confidence all over again.

'Now you're sure you're going to be all right?' Nick asked his brother.

'He'll be fine. Stop fussing like an old woman, or we'll miss all the excitement.' Ruby tugged on his arm, dragging him away.

Dora watched them hurry hand in hand down the alleyway, Ruby's excited laughter still echoing on the frosty night air after they had disappeared. Then she turned to Danny.

'All right, love? Shall we go in and get warm by the fire?'

'I like looking at the stars.' Danny shivered beside her, his pale face turned up towards the inky black night sky. 'Y-your Josie's been t-teaching me their names.' He pointed his long finger skywards. 'That one there ... that's the P-plough.'

'Is that right?' Dora peered upwards. 'It looks more like an old pan to me.'

'And that one is c-called Orion,' he went on. 'He's m-meant to be a man with a sword.'

Dora listened patiently as he pointed out more constellations in the sky. She'd often seen Danny perched on top of the coal bunker staring into space. Now she knew what he'd been looking at.

'You remembered all their names, Danny. Good for you,' she said. He gave a lopsided smile, proud of himself.

'D-do you think they have stars like this in Am-America, Dora?' he asked.

'I expect so, Dan. Why, are you going to do some star gazing when you get there?'

Danny nodded. 'N-Nick says he's going to buy me a tel-tel–' His face twisted as he struggled with the word.

'A telescope, you mean? Lucky you. That'll cost a few bob, I bet.'

'Nick s-says he'll have the m-money, once he's World Ch-champion.'

'I'm sure he will.' She wondered if Nick had

29

told Ruby about his secret plan to move to America with Danny once he'd saved up enough cash from his boxing. Like Dora, he dreamt of making a better life for himself. She was sure her friend Ruby would have something to say about it, once she found out.

But perhaps Ruby would approve? Somehow Dora could imagine her being right at home over there, rubbing shoulders with all her favourite Hollywood stars, like Claudette Colbert and Myrna Loy.

Dora sighed up at the sky. And meanwhile she'd probably still be here in Griffin Street, trying to stop her family from falling apart.

The bells of St Paul's suddenly rang out, breaking the stillness of the night air. A roar went up from the locals at the Rose and Crown as they spilled into the street, all trying to outdo each other with a loud and drunken rendition of 'Auld Lang Syne', welcoming in the start of 1936.

'Happy N-New Year, Dora,' Danny said.

Dora turned to smile back at him. 'I hope so, love,' she said.

Chapter Three

One hour into her duty on the first day of the New Year, Lady Amelia Charlotte Benedict, or Millie as she preferred to call herself, was being violently sick in the sluice.

Oh God. She stared down at the gaping hole in

the middle of the sink, her fingers clutching the cold stone rim for support. The chilly January air that whistled through the open grating did nothing to cool the sweat that prickled on her skin.

She shouldn't have run away like that. Yes, the stench had been overpowering and the sight that greeted her when she threw off that bedcover had been truly disgusting, but a real nurse would never have done what she had.

The memory of Sister Hyde's startled expression as Millie charged past her up the length of the ward, one hand clamped over her mouth, was enough to send her retching over the sink again.

She heard the sluice door open behind her and groaned in dread, bracing herself to hear Sister Hyde's voice ringing out. Sister needed little excuse to remind Millie of her shortcomings. She could lecture her for half an hour if she swept the ward in the wrong direction, so heaven only knew what she would make of her abandoning a patient to rush off and be sick.

But mercifully it was only Millie's room mate, Helen Tremayne. The pair of them had been assigned to Female Chronics together although Helen was in the year above, and superior to Millie in every other way, too.

'Sister sent me to find out where you'd gone.'

'Is she very angry?' Millie whispered.

'She certainly wasn't smiling when I left her.' As she crouched over the sink Millie saw Helen's stout black shoes, polished to military perfection as usual, come into view beside hers. 'You shouldn't have left Mrs Church, you know. No wonder Sister loses patience with you.'

'I couldn't help it!' Millie looked up at her friend, wincing as the bright lights of the sluice pricked her watering eyes. 'You didn't see the state she was in. It was horrible!'

'That's Messy Bessie for you.'

Bessie Church, or 'Messy Bessie' as the nurses nicknamed her, was a very sad case, an elderly woman who had lost her wits years ago. She was usually a placid old soul, but despite endless pleading – and a few stiff words from Sister – she still couldn't or wouldn't use a bedpan, preferring to let nature take its course and leave the nurses to worry about cleaning it up.

And this morning, much to her dismay, Millie had been given that particular job. She had arrived for duty feeling fragile, so cleaning up an incontinent patient was the last thing she needed.

Just the thought of it made her stomach roil again. She felt her cap sliding off her head as she threw herself over the sluice, and barely managed to rescue it before it ended up down the plug hole.

'You know you've only got yourself to blame,' Helen's voice echoed painfully in her ears. 'You wouldn't be in this state if you hadn't been out all night.'

'Shh! Sister will hear you. I wasn't out all night anyway.'

'What time did you get home?'

'I don't know ... about two?'

'Actually, it was nearer four.'

'Was it? Oh dear.' Millie bent down and rested her head on the edge of the sink, letting the cool stone soothe her fevered brow. 'I rather lost track

32

of time, I'm afraid.'

She'd lost track of quite a lot, unfortunately. Including how many Martinis she'd had.

'I'm surprised you didn't kill yourself when you came through our window. You shouldn't climb up drainpipes in that state, it's far too dangerous.'

'It's fine. I've done it lots of times.'

'You only have to break your neck once.'

Satisfied her stomach was finally settling, Millie sank to the floor, leant back against the cold tiled wall and started to pin her cap back in place.

'It was New Year's Eve, Tremayne. Don't tell me you weren't tempted to sneak out and celebrate with your Charlie?'

'Certainly not.' Helen blushed at the mention of her boyfriend's name. It never ceased to amaze Millie that the oh so perfect Nurse Tremayne had actually come down off her pedestal long enough to fall in love.

And with someone so gloriously unsuitable, too. Charlie was an absolute sweetie, but he was an apprentice carpenter and his father ran a fruit and veg stall. Helen's mother had been utterly livid.

'I studied until lights out, then went straight to sleep,' Helen went on primly.

'On New Year's Eve?'

'I have the State Final this year. I need to study if I'm going to pass.'

'But that's not for months!'

'I suppose you think I should leave everything until the last minute, like you do?'

Millie grinned at her through a mouthful of hairpins.

Helen had changed a lot since they'd first met, but she could still be an awful prig sometimes.

As if she realised what her friend was thinking, Helen smiled reluctantly. 'So what did you get up to last night?' she asked. 'I hope it was worth this morning's agony?'

'Oh, it was.' Millie smiled at the memory. She and her fiancé Seb had gone to the Savoy Hotel with their friends. They'd sipped Martinis in Harry's Bar, then danced in the ballroom under a vast hourglass suspended above their heads. As the last grains of sand trickled through, trumpeters from the Life Guards had played a rousing fanfare. Then there had been more cocktails, more dancing, and the hours just slipped by, until the next thing Millie knew she was in a taxi with Seb, kissing him a passionate goodnight outside the hospital gates.

She shuddered. How on earth Hopkins the head porter hadn't seen her she didn't know. It was sheer luck she wasn't explaining herself to Matron yet again this morning.

'We had so much fun,' she told Helen. 'And we drank the most marvellous new cocktail. It's called a Silent Third. I think it's lemon juice, Cointreau and Scotch. Have you tried it? Oh, you should, it's wonderful. The Prince of Wales drinks nothing else, so I'm told–'

'The Prince of Wales doesn't have to be ready to make beds and care for patients at seven in the morning, does he?'

Millie scrambled to her feet. Sister Hyde stood in the doorway. She was an imposing figure, tall and spare in her severe grey uniform. Her hair was drawn back under her starched bonnet, the jaunty bow under her chin a stark contrast to her gaunt face, etched with rigid lines that spoke of self-control and discipline.

'Perhaps if you devoted half as much time to your nursing as you do to your social life, Benedict, you might not be such a liability,' she said. 'May I remind you that Mrs Church is still awaiting your attention?'

'Yes, Sister. Sorry, Sister.'

'It's not me you should be apologising to, Benedict. It's poor Mrs Church.'

'She probably hasn't even noticed.' Millie didn't realise she'd muttered the words aloud until she saw the thunderous look on Sister Hyde's face.

'All the more reason why she needs us to take care of her!' she snapped. Her eyes were the hard, cold grey of flint.

'Yes, Sister.' Millie stared humbly down at her shoes, wishing the ground would open up beneath them.

'Well, don't just stand there, girl. Hurry up!'

Millie could feel Sister Hyde's disapproving gaze on her as she gathered soap, brush and comb, methylated spirits and dusting powder on her trolley, then filled the basin at the hot tap.

'Is that the correct temperature?'

'Yes, Sister.'

'Are you sure? You mustn't scald the patient.'

'No, Sister.'

'And don't leave the soap in the water while you're washing her, as you did yesterday,' Sister Hyde reminded her. 'It's a scandalous waste.'

'No, Sister.'

35

'And for heaven's sake, girl, try to look cheerful!' Sister's final words rang out after her.

She hates me, Millie thought as she pushed the trolley back up the ward.

She and Sister Hyde had got off to a bad start the previous year, when Millie had accidentally soaked her with soap enema solution during her Preliminary Training examination. The image of Sister Hyde standing there, her cap limp, soapy water dripping off the end of her long nose, had haunted Millie ever since.

And Sister Hyde clearly hadn't forgotten it either, because she never missed an opportunity to make her suffer. Millie had been dreading her assignment to Female Chronics.

Every day Sister Hyde took her to task for something. She was far harder on Millie than she was on any of the other nurses.

'It should take you less than three minutes to make an empty bed, Nurse,' she would say, standing behind her with watch poised. Or, 'Why are you shaking those sheets? For heaven's sake, girl, you're not putting out the flags.' She would follow Millie as she cleaned, running her finger along the locker tops and around the bathtubs, until she finally found something to complain about.

Millie tried to stay cheerful and to see the good in everything and everyone, but she was beginning to think there wasn't any in Sister Hyde.

Female Chronics, like most of the other wards at the Nightingale Hospital, was as cavernous as a cathedral, with twenty beds arranged down the two longer sides, each separated by a tile-topped locker. In the centre of the ward stood the Sister's desk and the fireplace, which crackled with a roaring fire throughout the winter months. Tall windows offered a view out over the courtyard, with its cluster of London plane trees in the centre where patients sometimes sat if they were well enough.

But none of the patients on Female Chronics ever ventured out into the courtyard. Few even got as far as admiring the view from the windows. They had come to the Nightingale not to get better, but to die.

It was another reason why Millie had been dreading her placement here. The women on Female Chronics were so sad. Many of them had been abandoned by their families, left to die alone and forgotten. Some of them had been sent here from the workhouse. No visitors ever came to this ward, bringing flowers, laughter or good cheer.

Not that it really mattered. Many of the patients were too old, sick or mad to know where they were. They would thrash and scream, rattling the bars of their cots and lashing out at the nurses. Or they would talk to themselves, carrying on conversations with unseen friends and family. And then there were the ones who lay staring at the ceiling, their faces devoid of hope. Those were the ones who tore most at Millie's heart.

Perhaps that was why Sister Hyde was so bitter and bad-tempered all the time, she thought. She would probably be the same herself if she had spent the last thirty years in such a depressing place.

Mrs Church gave her a wide, toothless grin

through the bars of her cot as Millie manoeuvred her trolley through the gap between the screens. She was no bigger than a child. Pearly skin stretched over the bones of her face, which was surrounded by a fluffy halo of sparse white hair. She didn't seem to notice the stinking mess that smeared her wrinkled hands and white nightgown. If anything she seemed to delight in it, much to the horror of the nurses. Messy Bessie had certainly earned her nickname.

Millie's stomach lurched violently as the stench hit her, but she fought against it, forcing a smile as she lowered the side of the cot. 'Right, Mrs Church, let's get you cleaned up, shall we?' she said bracingly, pulling on her rubber gloves.

'No!' Bessie Church galvanised herself, snatching at the bedclothes and yanking them up to her chin, her eyes round with terror.

Millie winced to see the palm prints smeared all over the blankets. 'Come along now, you can't stay in this mess, can you?' she encouraged. 'You'll feel so much better when you're all nice and fresh.'

But Bessie Church clung on, her fingernails rimed with filth.

'Nooo!' An unearthly wail of fear emerged from the gaping, toothless hole of her mouth.

'For heaven's sake, can you please shut that woman up?'

Maud Mortimer's voice rose imperiously from the other side of the ward. She was a grand lady in her seventies, and one of the few patients on the ward with all her mental faculties intact. Only her body let her down; she was bedbound, suffering from progressive muscular atrophy. But it seemed as if she had decided to devote her remaining time on earth to making everyone else as miserable as she possibly could.

Millie heard Staff Nurse Willis approach Mrs Mortimer's bed. She was a softly spoken woman, and Millie could barely make out her whispering voice. But she heard Mrs Mortimer's ringing answer, loud and clear.

'What do you mean, I'm disturbing the patients? Good heavens, you stupid woman, haven't you heard that dreadful racket going on? I have no idea what the idiotic nurse is doing behind those screens, but I sincerely hope she's putting that woman out of her misery with an elephant gun!' More murmuring from Staff Nurse Willis, then Mrs Mortimer said in outrage, 'I will spare a thought for the other patients when they spare a thought for me. Gracious, one can't even die in peace, it seems.'

Millie couldn't help smiling. Maud Mortimer reminded her of her own grandmother, the redoubtable Dowager Countess Rettingham, a woman so convinced of the rightness of her own opinions she saw absolutely no point in listening to anyone else's.

But then Millie turned around and saw what Bessie Church had just done, and her smile disappeared.

'Oh, no! Look at me!' She stared down in horror at her apron. She'd been so busy listening to Maud Mortimer, she hadn't noticed that Messy Bessie had released her hold on the bedclothes and was pawing at Millie instead.

Bessie Church just clapped her hands and

leered proudly back at her. Seizing her chance, Millie whipped off the bedclothes. Bessie's crowing laughter turned to a scream of outrage. She made a grab for the bedclothes and, when that didn't work, she made a grab for Millie instead.

'Ow! Let me go!' For such a tiny woman Mrs Church was surprisingly strong. Her dirty claws fixed on a handful of Millie's hair through her cap, pulling her off balance so that she pitched forward headlong on to the bed.

'What on earth is going on here?'

Sister Hyde rattled back the screens. Millie wrenched herself free and struggled off the bed, trying to straighten her cap. She didn't dare look down at herself, but she knew she was almost as messy as Bessie.

Sister Hyde's gaze raked her up and down. 'Go and get changed, Benedict,' she said at last through thin, almost unmoving lips. 'I will find someone competent to clean up Mrs Church.'

Millie slunk off, aware of the other nurses watching her with amusement as she made her way down the length of the ward. Even the pros, the lowest of the low, who spent their whole time up to their elbows in bedpans, were grinning.

When she got to the sluice she realised why. She pulled off her cap and apron in disgust.

Suddenly those cocktails at the Savoy seemed like a lifetime ago.

Chapter Four

The weekly ward visit by Mr Cooper the Chief Consultant always made Sister Wren nervous. She wasn't worried he might find fault with the way the patients on Gynae were cared for; her ward was far too well run for that. It was more the fluttery kind of nerves, like the girls in *Peg's Paper* felt every time they set eyes on their lover.

Yes, she loved him, even though she could only whisper it in her heart. She loved everything about him. His voice, so deep and thrilling. The way his mouth curved upwards at one corner when he smiled. His compelling blue eyes, and the sheen of his sleek black hair. His clever surgeon's hands that held the gift of life itself. How the sight of those long, sensitive fingers mesmerised her. Sometimes she had to force herself not to stare at them, imagining them caressing her face, or unbuttoning her blouse...

But like the girls in *Peg's Paper*, Sister Wren knew that her love was doomed. James Cooper was married. And even though she doubted very much if he could be happy, married as he was to a woman who dressed like a bohemian, sulked at public functions and, worst of all, was French, she also knew he was far too honourable to do anything that might sully his reputation or hers.

She gave herself a mental shake as she teased her ash-brown curls before the mirror in her sitting room. He was married, she reminded herself firmly. And no matter how much she – and he, for all she knew – might lament that state of affairs, she had to be practical.

Because Sister Wren had needs. And since those needs could never be met by the man she loved – unless a terrible accident befell Mrs Cooper – she had to find someone else.

She eyed that morning's edition of *The Times*, which lay across the arm of her chair, folded open at the Personal columns. There, among the births, marriages and appeals for missing people to come forward to 'hear something to their advantage', were the Lonely Hearts advertisements.

Sister Wren went through them every morning when the maid brought her breakfast, circling any likely prospects. Then, while having her midday meal in her sitting room, she would write letters to be posted discreetly at the Porters' Lodge that afternoon.

Rather discouragingly, most of her letters went unanswered. But every so often she would find herself taking tea with a gentleman. Unfortunately, the ones she met seldom bore any resemblance to James Cooper.

There was a soft knock on the door. 'Enter,' said Sister Wren, stuffing the newspaper out of sight behind a cushion. The door opened a fraction, and Ann Cuthbert, her staff nurse, peered through the crack.

'Sorry to disturb you, Sister, but they've just rung to say the new admission's on her way up.'

Sister Wren sighed with annoyance. She hated new patients arriving on the day of the consultant's visit. They took a long time to settle in and made her ward look messy. They had to be washed and prepared, there were charts to fill in, and then usually one or other of the nosy women in the nearby beds would want to start chatting, all adding to the general disorder.

'Thank you, Cuthbert. I'll be with you shortly.'

As soon as the nurse had gone Sister Wren placed her cap back on her head and tied the bow under her chin, being careful not to ruffle her artfully teased curls. She added a dab of rouge to colour her sallow cheeks and smudged on some pink lipstick – even though make-up was forbidden on the wards, she couldn't countenance meeting Mr Cooper looking anything but her best – then stepped out of her sitting room and back on to the adjoinmg ward, to find out which of her nurses needed the sternest reprimand.

Frustratingly, they seemed to have been hard at work in her absence. The ward was swept, dusted and scrubbed; the floors shone and a satisfying aroma of carbolic hung in the air. Even the leaves of her prize aspidistra gleamed like polished leather. The beds were neatly made and every patient was sitting propped up, hair brushed and wearing a fresh nightgown in honour of the consultant's visit.

The student nurses all stopped what they were doing and looked at her expectantly, waiting for her nod of approval. All except one.

Doyle was chatting to one of the patients again. Sister Wren felt her hackles rise as she watched them laughing together. Hadn't she warned her nurses not to be too familiar with the patients?

Most of them were coarse East End types with rough manners and loud voices – not the kind of women decent young girls should associate with, in her opinion. It made her shudder sometimes to see them in their shabby nightgowns, yelling to each other across the ward as if they were in Petticoat Lane, not a hospital. And as for their jokes ... no respectable woman should have to listen to some of the things they said.

And yet there was Doyle, laughing with one of them. Worse still, it was that awful Mrs Patterson, a costermonger's wife from Haggerston, who had been admitted with a prolapse. Hardly surprising, Sister Wren thought, since she had given birth to hordes of children. They swarmed to the hospital to see her every Sunday, and it took all Sister Wren's efforts to stop them all coming in at once. Time and time again she'd taken the trouble to explain that only two visitors at a time were allowed, but still it hadn't sunk in. They would stand outside the ward doors, sobbing and wailing and leaving sticky, smudged fingerprints on the glass.

Mrs Patterson was one of Sister Wren's least-favourite patients. And the feeling was mutual; she had overheard the patient telling her husband that the ward sister was 'a right snotty cow'.

Sister Wren stormed over to them.

'Doyle, I thought I told you to clean the bathrooms?'

She was used to students snapping to attention the moment she spoke to them. But Doyle faced her with an almost insolent calm.

'I finished them an hour ago, Sister. I've done

everything on the work list you gave me.' She had a rough way of speaking that made Sister Wren wince. Common girls like Doyle shouldn't be allowed to train as nurses, in her opinion. Only respectable, well brought up women like herself should ever be considered for a career in such a caring profession.

'Then why didn't you ask for more work?'

'I did, Sister. But Staff Nurse Cuthbert told me I could go for dinner when you came back. I should have gone an hour ago.'

Sister Wren's eyes narrowed. 'Are you complaining, Doyle?'

'No, Sister.' Her freckled face was bland, her muddy green eyes giving nothing away. But there was something about the way she faced Sister Wren that made her think Doyle wasn't nearly as afraid of her as she should have been.

'It's my fault, Sister,' Mrs Patterson interrupted. 'I've been feeling a bit down, what with being away from the kids, so I asked Nurse Doyle for a bit of company. I hope I haven't got her into trouble?' She looked anxiously from one to the other.

Sister Wren ignored her, her gaze fixed on Dora.

'Are you sure you don't have any complaints about the way I run my ward? Because I'm sure Matron would be happy to discuss them with you.'

Do it, Sister Wren urged her silently. Answer me back if you dare. All she needed was one word, a sideways look, and she could send Doyle straight to Matron.

She looked like the type who could fly off the

handle, with that square obstinate jaw and fiery red hair of hers. Common, uneducated types like her were notoriously bad at keeping their temper in check.

But somehow she managed it. 'No, Sister,' she said.

Sister Wren would have liked to try and provoke her further, but they were distracted by the arrival of the new patient. Sister Wren busied herself supervising the porter and making sure the woman, whose name was Mrs Venables, was made comfortable. At least she seemed a cut above their usual rabble of patients, Sister Wren thought. She was well spoken, and her suitcase was made from good-quality leather.

'Shall I have Ennis wash her and get her ready?' Staff Nurse Cuthbert asked.

Sister Wren considered the matter for a moment. 'No, have Doyle do it,' she said finally.

Cuthbert frowned in confusion. 'But Doyle is the only one who hasn't been for dinner yet. If she doesn't go soon, she'll miss it—'

'Who is running this ward, you or me?' Sister Wren interrupted her.

'You are, of course, but—'

'And I say Doyle has to prepare Mrs Venables. If she misses her dinner, then so be it. A good nurse should put her patients before everything,' Sister Wren said piously.

'Yes, Sister.' Cuthbert bobbed her head in agreement and went off to deliver the bad news to Doyle. She looked so grim, Sister Wren observed, anyone would think she was the one who was faced with the prospect of missing her dinner.

46

Mrs Venables was a very nice lady, and extremely apologetic when she found out she was keeping Dora from her dinner.

'Oh, that's no good at all, is it?' she tutted. 'It's such a shame. Why couldn't one of the other nurses do this?'

Because Sister doesn't have it in for the other nurses like she does for me, Dora thought. But as moaning to patients simply wasn't done, she smiled and said, 'I really don't mind. Now let's get you into your nightdress, shall we? Then you'll be all ready to meet our consultant, Mr Cooper. You'll want to look your best for him.'

She felt light-headed as she fastened the laces of Mrs Venables' nightgown. Not only had she not eaten, she hadn't sat down since she came on duty at seven that morning. But she didn't dare complain to Sister Wren. Students might be entitled to three regular breaks during their shift, but if the ward sister forgot or they were too busy, then they didn't get them.

Which would be fair enough if they really were busy. But somehow all the other students had been given leave to go for dinner except Dora.

She knew from talking to the other nurses that Sister Wren could be very spiteful if she didn't like someone, whether it was a patient or a student. But why she had taken against her Dora had no idea. She'd tried to do her best, did everything she was asked to do without complaint, even though she knew for a fact that she was given all the dirtiest jobs on her work list. But nothing she did could please Sister Wren.

It wasn't just Sister who was out to make her life a misery either. Her old neighbour Lettie Pike was the ward maid on Wren, and ever since Dora had arrived, she hadn't missed a chance to make a sly dig about the Doyle family.

'How's your mum?' She sidled up to Dora now as she pushed her trolley back to the sluice. Her narrow, pinched face was a mask of pretend concern. 'I saw her out the other day, but I hardly recognised her. Shocking, she looked. Really shocking. White as a ghost. And so thin! But no wonder, with all the worry she's got. I saw the rent man knocking again yesterday. That's the third time he's come looking for his money this week. And Rose was always such a regular payer, and all.'

She shook her head sadly, but her pretence of concern didn't fool Dora for a moment. Lettie had bitterly resented the upturn in Rose's fortunes when she'd married Alf Doyle, and now Dora knew she was rubbing her hands together in glee at the thought of her neighbour falling on hard times.

'As long as he's not knocking on your door, you haven't got anything to worry about, have you?' she replied shortly.

'There's no need to take that tone with me.' Lettie's beady little eyes turned cold. 'If you don't want me to show a bit of neighbourly concern, then I won't bother.'

'If by that you mean sticking your nose in where it doesn't belong, then no, I don't want you to bother.'

Dora barged at the sluice door with her trolley,

shoving it open and letting it fly back in Lettie's face.

By the time they served dinner to the patients, Dora's stomach was groaning in protest. She was so hungry, the smell of baked cod and mashed potatoes almost made her feel sick.

'Here, have mine. I'm not that hungry,' Mrs Venables offered, pushing her plate towards her.

'I can't.' Dora eyed it longingly, her mouth already watering. 'We're not allowed to eat on the ward.'

'But you must be starving. You'll pass out if you don't get something to eat.'

'I'll be all right. Now, can I get you a cup of tea to have with your dinner?'

But as she stood in the kitchen later, scraping the leftovers into the pig bin, Dora felt faint with hunger. It was so wrong to throw food away when it was almost untouched. And why should the pigs eat when she couldn't?

She lifted a plate to her face, letting the aroma waft towards her nostrils. Even the smell of the food made her head spin.

Her eyes darted towards the kitchen door. Surely no one would notice if she just helped herself to a morsel of cold cod?

She'd barely shovelled it into her mouth when the kitchen door was flung open and Lettie Pike stood there.

'Look at you, eating leftovers off patients' plates.' She shook her head. 'You know that's against the rules, don't you? What would Sister say about that? I wonder.'

'I expect you'll find out, won't you?' Dora helped

herself to another piece of fish off the plate. Lettie was going to tell anyway, so she might as well be hung for a sheep as a lamb.

But Lettie didn't get the chance to say anything. Sister Wren disappeared off to her sitting room again after dinner, to prepare for Mr Cooper's arrival. Meanwhile Dora and the other nurses changed into fresh caps and aprons and rushed around the ward, making sure everything was in place for the great man's visit.

Despite her hasty pickings in the kitchen, Dora was still feeling light-headed as she joined the line waiting outside the ward doors to greet Mr Cooper and his retinue of white-coated medical students, housemen and registrars. One of them, Dr Tremayne, gave her a brief nod of greeting. He was her room mate Helen's elder brother. He had also had a brief flirtation with their other room mate Millie Benedict before she had got engaged.

'Good afternoon, Sister.' Mr Cooper barely acknowledged the presence of the other nurses waiting in a neat line behind her. Such was their lowly place in life, Dora thought. She had already learnt that uttering any sound in front of a consultant, moving or even making eye contact, was forbidden.

'Good afternoon, Mr Cooper.' Any trace of harshness had disappeared from Sister Wren's manner, to be replaced by a barely recognisable simpering girlishness. 'The patients are ready for you, if you would like to come this way?'

Dora stayed at the end of the line as they progressed from bed to bed. It seemed to take such a long time for Mr Cooper to read every set of notes and talk to each patient, then question his students on the best treatment for them. Dora shifted her weight from one foot to the other, trying to stop her knees from giving way. She could feel beads of sweat trickling from under her cap.

'And what would it tell you if this patient were to present with a rigor, pyrexia and a severe headache?' Mr Cooper was asking his students, who stared blank-faced back at him.

'Meningitis?' one of them ventured.

'Possible, but unlikely since this is a gynaecology ward.' Mr Cooper tutted impatiently, his gaze scanning the group of students. 'Come along, surely one of you must have picked up a textbook at some point?'

As his eyes moved along the line, for some reason he caught sight of Dora. She saw the frown gathering between his dark brows.

'Nurse? Are you all right?'

She started at his unexpected attention. 'Y-yes, sir.'

'Are you sure? You look very–'

Everyone turned to look at her, their faces blurring in front of her eyes. She didn't hear the last of the sentence as her knees buckled. The last thing she saw was Dr Tremayne stepping forward to catch her as she slipped to the ground.

She jerked awake to the pungent smell of sal volatile being wafted under her nose, and found herself staring up into the deep blue eyes of Mr Cooper.

'You're back.' He smiled. 'You gave us all quite

a shock there, Nurse.'

'Wh-where am I?' Dora looked around, her senses slowly bringing the world into focus. The crisply starched pillows crackling under her head, the smell of lysol, the sight of Sister Wren scowling with rage... She tried to sit up, but Mr Cooper's hands closed on her shoulders, guiding her back against the pillows.

'No, you're not to get up for a moment,' he said. 'I've sent the maid for some hot sweet tea. You're to sit there and drink it before you even think about moving. And then I want you to go back to your room and lie down for the rest of the afternoon.'

Dora caught sight of Sister Wren's thunderous face behind him. If it had been anyone else but a consultant, she would have dragged Dora off that bed herself and forced her to wash bedpans for the rest of the day as punishment.

But since it was Mr Cooper, all she could do was smile and nod. Only Dora could see the bitter frustration in her thin mouth and narrowed eyes.

'Thank you, sir,' she whispered.

'Not at all, Nurse.' He addressed his students. 'We must look after our nursing staff as well as we look after our patients, for without them we doctors can do nothing.'

He gave Dora a final nod before sweeping off to the next bed. She was still blinking in disbelief about what had happened when Sister Wren appeared at her bedside.

'And when you've finished putting your feet up while everyone else does your share of the work,

I want you to report to Matron,' she hissed. 'Lettie has told me about you helping yourself to food in the kitchen. Perhaps you'd like to explain why you feel you're above the rules?'

Chapter Five

It had been a long, difficult night. They had lost two patients, one on Female Chronics and a particularly sad death on Male Surgical. A cancer patient, not yet thirty, with three children and his wife expecting a fourth. The young nurse left in charge of the ward hadn't yet learnt not to break her heart over every patient, so Violet had had to dry her tears as well as inform the duty registrar and see that last offices had been performed.

'But it's just not fair ... he was so young,' the young nurse wept as they gently washed the man's face and combed his hair.

'He was in great pain. At least his suffering is over now,' Violet replied. If you want to cry for anyone, do it for his wife, she added silently. The young man's troubles might be over, but with three mouths to feed and a baby on the way, hers were just beginning.

It was almost eight o'clock by the time she reached her lodgings in Shadwell. The January sky was still a dull slate grey and a damp fog had rolled in off the river, shrouding the cobbled alleyways. Violet pulled her scarf up around her mouth to keep out the metallic tang of the air and the damp, rotting smell of the river at low tide, visible between the looming Victorian wharves and warehouses.

She lodged in a room on the top floor of a tall tenement. A stale smell of overcooked cabbage mingled with the pungent odour of cat's urine greeted her as she pushed open the front door and entered a narrow hallway. From the depths of the house came the sound of shouting and a baby wailing.

As she climbed the stairs, Violet was seized by the familiar feeling of foreboding that lasted until the moment she pushed open the door to her room and saw her son again.

He was sitting cross-legged in the old armchair, frowning over his book. An eiderdown shrouded his skinny shoulders.

Seeing him like that, his brow puckered, lip pushed out in concentration, reminded her so strongly of his father that she felt her heart leap into her throat.

'Hello, darling. All dressed and ready, I see. What a good boy you are.' Violet smiled brightly as she pulled off her gloves. 'Did you sleep well, sweetheart? No nightmares?'

He shook his head. 'But I kept waking up because of the cold.'

'It is rather chilly, isn't it?' Violet shivered. She glanced at the blackened, empty grate. Still no coal, despite all her pleading and threats to the landlady.

'Don't worry, I'll talk to Mrs Bainbridge again.' She leant over and kissed the top of her son's dark head. He squirmed away, a typical seven year old who didn't want to be babied. 'Shall I make us some breakfast?'

She went into the tiny kitchenette that adjoined their room. It was barely more than a cupboard, with just enough room for a sink and an ancient gas stove, separated from their room by a thin, faded curtain.

The condensation on the tiny window above the sink had turned to ice, and the sills were rimed with black mould. Violet tested it with the end of her finger and frowned. It was no good for Oliver. His breathing was already heavy and troubled. The last thing they needed was a chest infection as bad as last year's.

She peered out of the grimy glass over the blackened rooftops. How did they ever end up like this? she wondered. She'd chosen the lodgings because they were cheap, far enough away from the Nightingale that she didn't risk being spotted, and the landlady hadn't asked too many questions. But it wasn't good enough. Oliver deserved a real home, somewhere with a garden where he could run and play. It was no life for a child, staying cooped up in one tiny room.

And it was no life for her, either. As she paced the hospital corridors every night, her mind was tormented by fears that he might wake up, scared and alone, wanting his mother. Or worse, that something dreadful might befall him while she wasn't there to watch over him.

She prepared some thin slices of bread and butter, and they chatted as they ate.

'Did you see any dead people?' Oliver asked through a mouthful, his dark eyes gleaming.

Violet thought about the poor man on Male Surgical. 'Heavens, what a question.' She reached over and brushed a stray lock of hair out of her son's eyes. 'It's much better to think about all the people who get well in a hospital, isn't it?'

Oliver considered this for a moment as he chewed. 'I prefer to think about dead people,' he said. 'Are people very scary when they're dead, Mummy?'

'Not at all,' Violet replied. 'They just look like people. People who are asleep, I suppose.'

'I want to work in a hospital when I grow up.'

Violet smiled at him over the rim of her teacup. 'Like Mummy, you mean?'

'No, I want to be a doctor like Daddy. He was a good doctor, wasn't he?'

It took less than a second for her to compose herself. 'Yes, darling, he was. A very good doctor.'

'Did he save people's lives?'

'Lots of people's lives.' She checked her watch. 'Now hurry up and finish your breakfast. We'll have to look smart if we don't want to be late for school.'

She bundled Oliver up in as many layers of jumpers, coat, scarves and gloves as she could find. Just before they left, she took her ring out of her pocket and slipped it on to the third finger of her left hand, then put on her own gloves.

Mrs Bainbridge must have been listening out for them, because she was waiting in the passageway when they came downstairs. A skinny, one-eyed ginger cat insinuated itself around her legs.

'Your rent's due.' She held out a callused palm for the money. 'I'll have it now, if you don't mind.'

Violet regarded her with disdain, taking in her stained crossover pinny with a shrunken cardigan worn over the top, and the cigarette dangling from her thin lips.

'The fire in my room has not been lit,' she said. 'I told you my son has a weak chest. The room needs to be kept warm and well ventilated. You said you would be able to make up the fire while I'm not here. I pay you extra to do it.'

'I do it every night before I go to bed.'

'Then why is the room freezing every morning?'

'Are you calling me a liar?' Mrs Bainbridge's pale eyes bulged in outrage.

'I'm saying I want you to keep to our agreement.'

'If you don't like it, you can always find somewhere else to live. Although I dunno as how there'd be many respectable places would take a woman on her own with a kid.' She glanced meaningfully at Violet.

'As I explained to you, I'm a widow.'

''Course you are, dearie.' Mrs Bainbridge smiled nastily, showing a mouthful of brown, stumpy teeth. 'And I'm Mae West.'

She stretched her palm out further. Violet took out her purse, counted a few coins and handed them to her.

Mrs Bainbridge checked the money then looked up sharply. 'What's this? I'm ten bob short.'

'I'll give you the rest when there's a decent fire in my room. And when you stop stealing my coal,' Violet added.

A dull flush crept up Mrs Bainbridge's face.

'Don't know what she's so uppity about,' Violet heard her mutter darkly to the cat as she shuffled back down the passageway. 'A widow indeed! Take more than a cheap secondhand ring to pull the wool over my eyes. I know a wrong 'un when I see one.'

They walked briskly to school, trying to keep warm. The fog had lifted, but their breath hung in the frosty air.

Violet gripped Oliver's hand, not letting him go until they were safely at the school gates.

'Now don't forget,' she warned him, 'wait for me by the door. Don't come out of the gates, and don't talk to anyone else. Do you hear me?'

'Why can't I walk home with the other boys?' he protested.

'I've told you, Ollie. It's not safe for you.'

'Why not?'

Violet tried to find the right words, then gave up. 'Just do as I say,' she said, holding him at arms' length, her eyes fixed on his. 'And promise me you'll never go off with anyone else. No matter what they say to you.'

'I promise, Mummy. I won't let the bad people get me.' Oliver looked so solemn, Violet couldn't help hugging him fiercely.

'Mummy!' He wriggled free, embarrassed. 'I'm not a baby,' he protested.

'No, you're not. You're growing up fast.' Too fast, she thought. One day he would be old enough to understand the truth. She wondered if she would ever find the courage to tell him.

She watched him go into the solid, redbrick school building with the other children. Only when he was out of sight and the doors had closed did she turn away and head back to her lodgings.

Oliver was her pride and joy, the only important thing in her life, but she had to keep him a secret, not least from her employers. Nurses were supposed to devote themselves to their work, so no one would have taken Violet on if they'd known she had a child to look after.

And there were other reasons why they had to remain in the shadows, reasons even Oliver couldn't know about.

On the way, she decided to stop off at the chemist's to buy some Friar's Balsam and cough medicine. She knew from past attacks that Oliver's bronchitis could come on suddenly, and she wanted to be prepared.

Out of habit, she kept to the narrow backstreets where she could, only emerging on to Cable Street when she had to. Even then she constantly glanced over her shoulder, eyes darting everywhere, searching the faces of passers-by.

There was a queue in the chemist's. The severe winter, with its snow, icy winds and freezing fog, had brought on all kinds of complaints, from chest infections to chilblains. And rather than pay to see a doctor, most people preferred to try to cure their ailments themselves, either with pills from the chemist or home remedies.

Violet had just given the chemist her order when the bell over the door jangled and Sister Blake walked in. Violet was so used to seeing her in a severe grey dress, her face framed by a starched white bonnet, that she almost didn't recognise the pretty, dark-haired woman in her crimson coat and neat felt hat.

She turned away quickly, pulling up her scarf so she wouldn't be seen. But it was too late. Sister Blake was already edging past the queue towards her.

'Miss Tanner?'

Violet turned around. 'Sister,' she greeted her. She was wearing gloves, but still instinctively hid her left hand in the folds of her coat.

'I think, since we're both out of uniform, you could call me Frannie.' Her smile was warm and friendly, lighting up her sparkling dark eyes. 'And I shall call you Violet, if I may?'

Violet tentatively returned her smile. She hadn't had much to do with Frannie so far, but her ward seemed happy and well run, and no one had a bad word to say about her.

'It seems odd, doesn't it, coming to a chemist's when we're surrounded by medicine all day?' Frannie said. 'But it's my day off and I'm going to visit my elderly aunt, and she's insisted I should bring her some of Dr Williams' Pink Pills. I've tried telling her they're a waste of money, but she's convinced they do wonders for her nerves, so what can you do?' She shrugged. 'What about you? I do hope you're not sickening for anything?'

'No, no, it's – um – for a friend.' Violet couldn't meet her eye as the chemist appeared with her medicines wrapped up in a brown paper bag.

'I'm glad to hear it. I don't know what we'd do without our Night Sister!' Frannie beamed. There was the trace of a northern accent in her voice. 'How do you like the Nightingale? I hope you're settling in all right?'

'Yes, thank you.' Violet edged away a few steps.

'I'm sorry we haven't been properly intro duced. We're rather like ships in the night, aren't we?'

'Mmm.' Violet eyed the door. A few more steps and she could escape.

But Frannie had other ideas. 'Tell you what, why don't you wait for me?' she suggested. 'If you're not in any hurry we could have a cup of tea. It would be nice to have a chat, get to know each other...'

'I am in a hurry,' Violet cut her off abruptly.

'Oh.' Frannie looked startled. 'Of course, how silly of me. I suppose you've not long finished your shift, haven't you? You'll be wanting your bed, I expect.' She smiled. 'Perhaps some other time?'

'Perhaps.'

'It would be nice for you to get to know all the Sisters, wouldn't it?' Her face brightened. 'I don't suppose you're interested in music at all? Only some of us like to get together and sing in a choir now and then – nothing serious, strictly for our own amusement. I don't know if you'd like to come along?'

'I can't sing.'

'Neither can most of our little group, but don't tell them I said that!' She smiled mischievously. 'I'm sure there must be some way we could all get together? It must be awfully lonely for you, working every night and never seeing anyone?'

'Actually, I prefer my own company,' Violet said bluntly.

'Oh.' Frannie's smile faltered a little. 'Right. I understand.'

'Now, if you'll excuse me...' Violet was out of the shop before Frannie had a chance to say any more.

She hurried home, her package tucked firmly under one arm. She felt a stab of guilt for what she'd done. She hadn't meant to be so sharp with Sister Blake; the poor woman was only trying to be friendly. And she seemed exactly the sort Violet might have chosen for a friend, if she had dared to allow herself such a luxury.

Chapter Six

The new patient on Female Chronics had been found sleeping rough under the railway arches. She was a deaf mute, breathless, coughing and barely able to stand when the police brought her in. But that didn't stop her scratching and kicking out at Millie and Helen as they tried to get her clothes off in the bathroom.

'But you'll enjoy it,' Millie coaxed, jumping backwards as the woman's boot caught her squarely on the shin. 'Look, lots of lovely hot water for you to soak in.' She tested it with the tip of her elbow. 'I jolly well wouldn't mind it myself, I can tell you.'

A deep, hot bath was one of the many luxuries she missed; junior students like her had to shiver in a couple of tepid inches after the seniors regularly nabbed all the hot water at the nurses' home. But at least they weren't as badly off as the first-year probationers, who regularly emerged from the bathroom with chattering teeth and blue extremities.

'I don't think you're going to persuade her like that,' Helen sighed. 'If you ask me, brute force is needed.'

Millie stepped back, hands on her hips. 'So what do you suggest? Should we–'

Before she had time to finish the sentence, Helen had sidestepped the woman's swinging boot and moved in swiftly to grab her from behind, pinning her arms to her sides and pushing her down to land with a thump on a chair. The woman gave a final grunt of defeat as all the fight went out of her.

Millie stared at Helen admiringly. 'Where did you learn to do that?'

'Fighting with my brother.' Helen paused for a moment, breathing hard. 'Right, you get her boots off while I hold her. Then at least she can't do so much damage if she starts fighting again.'

It took them ten minutes to peel off the layers of rags the woman was wearing. Her clothes, if anyone could call them that, were stiff with dirt and stank of stale urine.

'Poor old thing,' Millie said, as the woman stared balefully at her. 'How could anyone let herself get in this state?'

But there was worse to come. Underneath her clothes, her skin was ingrained with dirt and encrusted with oozing sores. And when Millie pulled off her shapeless hat, she jumped back with a scream of fright.

'Oh my God, Tremayne, her head is moving!'

Helen peered over. 'Lice,' she said.

Millie clamped a hand over her mouth. It was all she could do not to run screaming from the bathroom.

'For heaven's sake, Benedict, pull yourself together,' Helen said. 'It's only a few bugs.'

'A few?' The woman's scalp was crawling with them. Just looking at her made Millie's skin itch.

'I'm sorry, I can't touch her.' She backed away, scratching feverishly at her arms.

'Benedict—'

'I can't help it, I don't like the thought of things crawling around in my hair.'

'Benedict!' Millie caught the warning hiss in Helen's voice and suddenly realised she wasn't looking at her, but staring straight past her shoulder towards the doorway.

Millie turned slowly, a feeling of dread creeping up on her. There, as she knew she would be, stood Sister Hyde. How did she manage to catch Millie out so often? It wasn't fair, she thought.

'What are you making a fuss about now, Benedict?' she demanded, her face a rigid mask of disapproval.

'Nothing, Sister.'

Sister Hyde strode into the bathroom, closing the door behind her. Her expression softened when she saw the elderly woman shivering with fear under the towel Helen had wrapped around her.

'Poor wretch,' she murmured under her breath, then turned back to Millie. 'Perhaps, Benedict, you might stop thinking about yourself for a moment and imagine how this unfortunate woman is feeling? She is clearly confused and terrified by her surroundings. Can you imagine how humiliating it must be to have to suffer an idiot girl squealing in revulsion at the very sight of her?'

'Yes, Sister. Sorry, Sister.' Millie stared at the white-tiled wall, hot shame washing over her.

'It is not me you should be apologising to, Benedict. Never, ever forget that our patients, old and unfortunate as they may be, are still human beings with feelings.'

'Yes, Sister.'

Sister Hyde inspected the woman's head with a frowning glance.

'Yes, extremely pediculous,' she pronounced. 'Well, you're not going to be able to comb them out, there are far too many. You're going to have to apply a sassafras cap. You do know how to apply a sassafras cap, don't you?' Millie stared at her blankly. Sister Hyde tutted. 'Good heavens, what do they teach you in PTS these days?' She sighed heavily.

'Please, Sister, shall I do it?' Helen put in.

Sister Hyde gave her a withering glance. 'Have you done it before?'

'Yes, Sister.'

'Then you don't need to do it again, do you? How will Benedict ever learn if you keep helping her?'

'Yes, Sister.' As Helen hung her head humbly, Sister Hyde turned back to Millie. 'Go to the ward cupboard and find the oil of sassafras. It's in a large brown glass bottle. You must soak a piece of lint in it, then apply it to the patient's head. Cover it with a piece of jaconet, then a layer of wool, then fix it in place with a capelline bandage. You know what a capelline bandage is, I presume?'

'Yes, Sister.' Millie decided that now wasn't the time to tell her she'd never successfully dressed a patient's head in her life.

When Sister had gone, Millie and Helen managed to coax the woman into the bathtub. Once in, her whole body relaxed and she gave a blissful sigh as she slipped up to her neck in the warm water.

'You see?' Millie smiled over her shoulder, as she arranged a clean nightgown on the radiator. 'I told you you'd enjoy it.' She glanced across at Helen. 'Sorry I took fright earlier on. Sister's right, it was silly and thoughtless of me.'

'It doesn't matter.'

Millie frowned. Helen seemed preoccupied as she gently sponged the woman's scarred shoulders, as if she had something troubling on her mind.

'Is anything wrong?' Millie asked.

Helen was silent for a moment, concentrating on her task. Then, suddenly, she blurted out, 'William has a new girlfriend.'

Millie unfolded a towel and smoothed it out on the radiator to warm it. She was aware of Helen watching her closely, waiting for her to react.

'Your brother always has a new girlfriend,' she said lightly.

'We think this one might be serious. He's even talking about taking her home to meet Mother.'

'Gosh, then it must be serious. So who's the lucky nurse this time? Anyone I know?'

'She's not a nurse. She's a doctor. Her name's Philippa and they met years ago at university.'

'A doctor? That makes a change.'

'It does, doesn't it?' Helen looked up at her, her dark eyes anxious. 'You are all right about it, aren't you?'

'Why shouldn't I be?' Millie made a big effort to widen her smile. 'There was never anything serious between William and me. Besides, I'm engaged to Seb now. Why should I care what your brother gets up to?'

'No reason, I suppose,' Helen agreed. 'I just thought you'd want to hear it from me rather than the hospital grapevine.'

'That's very thoughtful of you, but really there's no need to worry about my feelings,' Millie assured her. 'Anyway, it's about time William settled down.'

'That's what Mother says. And as you know, my mother is always right.' Helen frowned at her. 'You aren't upset, are you?'

'I told you, I'm fine. Your brother and I had a silly, five-minute infatuation, nothing more than that. I like to think we're still friends, but that's as far as it goes.'

'I'm glad to hear it,' Helen said. 'So why are you folding up that towel you've just spread out on the radiator?'

Millie blinked at the folded towel in her hands, then sighed and unfolded it again. 'I'll go and get that sassafras cap ready.'

She stood at the ward cupboard, staring at the rows of glass bottles full of oils, fluids and various tinctures.

I don't care, she told herself. I'm engaged to Sebastian now. William Tremayne can have as many girlfriends as he likes.

God knows, he'd rarely been without a girl on his arm the whole time she'd known him. Dr Tremayne enjoyed a reputation as the scourge of the Nightingale's young nurses; no girl was safe from him.

Including Millie. She had fallen for him just like all the others. But unlike the others, she'd never become one of his conquests. She'd come to her senses, and found someone who truly loved her instead.

So why was she so shaken to hear that William had found someone too? It didn't make sense.

You don't want him but you don't want anyone else to have him, that's your problem, she told herself as she took the large brown glass bottle out of the cupboard and closed the door firmly.

Back in the bathroom, Helen had got the woman out of the bath, dried her off and was carefully dabbing disinfectant solution on her sores. The warm bath seemed to have subdued her, and she submitted with barely a whimper.

'She probably understands now that we're only trying to help her,' Millie said, as they bundled her into a hospital nightgown.

As Helen went to fill a hot water bottle for her bed, Millie set to work with the sassafras. It was a fiddly job, especially getting the capelline bandage tidy and secure. She was just tucking the final end in place when Helen returned.

'How are you getting on?' she asked.

'I think I've managed it.' Millie stood back and surveyed her handiwork. She'd done a good job for once, even if she said so herself.

That wasn't what Sister Hyde said, of course. She thought the bandage was very poorly executed, and she made sure she told Millie so several times as she and Helen put the woman into bed, where she fell into a deep, contented sleep.

'Poor old thing,' Millie said, looking down at her, 'I don't suppose she ever got much rest, sleeping in those cold, noisy railway arches.'

The following morning, the woman seemed much brighter. She was sitting up in bed eating toast when Millie arrived for her duty. She was pleased to notice the bandage was still in place – so much for Sister Hyde's dire predictions, she thought triumphantly.

But still Sister wasn't happy with her. 'When are you going to remove that patient's cap, Nurse?' she demanded, as she handed out the work lists. 'I know you have a horror of pediculi, but I'm sure you have nothing to fear by now.'

'I'll do it straight away, Sister.'

'And make sure you comb the hair out thoroughly before you shampoo it.'

This time the woman was as meek as a lamb as she followed Millie to the bathroom.

'You see,' Millie beamed at her as she unwound the bandage. 'Having a bath isn't so bad, is it? And you feel so much better when you're all clean and...' She stopped, the dressing falling from her hand. For a moment she stared at the woman's head, unable to believe what she saw.

'You stay there, I – um – won't be a moment.' Smiling encouragingly at the patient, she backed out of the bathroom and rushed to the kitchen where she found Helen making tea.

She looked up from warming the pot. 'Hello, aren't you supposed to be looking after our new patient?' Then she saw Millie's stricken expression. 'Oh Lord, please don't tell me you've done something awful to her?'

'You could say that.' Millie swallowed hard. 'You'd better come and see.'

Helen didn't quite believe what she saw either. 'But I don't understand,' she said. 'Sassafras shouldn't do that to anyone's hair.' She frowned at Millie. 'You're sure you put it on properly?'

'Of course I'm sure!' Millie stared at the woman's hair. No matter how hard she stared at it, it still looked the same. Overnight, it had gone from dirty brown to a halo of startling orange.

'You don't think it was shock, do you?' Helen ventured. 'You hear of that happening to people.'

'Shock turns people's hair white, not ... that colour.' Millie chewed her lip. 'Oh, Lord, what am I going to do? Sister Hyde is going to have an absolute fit.'

'Not if you don't tell her.'

'Tremayne, she can spot a speck of dust from the other end of the ward. Do you really think she won't notice something like this?'

'You could try to cover it up?'

'How?'

Helen looked thoughtful. 'A hat?' she suggested.

'You're not being very helpful.'

'I'm sorry,' Helen bit her lip. Millie could see she was making a supreme effort to stop herself from laughing.

'It's not funny. She looks like a marmalade cat.'

'She looks more like Doyle!' Then Millie caught sight of the orange hair out of the corner of her eye and felt her own mouth twitching treacherously.

'It's not funny,' she repeated. But then Helen started laughing and Millie couldn't stop herself from joining in. The patient joined in too, with a bellowing snort of a laugh that made Helen and Millie giggle even more.

'Something amusing nurses?'

Hearing Sister Hyde's voice was like having a bucket of icy water thrown over them. Even the patient sobered instantly, staring at Sister with round, fearful eyes.

'Really, Tremayne, I might have expected foolish high spirits from Benedict, but not from you. I thought you had more–'

Millie couldn't look, but she guessed Sister Hyde had spotted the patient, perched on her chair beside the bath, looking prim in her nightgown.

'What is this?' she said faintly.

'I don't know, Sister,' Millie replied.

'You don't know?' Sister Hyde swung round to face her, eyes narrowing. 'What do you mean, you don't know? Is this some kind of prank, Benedict?'

'It isn't, Sister, believe me. All I did was apply the sassafras cap as you told me, and then when I removed it this morning, it was – like this.' She looked at the patient. 'I thought perhaps it was supposed to do that?' she suggested hopefully.

Sister Hyde quivered with rage. 'Have you seen this woman's hair, Benedict? Have you?'

'Yes, Sister.'

'And do you honestly suppose that it is normal to turn a patient's hair orange while removing head lice?'

'Well–'

'No, Benedict, it isn't.' Sister Hyde closed her eyes briefly. She looked as if she was praying for strength. 'How on earth could you have done something like this? Are you sure you followed my instructions?'

'Yes, Sister.'

She and Helen glanced at each other as Sister Hyde picked up the lint she had taken from the woman's head and sniffed it.

'Odd,' she said. 'What exactly did you put on this, Benedict?'

'Oil of Sassafras, Sister. From the bottle in the cupboard.'

'Which bottle was that, Benedict? Show me.'

They made a humiliating procession to the ward cupboard, Sister Hyde in front, Millie and Helen trailing behind. Word had begun to spread, and a couple of the other nurses had sidled off to see for themselves what Millie had done now.

'This is what I used, Sister.' Millie took down the brown glass bottle and handed it to her. Sister Hyde examined the label, then unscrewed the cap and sniffed it.

'Tell me, Benedict, does this smell like the sassafras oil you used?'

She thrust it under Millie's nose. She recoiled as the pungent smell hit her. 'Ugh! No, Sister.'

'How about this?' Sister Hyde reached into the cupboard and took out another, identical brown glass bottle. Dread crept like ice through Millie's

72

veins as the truth began to dawn on her. She realised what she'd done even before Sister Hyde had unscrewed the cap and waved it under her nose. 'Perhaps this smells more familiar?'

It smelt familiar, all right. How many times had she used it to treat septic wounds? But she had been so preoccupied she hadn't even noticed. 'Yes, Sister.'

'And what does the label say?'

Millie didn't even have to raise her eyes to know. 'Hydrogen peroxide, Sister.'

'Which explains the patient's miraculous transformation, doesn't it?'

Millie heard a muffled giggle from the other side of the door. 'I'm sorry Sister. I don't know how it happened–'

'Oh, I do.' Sister Hyde's mouth thinned with contempt. 'You are, as I have always suspected, completely incapable of following simple instructions.'

Millie stared at the floor. She must have been so busy thinking about William, she hadn't read the label on the bottle correctly.

'Sorry, Sister.'

'Sorry indeed.' Her chilly gaze raked Millie from head to foot. 'I realise, Nurse Benedict, that this work is little more than a distraction for you, a way of filling in time before you get married, but I would thank you to remember that some of us take nursing very seriously. For some of us, taking care of patients is our life's work. And if you're not able to respect that, then perhaps you shouldn't be here.'

'But, Sister–'

'I really don't wish to hear any more from you, Benedict. Now I want you to go back to the bathroom and sort out that poor woman's hair. You'd better go with her, Tremayne, and make sure she doesn't leave her completely bald next time.'

'Yes, Sister,' they chorused.

'And while you're at it, Benedict, you can think about how you're going to explain this sorry incident to Matron, too. Because you can be sure I will be mentioning it in my ward report!'

Millie was still smarting over Sister Hyde's harsh comment when she got back to the bathroom.

'It's not fair,' she protested, taking off her stiff cuffs and rolling up her sleeves. 'She made me sound like some silly girl who is just doing this for fun. For heaven's sake, if I were out for fun, do you really think I would be here, disinfecting patients' sores and killing head lice?'

'You mustn't blame Sister Hyde,' Helen said. 'She's dedicated her whole life to nursing, and she expects the rest of us to do the same.'

'Who says I'm not devoting my life to nursing, too?'

Helen sent her a sceptical look. 'Everyone knows you're going to marry Sebastian as soon as you finish training.'

'You're going to marry Charlie.'

'Not for a few years. We agreed to wait before we got engaged, so that I could really make a go of my nursing.'

'I might do the same.'

'Do you think your grandmother would allow that?'

Millie was silent with resentment as she started to rinse the woman's hair.

Helen leant forward to peer at her. 'Are you crying?'

'Certainly not. I've just splashed myself in the eye, that's all.' She wiped her streaming nose on her sleeve.

She wouldn't give Sister Hyde the satisfaction of seeing her cry. Then she really would think Millie was an idiot.

'She said she wasn't crying, but I knew she was,' Helen told Charlie later. 'Poor Benedict, Sister really tore her off a strip. I've never seen her in such a temper.'

They were sitting in their favourite café, the place where Charlie had proposed nearly five months before. The cockney-Italian café owner had had a soft spot for them ever since, and often let them stay behind after hours while he cleaned up around them.

'I reckon that Sister of yours could do with a sense of humour,' Charlie grinned. 'It sounds like a right lark to me.'

Helen smiled in spite of herself. 'It was, but it could have been very serious. As nurses we can't afford to make mistakes like that. Someone could have died as a result of Benedict's reading a label wrongly.' She twirled a teaspoon between her fingers. 'The worst thing is, I can't help feeling it was all my fault.'

'How do you make that out?'

'I told her about William's new girlfriend. She put on a brave face, but I know she took it badly.'

Poor Millie. However much she might protest otherwise, Helen knew she still had feelings for William. She wished now she hadn't tried to keep them apart. She'd only done it because she was worried her brother would break Millie's heart, like he'd hurt so many girls in the past. But perhaps if she'd stood back and allowed the relationship to take its course, Millie would have realised for herself what he was like. Then her friend wouldn't be feeling so sad now.

'She would have found out sooner or later,' Charlie said pragmatically. 'Better it came from you than anyone else.'

'That's true,' Helen admitted with a sigh. 'William does seem rather besotted with this new girlfriend of his.'

'What's she like?'

'I only know what he's told me. She's a doctor and they met at university. They got back in touch recently, and William apparently fell head over heels in love.'

'How long's it going to last this time, I wonder?' Charlie's mouth twisted.

'That's the thing. I think he's really serious this time. He wants to introduce her to our mother. He's never done that before.'

'I hope she's a brave woman,' Charlie remarked. 'She's going to need to be.'

Helen looked across the table at him. He was smiling as usual, but she knew how hurt he was by the way her mother treated him.

Perhaps it was because he didn't come from the right background, or because an accident had left him disabled, or just because he had given Helen the confidence to stand up to her mother at last. But whatever the reason, Constance Tremayne made it clear she disapproved of her daughter's choice of boyfriend. No matter how well mannered and charming Charlie tried to be, her mother treated him with barely disguised contempt.

He certainly didn't deserve it, Helen thought as she looked into his smiling blue eyes. Charlie was simply the most wonderful man she had ever met.

'I'm sorry,' she apologised automatically.

'Whatever for?' He looked at her in surprise.

'My mother. I know she can be rather difficult...'

'She's protective of you, that's all.' Charlie put his hand over hers. 'Any mother would be. My mum's just the same.'

'No, she isn't.' Helen pulled a face. 'Your mother is an angel compared to mine.'

'Only because she's so relieved to find someone to take me off her hands!'

Helen smiled. 'She adores you, and you know it.'

The Dawsons had welcomed her into the family from the first moment she'd met them. Helen had been a little intimidated at first, faced with Charlie's extended tribe of brothers, sisters, aunts, uncles and cousins, who filled their cramped terrace house with constant noise and laughter. It was all so different from her own quiet, orderly upbringing in the Vicarage of St Oswald's, where laughing or speaking out of place were frowned on.

Not by her father, of course. The Reverend

77

Timothy Tremayne was a kind, loving man, but like the rest of the family he was dominated by his wife. Constance Tremayne controlled everything and everyone, and Helen, her father and her brother had learnt quickly that it was best to fall in with her plans.

Which was why Helen had ended up becoming a nurse in the first place. Constance had trained as a nurse herself, and it didn't occur to Helen to argue when her mother announced that she should do the same. But even when she started her training, Helen couldn't escape; her mother had seen to it that she became a nurse at the Nightingale, where Mrs Tremayne was on the Board of Trustees.

Helen might have gone on living under her mother's thumb if she hadn't met Charlie on her ward. He had lost his leg in an accident, and Helen had helped him come to terms with his anger and despair. But somewhere along the line professional caring had turned to friendship and then to love.

Knowing how horrified her mother would be at the idea of her daughter having a boyfriend, she and Charlie had kept their romance a secret at first. But inevitably Constance had found out. Of course she had tried to put a stop to it at once, even going so far as to pack Helen off to Scotland to finish her training. But by some miracle, and after an impassioned plea by Charlie, she had relented at the last minute and given her grudging approval to the match.

But that didn't mean she was happy about it.

'Tell you what, I wouldn't mind being a fly on

78

the wall when your mum meets William's new girlfriend,' Charlie said.

'You won't have to be a fly on the wall. We've been invited to lunch too.'

Invited, she thought with a smile. It made it sound as if anyone had a choice in the matter.

'Me?' Charlie looked surprised, as well he might. In all the months they had been seeing each other, he had only been allowed to visit the Vicarage once. And Helen knew even that had been for the sake of appearances, and nothing else.

'Yes.' She couldn't meet his eye. 'Mother says she's looking forward to seeing you again.'

She could sense his sceptical look. 'Are you sure about that?'

Helen bit her lip. 'You will come, won't you?' she blurted out. 'I mean, I wouldn't blame you if you didn't. But I'd like you to be there – for my sake?'

He squeezed her hand. 'Don't look so worried, love. Of course I'll be there. Don't want to let your mum down, do we?' he added mischievously. 'Not if she's looking forward to seeing me.'

Helen tried to smile back. It will all be all right, she told herself. But deep down, she couldn't help secretly hoping that William's new girlfriend would be awful. At least then it might make her mother more kindly disposed towards poor Charlie.

Chapter Seven

The chilly grey January dawn brought another so-called miscarriage on the Gynae ward.

In the two weeks Dora had been on Wren, not a day went by without at least one woman being admitted, screaming in pain and haemorrhaging badly. Some were young, some older, some married, some single. Some were lucky and survived, others were not.

It was too early to tell if the girl they'd operated on in the early hours of the morning was one of the lucky ones.

'Miscarriage, my eye,' Lettie Pike sneered as she made up the fire in the side ward where the patient had been put to recover from surgery. 'We all know what that one's been up to, don't we?'

'Have they made you a doctor now, Lettie?' Dora snapped.

'You don't have to be a doctor to see what she's done. Can you see a wedding ring on her finger?' Lettie shook her head. 'No, she's been caught good and proper. I expect she got a neighbour to help her out, or tried to do it herself. She made a right mess of it, too, from what I hear.'

'You hear too much.'

'I only hear what there is to hear.' Lettie straightened up, massaging her back.

Dora didn't bother to reply as she stroked a strand of pale hair back from the girl's ashen face. A pulse jumped feebly in her temple. She was as white as her pillows, her skinny frame swamped by the hospital nightgown.

It was the first time Dora had been entrusted to sit with a post-operative patient. She was so nervous she didn't dare take her eyes off the girl, just in case she missed the first flicker of consciousness.

Lettie looked down at her with a knowing eye. 'You're wasting your time with that one,' she said. 'She's a goner, if you ask me.'

'No one's asking you, are they?'

'Just giving my opinion.'

'Dr Tremayne seems to think she stands a chance.'

'Dr Tremayne isn't much more than a kid himself,' Lettie dismissed. 'That one might have stood more chance if she'd had Mr Cooper operate on her.'

'I expect next time she decides to collapse with massive haemorrhaging, she'll remember to wait until Mr Cooper's clinic hours,' Dora said.

'There won't be a next time, will there?' Lettie smiled nastily. 'From what I hear, she'd let it get so bad Dr Tremayne had to take it all away.' She looked down at the girl in the bed without sympathy. 'I wonder if she'd have been so quick to get rid of that baby she was carrying if she'd known it was her last chance?'

'Haven't you got any work to do, Lettie?' Dora turned on her, fighting to keep her temper.

'Pardon me for breathing, I'm sure. But I take my orders from Sister, not you!'

Lettie hauled the coal bucket out of the room,

slamming the door behind her. Dora turned back to the girl. Poor little thing, she thought. She looked so young, not much older than her sister Josie by the look of it. Her skin was as pale as pearl, her eyelids so translucent Dora could see the tracery of fine blue veins.

Lettie might be a vicious witch, but she was right about one thing, Dora thought. This girl, whoever she was, had said goodbye to her chances of ever having another child. But if she was desperate enough to turn to a backstreet abortionist, then perhaps she was too desperate to care anyway.

'Now then, little Miss No Name,' she whispered, covering the girl's small hand with hers. The skin on her palm was rubbed raw. 'How about you prove that old cow Lettie wrong and wake up, eh?'

It was just turned eight o'clock when the girl came round, and even longer before she was able to understand what was going on. Her eyelids fluttered open and she stared straight up at Dora. Her eyes were green, flecked with amber like a cat's.

'Hello,' Dora greeted her with a smile.

The girl's gaze darted around the room, then fixed back on Dora. 'Where am I?'

'In the Nightingale Hospital, love. You've been very poorly, but you're getting better now.'

Emotions passed like clouds across her face as realisation dawned. 'I collapsed.' She frowned, trying to put it all together. 'There was so much blood–'

'You were in a bad way, love.'

She drew in a deep, shuddering breath. 'She ...

she said it would be all right. She said I wouldn't feel a thing and no one would need to know anything about it. But there was so much pain, so much blood. I thought I was going to die–'

What little colour she had drained from her face and Dora grabbed the enamel receiver dish, just as the girl leant over and retched into it.

'Shh, don't say any more,' she said softly, stroking the girl's hair back off her face. 'You don't want to tell too many people what happened, all right? As far as anyone else needs to know, you lost your baby.'

The girl nodded dumbly. Even in her state, she understood that admitting to an illegal abortion could get her locked up. Most doctors and nurses turned a blind eye for the sake of the poor women, but Dora knew there were some who might not.

'Anyway, it's all over now, and you got through it. I'll fetch you some water, shall I?'

She felt the girl watching her as she filled a glass with water from the jug beside the bed. 'Does my dad know I'm here?' she asked fearfully.

'I don't think so, love. You turned up in the emergency department in the early hours, but I don't know who brought you.' Dora held the glass to her lips. 'We don't even know your name?'

'It's Jennie. Jennie Armstrong.' She pushed the glass away and looked up at Dora. 'I came here by myself,' she said. 'I started walking, but I ended up on my hands and knees when the pain got too bad.'

'That explains all these scratches and grazes.' Dora turned her palm over to show her. 'Your knees are rubbed raw too. You poor girl, why on earth didn't you call an ambulance?'

Jennie's chin tilted. 'I didn't want no ambulance coming to the house, in case someone told my dad.'

'He'll find out soon enough, surely?'

Jennie shook her head. 'Not if I get back smartish. He works two till ten at the docks. He won't know anything about it if I'm back before he gets home—'

She started to try and struggle upright, but Dora pinned her firmly back against the pillows by her shoulders. 'Sorry, ducks, but you're not going anywhere. The doctor will want you to stay in here for a couple of weeks.'

'A couple of weeks?' Jennie's green eyes filled with panic. 'But you don't understand, I can't stay here that long. My dad will kill me—'

'You'll kill yourself if you start getting upset. At least let me check you over.' Dora took the thermometer from its stand beside the bed, shook it and placed it in Jennie's mouth. 'You've had an operation, and the doctor needs to make sure you're well before you even think about leaving here.'

She took the thermometer out of the girl's mouth, checked it and noted the temperature on the chart. Then she took her pulse and checked her dressing. 'That seems all right,' she smiled. 'And you look as if you're getting some colour back into your cheeks, which is good. Now do me a favour and try to get some rest.'

'But I need to go home,' Jennie whimpered. 'My dad—'

'I'm sure he would rather you stayed here and got well.'

Jennie turned fear-filled eyes to meet hers. 'You don't know my dad,' she said.

Once she'd persuaded Jennie to go back to sleep, and finished making notes on her chart card, Dora went out to report to Sister Wren. But she was more concerned about the half-dozen eggs that had gone missing from the kitchen larder than she was about her newest patient.

'They were here yesterday morning, I know they were,' she insisted. 'Someone must have taken them.'

Her gaze raked the nurses assembled around her desk, settling finally on Dora. 'They belonged to a patient,' she said. 'Whoever has taken them is a thief. And I will be keeping a careful eye on you all until I find out who has been stealing.'

'Why on earth does she think we'd want to steal her wretched eggs?' another student, Katie O'Hara, whispered to Dora as they collected their work lists. 'It's not as if we can cook in the nurses' home, is it? If you ask me, it's more likely to be the night staff who took them, and left us to take the blame.' She consulted her work list. 'I'm doing beds, how about you?'

'Laundry, just for a change.' Dora looked down her list and sighed.

The morning was spent collecting and counting the soiled linen and entering the details in the laundry book, then packing it up in baskets to be sent off. Ennis brought in a couple of stained drawsheets, which Dora had to soak in cold water.

She worked as quickly and efficiently as she could, but even then Sister Wren wasn't satisfied. 'I hope you're not going to put those damp sheets in with the rest of the laundry?' She stood in the doorway to the sluice, watching Dora. 'You'll have the whole lot ruined with mildew.'

'No, Sister.'

'And when you've finished, clean the mackintoshes. And see you dry them properly, too. I don't want to see them folded up and shoved in a drawer while they're still damp.'

'No, Sister.' Dora gritted her teeth.

Fortunately she was saved from further nagging by Staff Nurse Cuthbert.

'There's a man in Emergency looking for his sister,' she said. 'Apparently she's gone missing.'

'And why are you telling me this?' Sister Wren demanded.

'They seem to think it might be the patient who was admitted during the night? Although we don't know her name...'

'Jennie,' Dora put in. 'It's Jennie Armstrong.'

Sister Wren turned slowly to face her, her eyebrows rising. 'I'm sorry, Doyle? Did anyone ask you to join in this conversation?'

'That's her! That's the girl he was looking for,' Staff Nurse Cuthbert said excitedly. 'I'll go and tell them, shall I?'

'You certainly will not,' Sister Wren retorted. 'I shall go down and speak to this person myself. When I am ready.'

'But, Sister, the poor man has been scouring the streets for her. He's exhausted–'

'And I shall go and talk to him in a moment,'

86

Sister Wren interrupted her. 'Goodness gracious, Cuthbert, I have a ward to run. I can't just drop everything and rush off willy-nilly, can I? Now, have you had any luck finding those missing eggs?'

Dora caught the flash of resentment in Staff Nurse Cuthbert's eyes, and realised they were thinking exactly the same thing. Sister Wren had no trouble dropping everything when Mr Cooper called in, or when she wanted to put her feet up and read *Peg's Paper*.

When she'd finished putting the mackintoshes on to rollers to dry, Dora went to Jennie Armstrong's room to check on her. She was still sleeping peacefully. It almost seemed a shame to wake her, but she needed to take her pulse and inspect her dressing.

Dora straightened the bedclothes and was tucking a towel around Jennie's neck in case of vomiting when Dr Tremayne came in.

He was as tall and good-looking as his sister, Dora's room mate Helen. But while she exuded an air of unruffled calm, William Tremayne was endearingly scruffy, with a lanky build and flopping dark hair. But he was still a senior houseman, and far out of Dora's orbit. She froze, not sure whether to speak to him or not.

Dr Tremayne smiled at her. 'How's our mystery patient?' he asked.

'She came round just after eight o'clock Doctor. And her name's Jennie Armstrong,' Dora added.

'Jennie Armstrong, eh?'

Dora watched him scanning the chart at the end of Jennie's bed. 'The patient was very anxious to go home, Doctor,' she ventured.

'She won't be going anywhere for a while yet.' He hung the chart back in its place. 'Any vomiting?'

'Only when she first came round.'

'Have you checked her dressing?'

'I was just about to check it again.'

'And her colour was good? She was talking?' Dora nodded. 'That's a relief. I really thought we were going to lose her.' He stood over her. 'Well, Miss Armstrong, you've had a very lucky escape, I reckon.' He ran his hand through his dark hair. 'Poor kid. It's a hellish business. She left it so late, too. She must have been a good few months pregnant, by my reckoning. It must have been agony for her.' His face was bleak. 'Whoever did this to her must have known what was going to happen. I bet they couldn't wait to get rid of her, in case she died there and then.'

Dora hesitated, her eyes darting towards the door. If Sister Wren came in and saw her talking to a doctor...

'I'd like to string these women up for what they do to young girls,' he said suddenly. 'Burning their insides with carbolic and mutilating them so they develop septicaemia. It's barbaric...' He saw Dora's look of dismay and stopped. 'Sorry, I don't mean to go on. But when you've stitched up as many of these girls as I have, you start to hate the women who do this to them. And make a good living from it, too.'

'They don't all do it for the money,' Dora said without thinking. 'Sometimes it's a friend or relative, doing it to help out.'

'Help out?' Dr Tremayne's mouth curled. 'You call this helping out?'

'It's better than the shame of having a baby and no husband.' Dora knew she was talking out of turn, but she couldn't help herself. 'I bet that's what drove this one to it. She's terrified of her dad finding out what's happened. I expect she's worried he'll beat her black and blue, or kick her out on to the streets.'

'Are you trying to tell me this girl is more afraid of her father than she is of dying?'

Dora looked at him steadily. 'You don't know what it's like where I come from.'

'Perhaps I don't,' Dr Tremayne agreed. He paused for a moment, considering. Then he said, 'I'd like you to keep an eye on her. Regular TPRs, make sure she's eating and drinking, and let me know if there are any symptoms you think I should know about.'

'I'll fetch Sister–' Dora started for the door, but Dr Tremayne stopped her.

'No, I'd like you to do it.'

'But I'm just a student.'

'You have compassion,' he said. 'Our Miss Armstrong is going to need that as much as good nursing.' He smiled at her. 'My sister told me you were a good nurse, Doyle. Between us, you and I are going to pull this young lady through.'

Dora was still feeling quietly proud of herself when she went down for her dinner break. Even when Sister Wren accused her of being slapdash with the laundry it couldn't take away the glow of pride she felt after Dr Tremayne's praise.

But as she crossed the courtyard towards the

89

dining room, something was troubling her.

Sister Wren had forgotten all about Jennie's brother. She was still preoccupied with searching for her missing eggs. Either that or she simply couldn't be bothered.

It's none of your business, Dora told herself firmly, hurrying her steps across the courtyard. These things should be left to Sister. You'll only get into trouble if you start sticking your nose in where it doesn't belong.

But then she remembered what Dr Tremayne had said about her having compassion. Surely Jennie's brother deserved a little compassion too?

She had almost reached the safety of the dining room when her conscience got the better of her and she found herself doing an about turn towards the main building.

She spotted him straight away, standing at the desk in the Emergency department.

'Please, Nurse, I've been here for hours,' she heard him saying. 'Surely someone must know if my sister's here? I've looked everywhere else.'

'I've told you, Mr Armstrong, someone will be here to talk to you shortly. In the meantime, please take a seat.'

'But that patient, the one you said they brought in during the night... That could be her, couldn't it? For God's sake, all you have to do is tell me!'

'It is her,' Dora blurted out.

They both turned to look at her. She saw the nurse roll her eyes with exasperation. 'At last!' she mouthed, and went back to her paperwork.

The young man stepped forward. He had fair hair like his sister and the same amber flecks in his green eyes. But he was as tall and muscular as Jennie Armstrong was slight and delicate.

'Jennie's here?' he said. 'Please, Miss, is she all right? Has she had an accident?'

Dora bit her lip. She knew she shouldn't say anything, but the poor man looked so sick with worry she couldn't leave him in such a state.

'Your sister is doing well,' she replied, choosing her words carefully. 'She's had to have an operation, but she is receiving excellent treatment so we expect her to make a full recovery.'

She parroted the words she had heard Sister use when talking to patients' relatives. But Mr Armstrong wasn't satisfied.

'An operation? I don't understand. What kind of an operation? What's wrong with her?'

Dora stared down at her shoes. 'Jennie has had a hysterectomy,' she revealed reluctantly.

'And what's that when it's at home?'

Dora was suddenly acutely aware that she shouldn't be having this conversation. There was a reason why this was best left to senior nurses. But now she'd blundered right in and it was too late to change her mind.

'Perhaps it's best you talk to Sister–'

'I'm asking you.'

'It's really not for me to say–' she began, but the young man cut her off.

'Tell me, Nurse, or so help me, I'll tear this place down brick by brick!' He closed his eyes briefly, and Dora could see he was forcing himself to calm down. 'She's my little sister,' he said, his voice shaking with the effort of controlling himself. 'I was out working all night, and when I came home there was blood everywhere and she was gone. For Christ's sake, nothing you tell me can be as bad as what's been going through my head!'

He looked so desperate, Dora couldn't help herself. 'It was – a miscarriage,' she said.

The blood drained from his face. 'A miscarriage?' He shook his head. 'No, that can't be right. There must be a mistake. Our Jennie wasn't pregnant. For God's sake, she's never even had a boyfriend.'

He ran his hand through his blond hair. He looked so pole-axed by the news, Dora's heart went out to him.

'You really should talk to Sister,' she said, an edge of desperation in her voice. 'If you stay here, I'm sure someone will be down soon.'

She turned and hurried away before he could ask any more. She was painfully aware she'd already said too much.

At the door she allowed herself a quick, guilty look back at him over her shoulder. He was still standing there, staring into space, trying to take in what she'd told him.

Poor man, she thought. Why had she interfered and made matters worse? Sister or a doctor would have taken him to one side, explained everything gently and in a way he could understand. They certainly wouldn't have blurted out the bad news in the middle of a busy emergency department and then abandoned him.

She'd thought she might spare him pain, but instead she'd blundered in and made him feel even worse.

Chapter Eight

A portrait of Charlotte, Countess of Rettingham, dominated the great hall of Billinghurst. She smiled down serenely, captured for ever in her youthful beauty, her gown draped off her shoulders, blonde hair upswept to show off her fine features and swan-like neck.

It was the closest Millie had ever got to her mother; Charlotte Rettingham had died of puerperal fever two days after her daughter was born.

'Do you think I look like her?' Millie asked.

'You have her blue eyes,' Seb replied.

She grinned. 'How tactful! What you really mean is I'm not remotely beautiful or graceful.'

'What I really mean is, you're utterly enchanting and I adore you.' Sebastian put his arm around her waist and kissed her neck tenderly. 'Even if you aren't remotely beautiful or graceful,' he murmured against her skin.

Millie pushed him away, her eyes still fixed on her mother's portrait. 'I wonder if she'd be proud of me, becoming a nurse?' she mused.

'Why wouldn't she be proud? We're all proud of you, Mil. Apart from your grandmother, of course, who thinks you're an utter disgrace.'

'Don't!' The dowager countess had done nothing but criticise Millie since they'd arrived the day before. Millie had been given a few days' holiday, and they were spending some time at Billinghurst before going on to a weekend house party at Seb's family home.

Unfortunately, her father had been called away shortly before they arrived, and was not due back until after they left. Millie was bitterly disappointed not to see him, but her grandmother explained that he had been summoned to Sandringham to see the King.

She didn't have to say why; on the morning they'd left London the newspapers were full of warnings that His Majesty's bronchial condition had weakened his heart. No one would say it, but everyone feared the worst.

Millie understood why her father had had to go, but after just a few hours in her grandmother's company, she was feeling utterly exhausted.

'Really, Amelia, do you have to slouch so?' were the dowager's first words as they joined her for breakfast. She herself sat ramrod-straight at the head of the table, the picture of haughty composure as ever, with her spectacles perched on the end of her long nose as she studied *The Times*. 'I can see all those classes af Madame Vacani's were utterly wasted.'

'Sorry, Granny.' Millie smiled at Seb across the table as they sat down. 'We don't have much chance to practise deportment on the wards.'

Lady Rettingham shuddered. It was an unspoken rule in the house that Millie didn't talk of her work to her grandmother. The only way the dowager countess could cope with such an aberration was to pretend it wasn't happening.

'And how is your sister, Sebastian?' Lady Rettingham changed the subject. 'When is her baby due?'

'Early April, Lady Rettingham.'

'So soon? Goodness, hasn't the time gone quickly? Such an exciting moment, the birth of one's first child. It's what every woman yearns for, isn't it? To be a mother and mistress of her own home.'

Millie felt her grandmother's meaningful gaze on her as she sipped her tea. Lady Rettingham thoroughly approved of Seb's sister Sophia. Not only had she been engaged by the end of the Season – and to the son of a duke, no less – but she had also managed to conceive an heir within weeks of her marriage. Her pregnancy put all Millie's achievements in the shade.

She tried to ignore her grandmother, and buttered her toast with a studied lack of concern. But the dowager was not to be put off.

'I see from *The Times* that Isabelle Pollard is to be married on Saturday. Do you remember her, Amelia? Her mother is the Duke of Horsley's sister. Rather a sullen girl ... very thick ankles? No? Oh, well, it doesn't matter.' She made a show of consulting the newspaper, although Millie knew exactly what was coming next. 'Didn't she announce her engagement after yours?'

'I don't know, Granny.' Millie stared down at her plate.

'Yes, I think she did. Now I recall, it was in November.' Lady Rettingham pretended to think, although her look of concentration fooled no one. She had a blade-sharp memory for other girls' marital arrangements.

95

'Only two months? That seems very hasty, if you ask me,' Millie said, taking a bite of her toast. 'Perhaps she had to get married?'

'Don't be vulgar, Amelia. And don't speak with your mouth full.'

Millie caught Seb's eye across the table. He was trying not to smile.

She counted slowly in her head. One ... two ... three...

'I really think you should at least set a date,' Lady Rettingham blurted out. Millie never got past three.

'There's no hurry, Granny.' Millie licked butter off her fingers. 'I told you, it won't be for at least another two years.'

'Two years!' Her grandmother quivered with outrage. 'That is quite ridiculous. Anything could happen in that time.'

'I think what my grandmother means is that you might change your mind,' Millie told Seb.

'Amelia!' Lady Rettingham turned to him. 'But I'm sure Sebastian must want to be married as soon as possible. Isn't that right, Sebastian?'

'I'm happy to go along with whatever Millie decides, actually, Lady Rettingham.'

The dowager countess looked down her nose at him, as if he'd bitterly disappointed her in some way.

'Well, I suppose you both know what you're doing,' she said heavily. 'I daresay you'll get round to setting a date in your own time. I just hope I'll still be here to see it.' She drew in a deep breath, the picture of injured dignity.

'Oh, Lord, I thought she was going to pull out her handkerchief and start dabbing at her eyes,' Millie said to Seb, as they headed for the stable-yard later. 'I know she's desperate to see me married off, but I never thought she'd stoop to suggesting she might die if I don't hurry up!'

If her grandmother had had her way, Millie would have been engaged by the end of her debutante Season. The dowager had done her best to prepare her granddaughter for her role as a society wife, training Millie like one of the thoroughbreds in her father's stables.

'She's only trying to protect your inheritance,' Seb pointed out.

'I suppose so.' Millie understood it was her duty to marry. As the only daughter of the Earl of Rettingham, she couldn't inherit the estate in her own right. If she married and had a male heir, Billinghurst would stay in the family. If not, it would pass on her father's death to an obscure cousin in Northumberland.

Millie didn't want that to happen. But nor did she want to spend her life as the chatelaine of a country estate, with nothing more demanding to do than order servants about and decide what to wear for dinner. She wanted to be independent, and to do something useful with her life.

She was distracted as the groom led her favourite horse, Mischief, out of the stable. They greeted each other warmly, Mischief greedily nuzzling her pocket for the treat he knew she would have brought with her.

Seb had chosen another of her father's horses, a sleek dark bay called Emperor. It was a big, powerful beast, and even though Millie had been riding almost since the day she learnt to walk, she was still wary of him. But Seb mastered him easily, swinging himself up into the saddle.

She smiled admiringly. 'He knows who's boss, doesn't he?'

'Shame I can't say the same about you!' Seb grinned. He turned Emperor's head and clattered out of the stableyard as Millie hoisted herself into the saddle.

She'd caught him up before they reached the gate. 'I'll show you who's boss. Race you!' she cried, breaking into a canter.

They galloped up to the ridge overlooking the estate which gave the best view of Billinghurst, nestling comfortably amid a rolling patchwork of fields. The wintry sunshine glinted off the house's mullioned windows and turned the thick stone walls to burnished gold.

They dismounted and allowed the horses to rest while they sat on the frosty grass. This kind of crisp, clear January day seldom happened in London, which seemed permanently shrouded in a low, depressing, yellowish-grey fog.

Millie sighed with pleasure. Much as she liked London, Billinghurst was where her heart lay.

'You really love it here, don't you?' Seb glanced across at her.

Millie nodded, her gaze still drifting across the fields. 'It's my home.'

He was silent for a moment, brooding. Then he said, 'You do want to get married, don't you? Only you didn't seem very enthusiastic about the idea when your grandmother was talking about it earlier on?'

'Not you, too!' Millie rolled her eyes at him. 'We talked about this, Seb. We agreed we wouldn't get married until I'd finished my training. Are you saying you want to do it sooner?'

He shook his head. 'As long as it's just the training that's stopping you?'

'What else would it be?'

He shifted his gaze to stare out over the fields. 'I sometimes wonder if you only decided to marry me because of what happened to your father.'

Millie was silent for a moment. She couldn't blame him for wondering. Their engagement had been sudden, after years of being nothing more than friends.

Perhaps they might have gone on being just that if her father hadn't been badly injured in a riding accident. For weeks his life had hung in the balance, and the future of Billinghurst had hung with it. For the first time in her life, Millie had had to consider the consequences of her decision not to marry.

'You're right,' she said. 'I did only decide to marry you because of what happened to Daddy. But not in the way you think,' she went on quickly, seeing his face fall. 'When he had his accident, I felt so horribly alone and afraid. And then you came along, and you made me feel safe.'

He'd driven all the way down from Scotland to be with her. Just when she thought she'd reached the lowest point of despair, suddenly Seb was there, holding her up. He'd taken so much of the weight off her shoulders, looking after the estate while her father was too ill to manage it. And he'd sat with her at her father's bedside, holding her hand through all those long, agonising days and nights.

'That was when I realised I loved you,' she said. 'And, that's why I never want to be with anyone else.'

'And you're not just marrying me so you can inherit Billinghurst?'

Millie laughed. 'What a question!'

'I'm serious.' He turned his head to look at her. For once there was no glint of laughter in his blue eyes.

'Seb, I'm marrying you because I love you.' She frowned at him. 'What on earth has brought all this on?'

'I don't know.' He shrugged. 'Perhaps it's just that I can't believe my luck.' He gazed back across the horizon. 'I've always loved you. Ever since the moment I met you at that first coming-out ball. But I never thought you'd look twice at me. And then, suddenly, a miracle happened, and you loved me. Now I keep looking over my shoulder, wondering if it's all been a fluke, if one day you'll wake up and come to your senses–'

Millie put her finger to his lips, silencing him. 'Don't you see? I came to my senses the day I realised I did love you.'

He took her in his arms and kissed her then. She had always thought it would feel strange kissing Sebastian, because she had known him for so long as a friend. But it felt like the most natural thing in the world.

They lay back, the damp grass soaking through their clothes, and stared up at the cloudless blue sky. Millie rested her head on Seb's chest, feeling the steady beat of his heart against her cheek.

'So you do want to marry me?' he asked again. 'Because if for any reason you want to call off this engagement, you know I'll understand–'

'Do shut up, Seb.'

She lifted her head from his chest and kissed him again. He kissed her back fiercely, his tongue sliding between her lips.

'Oh, God,' he said hoarsely. 'Is it wrong that I want to make love to you right here?'

'You know we can't. Granny would come after you with Daddy's hunting rifle.'

'It might be worth the risk.' As Seb bent to kiss her again, a resounding gunshot rang out across the fields. It was only the gamekeeper shooting rabbits in the lower field, but it shocked them both to their senses.

'What did I tell you?' Millie laughed, scrambling to her feet. 'Come on, let's get back before you do something you'll regret.'

'Who says I'd regret it?'

'You would if my grandmother caught you!'

Chapter Nine

Seb's family home, Lyford, was some thirty miles to the south-west of Billinghurst, over the county border. It was a breathtakingly beautiful Georgian house, with elegant symmetry and imposing frontage of Corinthian columns, sitting in the centre of beautifully manicured parkland. Millie always felt like a humble country cousin when she visited.

They arrived in the middle of the morning, but only Seb's sister Sophia was there to greet them. She was languishing sulkily on the chaise longue in the library.

'Thank God you've come,' she said, rousing herself with an effort, her pregnancy very evident under her loose dress. 'They wouldn't let me go shooting with them because of my condition. It's not fair.' She embraced them both. 'Never get pregnant, Millie,' she warned. 'It's unendurably tedious. I still have nearly three months to go and I'm already bored with this wretched baby.'

'You look very well,' Millie complimented her. Sophia's creamy skin positively glowed, and her hair – as dark as her brother's was fair – glinted in the wintry sunlight that streamed through the tall windows.

'I am well, that's what's so absolutely frustrating about it.' Sophia pouted. 'I'm blooming, as they say. And yet everyone insists on treating me like a piece of priceless Dresden. Every time I want to do something more taxing than getting out of bed, they shake their heads and talk in hushed tones about "my condition". Mother has engaged the services of Sir Charles Ingham as my obstetrician, and I believe she would have him accompany me everywhere if she could. And David's even worse!' She rolled her eyes.

'I'm not surprised. That's his son and heir you're carrying, remember?' Seb said.

'Oh, for heaven's sake, not you too!' Sophia turned to Millie. 'Anyway, you're here now. You

102

can keep me company while the others go off riding and hiking and shooting, and everything else I'm not allowed to do.'

The butler served them tea in the sunny drawing room as they discussed the rest of the house party.

'Who else is here?' Seb asked.

'Well, there's Mother and Father, of course, and Richard and David. And then there are the Carnforths and their daughter Lucinda. You know Lucinda, Mil – we did the Season together?'

Millie nodded. 'How could I forget Lulu?' Lucinda, daughter of Lord and Lady Carnforth, had like many other debutantes arrived in Society with a steely determination to bag herself a suitable husband. Except Lucinda's ambition bordered on the obsessive. She had already scared off one fiancé, and now she was on the hunt for a second.

'She's set her sights on our brother, would you believe?' Sophia said to Seb. 'She's probably out there now, stalking poor Richard with her gun.'

'He's evaded capture so far, I'm sure he can do it again,' said Seb. 'Isn't there another unsuspecting male she can hunt?'

'Only Jumbo, and he's here with Georgina Farsley.' Sophia pulled an apologetic face. 'Sorry,' she said. 'We had no idea he was bringing her until they arrived. It seems they're an item now.'

'Thank heavens for that,' Seb said. 'Perhaps now she'll leave me alone. Her and Jumbo, eh? Who would have thought it?'

Georgina Farsley was an American heiress who had made a play for Seb the previous year. The fact that he wasn't remotely interested in her hadn't stopped her blaming Millie for the failure of her quest. She had nursed a grudge ever since.

But it was the thought of Jumbo Jameson that really made Millie's heart sink. The Earl of Haworth's son was rich, handsome, and a conceited buffoon. He was also one of the reasons Millie had hated the Season so much. She had spent two thoroughly miserable months listening to the likes of Jumbo and his boorish friends showing off around her. The thought of having to spend any more time in his company made her feel quite ill.

The shooting party returned shortly before luncheon. Seb's mother Caroline, Duchess of Claremont, managed to look frighteningly regal even in her rough tweeds. The duke greeted Millie warmly. A little too warmly, for her liking; he might be her future father-in-law, but he was also a notorious old womaniser with a known weakness for blondes.

Lord and Lady Carnforth were a quiet, timid couple, unlike their ambitious daughter Lucinda who came in clinging proprietorially to the arm of Seb's older brother Richard, like a duchess in waiting.

And then there were Jumbo and Georgina. They made a handsome couple, both sleek, dark and exuding glamour.

Millie cringed as Jumbo's gaze fell on her. Just one smirking look from him was enough to send her back in time to the Grosvenor House Ball, standing in the corner with an empty dance card.

'Well, if it isn't Florence Nightingale!' he

104

greeted her.

Millie forced a smile at his tired old joke, for the sake of politeness. 'Hello, Jumbo. Georgina.' She nodded towards Miss Farsley. She was very beautiful, in a brittle kind of way. Her eyes had the cold sheen of polished jet; her painted lips were an uncompromising slash of crimson against her white skin. She was as thin as a whip in mannish trousers and a fitted tweed coat.

'Seb,' she drawled, her American accent even more pronounced since Wallis Simpson and her friends had made it fashionable. 'What a wonderful surprise.' She moved in to kiss his cheek, ignoring Millie completely. 'Are you staying all weekend?'

'We're going back to London tomorrow, I'm afraid. Millie has to report for duty on Monday.'

'Report for duty, eh?' Jumbo said, his eyebrows lifting. 'I suppose those bedpans won't empty themselves, will they?'

'We do more than just empty bedpans,' Millie said patiently.

'Oh, yes? Don't tell me they've let you loose on urinals as well?' He guffawed at his own joke.

'Actually, we save lives.'

She regretted it as soon as the words were out. Jumbo bellowed with laughter. 'Save lives?' he roared, as all heads turned their way. 'Ye Gods, I'm not sure I'd want you to save mine.'

'I'm not sure I would either,' Millie replied primly.

Seb snorted into his glass, but Jumbo was too busy chortling at his own wit to notice.

'From what I remember, you're a bit too accident-prone. I wouldn't fancy putting my life in your hands at all. Do you remember that time at the Wiltons', when you knocked a bottle of champagne over the Bishop?' He looked around, seeking out his audience. 'Tipped it all over him, she did – poor man was utterly soaked.'

'How awful,' Georgina smirked. Millie felt a tide of scalding colour rising up from the neckline of her dress.

'That was a long time ago,' she muttered.

'And then, just to make matters worse, she tried to make a dignified exit, slipped on the spilt champagne and skidded the length of the ballroom!' Jumbo went on, ignoring her. 'God, it was funny.'

He roared with laughter, and the others joined in appreciatively – especially Georgina. Even Seb was smiling, Millie noticed, shooting him a glare.

It started to rain during luncheon so they spent the rest of the afternoon indoors, playing games and listening to music. Millie left the others enacting a lively game of charades in the drawing room and retreated to the library to tackle a jigsaw.

It was a blessed relief to sit somewhere quiet, with nothing but the sombre ticking of the grandfather clock to keep her company.

She was still puzzling over the pieces when Seb found her.

'There you are,' he said. 'Why don't you come and join us?'

'And listen to Jumbo all afternoon? No, thank you. He gives me a headache.'

'He's harmless. Just ignore him.'

'It's all right for you. You're not the butt of his

106

incessant jokes.'

The sound of Lucinda Carnforth shrieking with laughter from down the hallway jangled Millie's nerves.

'Listen to them,' she said. 'I can't imagine anything more tedious than having to listen to that all day.'

'You used to enjoy it,' Seb reminded her. 'I remember a time when you would have been in there with them, joining in.'

He was right, thought Millie. Once upon a time she would have been taking centre stage, falling about as she tried to act out some impossible phrase. Now she found herself checking the time, and wondering if the consultant had finished his round on Hyde ward, and whether Mrs Mortimer had made any other nurses cry that morning.

She gave up trying to wedge in a fragment of sky where it didn't belong. 'Wretched thing. Why won't it go in?'

'Here, let me try.' Seb came round to her side of the table to study the puzzle. 'I know Jumbo can be a nuisance at times, Mil, but he's a good friend of mine. I do wish you'd make an effort. Here.' He took the puzzle piece from her and tried it in a few places, then gave up. 'It doesn't seem to fit in anywhere, does it?'

I know how it feels, Millie thought. She so wished she could fit in with Seb's friends, for his sake.

So for Seb's sake, she did make an effort. She gritted her teeth and tried very hard not to let Jumbo irritate her for the rest of the afternoon. She even gave up on the jigsaw and joined the others, watching Jumbo teaching Georgina to play chess. He was a terrible, impatient teacher, but Georgina was an even worse pupil; several times she allowed Jumbo to capture her pieces, even though it was obvious even to Millie what her next move should have been.

'I don't understand,' she whispered to Seb when Georgina conceded yet another game, laughing at her own foolishness. 'She could have won easily.'

'Perhaps she has a bigger prize in mind?' he suggested.

Millie scowled. Georgina Farsley might not be the nicest person she knew, but she certainly wasn't stupid. Millie couldn't imagine why she would want to win over a pompous dullard like Jumbo Jameson.

She managed to keep her feelings to herself right through dinner. She bit her tongue as Jumbo bragged about how he had flown to Munich with his parents to visit Herr Hitler, and what a charming host he had been.

'He isn't interested in going to war with us,' he reassured everyone with a wave of his wine glass. 'On the contrary, he utterly respects Great Britain. He only wants what rightfully belongs to Germany.'

She also resisted the urge to tell him he was talking tosh when he enthused about what a 'breath of fresh air' the Prince of Wales would be as King – even though she could see from the thunderous expressions of Seb's father and Lord Carnforth that they found it distasteful to discuss the matter when the old King wasn't even dead yet.

The duchess, ever the perfect hostess, skilfully steered the conversation away.

'Did Sophia tell you, she and David are moving into their new London house next week?' she addressed Lady Carnforth.

'Really?' Lady Carnforth said. 'I'm surprised you would want the upheaval in your condition, Sophia.'

'That's what I said,' the duchess sighed. 'But you know what girls are like these days, Eleanor. They simply won't listen to reason. They have to have their own way in everything, don't they?'

She eyed Millie down the length of the table when she said it. Millie wondered if she was as irritated as her grandmother at having to wait for the wedding.

'Honestly, Mother, there's no need to fuss,' Sophia said airily. 'This baby will arrive whether I'm sitting here staring out of the window, or in Smith Square hanging curtains in the nursery.'

'Good gracious!' Her mother stared at her, wide-eyed with horror. 'I hope you're not considering hanging curtains, Sophia?'

'No, Mother, of course not,' she sighed. 'But I am thinking of having a housewarming party,' she added, smiling around the table.

'Surely not?' The duchess turned to her son-in-law. 'David, you can't possibly think this is a good idea?'

He gave a shrug. 'If it's what Sophia wants.' He gazed adoringly at his wife across the table.

'Quite right,' the duke guffawed. 'Let the fillies have their head, eh? It's the only way to keep them quiet.'

The duchess pressed her lips together. 'But are you sure a housewarming party is a good idea, darling?' she asked her daughter.

'Mother, I'll be fine. Ask Millie, she'll tell you.' Sophia turned to her. 'Tell her, Millie. Being pregnant isn't like being ill, is it?'

'Well, I–'

'What would Amelia know?' the duchess cut her off impatiently. 'She's not a doctor, is she?'

'No, but she does save lives, remember?' Jumbo put in. Millie stared at him. If he mentions bedpans again, I will empty this sauce boat over his head, she thought, her fingers twitching towards it.

'I know you think what I do is very amusing, Jumbo, but at least it is useful,' she said with as much dignity as she could muster. 'The most purposeful thing you do is order a cocktail at White's!'

An embarrassed hush followed her outburst. Out of the corner of her eye, Millie caught Seb's frown of disapproval.

'I say,' Lucinda Carnforth broke the tense silence with a loud whisper. 'I don't know if I should mention this but ... there's something moving in your hair.'

They drove back to London that night. The duchess had made a great show of insisting they should stay the night as planned, but she couldn't hide her relief when Millie declined the invitation.

'I quite understand, under the circumstances,' she'd whispered.

Millie slumped back in the passenger seat, silent with shame, her hat pulled down low over

110

her ears.

Seb glanced sideways at her. 'You can take it off, if you like?' he suggested. 'I'm sure I won't catch anything.'

'Don't.' Millie shuddered. 'I don't even want to think about it. I've never been so humiliated in my life.'

She could never face them again, she was certain of that. In fact, she probably wouldn't be able to face anyone again. She could just imagine the gossip that would already be circulating in the country homes and London houses.

'Did you hear about Rettingham's daughter? Turned up to the Claremonts' with head lice. Yes, head lice. Can you believe it? Quite extraordinary.'

It would only be a matter of time before news reached her grandmother's ears, and then all hell would break loose.

'It wasn't that bad,' Seb said. 'I think some people found it quite amusing–'

'Like your friend Jumbo, you mean?' Millie snapped. The sound of his braying laughter would haunt her nightmares for ever. 'Oh, yes, he loved it, didn't he? He thought it was an absolute hoot.'

'You have to admit, Mil, it was quite funny. The look on Georgina's face–' He caught her grim expression and stopped smiling. 'Oh, for heaven's sake. It's not the end of the world, is it?'

'Isn't it?' Millie stared bleakly ahead of her. 'I expect your mother will want you to call off the engagement.'

'Of course she won't.'

'Seb, she couldn't get me out of the door fast enough! She's probably having my room fumigated and all the bedding burnt as we speak. I'm surprised she didn't try to throw me on the bonfire, too.'

They drove in silence for a while. Then he said, 'Look on the bright side. At least if you're shunned by polite society, you won't have to see Jumbo Jameson again.'

Millie ventured a cautious look at him from under the pulled-down brim of her hat. He grinned back at her, his blue eyes crinkling.

'Stop it,' she said, her mouth twitching. 'I'm trying to be mortified.'

'Can I help it if my smile is infectious?'

Millie tugged at the brim of her hat. 'Please don't say that word!' she begged.

Chapter Ten

It was visiting day on Wren ward. The first in line outside the doors was Jennie's brother Joe.

'You see? I told you he'd be here,' Dora said as she straightened the girl's bedclothes. She had been moved on to the main ward. 'And you've been worrying all week that he wouldn't come.'

Jennie's eyes flicked anxiously towards the doors. She had been recovering well, but seeing her brother had drained away what little colour there was in her face. 'I don't think I can face him. He'll never forgive me for what I've done, I know he won't.'

'He's here, isn't he?' Dora turned down the

sheet to the regulation eighteen inches. She didn't even need to measure it now, she could judge it by eye.

'He's probably come to tell me they don't want me home.' Jennie's eyes brimmed with tears.

'Do you think he'd have brought flowers if he was going to tell you that?' Dora tweaked the cover into place. 'Just hear him out before you start getting upset, all right?'

'Don't leave me,' Jennie begged as Sister Wren finally opened the doors and the visitors began to stream in.

'I can't stay here, I've got work to do.'

'But what if he gets angry with me? What if he loses his temper?'

Dora squeezed Jennie's hand. 'Don't worry, I'll be keeping an eye on you.'

'Promise?'

'I promise.' She glanced round, smiling, as Joe arrived at the bedside. He looked ill at ease in his best suit, clutching a bunch of flowers.

'Hello, Mr Armstrong.' She smiled at him while his sister stared dumbly down at her hands.

'Nurse,' he nodded, his eyes fixed on Jennie. 'All right, Jen?' He looked as nervous as his sister.

'What lovely flowers. I'll put them in water, shall I?' Neither of them replied. 'Well, I'll leave you to it,' Dora went on, taking the flowers from him. 'I'll be coming round with the tea trolley later. Perhaps you'd like a cup?'

Dora went off to get on with the list of jobs Sister Wren had given her to do. While she worked, she kept glancing over at them. Joe was sitting beside Jennie's bed. At least they seemed to be talking to each other.

She hoped he wouldn't be too hard on his sister. Dora had grown to know and like Jennie Armstrong in the week she'd been nursing her. She was seventeen years old, but very young and naïve for her age. Dora got the impression that she didn't have much of a life, working long hours at a textile factory as well as looking after her father and brother since her mother died. She was just the type to end up getting into trouble. A frightened little girl who was easily led astray and didn't know any better.

Not that she ever talked about her baby's father. The only time Dora had mentioned him, a blank look had come into Jennie's eyes. 'I don't want to talk about it,' was all she would say.

When Dora went round with the tea trolley later, Jenny and Joe were still talking. Her face was puffy with tears, but from the way she gripped her brother's hand, Dora guessed it wasn't he who had caused them.

'Doyle, why do you keep making eyes at that young man?' Sister Wren's shrill voice interrupted her thoughts.

'I – I don't, Sister.'

'Don't argue with me, I've been watching you.' She stood in front of the trolley, blocking the way. 'Keep your mind on your work, please. If I catch you looking at him again, I'll have to teach you a lesson with a cold bath punishment.'

'If you ask me, she's the one who needs the cold bath punishment,' Katie O'Hara whispered as Dora passed her on her way to the kitchen. 'Have you seen the way she's been looking at Mrs Venables' son? She can't take her eyes off him.'

'What's a cold bath punishment when it's at home?'

'Haven't you heard of it before? Sister's always handing it out to nurses she thinks are man-mad. You have to get up at the crack of dawn and report to Night Sister for an ice cold bath. And I mean ice cold. Even colder than the baths at the nurses' home after the seniors have been at the hot water! Mind you,' she added, 'I think that one might be worth risking a cold bath for, don't you?' She nodded towards Joe Armstrong.

'You think any man is worth risking a cold bath for!' Dora laughed. Plump, pretty Katie O'Hara had come over from a small village in Ireland to be a student at the Nightingale like her elder sisters. She was making the most of being in the big city, away from her mammy.

Visiting time finished, and the usual routine of beds and backs, changing dressings and handing out bedpans, began. But first they had to search all the patients' lockers, confiscating anything that might go mouldy. Any food that could be used went into the ward larder for safekeeping, or to be shared among the rest of the patients.

Sister Wren stood at the larder, greedily eyeing the food as it came in. She was particularly impressed with a jar of home-made jam Mrs Venables' son had brought in, a gift from her sister.

'The patients can have that with their breakfast,' she announced.

'And she can have it with her tea and toast while she's putting her feet up this afternoon!'

Katie grinned to Dora as she handed over a box of eggs she'd found.

Jennie Armstrong seemed a lot more cheerful when Dora went to treat her back for bedsores.

'How did it go?' she asked, as she carefully washed and dried Jennie's shoulders and hips. She was so thin, Dora could trace all the knobbly bones of her spine under her skin.

'It was all right. He was upset, but he wasn't angry. And he's told Dad I got rushed into hospital with appendicitis, so he's none the wiser.' She sounded relieved. 'I'm glad about that, at least. I don't want him finding out what happened.'

'I'm surprised he hasn't come in to see you too?'

There was a long silence. Then Jennie said, 'Dad would never come. I wouldn't want him to, anyway.' Her voice was heavy with resentment.

'You don't get on with him, then?' Dora said, dabbing on methylated spirits.

Jennie didn't reply. Dora wondered if the faded bruises and scars that covered the girl's back were answer enough.

'At least you've made it up with your brother, that's a good thing,' she said.

'Yes, I'm pleased about that. Joe's always looked after me. He's the strong one, you see. Even my dad listens to him.' Then her smile faded. 'I just wish he hadn't kept going on about my ... the baby's father.'

'What did he say?'

'He kept on at me, wanting to know who he was and where he lived.'

'I expect he just wants him to face up to what

he's done.'

'He wants to kill him, more like. Joe would rip him apart with his bare hands if he ever got hold of him.'

'So you didn't tell him?'

Jennie shook her head. 'It doesn't matter anyway. He'd never find him.' Her voice was dull. 'He's long gone.'

'You mean he did a runner after he found out about the baby?'

Jennie kept her mouth tight shut, trapping the words, as if she'd already said too much.

'It's all right,' Dora went on. 'You don't have to tell me if you don't want to.'

Jennie regarded her warily. 'You wouldn't tell Joe?'

''Course not. I know how to keep a secret, believe me.'

Jennie hesitated for a moment, then shook her head. 'I can't,' she said. 'I'm too ashamed. It turns out … he wasn't the man I thought he was.'

'In what way?'

But Jennie didn't reply. Dora saw a tear squeezing out from between tightly shut lids, and understood that, whatever had happened with Jennie's mystery man, it was too painful for her to talk about.

She didn't think any more of it until she was sent off duty at five. She was crossing the courtyard when she spotted Joe Armstrong sitting on a bench under the plane trees. A freezing wind whipped his fair hair across his face but he hardly seemed to notice as he smoked a cigarette, his gaze directed into space. He looked as if he had the worries of the world on his broad shoulders.

Dora hesitated. Should she go over? She remembered the last time she'd taken it upon herself to speak to him. She'd caused more harm than good that day, and didn't want to repeat it. Besides, they were right outside Matron's office. She would only have to look out of the window and Dora would be in for a lot more trouble than Sister Wren's cold bath punishment.

But Joe Armstrong looked so desolate, she was walking towards him before she could stop herself.

'All right, Mr Armstrong?'

He looked up at her sharply. 'Oh, it's you, Nurse. Sorry, I was miles away.'

'Is there something on your mind?'

'Just thinking, Nurse.'

'Visiting time finished over an hour ago.'

'Yeah, well, I've got a lot of thinking to do, haven't I?'

Dora took a quick glance towards Matron's window, then sat down beside him. 'Jennie will be all right, you know.'

'Will she?' Joe Armstrong looked at her, his eyes narrowing. 'She told me she can't have kids now. What kind of life is that going to be for her, tell me that.' He took a long drag on his cigarette. His hands were shaking, Dora noticed. 'Our Jennie's always loved babies. All she's ever wanted is to get married and have a family of her own. Who's going to want her now?'

'I – I'm sorry.'

Joe's shoulders slumped. 'No, Nurse, I'm the one who should be sorry. I didn't mean to snap at you like that.' He managed a weary smile. 'Our Jennie couldn't stop talking about you... Nurse Doyle this, Nurse Doyle that. I don't think she would have pulled through if it hadn't been for you.'

'Oh, I don't know about that–'

'I do. You've been kind to her. And Jennie's not had a lot of kindness in her life, I can tell you.'

Their eyes met and held. Dora rose to her feet, feeling suddenly awkward. 'I have to go,' she said. 'If Matron sees me talking to you, she'll have my guts for garters.'

As she started to walk away, he called her back. 'Nurse?'

'Yes?' She looked over her shoulder.

'I don't suppose she's said anything to you ... about who did this to her?'

Dora thought about her promise to Jennie, and shook her head. 'Not to me.'

'Probably just as well.' Joe Armstrong dropped his cigarette end and ground it out viciously with the heel of his boot. 'But I daresay I'll find him soon enough.'

Nick Riley was having a cigarette behind the Porters' Lodge when he spotted Dora talking to Joe Armstrong.

He recognised Armstrong immediately. The man belonged to the Poplar Boxing Club, and they'd faced each other in the ring a few times. He had a reputation as a dirty fighter and most of the lads were afraid of him. But not Nick.

Why was he talking to Dora? Nick immediately felt his hackles rise.

It seemed to him sometimes as if he'd spent most of his life watching Dora Doyle, never quite getting up the courage to speak his mind. They had lived next door to each other for more than ten years, his family and hers, always in and out of each other's houses. He had been eleven years old when she first arrived in Griffin Street, already on the verge of manhood and responsible for putting food on his family's table. He'd watched Dora play with the younger kids, and envied her her freedom. He'd listened to her sitting on the pavement, telling them stories, and wished he could sit at her feet like they did. He'd felt so tongue-tied and foolish around her, all he could do was lash out and tease her. But even then she was more than a match for him. When he'd made fun of her frizzy ginger hair she'd kicked him in the shins, so hard it had brought tears to his eyes, although he would never let her see how much she'd hurt him.

And she'd hurt him again, just a few months ago, when he'd finally plucked up the courage to kiss her. It was the first time he'd ever shown his real feelings, the first time he'd made himself vulnerable to anyone.

And she'd rejected him.

The memory of it still burnt. He'd made up his mind in that moment that he would forget her. He had even started courting Ruby Pike in an effort to push all thoughts of Dora from his mind and his heart.

But he had never realised how hard it would be.

He watched her turn away from Joe and head across the courtyard towards him. As she drew level with the Porters' Lodge, he stepped out in front of her.

'Oh, Nick! You nearly gave me a heart attack!' Dora put her hand to her chest.

'Was that Joe Armstrong you were talking to?'

She frowned. 'You know him?'

'I've been in the ring with him a few times.'

'He's a boxer?' She considered it for a moment. 'That doesn't surprise me.'

'What's he doing here?'

'He's been in to visit his sister.'

'The girl who had the backstreet abortion?'

He saw the flash of anger in Dora's face. 'Who told you that?' she snapped. Then, before he could answer, she said, 'I suppose it was Lettie Pike?' Her mouth tightened. 'That old bag shouldn't go around gossiping.'

'Asking Lettie Pike not to gossip is like asking her not to breathe.'

'True.' Dora smiled reluctantly. She wasn't even pretty Nick thought. Her mouth was too wide, her nose was too pudgy and smattered with far too many freckles. And as for that hair... He'd always gone for lookers in the past. Real glamour girls, like Ruby. The kind who turned men's heads in the street.

Dora would never turn any man's head. And yet when she looked at Nick in a certain way, it was like someone had lit a firework inside him.

'So why was he talking to you?' he asked.

'You're a nosy one, aren't you? It's not like you to want to know everyone's business. If you ask me, you've been spending too long with Lettie Pike!' There was a teasing glint in Dora's eyes. 'If

121

you must know, he's worried about his sister.'

'I daresay he'll want to know who got her into trouble, too. I know if I were him, I'd want to make someone pay for what they did to her.' Someone always had to pay. It was the East End way.

'And you think that would help his poor sister?'

'You've got to protect the people you love,' Nick insisted stubbornly.

Perhaps if he'd stepped in sooner, he could have protected his brother Danny from their dad. As it was, he'd made Reg Riley pay in the end, giving him a taste of his own medicine and then running him out of Bethnal Green for good.

'Violence isn't the answer to everything, Nick,' Dora said.

It got rid of your stepdad, didn't it? he wanted to reply.

He would never have interfered in anyone else's business, but when Danny told him he'd seen Alf Doyle beating Dora that day, it was as if someone had flicked a switch inside Nick's head, rekindling all his old rage. A few days later he'd cornered Alf in an alleyway and convinced him to pack his bags and leave Griffin Street. And, coward that he was, Alf hadn't argued.

Perhaps he shouldn't have interfered, thought Nick. But as he'd said to Dora, you had to protect the people you loved.

It was the way he looked at her. In all the months they'd been courting, Lettie Pike had never seen Nick look at her Ruby the way he looked at Dora Doyle.

122

She had stopped for a moment by the window to rub her aching back. Those nurses thought they had it so hard, but they should do her job, she thought. She was getting too old for sweeping and scrubbing and laying fires. She should have been putting her feet up. And she would have been, too, if her lazy husband Len ever managed to stay away from the bookies long enough. Between the horses and the drink, he somehow managed to squander every penny she brought home, and a lot more besides. He'd even found the few quid she'd hidden in a toffee tin under the bed, the thieving sod. And when she'd complained, he'd given her a clout round the ear for hiding it in the first place.

She glanced out of the window and caught sight of Dora Doyle talking to a young man under the trees in the middle of the courtyard. And she wasn't the only one watching. From the shadows behind the Porters' Lodge, Nick Riley was watching them too.

Lettie felt a prickle of unease.

She stood rooted to the spot as Dora finished talking to the young man and headed across the courtyard. Then Nick stepped out in front of her.

Lettie pressed her nose against the glass, but she didn't have to hear what they were saying. It was there, in the way they looked at each other.

'Sister?' she called out.

'What is it, Lettie?' Sister Wren came over straight away.

They'd worked together on the ward for many years. Sister didn't treat her like she did the nurses. She understood Lettie's value too much for that.

The maid was her eyes and ears on the ward; she let Sister know when the nurses were getting up to no good.

Like now, for instance.

'Look at that,' she said, pointing. 'Bold as brass, that one.'

Sister Wren looked, then looked again. A dull flush spread up her neck, a sure sign she was heading for one of her rages. 'Doyle,' she hissed. 'I might have known.'

'Terrible, isn't it?' Lettie said. 'Her hanging about chatting up lads when she should be working. And in uniform, too. I call it a disgrace, I really do.'

'So do I, Lettie. But don't you worry, she'll get what's coming to her.'

'Are you sending her to Matron, Sister?'

Sister Wren looked at her, and Lettie had the satisfaction of seeing a gleam of spite in her eyes. 'Oh, no,' she smiled with relish. 'I'll deal with her myself.'

Ruby was already in when Lettie got home. She was sitting at the kitchen table, painting her nails. Lettie suppressed her annoyance that the dishes were still piled up in the sink and no one had bothered to put the dinner on.

She dumped her shopping bag on the floor. 'I'll put the kettle on, shall I? she said grumpily.

'I'll have one, if you're making it.' Ruby didn't look up as she blew on her nails.

Lettie went over to the sink and filled the kettle under the tap. 'Where are the boys?' she asked.

'God knows. Up to no good as usual, I s'pose.'

Ruby raised her scarlet-tipped nails to show her mother. 'What do you reckon to this colour? I bought it from Woolworth's.'

'Very nice.' Lettie looked at her daughter's artfully arranged golden curls, and felt her heart lift with pride. She might be a lazy cow, but Ruby was easily the prettiest girl in Bethnal Green.

She sometimes wondered how she had ever managed to bring such a beauty into the world. Lettie herself was no oil painting. Even as a young girl she had been skinny and sallow-looking, with thin mousy hair and teeth so crooked her mother said she could 'eat an apple through a letterbox'. Len Pike wasn't much to look at either. And yet somehow, between them, they had managed to produce a glorious creature like Ruby.

From the moment Ruby was born, she had been Lettie's angel. She'd treated her like a princess, going without herself so she could buy her daughter dresses, combing her halo of golden curls for hours, telling her how special she was. It wasn't Ruby's fault she'd turned out spoilt rotten, her mother thought.

She swelled with a pride she'd never known before when the other mothers commented on how pretty little Ruby was. And when the young men started courting her, Ruby took it all as her due. But Lettie, who had never had an admiring glance from anyone in her life, was thrilled by all the attention her daughter received. Ruby would never be like her, she decided. She would never have to make do with the likes of Len Pike, with his flabby body and bad temper. Ruby could have any man she wanted.

And she wanted Nick Riley.

He wasn't the man Lettie would have chosen for her daughter. She had hoped Ruby might be a bit more ambitious, go for someone with a trade, perhaps even a businessman, someone with a bit of money who could give her all the finer things in life that she deserved.

Lettie doubted if Nick Riley would ever be able to afford a motor car, or a house in the suburbs. He was good-looking, there was no doubt about that, and he was a grafter. But he was a surly bugger, with a nasty temper when he was roused. And Lettie's heart sank at the thought of her Ruby saddling herself with in-laws like that old drunk June Riley and her imbecile son.

But if Nick was the man Ruby had set her heart on, then he was the one she must have. The thought that he might not realise how lucky he was, or that he might not feel the same way, had never even occurred to Lettie until she saw him with Dora.

She glanced at Ruby, wondering how best to approach the subject.

'I saw your Nick earlier on,' she said casually, as she spooned tea into the pot.

'Yeah?'

'He was talking to Dora Doyle.' Lettie glanced at her daughter. 'They seemed very thick together.'

'Why, what were they doing?'

'I told you, they were talking. And they were smiling,' she added, filling the teapot.

'Smiling, eh? Ooh, I'd better watch out, hadn't I?'

'You might laugh, my girl, but you didn't see

them together. I'm telling you, they were very thick.'

Ruby set down her nail-polish brush. 'Blimey, Mum, we've all known each other years. They're bound to talk to each other, ain't they? It don't mean anything. What's he meant to do, ignore her just because we're courting?'

Ruby held up her hands again, turning them this way and that to admire the light glinting off her shiny painted nails.

Lettie stirred the leaves in the teapot. 'He looked a bit too pleased to see her, if you ask me,' she mumbled. Then, when Ruby didn't reply, she repeated, 'Are you listening to me? I said–'

'I heard what you said!' Ruby's voice was sharp. 'Are you telling me my Nick is messing about with Dora Doyle?'

'I'm not saying anything. But you know he's got a name for himself round here. There's lots of girls who've tried to catch his eye, and they've all fallen by the wayside...'

'Yes, but that was before he met me, wasn't it?' Lettie met her daughter's gaze. Ruby's blue eyes were hard and determined. 'Anyway, Dora's my best mate. She knows better than to mess about with my boyfriend. Even if she was interested in him, which she's not.'

'She might not be interested, but how do you know you can say the same about him?'

'Oh, Mum!' Ruby gave an almost pitying laugh. 'Look at me. Do you really think Nick would look twice at someone like Dora?'

Lettie stared into her daughter's pretty face. She could have been in the films, she was so beautiful. Then she thought about Dora Doyle, as plain as a pikestaff, her broad nose smothered with freckles.

'You're right, love, I'm just being daft,' she agreed. But as she turned to pour the tea into chipped cups, she didn't see the troubled look in her daughter's eyes.

Chapter Eleven

The news finally came at midnight.

Ever since the sombre announcement just after half-past ten that night, that the King's life was 'moving peacefully towards its close', wireless sets in kitchens and sluices all over the hospital had been tuned in for further bulletins.

Violet was supervising an emergency admission to Male Surgical when a tearful student whispered the news.

'Thank you for letting me know, Nurse,' she said calmly. Later, she was sure the nurse would tell her friends Miss Tanner took the news with no emotion; how it proved everyone right when they said she was a 'cold fish'.

But although Violet was moved by the King's death, she felt more wretched for the young man behind the screens, rapidly losing the struggle for life after being knocked off his bike on the way to his night shift. Of course she felt sorrow for His Majesty's passing. But at least he had lived a long, full life, and had died with dignity. There was no dignity for poor Mr Parsons, lying bleeding in a gutter, his life over almost before it had begun.

She pushed open the door to the visitors' room and was confronted by a set of anxious white faces. Mr Parsons' mother, his father, brothers and sisters, all roused from their sleep, overcoats thrown on over their nightclothes in their rush to get to the hospital.

It was a sight she often faced, but it didn't get any easier. Patients who clung tenaciously to life during daylight hours seemed to lose the will during the long hours of darkness. As Night Sister it was her job to prepare relatives for the worst, or give them the news they dreaded.

'Is he ... is he going to be all right, Nurse?' Mrs Parsons whispered.

Violet took a deep breath, composed herself, and quietly closed the door.

News of the King's death drifted through the hospital on a wave of sorrow. Nurses wept; patients woke up, grew restless, needed to talk. Violet spent the night going from ward to ward, soothing and comforting, holding hands and making endless cups of tea.

As dawn broke the following morning she was exhausted. All she could think about was going home and crawling into her bed.

She wasn't sure if she was imagining it at first when she heard the sound of a tap running in the bathroom of Wren ward just before six in the morning. She investigated, and found an un-happy-looking young nurse filling the bathtub. The night student stood in the doorway watching her, looking almost as wretched.

They both glanced round sharply when Violet appeared. 'What do you think you're doing, Nurse?' she demanded.

'It's for my punishment, Sister.' The young woman's voice was almost drowned out by the roar of the tap. She looked as weary as Violet felt, her face haggard from lack of sleep, her red hair a frizzy, unbrushed halo.

'I beg your pardon?'

'My cold bath punishment. Sister Wren says you're to supervise it.'

Violet rubbed her eyes with a weary hand. 'I'm sorry, Nurse, you're going to have to explain yourself.' She looked from one to the other of the two girls.

It was the night student who spoke up first. 'Sister Wren makes us take a cold bath at dawn if we're caught talking to men, Sister,' she explained.

'I see. So I'm to see that this punishment is carried out?' They both nodded. 'And suppose I don't want to?'

The nurses looked at each other in confusion. 'I – I'm sorry, Miss,' said the red-haired student. 'I don't understand–'

Violet sighed. 'What is your name, Nurse?'

'Doyle, Sister.'

'Tell me, Doyle, were you talking to this man?'

'Yes, Sister.' She met Violet's eye when she said it. Not boldly or cheekily, but in a steady, straight-forward kind of way. She didn't look like the flirtatious type, Violet thought.

She reached over and turned off the tap. 'Go away, Doyle,' she said wearily.

'But Miss–'

'Doyle, it's been a very long night, and now I have to check all the ward reports and make sure all the patients are fed and everything is in order before the day staff come on duty at seven. Do you really think I also have time to supervise you taking a cold bath as well?'

'No, Sister.' The girl's broad, freckled face filled with hope.

'No, I do not. And I'm sure you have better things to do with your time, too. So go and have your breakfast, and make sure you report back on the ward promptly for duty.'

'But Sister Wren will be–'

'I will deal with Sister Wren,' Violet said firmly.

'Isn't it awful about the poor King?'

Millie heard it everywhere she went on that bleak, cold Tuesday morning. All the nurses were talking about it over breakfast, and the old ladies on Female Chronic – the few who were aware of what was going on around them, anyway – all wanted to share their fond reminiscences with Millie as she went about her chores on the ward.

Outside the hospital, church bells rang out. Sister Hyde had allowed a wireless into the ward, but Millie began to wish she hadn't as they were treated to hour after hour of solemn music.

'Why do we have to listen to this?' Maud Mortimer demanded as she submitted unwillingly to Millie wielding a hairbrush. 'Isn't this place depressing enough without having to listen to these dreadful dirges?'

'It's for the King,' Millie said, carefully untang-

131

ling a knot in Maud's long, silky white hair.

'Why? He can't hear it, can he? For heaven's sake, girl, do you have to be so rough?' she snapped, jerking her head away.

'Sorry.' Millie slowed down her brushing. 'But the music is a mark of respect, don't you think?'

'Respect, my eye,' Maud tutted. 'It's nothing but a lot of mawkish sentimentality, if you ask me. Although I'm not remotely surprised at you getting so emotional about it – you strike me as the mawkish type,' she added.

'It's always sad when someone dies.'

'What utter nonsense,' Maud dismissed. 'For most people it's a blessed release. Or it would be, if it weren't for the likes of do-gooders like you,' she added accusingly. 'You nurses and doctors, coming in here with your face flannels and your feeding cups and your sickening, relentless cheerfulness, trying to keep us alive when all we want to do is die in peace.'

'It's our job to care for people, Mrs Mortimer.' Millie's smile wobbled uncertainly.

'You call this caring? If you really cared you'd put us all out of our misery.'

'You mustn't talk like that.'

'Why not?' She gestured around the ward. 'Have you ever taken the trouble to look around you? Do you believe these women want to be helpless and in pain? Do you think they enjoy having to have someone to feed them and wash their hair and wipe their backsides? Don't you think every one of them would choose to go to sleep and never wake up if they could? I know I would. Oh, don't look so shocked,' she snapped.

'If I have nothing left to live for, why shouldn't I go when I please?'

'There's always something left to live for.'

Maud Mortimer sent her a look of pure contempt. 'You foolish, foolish girl!' she hissed. 'You only say that because you're young. You wait until you're my age, and everyone you care about has passed away or forgotten you exist. Wait until your mind is fading and your body is letting you down, and you're at the mercy of stupid girls with sunny smiles and hairbrushes, then tell me you want to live.'

The bleakness in her hard, bright eyes made Millie want to cry. She could feel hot tears pricking the back of her eyes.

'Oh, for heaven's sake!' Maud snatched the hairbrush from her, but it fell from her weak grasp and rolled away under the bed. 'You see?' she said. 'I can't even brush my own hair now. What kind of life is that?'

Millie dived under the bed to retrieve the brush, but Maud waved her away. 'Just leave me alone,' she said wearily. 'You're giving me a headache.'

'But–'

'Did you hear me? I said go away. Go and torment one of these other wretched women. Perhaps you can have a good old weep together about the poor old King.'

Millie was still shaking as she pushed her trolley back towards the sluice. She tried to tell herself that Maud was just having a bad day. But the bitterness she'd seen in the old woman's eyes haunted her.

She avoided Maud Mortimer for the rest of the

morning. Luckily Sister Hyde gave Helen the job of feeding Maud at dinnertime. Millie watched from the other end of the ward as her friend sat beside the bed, a feeding cup in her hand.

'I don't want it,' Maud said, turning her head away. 'I refuse to be fed like a child.'

'Come on, Mrs Mortimer, you have to keep your strength up,' Helen pleaded. 'Just try one sip for me–'

'I told you, I don't want it!' Maud shoved the cup away from her with such force, it flew out of Helen's hand and skimmed across the floor.

There was an appalled silence. Sister Hyde stalked over to Maud, her expression stern.

'Really, Mrs Mortimer, you must let Nurse Tremayne feed you,' she warned her. 'Otherwise–'

'Otherwise what?' Maud faced her defiantly. 'I'll starve to death?'

'Otherwise we will have to use a feeding tube,' Sister Hyde said quietly.

There was a long silence. Even from the other end of the ward Millie caught the brief flash of fear in Maud's face.

'Very well, then,' she said with dignity. 'You may feed me.'

Sister Hyde smiled. 'That's better. Tremayne, prepare another feeding cup. And Benedict,' she called over to her, 'see this mess is cleaned up at once.'

As Millie mopped the floor, she watched Helen feeding Maud.

'There,' she said soothingly, holding the cup to her lips. 'That's not so bad, is it?'

Millie caught the bleak look in Maud's eyes,

and remembered what she had said about being at the mercy of girls with sunny smiles. It was bad, she thought. As far as Maud Mortimer was concerned, it couldn't get much worse.

Chapter Twelve

'I'm sorry, love. The room's gone.'

Violet stared at the woman who stood on the front doorstep, arms folded across her chest. She looked straight back at her, her face a blank mask.

'But it was available this morning.' It had been perfect. Large, filled with light, with a door that led out on to the garden. 'I told you I wanted it. I said I was coming back this afternoon with the money–'

'Yes, well, someone beat you to it, I'm afraid.'

Violet drew herself upright. 'You told me the room had been available for weeks. It's very strange that two people should turn up and want it on the same day, don't you think?'

'These things happen.' The woman shrugged.

Violet held on to Oliver's hand. 'So it has nothing to do with my son?' she said quietly.

The woman's darting gaze gave her away. 'I thought you were a respectable single lady,' she muttered.

'I'm a widow.'

'Is that right?' The woman glanced meaningfully at Violet's cheap ring, glinting unconvincingly in the pale sunlight. 'You weren't wearing that this morning?'

'I have to take it off when I'm working.'

'Oh, yes? And what kind of work would that be, then?'

Colour scalded Violet's cheeks. 'I'm a nurse!'

'If you say so, dearie.' The woman looked at her sceptically.

Violet held in her anger, determined not to let Oliver see her upset. She hated the way the other woman looked down her nose at her, but at the same time she couldn't blame her. She wouldn't be the first young mother to buy a cheap ring from a pawnshop and try to pass herself off as a widow for the sake of respectability.

It's not what you think, she wanted to cry out. But fear kept her silent.

'Look, love,' the landlady said kindly. 'I'm sure it can't be easy for you. You seem like a nice woman. But I can't let you have the room. Not with–' Her eyes flicked to Oliver and away again. 'Haven't you got any family that can help you out?' she asked.

'No,' Violet's voice faltered. 'I don't have anyone.'

'Then I feel sorry for you, I really do.'

Violet stood on the doorstep for a moment after the front door had closed in her face, blinking back the tears.

'Mummy?' Oliver pulled on her hand, his voice uncertain. 'Are we going to live here?'

'No, sweetheart. It turns out it's not the right place after all.'

'But I don't want to live with Mrs Bainbridge any more.'

136

Neither do I, Violet thought. But we don't have a lot of choice.

'We'll find somewhere soon, darling,' she promised. By the time she looked down at him, she'd managed to summon up a smile. 'Now then, shall we go home through the market? We'll buy some apple fritters from the van, how about that?'

'Yes, please!' Oliver did a little dance, wriggling and jiggling while she held his hand. 'And can we have fish and chips for tea?'

'Why not? I think we deserve a treat.'

They walked home, past shops decked out in sombre black crepe to mark the King's death. It was freezing cold and a biting wind blew through the narrow streets but at least it had blown away the choking fog. Violet stayed out for as long as she could, partly because she dreaded going back to the damp, dark tenement, and partly to give Oliver the chance to get some fresh air. She'd noticed his breathing was getting worse recently, his little chest rising and falling as he gulped for air. Mrs Bainbridge had also complained that his coughing kept her awake.

But finally she couldn't put it off any longer, and they trudged back home, stopping for fish and chips on the way.

Their little room reeked of damp and decay. Violet tried not to notice the patches of black mould creeping up the plasterwork under the window as she helped Oliver out of his coat, then went into the kitchenette to set out their fish and chips.

'Can't we eat it out of the newspaper?' he begged.

'Certainly not.'

'But that's how Mrs Bainbridge eats it.'

'All the more reason for us not to,' Violet murmured to herself as she pulled two plates out of the cupboard.

That was when she noticed the cocoa tin was gone.

The place might be rotting around their ears, but she kept it spotlessly clean. The wooden surfaces were scrubbed with lysol, and everything was lined up neatly in the cupboards. So it was easy for her to spot when something had been moved. Or taken.

A cold feeling washed over her. She reached to the back of the cupboard, scrabbling among the tins and packets, already knowing that what she was looking for was missing, but not wanting to give up hope.

'Mummy!' Oliver called out.

'Just a minute, darling. Mummy's looking for something.'

But the old Rowntree's cocoa tin in which she kept her money and the few treasured belongings she had, was gone.

Forcing herself to stay calm, she gave Oliver his fish and chips, then went downstairs and knocked on Mrs Bainbridge's door.

It was a few minutes before she came to the door, wiping her hands on her flowery pinny. Over her shoulder the kitchen was a chaos of babies wailing, children arguing and the rancid smell of frying fat.

'Yes? What do you want?'

Violet had meant to stay calm. But seeing Mrs

Bainbridge's narrow, sly face was too much for her.

'Where's my tin?' she demanded.

Mrs Bainbridge blinked at her. 'What are you talking about?'

'You know very well. I had an old cocoa tin in my cupboard and it's gone.'

'What are you looking at me for? I ain't had it.'

'Someone has.' Violet looked past her into the kitchen. Half a dozen children stared back at her, all with eyes as sly as their mother's.

'Are you calling me a thief?'

Violet struggled to keep her temper. 'I just want my belongings back,' she said patiently. 'I don't even care about the money. But there was jewellery in that tin. A locket my mother gave me. It's all I have left...'

'Then you should have taken better care of it, shouldn't you?'

'And you should stop helping yourself to other people's things!'

Mrs Bainbridge looked outraged. 'I ain't had your rotten locket,' she snarled. 'You're welcome to search the place if you don't believe me. But I'm telling you, you won't find anything here.'

She stepped back from the doorway. Violet stared past her into the steamy fug of the kitchen. What was the point? she thought. Her jewellery would have found its way to the pawnshop hours ago.

'Or maybe we should call in the police?' Mrs Bainbridge suggested. 'Let them sort it out?'

'No!' Violet saw the flare of triumph in Mrs Bainbridge's eyes and realised she'd spoken too quickly. 'Just stay away from what's mine,' she said quietly.

'And does that include your boy?' the landlady called after her as she headed back towards the stairs. 'I s'pose that means you don't want me keeping an eye on him while you're out any more?'

'Of course I do.'

'Well, I'm not sure as I want to. It's not nice, y'know, being called a thief when you're just trying to be neighbourly. I reckon I might need an apology from you before I put myself out again.'

'I'm sorry,' Violet whispered.

She walked back up the stairs to the top of the house, burning with fresh anger and frustration at each step. How she hated that evil woman! But Mrs Bainbridge was right. Violet couldn't even put a lock on the door because she relied on her to look after Oliver while she was at work.

He looked up at her as she let herself back into their room. 'Mummy, your fish and chips have gone cold.'

'I'm not very hungry any more.' She picked up her plate and tipped its contents into the bin.

After tea, she got Oliver washed at the sink and into his pyjamas, read to him and put him to bed.

'I've left you some milk and biscuits in case you get hungry in the night,' she said, stoking up the fire. 'Now remember, sweetheart, what Mummy always tells you?'

'Don't touch the fireguard, and don't let any strangers into the room,' he parroted dutifully. 'And don't go off with anyone, no matter what they tell me.'

'That's right.' Violet sat down on his narrow

bed and kissed her son goodnight. As always, she hugged him fiercely, gripped by a terrible fear that this would be the last time she saw him.

'I wish you didn't have to go away every night, Mummy,' he said.

'So do I, darling.'

'I liked it better when we lived with Mr Mannion in the big house.'

'Me, too,' Violet sighed. There had been fresh air there, and a big garden for Oliver to play in. And old Mr Mannion, poorly as he was, had loved to watch him from the French windows. He said Oliver brought a breath of life into the old, decaying house. His own children had grown up and moved away long ago, and never visited him. In fact, they seldom had any visitors. Which was why Violet had felt so safe there.

But then Mr Mannion had died, and his sons and daughters had finally remembered they had a father. They had descended on the house, picking over Mr Mannion's belongings like crows on carrion. The house had been sold, and Violet had been sent away.

But coming to London had been a mistake, she thought. She had imagined she could get lost in the big city, that she could make a new life for herself and her son without arousing anyone's curiosity. But she had been wrong.

She arrived at the Nightingale and headed straight for the Porters' Lodge. Mr Hopkins the head porter greeted her at the door. He was a fussy little man, with a bristling moustache and a military bearing enhanced by his polished shoes and well-pressed brown overall. A stickler for protocol, he wore a black crepe armband out of respect for the King.

'They're all waiting for you round the back, Miss,' he said in his lilting Welsh accent. 'Quite a turn-out tonight.'

'Thank you, Mr Hopkins.' Violet went around to the back of the Lodge, where the would-be night cleaners clustered together, sheltering from the wind.

Violet looked at the gaggle of hopeful faces all turned towards her. This was her least favourite task of the night. She took a deep breath and chose quickly.

'It's not fair, she got picked last night,' one of the women protested as Violet ushered the lucky few away.

Violet steeled herself. There was always someone who wasn't happy.

'Come back tomorrow night,' she called over her shoulder.

'And what am I going to tell my husband when I go home empty-handed? He's going to kill me if I don't bring some money in tonight.'

Violet heard the pleading note in the woman's voice but walked on.

'That's right, walk away from me. It's all right for you, you snotty cow!' the woman called after her. 'You don't know what it's like to have an old man at home who batters you black and blue, do you?'

Violet set the night cleaners about their duties then crossed the courtyard to her small sitting room on the night corridor and changed into her uniform. She could almost feel herself becoming a different person as she fastened the starched cuffs on her grey dress and tied the long strings of her cap under her chin. For a few hours, she could cast off the cares and troubles of Violet Tanner to become the Night Sister.

But the Night Sister had woes of her own to deal with, she realised, as she met Sister Wren on the sisters' corridor.

Violet's heart sank when she saw her approaching with Sister Blake from the other end of the passageway, a tight-lipped expression on her face. She was clearly on the warpath about something.

'I want a word with you.' She bore down on Violet, her small face full of spite and fury. 'What do you mean by undermining me?'

Sister Blake looked dismayed. 'Really, Sister Wren—'

'Undermining you? I don't know what you mean,' Violet replied calmly.

'Don't be obtuse! I asked you to supervise the punishment of one of my students, but you refused.'

'Perhaps you should discuss this in private?' Sister Blake suggested tactfully.

'Mind your own business!' Sister Wren turned on her.

Violet Tanner straightened her shoulders. 'Yes, I did refuse to supervise the punishment,' she said.

'May I ask why?'

'I thought it was spiteful and pointless.'

Sister Wren's dishwater-grey eyes blazed. 'Spiteful ... pointless?'

143

Violet nodded. 'As far as I could see, it served no useful purpose.'

'It was a punishment!'

'If you were out to punish the girl, then surely sending her to Matron would have been just as effective? There was no need to subject her to humiliation. Unless that was your aim, to bully and humiliate her?'

Cords of rage stood out on Sister Wren's scrawny neck.

'How dare you!' She choked on her words. 'You have no right to speak to me like that. You're only the Night Sister!'

Violet stared down at Sister Wren. Her little fists were balled at her sides, her face contorted with rage. She was so small and so furious, she reminded Violet of Oliver stamping his feet in the middle of a tantrum.

Suddenly she saw the woman on the doorstep earlier on, looking at her as if she was something on her shoe. Then she saw Mrs Bainbridge, casually helping herself to Violet's belongings, knowing she was trapped and couldn't fight back.

She might have to accept the way they treated her. But she didn't have to accept it from Sister Wren.

'May I remind you, Sister Wren, that I am still a Sister at this hospital, and not one of your students to be ordered about?'

'Now, you listen to me–'

'No, _you_ listen.' The quivering anger in Violet's voice was enough to silence Sister Wren. She stood there, her mouth a tight line of seething indignation. 'I am happy to carry out your instructions

144

when it comes to the welfare of your patients. But in future, if you wish to inflict a cold bath on someone at the crack of dawn, then you will have to do your own dirty work. Is that clear?'

There was a brief silence. 'Have you quite finished?' Sister Wren spat out.

'Yes, thank you.'

'In that case, we will hear what Matron has to say about this!'

Sister Wren stalked off, her spine rigid with resentment.

Sister Blake watched her go. 'Good for you,' she said to Violet. 'It's about time someone told her what she can do with her wretched cold bath punishment. We've all been trying to tell her for years, but she wouldn't listen. Looks like you might have got through to her at last!'

Violet didn't reply. Her eyes were still fixed on Sister Wren.

'Don't worry, you won't get into any trouble,' Sister Blake said. 'If I know Matron, she'll agree with you.'

It's not Matron I'm worried about, Violet thought. The last thing she wanted was to make an enemy at the Nightingale.

And she had the feeling Sister Wren could be a very vindictive enemy indeed.

Chapter Thirteen

Ruby stood in front of the mirror, frowning at her appearance. Most girls would have been pleased with what they saw, but she noticed only faults. The calluses on her fingers from machining ten hours a day, her skirt straining over her too-plump hips. Even her blonde curls, despite all her efforts with the tongs, hung limply around her face.

She cursed her reflection. Why did her mum have to go and say that about Nick? She hadn't been able to look at herself since without her confidence sinking.

Because in spite of what she'd told her mother, Ruby was worried.

It was the little things that troubled her. She had to hold Nick's hand when they walked down the street, he never reached for hers. Sometimes when she was talking to him, prattling on about the new film she wanted to see at the Rialto or what that bitch Esther Gold had said to her at the factory, she would sense his thoughts were elsewhere.

And he had never, ever told her he loved her.

It was a strange sensation for her. No young man had ever lost interest in Ruby Pike. It was always the other way round. Now she knew how the boys felt when she turned cool with them, stopped smiling at their jokes and stiffened when they tried to put their arms around her. It wasn't a nice feeling.

She didn't want it to happen with Nick Riley. Everyone in Griffin Street knew they were courting; Ruby wasn't sure she would ever be able to hold her head up again if she let him get away from her.

But it was more than just hurt pride. She had started to have feelings for him. True, real feelings, not just the fluttering in her belly she usually got when she looked into his gorgeous blue eyes.

He was deep, as her mother would say. He didn't give his feelings away, didn't show off or try to impress her like some of the other boys she'd been out with. He didn't flash his cash around, act the fool to make her laugh, or pick fights with other blokes to prove how manly he was, either.

Nick didn't need to prove anything. Ruby felt a surge of pride when she walked down the street on his arm. He was so handsome, she could feel all the other girls watching her enviously. And he was so big and powerful, she felt protected too. Nothing and no one could hurt her when Nick Riley was around. Even her dad treated him with wary respect.

She knew she would never find anyone else like him. She had to keep him, it was as simple as that. And as far as Ruby knew, there was only one way to make sure of it.

She didn't doubt it would work. It was what all men wanted, wasn't it? She'd tussled with enough of them in the back row of the pictures to know that. And deep as he might be, Nick Riley was just a red-blooded man like all the rest.

Not that he'd ever tried it on, or anything like that. They'd done plenty of kissing and cuddling, but unlike the other boys Nick never tried to push it further. Ruby liked to tell herself it was because he respected her too much. She didn't want to consider the possibility that he just wasn't interested.

She twiddled nervously with a curl, teasing it into place. In spite of what people might have thought from the way she looked and acted, she had never gone all the way before. Her mother had cautioned her not to give it away, to make sure she had a ring on her finger first. But it hadn't done *her* much good, had it? All that waiting, and she'd still ended up married to a lazy loser. Ruby didn't plan to end up like her mother, not in a million years.

No, the good Lord had given her looks that drove men wild, and she meant to use them.

She had been thinking about it for days, and now she had her chance. Her dad was at work, and her mum was taking her brothers to see the King lying in state in Westminster. Nick's mother June was going too, and for once she was taking his brother Danny with her. They would have the whole house to themselves.

Not that Nick seemed excited at the prospect. He was more concerned about his brother.

'You'll keep an eye on him, won't you?' he warned his mother for the hundredth time as he followed her and Danny into the backyard.

''Course I will. I'm his mother, ain't I? You don't think I know how to look after my own bleeding son?'

148

June Riley rolled her eyes at Ruby. She grinned back, but she understood why Nick was worried. She had already caught a whiff of gin on June's breath and seen the way her hands shook. The state she was in, they'd probably both end up under a tram. If they even made it up West – June had to pass a good few pubs on their way to the bus stop.

She watched Nick fastening the woollen scarf around his brother's neck, tucking it inside his jacket to keep out the cold. Danny gave her the creeps, with his vacant eyes and slack, drooling lips, but Nick never showed such tenderness to anyone as he did to his brother.

'Have a nice time, won't you, Danny?' Ruby forced herself to smile warmly at him. Danny gave her one of his scared-rabbit looks, and ducked his head away.

'Are you sure you don't want to come with us?' Her mother came out of the house, buttoning up her coat, followed by Ruby's younger brothers, who were scrapping as usual. 'It's disrespectful, if you ask me, not to wanting to see the King.'

'He ain't going to notice if I'm not there, is he? Besides, I want to stay here with Nick. I promised to give him his tea.'

Her mother glanced across at Nick, then back at Ruby. 'As long as that's all you give him,' she warned.

Ruby laughed. 'Don't you worry about me. I know what I'm doing.'

Her mother sent her a shrewd look. 'I hope you do, my girl.'

Half an hour later Ruby stood at the stove,

frying bacon with the eggs her mum had just brought home. She was beginning to wish she'd never offered to cook for Nick. She'd already spattered her new frock with fat, and she felt sure her hair smelt of frying.

She glanced over her shoulder at Nick, who was pouring himself a beer. She wasn't used to seeing him sitting at their kitchen table. He rarely came upstairs to the Pikes' part of their shared house. Ruby knew he didn't have much time for the rest of her family – especially not her mum, who never held back with her opinions of the Rileys, or anyone else for that matter. Ruby had tried telling Nick her mum didn't mean anything by it, but he didn't seem convinced.

'I wouldn't do this for everyone, you know,' she told him, as she prodded the eggs with a spoon. 'You should be honoured.'

'I'll tell you when I've tasted it.'

'Don't be cheeky.' She smiled at him, flashing her dimples, then promptly forgot she was supposed to be charming as she accidentally put the spoon through one of the eggs. 'Oh, sod it. Now look what I've done!' she cursed, as the yellow yolk oozed out into the sizzling pan.

'Here, let me.' Nick came over and took the pan out of her hands. 'You're making a right mess of it.'

'I'm not much of a cook,' she admitted helplessly, watching him expertly scraping blackened bits of bacon from the edges of the pan. 'Mum does all the cooking.'

'You'll have to learn sometime.'

'Unless I marry a man who can cook?' she said hopefully.

'Or doesn't mind burnt offerings.' He glanced over his shoulder at her. 'Don't just stand there batting your eyelashes. Make yourself useful and lay the table, will you?'

They sat across the table from each other. Ruby did her best to act sophisticated, playing languidly with her food as she'd seen Bette Davis do in a film once.

'Why aren't you eating?' Nick looked across at her plate, frowning. 'You've been waving that food around for five minutes.'

'I'm not hungry.'

'Give it here, then.'

She passed her plate across the table to him. 'You must be starving, if you can eat my cooking,' she joked.

'It's not that bad.'

'Is that a compliment?' She smiled archly at him. 'Careful, you silver-tongued devil, you'll sweep me off my feet.'

He didn't respond, so she slipped off her shoe and reached under the table with her foot, sliding it slowly and suggestively up and down his leg.

Nick stared across at her, his eyes darkening. 'You're the one who should be careful,' he said softly.

'I know what I'm doing.'

'Do you? I wonder.'

After that, much to her frustration, Nick insisted on washing up, even though Ruby did her best to lure him on to the couch.

'Isn't it nice to have the house to ourselves?' she purred. 'I can't wait until I have my own place. Then I can shut the door on the rest of the world.'

She loved her family, but the house was too crowded, always full of noise, what with her brothers fighting and her dad shouting and her mum always sniping about the neighbours. She hated sharing a bedroom with Frank and Dennis, having to put up with them nosing in her belongings, helping themselves out of her purse and scrawling all over her Picturegoer with her best lipstick. 'I really want a place of my own. One of those nice modern flats the Corporation is building, with a bathroom where I can just turn on a tap and soak in a proper tub any time I like, instead of having to drag in the old tin bath from the backyard.' She looked at Nick. 'What about you? Don't you want to get away from here one day?'

Nick scrubbed away at a frying pan, his back turned to her. 'I've got plans,' he admitted.

'What kind of plans?'

He laid the pan down on the draining board. 'I'm going to America,' he said finally.

Ruby sat up and stared at him over the back of the couch. 'America? You mean, like Hollywood?'

'New York. I've read there are doctors over there who might be able to put our Danny right.'

Ruby frowned. Why did it always have to be about Danny? Anyway, surely Nick must know it would take a miracle, not medicine, to get that boy straight.

'Doctors cost money, don't they? How are you going to afford it?' she asked.

'I'm saving.'

'On your wages? You can hardly afford the bus fare to Bow, let alone America!'

'I've got my winnings from boxing.' His chin lifted proudly. 'And if I do well enough, they might even pay for me to go over there and fight.'

Ruby watched him, impressed. He had plans, ambition. She liked that.

'I'd love to go to America,' she sighed. She read avidly about the lives of the Hollywood stars in *Picturegoer* every week. 'I want to be like Olivia de Havilland, dressed in the latest fashions and going out to fancy parties every night. That would be the life, wouldn't it?'

Nick gave her one of his rare smiles. 'You'd best start saving, then.'

'Unless you take me?' she suggested boldly.

'Now why would I want to do that?' But he was still smiling, which was a good sign.

He finished washing up and dried his hands on the tea towel. 'Right, I'd best be off,' he said.

Ruby jumped to her feet, panicking. 'Aren't you going to stay?'

'I can't. I've got training at the club.'

'Can't you give it a miss, just for one night? It's not every day we get the house to ourselves, is it? I thought we could have a nice night in together. Just the two of us,' she added meaningfully.

'I don't know if that's such a good idea.'

'Why not?' She feigned innocence.

'You know very well why not.'

Their eyes met, and Ruby felt a jolt of desire that almost turned her legs to liquid.

She sent him a look from under her lashes. 'What's wrong, Nick?' she pouted. 'Don't you want me?'

His eyes were dark, almost black. 'I don't want

153

to take advantage. It wouldn't be right,' he said gruffly.

'You wouldn't be taking advantage if I wanted it to happen, would you?'

Nick frowned, but she could see he was already weakening. He wanted to touch her, she could feel desire running through him like electricity.

Holding his gaze, she reached up and began to unbutton her dress.

'Don't.' It came out as a groan of longing. He couldn't take his eyes off her as she pushed her dress from her shoulders and let it fall at her feet.

She had to stop herself from trembling as she faced him, exposed in her camisole and knickers. She could feel her nipples hardening under his dark gaze, pressing against the thin silk.

'We mustn't,' he said softly. But she knew he didn't mean it. He was looking at her yearningly, like a thirsty man staring at a pool of water in the middle of a hot desert.

'Suit yourself.' Nimbly she stepped out of her dress. Then, she turned slowly and walked out of the room and into her bedroom, closing the door behind her.

She wondered if she'd overplayed her hand as she lay in bed five minutes later, nervously pleating the frayed silk of her eiderdown between her fingers.

She heard the front door bang shut and her heart sank. She had been so sure he would follow her. But as she shivered in the chilly darkness, she began to feel rather foolish. She sat up, hugging her knees. So that was that. Nick obviously wasn't interested.

'It's his loss,' she said out loud, but the words had a hollow ring.

She was just wondering if she should get up and turn on the lamp when she heard the creak of her bedroom doorknob as it turned slowly. The door opened and she saw Nick's tall, broad-shouldered shape outlined in the light from the hallway.

He stood in the doorway for a moment, and even though she couldn't see his face she could feel his hesitation.

She lay back against the pillows and held out her arms to him.

'Are you coming in, or what?' she said softly.

Another moment's hesitation, then he came in and closed the door quietly behind him, shutting out the light.

Chapter Fourteen

On a damp, misty Tuesday morning in late January, Dora and her family packed in with thousands of others outside Paddington Station to wait for the arrival of the King's funeral cortège on its way to Windsor.

'Talk about being late for your own funeral!' Nanna Winnie mumbled through a mouthful of bread and dripping. As usual, she never went anywhere without a picnic, even a solemn state occasion. 'It was meant to come past an hour ago. What's keeping it, I wonder.'

'We heard they can't get up the streets because of all the people,' a man close by told them. 'The streets are packed round Hyde Park, so they say. Police can't hold them back.'

'Quite right, too,' Nanna agreed piously. 'We all have to pay our respects to His Majesty. I wouldn't have missed this for the world. Even if this cold wind is doing nothing for my rheumatics,' she grumbled, pulling her coat tighter around her.

Dora smiled. It took a lot to get Nanna Winnie out of Griffin Street, let alone all the way up west. Dora had never known her go beyond Aldgate before. And yet here she was, done up in her best coat, the one she always wore for funerals, reeking of mothballs.

'I can't see!' Bea complained. 'Why do we have to be right at the back? It's not fair!' She scowled at the towering head and shoulders of the man standing in front of her, as if she would have liked to knock his hat off.

'Oh, stop moaning, Bea. It's a funeral, not a flipping circus!' Josie scolded her. 'It don't matter if you can't get a front-row seat.'

'It's all right for Little Alfie. He's sitting on Dora's shoulders,' Bea pouted.

'Well, if you think I'm putting *you* on my shoulders, you've got another think coming!' Dora laughed. 'Little Alfie weighs a ton as it is.' She tickled her little brother's chubby leg, making him giggle.

Then she looked at her mother and her smile faded. Rose Doyle was scanning the crowd restlessly. Dora knew exactly who she was looking for.

She tugged at the sleeve of her coat. 'I don't think Alf will be here, Mum,' she whispered.

Rose gave her a tired smile. 'I know I'm being daft. I just thought with all these thousands of people... I mean, he's got to be somewhere, hasn't he? He can't just disappear into thin air.'

'I suppose not, Mum,' Dora agreed wearily.

'I know he'll come back when he's ready, but I wish he'd hurry up. We could do with him being home, especially now–' She caught Nanna's eye and stopped abruptly. Dora looked from one to the other.

'Especially now what?' she asked.

'It's nothing, love. Ooh, listen.' Her mother looked up at the sound of a distant marching band. 'Sounds like the King's on his way!'

'Here we go.' Nanna wrapped up the remains of her bread and dripping and stuffed it back into her battered handbag. 'About time, too, I reckon.'

'I can't see!' Bea protested, jumping up and down. They watched as the gun carriage and coffin, with the Imperial Crown glittering on top, rumbled past, pulled by a company of sailors, eight abreast and twelve deep. 'Look at them,' Josie whispered admiringly, her voice almost lost under the mournful strains of the Scottish regiments' bagpipes. 'Have you ever seen anything like it? The way they all move in perfect time. It's like they're a machine.'

The coffin was followed by the new King and his brothers, on foot. Dora and her sisters strained to get a glimpse of King Edward, shrouded in his overcoat, his eyes cast down as he passed.

'He looks so sad, doesn't he?' Josie said.

157

'It's his father's bleeding funeral, girl. He's not going to be doing handstands, is he?' Nanna hissed back. 'Oh, look, here comes Queen Mary. Doesn't she look dignified?' They watched the Queen's carriage roll slowly past, with Her Majesty in the back, dressed all in black. 'What a shame we can't see her face behind that thick veil, though.'

When it was finally all over Nanna smiled with satisfaction, showing off her dentures, which she'd put in for the occasion. 'Ooh, I wouldn't have missed that for the world. I do love a good funeral,' she sighed. 'Not sure about them bag-pipes, though. Haven't heard a racket like that since Mrs Peterson's cat got its tail stuck in the mangle.'

'I s'pose we'd better try and find a bus to get home,' Rose said. 'I daresay that'll take a month of Sundays, too, with all these people.' She looked around. 'Where's Bea?'

They all looked, but no one could remember seeing her since the procession started. 'She kept saying she couldn't see. Perhaps she's tried to get nearer the front?' Nanna suggested.

'Mum, you wait here with Little Alfie in case she comes back,' Rose said. 'Dora and Josie and I'll split up and start looking for her.'

'Hang on,' Josie said, pointing. 'Here she comes now.'

Sure enough, there was Bea, pale with terror, being steered through the crowd towards them by a policeman. When she saw them, she broke away from his hand and, dramatic as ever, launched herself tearfully into her mother's arms.

158

'Blimey, look at her carrying on,' Nanna whispered. 'She's only been missing five minutes.'

'I take it you're her family?' The policeman smiled.

'Yes, Constable, thank you–' Dora swung round and found herself looking up into a familiar face. Those amber-flecked green eyes were shaded by his helmet, but she would have known them anywhere. 'Mr Armstrong?'

'Nurse Doyle?' He looked her up and down. 'Sorry, I didn't recognise you out of your uniform.'

'And I didn't recognise you in yours!' Dora laughed.

'Do you two know each other, then?' Nanna said, muscling in between them.

'Nurse Doyle has been looking after my sister while she's been in hospital,' Joe Armstrong explained.

'You can call me Dora, now Sister's not watching.'

'And I'm Joe. Pleased to meet you, Dora.' He held out his hand and she shook it. 'Seems funny to be able to talk to you without you looking over your shoulder all the time.'

'So you're an East End lad, then?' Nanna Winnie butted in.

'We live in Whitechapel.'

'Fancy that.' Dora didn't like the way Nanna was staring at Joe. She'd seen that look in her eye before.

'Anyway, we'd better be getting off home.' She swooped down and gathered Little Alfie into her arms. His plump cheek was as cold as marble against hers. 'We don't want to keep Joe from his

159

work, do we?'

'I'm sure he doesn't mind. Do you, son?' Nanna flashed her false teeth at him.

'Actually, I am meant to be on duty.' He grinned at Dora. 'Makes a change for me to be saying that and not you, doesn't it?'

'You'll have to come round for your tea sometime,' Nanna said, as Dora groaned inwardly. 'Any friend of our Dora's is always welcome. Isn't that right, Rose?'

Dora looked imploringly at her mother, who smiled and said, 'Come on, Mum. Let's get you home. I think all the excitement of the day's been too much for you.'

The bus back to Bethnal Green was crowded, so at least Dora didn't have to endure her grandmother's interrogation. But she could hear her whispering loudly to Rose at the back of the bus.

'Did you see the way he looked at our Dora? He seemed very keen, didn't he?'

'It's none of our business, Mum,' Rose said patiently.

'Well, I think there's something going on there. You should have a word with her, Rosie, tell her to give him some encouragement. Lord knows, that girl isn't going to get offers every day. She's nearly twenty ... high time she was courting, I reckon. I was married with a baby on the way by the time I was her age.'

Dora caught Josie's eye and they grinned sheepishly at each other. 'She never stops, does she?' said Dora, shaking her head.

'Remember that time she tried to pair you off with Nick Riley?' Josie reminded her. 'Imagine you two together!'

Dora looked away so her sister wouldn't see her blushing face. 'Imagine that,' she said quietly.

'So is there anything going on between you and Joe?' Josie asked.

'No! We've passed the time of day a couple of times, that's all.'

'Nanna's right, though. I reckon he likes you.'

'Not you, too!' Dora rolled her eyes in exasperation. 'For once and for all, Joe Armstrong doesn't like me. Not in that way anyway. And even if he did, you know I wouldn't be interested in him. And you know why, too.'

They were both silent for a moment. Josie cleared a spot with her sleeve on the steamy window and stared out at the grey city streets. Dora wished she hadn't said anything. She knew her sister was as haunted by Alf Doyle's memory as she was. He might be gone, but he still cast a shadow over their lives.

The house was cold when they got home.

'I'm freezing,' Bea complained as Nanna lit the lamps.

'Let's put some coal on the fire.' Dora went over to the fireplace and picked up the scuttle. 'Oh, this is empty.'

'It's all right,' her mother said. 'Bea can put an extra jumper on.'

'But I might as well fill it anyway–'

'You can't. There's no coal left,' Nanna said bluntly.

'No coal?' Dora looked from one to the other. The atmosphere suddenly seemed charged with tension. Even Josie looked uneasy. 'What's going on?' she asked. 'What aren't you telling me?'

An anxious glance passed between her mother and grandmother. 'You'll have to tell her, Rose,' Nanna said quietly.

'Tell me what? For God's sake, someone tell me something!'

Her mother took a deep breath. 'Your brother's lost his job,' she said.

'It's the Jews' fault,' Bea piped up. 'That's what our Pete says. He reckons they get rid of decent British working people like him just so they can – ow!' she wailed, as Nanna lashed out with a stinging slap around her ear. 'What was that for?'

'For talking nonsense.'

'But Pete says–'

'Your brother doesn't know what he's talking about, and nor do you!' Nanna snapped. 'Don't you think we're all in enough trouble, without you going about spouting that Blackshirt rubbish? And you can stop yelling, too, or I'll give you one on the other side!' She lifted the back of her hand. Bea ducked.

Dora dug in her coat pocket for her purse and took out a couple of coins. 'Josie, take this down to the coal yard and bring us some coke. And take Bea and Little Alfie with you,' she said.

Josie took the coins but Bea folded her arms stubbornly. 'I don't want to go. You're going to be talking about secrets while we're gone and I want to hear what's going on.'

'Hark at you, nosy little beggar!' Nanna glared at her.

'We all know who I get it from, don't we?' Bea glared back at her from a safe distance.

162

'Go on,' Dora coaxed. 'You can buy yourselves some sweets with the change,' she added.

Bea looked from Dora to Josie for a moment, her green eyes gleaming greedily. Then, taking Little Alfie by the hand, she flounced out, Josie following.

'And make sure they don't give you no dust down at that yard!' Nanna called after them, as the door slammed shut.

'Right,' Dora said when they'd gone. 'I want you to tell me what's been going on.'

'It's nothing,' her mother replied. 'It's just Peter being laid off has left us a bit short, that's all.' She couldn't quite meet Dora's eye as she said it.

'How short?'

'We're two weeks behind on the rent,' Nanna filled the silence.

'But we'll manage,' Rose added cheerfully. 'Things will be all right. It's nothing for you to worry about.' Her smile was bright, but Dora could see the lines of strain around her eyes.

'How will you manage?' she asked.

Another silence. 'You'd best tell her, Rosie,' Nanna said heavily. 'She'll find out soon enough.'

'Find out what?' Panic fluttered in her chest.

Her mother stared down at her hands. 'I'm going to the Public Assistance,' she said.

Dora stared at her in horror. 'Mum, no! You can't!'

'What choice do I have, love?' Rose turned pain-filled eyes to meet hers. 'I feel wretched about it, I really do. But the kids have got to eat, and however you look at it we haven't got enough money coming in. Look, it might not be that bad,' she said

163

in a forced voice. 'And if it means we get some help...' Her voice trailed off hopelessly.

'But the Public Assistance, Mum!' Things must be even worse than her mother was letting on, if she was even thinking about going cap in hand to them.

All around them in the East End, people still lived in fear of the workhouse. Nanna often told stories about how she and her brothers and sisters were put there when her father died and her mother couldn't afford to keep them. It was a harsh, cruel life. One of Nanna's brothers had died of TB in there.

Things were supposed to be better now, of course. But asking for help still meant letting the Public Assistance Committee pry into your affairs. The Means Test man would come round with his clipboard and make notes of everything you owned and how much it was worth. Then he'd decide what had to be sold before you could claim any money.

It was a degrading process, and Dora knew there were many in Bethnal Green who would starve on the streets before they let the Means Test man over their doorstep.

'There must be something else we can do?'

'Like what? Believe me, love, I've done everything. I work night and day at the laundry, and Nanna and Josie are doing piecework from the box factory.'

Dora looked up sharply. 'Josie's working?'

'Only part-time, evenings and weekends.'

'But what about her schoolwork?'

'She can still keep up with her schoolwork,

164

don't you worry.' Dora saw Nanna shake her head warningly, and looked at her mother. Rose's head was bowed, her dark hair streaked with grey that hadn't been there recently. She was such a proud woman, it must be breaking her heart to be in this position.

'I should do something too,' Dora said.

'You already do more than enough, handing over your keep every week.'

'I could give you even more if I went back to work at Gold's.'

'No, Dora.' Rose shook her head. 'I won't hear of it.'

'I mean it, Mum. We're a family, we've all got to pull together. I can earn more as a machinist at Gold's than I do as a student–'

'Please, love. ' Her mother's dark eyes appealed to her. 'I've already had Josie risking her future. I don't want to see another of my girls do it.' Her voice cracked. 'I haven't done much with my life. All I've got to be proud of are my kids. Just to see you in that uniform, to know you're going to have a proper career, not taking in washing or skivvying for a living – well, it gives me some hope to cling to when things get bad.' She reached for Dora's hand and squeezed it.

She looked down at her mother's callused fingers wrapped around hers. 'It just doesn't seem fair,' she said. 'Not when everyone else is working so hard... At least let me give you all my wages?' she offered. 'I know it's not much, but it might help?'

'Won't you need it?'

'What for? My board and lodgings are already

found, and it's not as if I get the time to spend anything!' Dora smiled wryly. 'And I'd like to do my bit to help, if I can. Please, Mum. It'll make me feel better.'

'Well, if you're sure...?' Her mother looked grateful. 'Thanks, love.'

'You never know, it might help keep the Means Test man away!' Dora joked feebly.

But when she saw the look that passed between her mother and grandmother, she had the uneasy feeling that he would still be knocking on the door one day soon.

Chapter Fifteen

'Acute bronchial catarrh,' the doctor pronounced, unhooking his stethoscope from his ears.

'Are you sure?' Violet asked. 'His temperature is rather high–'

'My dear lady, a slight fever is to be expected with this condition. I assure you, it's nothing to worry about.'

He patted her arm when he said it. He had a typical doctor's way of speaking, a mix of arrogance and condescension that made her hackles rise.

'This is not a slight fever,' she said, holding on to her temper. 'A slight fever is less than one hundred and two degrees. My son's temperature was one hundred and three the last time I checked it. I'm a nurse,' she explained, as the doctor raised his eyebrows.

'If you're a nurse then I'm sure you'll know that living in damp conditions like these is not helping your son's weak chest?' he retorted, glancing meaningfully at the black patch of mould under the window.

Violet fell silent. Having put her firmly back in her place, the doctor smiled kindly at her. 'I realise you have some medical knowledge, Mrs–' He consulted his notes vaguely.

'Gifford,' Violet said automatically.

'Mrs Gifford. But in this situation you are first and foremost an anxious mother. Of course you will exaggerate the importance of certain symptoms, or even notice symptoms that aren't there. Mothers imagine the worst, my dear. It's their job.'

'And am I imagining the way he's breathing, too?' Violet looked anxiously at Oliver. His sternomastoid muscles were struggling, drawing his head back and thrusting his chin forward with every breath.

'An inhalation of Friar's Balsam or turpentine will soon sort that out.' The doctor was already packing up his bag to leave. 'If he's no better in a couple of days, send for me again. And in the meantime, try to do something about your lodgings.' He gazed around him, his mouth curling with distaste. 'Living here really isn't doing your son any good, you know.'

Tell me something I don't know, thought Violet. She was tempted to show him all the advertisements for accommodation she had answered, only to be turned away because no one wanted a single

167

mother and her child. Even if she did tell them she was a widow.

The doctor packed up his bag. Panic rose in her chest as he headed for the door. 'You can't leave Oliver like this!' she cried out.

He turned back to look at her. 'I'm sure he will do very well under your excellent nursing.'

Violet listened to him going down the stairs. Why hadn't he listened to her? She wasn't just another anxious mother. Oliver was sick, really sick, and he had done nothing about it.

'Mummy?'

'I'm here, sweetheart.' She summoned a smile for her son. She had rigged up a bedrest with an upturned chair covered with pillows so that he could sit up, but he was still struggling for breath.

She sat on his bed and brushed away a dark lock of hair that clung damply to his forehead. 'How are you feeling?'

'A bit better.' He looked up at her, his dark eyes huge. 'You won't leave me, will you, Mummy?'

'No, darling, I'm not going anywhere.' She had already made her mind up she would call the hospital and make an excuse not to go in. 'I have to stay here and nurse my baby, don't I?'

She got up and threw a couple of lumps of coal on to the fire, watching as the flames stirred back into life. Then she replaced the fireguard and adjusted the makeshift screen of sheets thrown over a clothes horse that she'd assembled to protect Oliver from the draught coming through the open window.

She rubbed liniment into his little chest, feeling his ribs rising and falling under her hand.

'It hurts, Mummy,' he complained.

'I know, darling.' She felt the pain of every breath he took as if it were her own lungs that were clogged. 'This will make you feel better.'

But as she rubbed the liniment into his skin, she knew it wasn't enough. Anxiety flowed through her, filling all the space inside her head like black ink.

Once she'd done her best to make him comfortable, she washed her hands and dried them.

'Right, I have to go out for a moment – don't worry, I'll be back very soon,' she added, seeing her son's look of dismay. 'I just have to telephone the hospital and tell them I won't be coming in. They'll need to find another nurse to look after the patients tonight if I'm not there, won't they?'

Oliver still cried as she left and Violet wept too as she hurried down to the phone box on the corner.

The Matron, Miss Fox, was very good when Violet explained that she was running a slight fever and couldn't come in.

'Of course you must go to bed immediately,' she said, full of concern. 'Don't forget to take plenty of fluids. Do you have anyone looking after you?'

Hearing the warmth and concern in her voice, Violet felt herself cracking. She wanted to break down and cry like a child. She wanted to tell her the truth, that she was alone and frightened and she didn't know what to do. But instead she held herself rigid and assured Miss Fox that she was perfectly capable of caring for herself, and that all being well she would be back on duty the following evening. When had lying become second nature to her? she wondered.

Mrs Bainbridge intercepted her in the hall, carrying a large saucepan. Violet steeled herself for another bruising encounter, but Mrs Bainbridge surprised her by handing her the pan.

'I've made some broth. I thought you might want some for your boy?' she offered. 'I know the little mite's proper poorly, so I thought it would help.'

Violet could see from her expression that Mrs Bainbridge was acting out of guilt for all those times she had neglected him and not made up the fire. She would have liked to refuse it on principle, but was so exhausted by worry she welcomed even the tiniest scrap of comfort and kindness.

'Thank you,' she said, taking the pan from her hands.

That afternoon she prepared an inhalation of Friar's Balsam and rigged up a steam tent around him while she heated up the broth. To her great relief, Oliver managed to eat everything she gave him, then announced he was bored.

'Why can't I get up and play?' he mumbled through clenched lips as Violet checked his temperature.

'When you're better, darling.'

'But I feel better now!'

'Let's see, shall we?' She checked the thermometer. A hundred and one. Perhaps the doctor was right, after all? 'Tell you what, why don't I fetch the cards and teach you a new game?'

The rest of the afternoon and evening were spent playing cards and reading. Oliver demanded his favourite book, *The Water Babies*, even though he'd heard the story a hundred times.

Afterwards, Violet got into his bed with him and held his feverish little body to hers until he fell asleep. It was a treat to be with him. She had missed talking and singing to him, and reading him a bedtime story.

'Did my daddy know about me?' he asked sleepily, his eyelids already drooping.

Violet stopped stroking his head. 'Why do you ask?'

He shrugged his thin shoulders. 'I don't remember him at all.'

Violet let her hand run slowly over his sleek dark head, so like his father's. 'Yes, he knew all about you,' she replied carefully.

'And did he ever play with me, and read to me like you do?'

'You were just a baby when he knew you. But he loved you. He loved you with all his heart.' A lump rose in her throat and she swallowed it down determinedly.

'I wish he wasn't dead,' Oliver said firmly. 'I think I would like a daddy.' He twisted his body to look up at her. 'You should get married to someone else,' he decided.

Violet laughed. 'There's only room for one man in my life, sweetheart.' She eased him gently off her shoulder and stood up. 'Now it's time for you to go to sleep.'

'Promise you'll think about it,' he said as she settled him back against the pillows and tucked the covers under his chin. 'Promise you'll think about getting married to someone else.'

'All right, I'll think about it,' she agreed. 'Now

171

get some sleep.'

She sat with him, holding his little hand in hers, until his eyelids finally fluttered closed and he drifted off to sleep. Then she gently let go of him and stood up, massaging her stiff muscles.

She made up the fire again and then went over to pull the curtains. It was a clear, starry February night, with fresh, mild air that held the promise of spring. Soon winter would be over and the weather would be fine enough to take Oliver out every day, she thought. He could breathe fresh air and she wouldn't have to worry about his weak chest for a few blessed months.

Then she realised with a shock what day it was. She had been so worried about Oliver, she hadn't even remembered it was her birthday.

She gazed over the moonlit rooftops and wondered if anyone else out there had remembered. Had her mother thought about her at all? If she had, it probably wouldn't be with fondness. Violet dearly wished she could write to her, but her mother had made it very clear four years ago that she no longer wished to hear from her daughter.

A tear rolled down her cheek, and she dashed it away. Perhaps Oliver was right, she thought. Perhaps she should find a husband, someone to take care of her.

But even as she thought it, she knew it was never going to happen. She was on her own now, and for her own sake and Oliver's, it had to stay that way.

'I'm sorry,' Millie said.

'But it's my birthday, Mil. We arranged all this

ages ago. You said you could come.'

'Yes, but I didn't know Mrs Tremayne and the Board of Trustees would choose that day to pay a visit to the ward, did I? We were only told about it this morning.'

Millie shivered in the frigid chill of the nurses' home corridor as she listened to Seb on the other end of the telephone line. She didn't blame him for being upset. She had been looking forward to flying over to Le Touquet for his birthday. But now Sister Hyde had cancelled all leave.

'Yes, well, we mustn't let Mrs Tremayne down, must we?' he said bitterly.

'Don't be like that, Seb, please,' Millie begged. 'You know I can't help it.'

'I suppose not.' He paused. 'This Mrs Tremayne – she wouldn't be any relation of your friend William, would she?'

'She's his mother. Why?'

'No reason. So when am I going to see you again?'

'I'll definitely be able to come to Sophia's house party.'

'That's a whole month away. Can't I see you before then?'

'I'll try, but I can't promise anything. They never tell us when we're allowed a day off until the last minute. I only managed to get to Sophia's party by telling them my cousin was getting married in Scotland. I just hope Sister Wren doesn't check the Society pages!' She listened to the silence at the other end of the line. 'You are all right about this, aren't you?'

'I don't have much choice, do I?'

173

'I'll make it up to you, I promise.'

He laughed. 'Sounds intriguing. Tell me more.'

She heard the sound of a dog yapping in the distance. 'Look, I'd better go. I can hear Sister Sutton coming. She's bound to catch me for something.'

'I love you–'

'Love you, too. Sorry, Seb, I'll call again as soon as I can.'

She hung up the phone just as Sister Sutton rounded the corner, her Jack Russell terrier Sparky as ever at her heels.

'Benedict?'

Her voice rang out down the hallway, stopping Millie in her tracks. Sister Sutton's squat, wide body almost filled the hallway.

'Sister?'

She had no choice but to stand and wait as Sister Sutton lumbered down the hall towards her, flat-footed in her stout black shoes. Her uniform strained over her vast bosom, and the bow of her starched cap was almost lost in the fleshy folds of her chin.

'I went up in your room earlier, Benedict. It's a disgrace,' she snorted. 'Your belongings were strewn everywhere, your bed wasn't made properly, and when was the last time you turned your mattress?'

Millie glanced down at Sparky, who was baring his teeth dangerously close to her ankle. 'Last week, Sister.'

'Last week? A likely story.' Her eyes were like tiny black raisins in her big doughy face.

As Home Sister, she was in charge of the welfare

174

of the students living in the nurses' home. Before she'd started her training, Millie had looked forward to having someone motherly in her life. But she soon found out Sister Sutton was as maternal as a regimental sergeant major.

Sensing Sister Sutton was about to go into one of her lectures, Millie did the only sensible thing she could, and burst into tears.

'Good gracious, girl!' Sister Sutton stepped back, startled. Even Sparky stopped snarling. 'What on earth is the matter with you?'

'I – I'm sorry, Sister,' she gulped, fumbling in her pocket for a handkerchief. 'I've just been on the telephone to my boyfriend, and he told me–'

'Yes, well, that's enough of that, thank you very much!' Sister Sutton flapped her hand. 'Go up to your room and pull yourself together.'

'Y-Yes, Sister.'

Millie hid her smile behind her handkerchief as she watched Sister bustle away. She might be an authority on a well-made bed or a properly starched apron, but if there was anything that threw Sister Sutton into confusion, it was having to deal with young girls' emotional problems. Bringing a troublesome boyfriend into the conversation had saved her from endless lectures recently.

Millie hurried upstairs to the attic bedroom she shared with Helen and Dora. Dora was sitting cross-legged on the bed, her head in a textbook, while Helen craned her neck to apply her make-up in the small square mirror above the chest of drawers. Both of them were managing to ignore Millie's upended bed in the middle of the room.

'Not again!' she sighed, picking up a pillow. 'Honestly, doesn't Sister Sutton ever get tired of doing this?'

'I'll give you a hand.' Dora put down her book and slid off the bed.

As she and Dora hauled the heavy horsehair mattress back on to the iron bedstead, Millie told them about having to let Seb down on his birthday.

'This is all your mother's fault.' She glared at Helen. 'Couldn't she and the other Trustees pick another day to visit?'

'Don't talk to me about it. I'm not looking forward to it any more than you are.' Helen pulled the pins out of her hair and fluffed it out around her face. 'She's bound to find fault with me. She always does.'

'I thought you two had called a truce?' After sharing a room with her for nearly two years, Millie knew only too well how Helen used to live in fear of her over-critical mother. But recently Constance Tremayne seemed to have relaxed her tight grip on her daughter's life.

'Oh, we have. But that doesn't stop her disapproving of everything I do.' Helen ran a brush through her hair. 'She's even worse since I started going out with Charlie. She's convinced he's somehow going to stop me finishing my training.'

'That's never going to happen, is it?' Helen had blossomed and lost much of her shyness since she'd met him. But she was still the hardest-working student Millie knew. 'So where's he taking you tonight?'

'Just to the pictures. There's a new John Wayne

film on at the Rialto. Not that I really mind what I scc, as long as I can sit down and rest my feet!' she grimaced.

'Why don't we go to the pictures?' Millie suggested to Dora. 'I could do with a night out.'

Dora shook her head. 'I'm back on duty in half an hour. I don't finish until nine tonight,' she said, as she tucked in the sheet on Millie's bed.

'Some other night, then?'

'I can't afford it.'

'But we only got paid yesterday! You can't have spent it all already?' Millie laughed in disbelief.

Dora kept her head down as she smoothed the blanket into place. 'That's my business,' she muttered.

'Then I'll pay.'

'No, thanks.' She straightened up, shook the pillow and put it in place. 'I've told you before. I'm not a charity case.'

'I didn't say you were.' Millie frowned as Dora headed for the door. 'Where are you going? Doyle–' But she'd already gathered up her books and disappeared out of the door.

Millie turned to Helen. 'What's wrong with her?'

'Search me.' Helen shrugged. 'You know how prickly she can be, especially about money.'

'Don't tell me I've put my foot in it again?' Millie sighed. She always seemed to be doing that with Dora.

Chapter Sixteen

By the middle of February, Jennie Armstrong was well enough to go home.

'Never underestimate the healing power of youth!' Dr Tremayne grinned, when he'd finished examining her. 'And excellent nursing, of course,' he added, winking at Dora.

She felt herself blushing as she fumbled with the notes he'd handed her. Having worked on the ward with him, she now understood why William Tremayne was so popular with the nurses at the Nightingale. He was so warm and charming, she could imagine him sweeping any woman off her feet.

'Nurse Doyle, are you and Dr Tremayne – you know?' Jennie was agog when he'd gone, and Dora was emptying her locker.

'No!' she laughed. 'Although I think I'm probably the only nurse in this hospital who can say that,' she added with a conspiratorial grin.

'You don't have a boyfriend then?'

Dora shook her head. 'Not me. Do you want to take these flowers with you? It seems a shame to throw them away.'

'Leave them here, if you like,' Jennie said. 'My brother probably meant them for you as much as me anyway,' she added archly. She looked much younger than her seventeen years, with her big shining eyes and impish face.

'So are you looking forward to going home?' Dora changed the subject swiftly.

Jennie's smile faded. 'Going back to cooking and cleaning and getting beatings off my dad, you mean? I can't wait,' she said bitterly.

Dora looked at her. 'Is it that bad?'

'I hate it.' The vehemence in Jennie's voice surprised her. 'He's made my life a misery ever since Mum died. I can't wait to get away.' She pulled a dead petal off one of the flowers. 'I thought I was going to get away with ... him,' she said quietly.

'Your boyfriend?'

'He said he'd look after me. He promised we were going to get married, have a place of our own...' she trailed off miserably.

'But then he cleared off?'

Jennie looked up at her, her green eyes pools of unhappiness. 'Turns out he was lying about everything,' she said. 'He was never going to marry me. How could he when–' She stopped herself from finishing the sentence.

'Sounds as if you're better off without him,' Dora said. 'Any man who can walk out on a young girl in trouble isn't worth knowing, in my opinion.'

'You don't understand,' Jennie said. 'It wasn't because of the baby. He didn't even know I was pregnant when he – left me.'

'And you didn't tell him?'

'I wanted to, but I didn't get the chance. And then I found out he was married.'

'Ah.'

I didn't know,' Jennie insisted, tears filling her eyes. 'I would never have gone with him if I'd known he already had a wife and kids.'

'Don't cry, ducks.' Dora pressed a handkerchief into Jennie's hands as she started to sob.

She looked at the young girl's anguished face. She was so naïve and desperate for love, she would have been easy pickings for a smooth-talking married man looking for a bit on the side. It was such a shame.

Sister Wren kept them busy for the rest of the morning, searching for – of all things – Mrs Venables' jar of jam, which had gone missing.

'Someone has stolen it from the kitchen,' she announced dramatically. 'I want you to search the whole ward, including the lockers and under the beds. Leave no stone unturned, Nurses!'

'This is ridiculous,' Laura Ennis whispered as they pulled out the kitchen cupboards to search. 'It's only a jar of jam, not the crown jewels!'

'True, but you know what she's like when she's got a bee in her bonnet,' Dora replied, sighing. 'And since those eggs disappeared, she's convinced we've got a thief in our midst.'

She was searching under a bed when Joe Armstrong arrived to collect his sister. Dora saw a pair of polished shoes a few feet from her nose, then shifted her gaze up to his face.

He stared down at her curiously. He was clutching a large bunch of flowers. 'Looking for something?' he asked.

'A jar of jam, would you believe?' She stood up, dusting invisible specks off her apron. 'For heaven's sake, don't let on to Sister that you're a policeman, or she'll have you clapping us all in handcuffs.'

'Come again?' he frowned in confusion.

'It doesn't matter.' She smiled brightly at him. 'You've come to collect Jennie? She's all ready for you.'

She started to lead the way to Jennie's bed, but Joe stopped her.

'Just a minute, Nurse. These are for you.' He thrust the flowers at her. 'To thank you for everything you've done for our Jennie,' he explained.

'They're lovely, Mr Armstrong. Thank you.' Dora buried her face in the blooms, enjoying their scent. 'But you didn't have to do that.'

'I know, but I wanted to.'

He slicked down his blond hair nervously. He was blushing, Dora noticed. In a sudden flash of intuition, she knew he was going to ask her out.

'Dora–' he began.

'We're all very pleased with the way your sister has recovered,' she interrupted him, her mouth dry with panic. 'She'll still need plenty of rest to keep her strength up, but if you look after her she should be as right as rain–'

'I'll look after her, don't you worry. Dora, there's something I wanted to ask you–'

Dora stared at him, panic-stricken. Oh God, she thought. Please don't ask me. Please...

'Doyle? Don't you have anything better to do than gossip?' Sister Wren's shrill voice sounded like music to her ears.

'I was just saying goodbye to Miss Armstrong, Sister.'

'Yes, well, now you've said it.' Sister Wren bustled over, her starched apron crackling as she walked. 'Now get those flowers in water quickly and get on with your work. Have you found that jam yet?'

'Not yet, Sister.'

'Then get on with it!'

Dora turned to Joe. 'Sorry, I have to go,' she whispered.

'But I wanted to–'

She gave an apologetic shrug and hurried off before he could finish, for once sending up a silent prayer of gratitude for Sister Wren's bossiness.

Chapter Seventeen

'It has been three days now, Matron. Surely this situation cannot be allowed to continue?'

Kathleen Fox glanced at the polished wooden clock on her office wall and sighed. It was five minutes past ten. Her Assistant Matron usually liked to complain about the Night Sister's continued absence by ten o'clock sharp every morning.

'There isn't a problem surely, Miss Hanley? Miss Wychwood is managing perfectly well as relief Night Sister.'

'That's as may be, but it's most inconvenient that we have to cover for Miss Tanner's absence.' Miss Hanley's broad, square face was indignant. 'The rotas are all over the place.'

Ah, the rotas. Kathleen Fox smiled to herself. Her Assistant Matron had an obsession with lists and timetables that bordered on the fanatical.

Kathleen was sure it must have something to do with Miss Hanley's father's military background.

'I'm sure Miss Tanner didn't become unwell with the intention of deliberately disrupting your rotas,' she said mildly.

'Unwell! Sisters do not become unwell. The former Night Sister did not take a day off sick in nearly twenty years of working here.'

'The former Night Sister dropped dead on duty. She is hardly a shining example.'

Miss Hanley's eyes narrowed with suspicion. 'Is that one of your jokes, Matron?'

Their sense of humour was one of the many things that divided them. It was no secret that Veronica Hanley, or 'Manly Hanley' as many of the nurses called her, had wanted the Matron's job. Many agreed she should have had it, too. She was tough and self-disciplined, and would have commanded the hospital like her father commanded the Hampshire Regiment in Lucknow.

But Kathleen Fox had been appointed instead, much to Miss Hanley's dismay. The Assistant Matron had made life difficult during Matron's first year, although the pair had settled into an uneasy truce lately.

But that didn't stop the occasional moments of friction.

'So what do you suggest I should do, Miss Hanley?' Kathleen asked wearily. 'Go to her home, drag her out by her hair and insist she returns to her duties?'

'It might not be a bad idea to find out if and when she intends to return,' Miss Hanley sniffed.

Kathleen Fox studied the blotter on her desk in

front of her. For once, she had to admit Miss Hanley had a point. It would be an imposition to expect the relief Night Sister to continue indefinitely.

And there was something else, too. Something that had been troubling her ever since Miss Tanner had first telephoned to say she was unwell. Matron couldn't think what it was, but there was something in the tone of her voice that had made her think Violet Tanner wasn't telling her the full story.

'Very well, Miss Hanley,' she said. 'I shall pay a visit to our Miss Tanner.'

'Nurse! Come here immediately.'

'Yes, Mrs Mortimer, what is it?'

Millie was pleased with herself for remembering to call her by her full name. Last time she'd chummily called her 'Maud' by accident, and had received a dressing down from both her and Sister Hyde. Mrs Mortimer's was far, far worse.

'For heaven's sake, I don't want you!' Maud dismissed her. 'I want a proper nurse. What about that dark-haired girl?' She nodded towards Helen at the far end of the ward. 'She seems to know what she's doing.'

'Nurse Tremayne is busy, Mrs Mortimer. I'm afraid you're stuck with me,' Millie said cheerfully. 'Now, what can I do for you?'

'Very well.' Mrs Mortimer gave a martyred sigh. 'My pillows need adjusting.'

Not a please or thank you, Millie thought as she shook and plumped the pillows and put them carefully back in place. Maud Mortimer always addressed the nurses as if they were servants.

184

'There. Is that better?' she said.

Mrs Mortimer leant back against them. 'It will have to do, I suppose,' she said grudgingly. 'Although I daresay a real nurse would have made a better job of it.'

'I daresay you're right, Mrs Mortimer,' Millie agreed. She picked up the patient's copy of *The Times*, still neatly folded on her locker. 'Are you not doing the crossword today?'

'I'm not in the mood.'

'I love *The Times* crossword. I always helped my father do it when I lived at home.'

Maud raised an imperious eyebrow. 'I'm sure you were a great help,' she said witheringly.

'You'd be surprised.' Millie looked down at Maud's wrinkled hands, lying limp on top of the bedcover. 'I could help you, if you like?' she offered. 'Perhaps I could fill in the answers for you.'

Maud's sharp gaze fixed itself on her. 'What are you saying? Are you implying I'm too feeble to hold a pen?'

'Well—'

'I told you, you stupid girl, I'm not in the mood. Good gracious, is it compulsory to be usefully occupied in this place?'

'No, but—'

'Now I'm finding you rather tiresome. Please leave me alone.'

She turned her head away, dismissing her. Millie opened her mouth to speak, then closed it again.

Helen was sympathetic. 'She really is an absolute horror, isn't she?' she whispered.

Millie shrugged it off. 'I feel sorry for her. She's

such a proud woman, it must be awful for her to have to admit she needs help.'

'That's no reason to take it out on us,' Helen replied. 'I'm dreading dinnertime. She's bound to make another horrible fuss about being fed. I just hope I'm not the one who has to do it today.' She shuddered at the thought. 'I don't know why they don't just give her a feeding tube. It would be far easier.'

'Would you like a feeding tube shoved down your throat?' Millie asked. 'It might be far easier for us, but it wouldn't be easier for her.'

She glanced back at Maud Mortimer who was lying back against her pillows, eyes closed. But even from the far end of the ward, Millie could tell she wasn't asleep.

'She was a suffragette when she was younger,' she said. 'I overheard Sister telling Staff Nurse Willis the other day. Apparently she was arrested and force fed because she refused to eat. That's why she's so terrified of the feeding tube.'

'Oh God, I had no idea.'

'That's the point, isn't it? None of us knows anything about these women.' Millie gestured around the ward. 'To us they're just old ladies who wet their beds and won't eat. We forget they were once like us, girls with hopes and dreams and lives ahead of them.'

'Yes, but they're old and they need our help now,' Helen reminded her. 'We've still got to nurse them.'

'And what if we end up like them one day? I don't know about you, but I'd hate it if some young nurse kept trying to treat me like a child,

186

just because she'd learnt it from a textbook.'

Helen smiled. 'Now you're even starting to sound like Mrs Mortimer!'

Sister Hyde was called away to attend a meeting in Matron's office, leaving Staff Nurse Willis in charge of supervising dinner.

Much to Helen's relief, the job of feeding Maud Mortimer fell to Millie.

'And try to see she has it all this time,' Staff Nurse Willis warned her as she handed her the cup. 'Sister is very concerned that she is not keeping her strength up.'

Millie looked at the feeding cup. It was like something a small child would use. How humiliating it must be to have to subject oneself to it. Especially at the hands of a stranger young enough to be your grandchild.

She took a deep breath. If Sister Hyde had been supervising dinner as usual, she doubted if she would have had the courage to speak. But Staff Nurse Willis was a kindly woman.

'Please, Staff, may I make a suggestion?' she said.

She quailed as Staff Nurse Willis frowned at her. Kindly or not, she still wouldn't appreciate any interference from a student.

'Go on,' she said shortly.

Millie could already see Maud's forbidding expression as she approached with the tray a few minutes later.

'If you think you're going to feed me with that slop, you're wrong,' she snapped, her mouth already tightening in refusal.

'If you think I'm going to feed you at all, then

you're wrong.' Millie set the cup down. 'Sister isn't here, and I'm far too busy to sit here holding this cup. If you want feeding, you'll have to do it yourself.'

Maud Mortimer's eyes widened. 'I beg your pardon?'

'You heard me.' Millie picked up the cup and showed her. 'I thought this might help. I've wrapped the handles in lots of clean dressings to make them easier for you to grip, you see?'

Maud stared at the cup, then back at Millie. Her face was unreadable. Looking into her cold eyes, Millie felt her confidence wilting. 'Anyway, I'll just put it down for you on this tray...' She set it down carefully.

Maud looked from the cup to her and back again. Millie noticed her flexing her fingers tentatively. Then, gearing herself up, she reached for the cup. Millie held her breath, only letting it out as Maud grasped the handles and lifted the cup shakily to her lips.

'Busy, indeed!' Millie heard her mutter as she walked away. 'Busy gossiping with her friends, more likely.'

Typical Maud, Millie thought as she walked away. She always had to have the last word.

She was still smiling to herself when Sister Hyde returned to the ward. Millie was in the kitchen, washing up the dishes with the pro. Through the crack in the door, she saw Sister talking to Staff Nurse Willis. Sister Hyde looked down the ward at Maud Mortimer, then back over her shoulder at the kitchen door. Millie caught her frosty grey glare, and her stomach plummeted.

'Nurse Benedict?' A dish slipped from her hands at the sound of Sister's voice. It fell back into the sink, splashing her and the pro with soapy water.

'Yes, Sister?' She turned, soap suds running down her face.

Sister Hyde suppressed a sigh. 'Staff tells me you came up with an idea to help Mrs Mortimer feed herself?'

'Yes, Sister.' She stared at the ground. This is it, she thought. This is where I get hauled over the coals yet again.

'It was a good idea, Benedict. Mrs Mortimer struggles with the loss of her independence, so you showed great sensitivity. For once,' she added.

Millie looked up at her, hardly able to believe what she'd heard. It didn't even matter that Sister Hyde managed to make praise sound like stinging criticism. Just to hear the words was more than enough. 'Thank you, Sister.'

Sister Hyde looked her up and down. 'It's just a pity you can't manage a simple task like washing up,' she said.

Chapter Eighteen

Kathleen Fox consulted the piece of paper in her gloved hand, then looked back up at the dank tenement building. Surely this wasn't the right address?

Her doubts had been growing ever since she'd

got off the bus at Cable Street. The narrow, cobbled streets around her were straight out of Dickens. Grubby washing hung listlessly from lines strung between houses so tall and close together that only the dimmest strip of daylight penetrated the gloom. A sway-backed horse clopped past, slowly dragging a cart, while children in ragged clothes played in the gutter. In the distance the skyline was scarred by dockside cranes and the smoke stacks of ships, while seagulls screeched overhead, searching for pickings.

Even as she knocked on the door, Kathleen couldn't imagine someone as refined as Violet Tanner choosing to live in such a place.

The woman who answered had a cigarette dangling from her lips.

'Yes?' She squinted at Kathleen through the drifting smoke. 'What do you want?' She looked her up and down. 'If you've come round collecting for the church, you can sling your hook, 'cos I ain't got nothing to give.'

She went to shut the door in her face, but Kathleen held out her hand. 'I'm looking for Miss Tanner,' she said.

The woman regarded her with hostile eyes. 'There's no one here by that name.'

From somewhere inside the house, Kathleen heard the distant sound of a child coughing.

'Are you sure? This is the address she gave me.' Her tone was pleasant, but the look she gave the woman was capable of reducing a student to tears in under ten seconds.

'Then she's pulling a fast one, ain't she?'

'I hardly think Violet Tanner would pull a fast

190

one, as you call it.'

The woman cocked her head. 'Violet, you say?'

'That's right. Violet Tanner.'

A malevolent smile edged across the woman's face. 'I knew it,' she muttered to herself. 'I knew the uppity cow was hiding something. Tanner, eh? She's got some front.'

'I beg your pardon?'

The woman looked at her, considering for a moment, then stepped aside. 'Top floor,' she said, jerking her head towards the narrow staircase. 'That's where Violet Gifford lives, at any rate.'

Kathleen edged past her into the hall. The greasy, yellowing wallpaper and smell of over-boiled cabbage made her feel sick. Poor Miss Tanner, she thought. Why on earth would she choose to live in such a hellhole?

She found out when she reached the top floor. She stood outside the door for a moment, listening to the sound of the child's rasping cough. Then she knocked.

There was no reply, so she quietly let herself in.

The room was small, cramped, and stank of mildew and liniment. Violet Tanner had turned it into a sick room, rigging up a makeshift screen around one of the beds. Kathleen barely recognised the usually composed Night Sister in the woman who sat sponging the face of a feverish small boy.

'Hello, Miss Tanner,' she greeted her. 'Or is it Mrs Gifford?'

'Matron?' Her ravaged face barely registered shock. Kathleen saw at once that she was utterly exhausted. Her skin was the colour of putty, except for two dark circles like bruises around her eyes. Strands of hair escaped from an untidily fastened bun.

Kathleen didn't bother to ask for an explanation. All her professional attention was immediately fixed on the child.

'How long has he been like this?' she asked, slipping off her coat and rolling up her sleeves.

'A few days. He usually gets a bout of bronchitis every winter, but this time it's much worse.' Violet gently pressed the sponge to his sweating forehead. The boy twitched away from her, his eyes closed, lips moving in a stream of delirious chatter that neither of them could hear.

'I thought he was improving. His temperature went down for a while, but now it's increased again. I've been giving him steam inhalations and linseed poultices.' Violet's voice was shrill with worry. 'I've had the doctor in twice, but he just told me I was being over-anxious.'

Then the doctor is a fool, Kathleen thought. She put her hand on the child's chest. His breathing was rapid and shallow, his sternum drawing in with effort on every breath. There was a tinge of blue around his lips.

'And what do you think?' she asked.

Violet looked down at the child. 'I think he needs to be in hospital.'

'I agree.' Kathleen reached for her coat. 'Where is the nearest telephone box?'

'On the corner.'

'I'll go and call for an ambulance. You stay here with your son. He is your son, I take it?'

Violet bit her lip and nodded. 'Oliver,' she said.

192

'His name is Oliver.'

Violet was too exhausted to lie any more. Too exhausted and far, far too afraid.

She was glad Miss Fox was there to take charge. She organised the ambulance, then helped Violet pack up some things for herself and Oliver. It felt such a relief to have someone else to share the burden.

They travelled together in the ambulance with Oliver. Violet clutched his little hand in hers and tried to shut her mind to all the nameless terrors that threatened to overwhelm her.

She should have called the ambulance, she told herself over and over again. She knew Oliver was ill, but she had allowed herself to be persuaded by that arrogant doctor instead of trusting her own instincts. If her son died, it would be her fault. Her fault for making him live like this, for not providing for him properly.

If he died, it would be her punishment for all the terrible mistakes she'd made in her life.

Miss Fox seemed to read her thoughts. 'It will be all right,' she said softly. 'He's in safe hands now.'

Her voice was calm and reassuring, but Violet had used that tone herself on too many patients' families to be fooled by it.

At the hospital, she followed matron, moving like a ghost through the corridors she knew so well, but which suddenly seemed strange and terrifying to her. Even the nurses in their crisp uniforms looked like beings from another world.

On the Children's ward, Sister Parry frowned

at the sight of Matron, dressed in her coat and hat and not her uniform. She didn't recognise Violet at first. She tried to hustle her out into the parents' room until Matron intervened.

'I think we can allow Miss Tanner to stay, under the circumstances, Sister,' she said.

Sister Parry frowned at her in confusion. 'Miss Tanner?' Recognition dawned on her face. 'Sister? But I don't understand – what are you doing here?'

Once again, Miss Fox answered for her. 'There will be plenty of time for questions later, Sister. The first thing we must do is to get this young man well again.' She smiled down at Oliver as the porter lifted him on to the bed that had been made up for him. 'Now, we will need to get an inhalation tent set up. Has the consultant been informed?'

'He's in surgery. But the registrar is on his way, Matron.'

'Very well. I will arrange to have a word with Mr Joyce when he comes out of theatre. I would like his opinion.'

Violet was allowed to stay on the ward until Oliver was settled, and the registrar had arrived. She wanted to stay with him then, but Miss Fox took her arm and steered her gently out of the ward.

'He'll be all right for a few minutes,' she said. 'You and I need to have a talk.'

She took Violet to her office, a book-lined study full of heavy, dark furniture. Kathleen sat her down in one of the leather armchairs on either side of the fireplace, and ordered some tea. Violet stared into the crackling flames, grateful that she didn't have to think at all. She had been galvanised by fear and terror for so long, she hadn't realised how utterly exhausted she was. Embraced by the fire's welcome warmth, all she wanted to do was close her eyes and sleep.

The maid brought in a tray of tea. Miss Fox poured it, put a cup into Violet's hands and then sat back.

Violet understood she was waiting for an explanation. She took a deep breath. 'It's not what you think,' she began. 'I am – I was – married. I've been a widow for five years. Tanner is my maiden name.'

'I see.' Miss Fox considered this for a moment. 'Why didn't you tell me you had a child?'

'Would you have given me the job if you'd known?'

Miss Fox met her gaze steadily. Out of her severe black uniform she seemed so much younger and more human. Wavy chestnut hair softened her face, but her grey eyes were as direct and challenging as ever.

'Probably not,' she conceded, and set down her cup. 'But it can't have been easy for you, living this curious double life. How have you managed to look after your son?'

'I've managed.' Violet's chin tilted, sensing criticism. 'My landlady Mrs Bainbridge keeps an eye on Oliver while I'm working here. And working nights means I can be with him during the day.'

'All the same, I'm surprised you chose to live in such a place. That appalling damp room can't have been good for your son's chest.'

'I didn't have much choice!' Violet felt her

frustration flaring. 'Don't you think I've tried to find somewhere better to live? But people don't like to rent rooms to mothers without husbands. It's not respectable, you see.'

'I suppose it doesn't help that you wear no ring?'

'I do sometimes. But it's only a cheap second-hand one so no one believes it.' Violet looked down at her bare hand. 'I sold my real wedding ring,' she said quietly.

She heard Miss Fox sigh. 'Please don't think I'm criticising you, Violet,' she said. 'On the contrary, I admire you for coping so well. As I said, it can't have been easy for you.'

Her gentle sympathy thawed Violet's defences. 'It was easier when I was caring for a private patient,' she admitted. 'We lived in, so I was able to look after Oliver while I was nursing.'

'I wonder you didn't look for a similar job after you left?'

Violet managed a small smile. 'Not every invalid wants a child around the place. I was very fortunate to find an employer like Mr Mannion.'

'Indeed.' Miss Fox sipped her tea thoughtfully. Then she said, 'Well, obviously this situation cannot continue.'

Violet took a deep, steadying breath. She had expected it, but it was still a blow.

'I understand.' She put down her cup and stood up. 'Would you like me to work out my notice, or would you prefer it if I left immediately?'

Miss Fox stared up at her. 'Who said anything about your leaving?'

'But I assumed–'

'I was referring to your living arrangements. You can't stay in that awful place. And you can't go on leaving your son night after night to the tender mercies of that landlady. I only met her briefly, but I have to say, I wouldn't trust her to take care of a cat!' She had a down-to-earth northern edge to her voice that Violet had never noticed before. It made her seem warm and approachable.

'Actually, Matron, the only creature Mrs Bainbridge has any time for is her cat,' she said.

Miss Fox smiled. 'That doesn't surprise me at all.' She waved Violet back into her seat. 'I know you've done your best, but that house is riddled with damp and no good at all for your son's health. Which is why you must come and live here.'

Violet stared at her. For a moment she wondered if she'd heard her correctly. 'Here, Matron?'

'Why not? There is plenty of room in the sisters' block for you and Oliver. Although it might be better if you had somewhere bigger, so he could have a room of his own. I know...' Her grey eyes brightened. 'You could have my flat.'

Violet's mouth fell open. 'I couldn't do that!'

'Why not? It's far too big for one person anyway. I'd be perfectly happy in a smaller set of rooms.' She smiled. 'It seems like the perfect solution, don't you agree?'

Violet was certain she must be going mad. Or perhaps she had fallen asleep and this was all a dream? 'You can't do that,' she whispered.

'Mrs Tanner, I am Matron here. I can do as I please.' There was a hint of amusement in her eyes. 'So what do you think?'

Violet felt herself smiling reluctantly, but still she didn't dare allow herself to hope.

'What about the other sisters?' she asked.

'What about them?'

'They might not like the idea of Oliver and me moving in.'

'I'm sure most of them will find it perfectly acceptable.'

'And the ones who don't?'

Miss Fox gave her an imperious smile. Suddenly she seemed every inch the Matron. 'Leave them to me.'

She stood up. 'Now,' she said, 'I'm sure the registrar will have finished examining your son, so we should go up and see what he has to say. I suggest you move your things into the Night Sister's room for now, until we can sort out something more permanent.'

'Yes, Matron.' Violet stood for a moment, at a loss for words. It took all the restraint she could summon up for her not to throw herself into Miss Fox's arms in sheer gratitude. But instead, she managed a quiet, 'Thank you.'

'That's quite all right.' She was almost at the door before Miss Fox called her back. 'Mrs Tanner?'

She turned. 'Yes, Matron?'

'You don't have any other secrets you're not telling me, do you?'

Violet paused. All kinds of thoughts chased one another through her mind, but she cut them off. 'No, Matron,' she said.

Chapter Nineteen

The Means Test man was small and wiry, with a pencil moustache and slicked-back hair that smelled of brilliantine. Dora and her family watched helplessly as he walked around their home, his clipboard under his arm, peering into drawers and cupboards.

'Look at him, poking his nose in as if he owned the place!' Nanna hissed furiously.

'But I don't understand. Why is he writing everything down?' Bea asked.

'He's working out what can be sold.' Dora fought to keep the emotion out of her voice. 'We're allowed to keep what we need, but everything else has to go.'

'He's stripping us bare, that's what he's doing. I dunno how he can sleep at night, doing this to decent people,' Nanna said, loud enough for the man to hear.

'Shh, Mum. He's only doing his job,' Rose replied under her breath.

'Your daughter's right, Missus. I wouldn't be here if you hadn't applied for Public Assistance, would I?' He pointed his pencil at Nanna's rocking chair. 'That should fetch a few quid.'

'Not my chair!' Nanna stood in front of it. 'You can't take that. It's been in my family for years. My mum used to sit in it, and her mum before her.'

The man shrugged. 'You've got other chairs. I'm leaving you enough furniture for your basic needs. That's the rules, I don't make 'em up.'

'Yes, but you enjoy carrying 'em out, don't you?' Nanna glared at him.

Dora heard a whimper, and looked around. Her mother was holding herself rigid, but tears were running down her ashen cheeks.

'This is all my fault,' she whispered. 'I'm so sorry, kids. I've let you all down.'

Josie put her arms around her mother. 'Don't, Mum. You haven't let us down.'

'Look at us. Look what we've sunk to. Having to sell off all our possessions just so we can pay the rent.' She dashed tears away with her sleeve. 'We wouldn't be in this position if your dad was here. And it must be my fault he's gone, mustn't it? I did something to drive him away, I must have done.'

'Oh, Mum.' Dora wrapped her arms around them both. 'It'll be all right, honest. We'll get back on our feet soon.'

Nanna twitched back the net curtain and peered outside. 'At least the neighbours are enjoying it,' she commented grimly. 'Look at 'em out there, gawping over their fences. I'm surprised Lettie Pike isn't putting out the flags.'

Next door, Lettie Pike already had a grandstand view out of the upstairs window.

'He's been in there a long time, hasn't he? Honestly, you wouldn't think they'd have that much stuff, would you?' She twitched with excitement.

'Enjoying it, are you?' Nick sat at the kitchen

200

table, his thumb tracing a scratch in the wood so he wouldn't have to look at Lettie's gleeful face. Any minute now he would pick her up and throw her out of that wretched window.

'Come away, Mum, for gawd's sake.' Ruby shot him a wary look. 'Ain't you got nothing better to do on a Saturday morning than spy on the neighbours?'

Her mother ignored her, her nose still glued to the glass. 'Ooh, look, the Means Test bloke's come out now... He's calling to those other two in the van... They'll be moving the furniture out in a minute, I expect!'

She let the curtain drop and went to put on her coat. 'Where are you going?' Nick asked.

'Downstairs, of course. I'm not going to miss this, am I?' She looked at Ruby. 'Are you coming, or what?'

Ruby glanced at Nick. 'No,' she said, hesitating just a fraction too long for his liking. 'What do you think I am? Dora's my mate. And you didn't ought to go either,' she added.

'Why not? All the neighbours are out there. I'm not going to miss the chance to see the Doyles taken down a peg or two, am I?' Lettie's narrow face gleamed with relish.

'What have they ever done to you?' Nick asked.

Lettie stared at him, lost for words. 'That's not the point,' she snapped.

The door slammed behind her, and Ruby turned to Nick. 'Take no notice of her, she doesn't mean any harm by it.'

'Your mum's a vicious old witch.'

'I can't argue with that.' Ruby smiled. She

came round to his side of the table and slid on to his lap, winding her arms around his neck.

He jerked his head away. 'Your mum'll be back in a minute.'

'Then we'd best make the most of it, hadn't we?' she purred, moving in for a long, lingering kiss.

Nick breathed in the scent of eau de cologne in her blonde hair and felt his treacherous body respond instantly. Ruby was such a gorgeous girl, a man would have to be dead from the neck down not to be aroused by her. Every time he touched her he was lost, and every time he hated himself for it.

He hadn't meant to get so involved. She had made all the moves the first time, and every time since, but that was no excuse. He knew whenever he touched her he gave her false hope, and he cared for her too much to do that.

'No.' He pulled away from her kiss, pinning down her hands.

'Why not?' Ruby looked hurt, her full lips pouting. 'It's been so long, Nick. Almost a week since we last ... you know.' She looked up at him coyly through her long, sweeping lashes. 'Anyone would think you've gone off me?'

Nick didn't reply. He stood up, gently tipping her off his lap, and went over to the window.

'Don't tell me you're spying on the Doyles too?' Ruby teased him. 'Shame on you, Nick Riley. And after you had a go at my mum, too!'

She tiptoed over to stand behind him, wrapping her arms around him. Nick ignored her, gazing down into the cobbled backyard. Two men were carrying furniture out of the Doyles' house.

'Look at them,' he said. 'They're just old bits and pieces to them. They don't realise what they're doing, do they?'

'Don't watch if it upsets you so much.' Her hands roved up his chest, unbuttoning his shirt.

Nick's body tensed when he saw Dora following the men out of the back door. He watched her turn to confront the neighbours, proud and utterly defiant. But her hand shook as it pushed back the red curls that were whipping across her face, and Nick could tell how much the fearless gesture was costing her.

'We should be down there with her,' he said.

'Why?' Ruby's hands stopped moving.

'Because she's your mate.'

'Dora's a big girl,' Ruby replied dismissively. 'She can take care of herself.'

Nick stared down at the solitary figure, standing in the yard.

Not while I'm around, he thought.

She didn't blame the neighbours for staring. Most of them didn't mean any harm by it, they were just curious. But Dora felt her anger flaring all the same as she faced them all on the other side of the low, broken fence. These people had known them for years. They were supposed to be their friends.

'Seen enough, have you?' she challenged as the men marched past her carrying a chest of drawers. 'Don't be shy, come a bit nearer ... get a better view. You don't want to miss anything, do you?' She fixed her eyes on Mrs Peterson, who was hovering near the edge of the crowd. 'Tell you what, why don't you all bring your chairs out, make yourselves comfy? We could have a bit of a party. It'll be just like the flaming Jubilee all over again!'

The neighbours shuffled their feet and looked embarrassed. All except for Lettie Pike, who stared straight back at her.

'You want to know why we're watching? To see you lot get what you deserve,' she shot back. 'That mother of yours was always looking down her nose, reckoning she's better than the rest of us. Now look at her.'

Dora swung round to face her. 'She could be on the streets and starving and she'd still be better than you, Lettie Pike!' she spat.

'And I expect that's what will happen to her!' Lettie's face was twisted with spite. 'You wait, it'll be the workhouse next.'

'Shut it, Lettie.'

They all looked round at the sound of Nick Riley's voice. He rarely involved himself with the neighbours' petty squabbles, so Dora was as surprised as any of them to see him shouldering his way through the crowd towards her.

Lettie gave a squawk of indignation. 'Now listen here–'

'No, you listen. All of you.' He pushed through the crack in the fence to stand at Dora's side. 'The show's over, all right? Any of you lot got anything to say to this family, you can say it to me first.' He stood eyeing them all menacingly, his arms folded across his muscular chest.

Dora couldn't bring herself to look at him but

she felt his presence through her skin, tall, strong and protective.

The neighbours started to move away. A couple of them mumbled apologies, although none of them could meet her eye. Except for Lettie, of course, who gave them both an icy glare.

'Are you coming back upstairs?' she said to Nick.

'In a minute.'

'But my Ruby will be waiting–'

'I said, in a minute!'

Lettie flinched at his raised voice. 'All right, keep your hair on.' She shuffled back inside, slamming the door.

He turned to Dora. 'Are you all right?'

'I think so.' She took a deep, shaky breath. 'At least we've given the neighbours something to talk about!'

He smiled grimly. His face was all hard planes, too dangerous-looking to be truly handsome. 'It makes a change from them talking about my mum.'

Dora looked around. 'Where is your mum? I didn't see her.' For all her faults, June Riley was one of her mother's best friends. It wasn't like her to miss a ding-dong.

'Sleeping it off, as usual. She didn't get in till the early hours.'

'I'm surprised she managed to kip through all this.'

'My mum could kip through the Second Coming if she'd had a skinful!' He fixed his gaze on Dora intently. She could never get over how intensely blue his eyes were, fringed by thick dark lashes. 'Are you sure you're all right?'

She nodded. 'I dunno about Mum, though. This has hit her hard. She feels like she's let us all down.' Dora would never have admitted it to anyone else, but somehow she felt Nick understood her better than anyone else did.

He glanced towards the house. 'Have they taken much?'

'I don't know.' She shuddered. 'I'm scared to go in and look.'

'Want me to come in with you?'

'Better not,' she said. 'I don't think Mum would want anyone to see us ... you know...'

Nick nodded. 'She's a proud woman, your mum.'

'She is,' Dora sighed. 'I'm not sure what this will do to her, though.'

'She'll be all right. You all will.' She knew they were just words. But somehow when Nick said them she believed him.

She looked into his eyes, and felt her stomach lurch with longing. He stared back at her and she saw his lips part, as if he was about to say something. And then–

'Nick!'

Ruby's scream was like a bucket of icy water, drenching them. They looked up to see her hanging out of a window above them.

'Are you going to be down there all day, or what?' she yelled.

He winced. 'I'm coming, all right?'

Dora smiled at him. 'You'd better go.'

'She can wait a minute.' His eyes stayed fixed on Dora's. 'Are you sure you're all right?'

'I'm fine. Thanks again for coming to my rescue.'

'Any time. You only have to ask, you know that.'

'Nick!'

'I'm coming. Keep your hair on.'

He walked off. Dora looked up and waved to Ruby. She ducked back inside and slammed the window shut, her face set like stone.

Chapter Twenty

Sunday lunch at the Vicarage was always an ordeal for the Tremayne children. But today it was even worse for William. Because today was the day he introduced his mother to Philippa Wilde.

It was the first time Constance Tremayne had met any of his girlfriends. For one thing he never liked his romances to become that serious, and for another he'd never met a girl he thought could withstand a bruising encounter with his mother.

But Phil was more than up to it. He watched with open admiration from across the table as she dazzled his parents, flirting with his father and fielding all his mother's questioning with her usual breezy charm.

It hadn't started too well, though. Constance Tremayne had gone straight on the attack, before they'd even made it to the table.

'William tells me you're a doctor, Philippa. That seems like an odd choice of career for a woman. I wonder why you didn't think about becoming a nurse?'

William gripped the narrow stem of his sherry glass so hard it was a wonder it didn't break. He waited tensely for Phil to deliver her usual stinging verbal assault on anyone who dared suggest women should not become doctors. She'd been fighting her corner and slapping people down about it ever since he'd known her at university.

She might even say something scathing about the submissive role nurses played on the ward – he had known her do that before, too. That would go down very well with his mother, he thought, especially when Constance was so very proud of her own nursing training.

But Phil merely smiled, that quirky little smile of hers, and replied tactfully, 'You know, Mrs Tremayne, I really don't think I have what it takes to become a nurse.'

Constance Tremayne smirked with approval, and William allowed himself to breathe again.

'Well, yes, my dear, I suppose you're right,' she agreed. 'Nursing does demand rather a lot of a girl. I always think it's much more of a vocation than simply a career. When I was on the wards...'

And she was off again, on another of her fond reminiscences. William shot a quick, grateful look at Phil. She raised her glass in a teasing salute.

He looked around at his sister, sitting next to her boyfriend Charlie on the sofa. Helen was as taut as a piece of stretched elastic, knees locked together, elbows clamped by her sides, as if by making herself as small as possible she could evade her mother's watchful eye. Charlie sat equally upright beside her, his fair hair slicked down smartly, his neck reddening under his tight shirt collar. Poor Charlie, William thought. As if a haircut and his best suit would cut any ice. Constance had done her best to ignore him ever since he'd walked in.

At least Father seemed to take pity on him.

'And how are you, Charlie?' Timothy Tremayne asked kindly, peering over his half-moon spectacles at the young man. 'You're working at your uncle's joinery firm now, aren't you?'

Charlie looked pleased at the unexpected attention. 'That's right, sir. I'm getting on well, too. My uncle says I'm a natural with my hands. Just as well, really, I s'pose, since my legs have let me down!'

He smiled around the room, then caught Constance Tremayne's disapproving glare and his expression faded.

'How marvellous that you have a trade,' Phil spoke up. 'I've always admired men who can actually do something useful.'

'Indeed,' Reverend Tremayne joined in enthusiastically. 'Which reminds me, I wonder if perhaps you could look at the window frame in my study? The wind rattles through it so loudly I can hardly hear myself think.'

'I'd be glad to, sir.'

'Would you? I keep meaning to telephone a joiner, but–'

'That really won't be necessary,' William's mother cut in. 'We couldn't possibly impose on Charlie's good nature.'

'Oh, but it's no trouble,' Charlie said. 'Probably just needs a bit of putty replacing.'

'All the same, I wouldn't hear of it,' Constance

Tremayne stated firmly, a forbidding glint in her eye.

'But–'

'Really, that is my last word on the subject.' She rose to her feet, her taut smile back in place. 'Shall we go through to the dining room?'

As they left the drawing room, William heard his mother say to his father in a stage whisper, 'Really, Timothy, I'm surprised at you for even suggesting such a thing. Isn't it mortifying enough that our daughter is consorting with a tradesman, without engaging him to do odd jobs around the house?'

William glanced at Charlie, hoping he hadn't caught her remark. The young man's genial smile was fixed in place, but the hurt look in his eyes told him he had heard every word.

It obviously pained Constance Tremayne that her daughter had fallen in love with a coster-monger's son from Bethnal Green. William knew she'd tried to put a stop to the romance. But when her plan had failed, she had resorted to her usual trick when faced with an unpleasant situation she could not control. She simply ignored it.

Poor Charlie did his best to get on with Mrs Tremayne, and it upset William to see his efforts rebuffed. He felt ashamed of his mother; Constance Tremayne always fancied herself a paragon of the social virtues, and yet she was being un-utterably rude.

If only his mother had realised it, Helen could have done a lot worse than Charlie Dawson. He was kind, polite, and obviously adored her. William watched them holding hands under the table and felt pleased that his sister had finally found someone who made her happy. She had suffered so dreadfully under their mother's iron control before this, putting up with far more than he had ever had to endure.

Perhaps that was why Constance resented Charlie, he thought. But it was still no excuse for making him feel so unwelcome.

William turned his attention to Phil instead. She really was magnificent, he thought, as he gazed at her across the table during lunch. She wasn't an obvious beauty – her chin was too pointed, her mouth too wide, and her hair couldn't seem to decide whether it was brown or blonde, or just a streaked mass of both. But her imperfections, and the way her bronze eyes sparkled in challenge above her high, jutting cheekbones, gave her an irresistible sex appeal. She was also intimidatingly clever, frank, funny, and frighteningly well connected. No wonder he was utterly besotted with her.

But what really attracted him was that Philippa Wilde was a challenge.

'So where are you working now?' Constance asked as they handed round the vegetables.

'St Agatha's, in Berkhamsted. I specialise in Orthopaedics.'

'Oh? I would have thought you'd prefer Paediatrics?'

He saw the light of combat in Phil's eyes. 'What makes you say that?'

'Helping to heal sick children seems so much more feminine, don't you think?'

'Actually, Mrs Tremayne, I don't really like

children,' Phil replied, spooning peas on to her plate.

'Phil's terribly clever,' William put in hastily, seeing his mother's expression darken. 'She got a double first at university. She was always by far the brightest in our year.'

'There wasn't a great deal of competition,' Phil replied, passing on the bowl.

'And yet you're only a junior houseman, while my son is a senior?' Constance said. 'How odd.'

'Not when you consider that most hospitals are run by the old boys' network of male consultants who feel threatened by a woman in their midst.'

'I think you'll find most patients prefer a male consultant,' Constance replied. 'So much more reassuring, don't you think, to know you're in a man's safe hands?'

'I daresay you're right,' Phil said. 'I know I like to be in a man's hands.' She sent William a smile across the table that almost stopped his heart.

'So you two knew each other at university?' Helen broke in quickly, before Constance had a chance to realise what had been said. Like William, she was on edge, permanently alert for anything that might set their mother off.

Mercifully, Phil took the hint. 'That's right,' she said. 'Although our paths didn't cross a great deal in those days,' she sighed. 'I was too busy studying, and your brother was too busy with his—'

'Carrots?' William thrust the bowl across the table at her, shooting her a warning look.

'Thank you.' Phil took it, her smile teasing. 'As I was saying, I was too busy studying, and Will was too busy with his studies, too.' William shook his head at her, but she ignored him. 'We lost touch for several years when we went our separate ways. But we met again at a college reunion at Christmas. Isn't that right, Will?'

The searing look she gave him made him blush. That night had been one of the most memorable and extraordinary of his life. He had never met a woman who was so confident, so sure of what she wanted.

'It must have been nice for you, to catch up on old times?' Constance remarked.

'Oh, yes. We had a lot of catching up to do, didn't we?'

She simply didn't give a damn, he thought. That night they had gone back to his hotel room and made love, and then the following morning Phil was gone before he'd woken up. When he'd finally managed to track down her telephone number, she had seemed almost irritated to hear from him again. It came as an unpleasant shock to William, who was more used to dealing with clinging, tearful girls than fiercely independent ones.

It had been the same ever since. Phil called the shots completely. He thought he knew how to play games, but he was a beginner beside her. Not that she played unfairly; she was utterly candid, and made it absolutely clear that William was by no means the only man in her life. He had to fight for her attention, and when he finally won it, it felt like a real victory.

Phil turned her attention to Helen and her boyfriend. 'Will told me you two met in hospital. How divinely romantic!' she said.

'How unprofessional, more like.' Constance glared down the table at Helen as she crossly attacked her roast beef. 'Romantic associations between patients and nurses are not permitted at the Nightingale. I'm surprised my daughter wasn't dismissed.'

'We didn't have an association while Charlie was a patient, Mother,' Helen pointed out. William stared at her, impressed. Six months ago, a harsh word from her mother would have been enough to turn his sister into a nervous, stuttering wreck.

'But I did have my eye on her,' Charlie admitted with a sheepish grin. 'Not that I thought she'd look twice at me, after my accident,' he added. He turned to Constance. 'Lovely dinner, Mrs Tremayne.'

'In polite circles, it is referred to as luncheon,' she corrected him frostily.

'Oh. I beg your pardon.' William saw Charlie redden, and exchanged an anguished glance with his sister across the table.

Phil turned to Charlie, her face animated. 'Do you mind if I ask you about your leg?'

William laughed, thankful that she'd changed the subject. 'I forgot to warn you, Charlie old man, Phil has an absolute obsession with limbs, especially lost ones.'

'I merely have a professional interest.' She turned back to Charlie. 'You don't mind my asking about it, do you?'

''Course not,' he replied good-naturedly.

'Not at the table, Philippa, please!' Constance said with a tight smile.

Phil ignored her. 'So how did it happen?' she asked.

'It was an accident at the factory where I was working. Got my trouser leg caught in a bit of unguarded machinery.'

William saw his mother's narrow mouth purse with distaste. 'Some of us are still eating...'

'How fascinating. What happened then?' Phil asked

'Well, my leg got trapped. It ended up being pulled into the machinery and crushed.'

'Completely crushed?'

'There was nothing left of it, once they cut my trouser leg off.'

'Goodness, I would have loved to have seen that. I've been present at amputations before, but nothing as dramatic as that. I don't suppose they took photographs?'

'I don't think there was much left to photograph, to be honest. The doctor reckoned–'

'Really, I hardly think this is suitable conversation!' Constance let her knife and fork drop with a clatter, silencing them. 'Timothy, perhaps you would like to tell the children about your sermon this morning, since they missed the service?' She turned pleadingly to her husband.

William noticed the mischievous wink that passed between Phil and Charlie, and smiled to himself. He didn't blame either of them. Charlie deserved some revenge after the way Mother had treated him.

It was a relief all round when the afternoon ended. Phil drove them back, since William's beloved car Bessie was in the garage yet again.

'Nice car,' Charlie commented. 'Hillman Minx?'

Phil nodded. 'Pressed steel body and a thirty brake horsepower engine.'

'Synchromesh?'

'Of course. Got it new last year.'

'Phil knows about cars,' William said.

'Phil knows about everything,' she corrected him, gunning the motor into life.

'But she's incredibly modest with it,' he added, grinning at her.

The atmosphere in the car was much more relaxed on the way back to London. They chatted, and laughed, and were generally relieved that they had survived another Sunday at the Vicarage.

'Your mother's not that bad,' Charlie said tolerantly. 'Well, she isn't,' he insisted, to a chorus of groans.

'Why do you insist on seeing the best in everyone, Charlie?' William asked, exasperated. 'You make the rest of us look terrible.'

'I'm dreading her official visit with the Board of Trustees next week,' Helen sighed. 'I know she's going to find fault with everything. And poor Millie's already having sleepless nights at the thought–' She stopped dead, her mouth clamping shut.

'I'm not surprised,' Charlie laughed. 'That mate of yours is an accident waiting to happen. Did you tell your brother what she did the other week?'

'What did she do?' William asked.

'It doesn't matter,' Helen muttered.

'It was a riot.' Charlie grinned. 'Millie only went and accidentally bleached some woman's hair when she was meant to be delousing it, didn't she?'

'She sounds like an idiot,' Phil said, her eyes fixed on the road.

'She isn't. She's actually a very sweet girl,' William said, a little too quickly.

He hoped Phil wouldn't notice, but she was far too sharp for that. 'What's this? Why do I get the feeling there's something you're not telling me about this Millie? Is she yet another of your old flames, by any chance?'

'No.'

'But you wanted her to be, is that it?'

William glanced at Helen, but she was staring out of the car window, refusing to meet his eye. She had never approved of his friendship with Millie, had even warned him off getting too close to her. 'She's a sweet girl,' he said again. 'Very naïve, very innocent.'

'She doesn't sound like your type at all!' Phil laughed.

'No,' he said. 'She wasn't.'

'Oh, dear,' Phil said. 'Don't tell me she rejected you? Should I be jealous?' She gave him a sidelong look. 'Don't look so worried, I'm only teasing you. I'd like to meet her. She sounds utterly charming.'

They dropped off Helen and Charlie outside the hospital, then Phil drove William the short distance to his lodgings on the other side of Victoria Park.

'Well?' she said, as she pulled up at the kerb. 'Did I pass muster with your mother, do you think?'

'You did wonderfully. I was very impressed.'

'I was on my very best behaviour. I hope you noticed?'

'I did. Thank you. And thank you for biting your tongue on several occasions.'

'Actually, I quite enjoyed playing the dutiful girlfriend. Even though, as you know, I'm far from the dutiful type.'

'I'd be disappointed if you were.'

'Wouldn't you just?'

She slid along the polished leather seat towards him, and for a moment he thought she was moving in for a kiss until she leant over and opened his door for him.

Disappointment flooded through him. 'Aren't you coming in? I thought we could spend the evening together?'

'Not tonight. I'm meeting someone.'

He felt a stab. 'A man?'

'Yes.'

'Who is he? Do I know him?'

She put a finger to his lips. 'So many questions,' she whispered. 'I don't ask you about your mysterious Millie, do I?'

'There's a difference,' he said bitterly. 'I'm not sleeping with Millie.'

'How do you know I'm sleeping with my friend?'

'Are you?'

She sighed. 'Jealousy really doesn't suit you, William.' She kissed his cheek and then slid back behind the wheel. 'I'll see you,' she said.

'When?' He hated the pleading note that crept into his voice, but he couldn't help it.

'Soon,' she promised. 'I'll call you.'

He got out of the car and slammed the door. She blew him a kiss and roared off straight away, leaving him standing on the pavement.

A sour taste filled William's mouth. It always ended like this with Phil. She seemed to enjoy going off and leaving him full of fear that he might not see her again. He knew he would spend the rest of the evening torturing himself with thoughts of who she was with, and what she was doing. He hated himself for it, but he couldn't help it.

Phil was right, he thought. Jealousy really didn't suit him.

Chapter Twenty-One

Dora's brother Peter was built like a brick out-house. But Nanna's ringing slap nearly knocked him off his feet.

'I won't have it,' she declared fiercely. 'I will not have you bringing your Blackshirt nonsense into this house, d'you hear me?'

'It's not nonsense,' he muttered, rubbing his ear. 'Anyway, you should be thanking us. At least we're standing up for the East End.'

'I don't need a bunch of thugs standing up for me, thank you very much,' Dora retorted, as she helped her mother fold damp laundry and drape it in front of the fire to dry.

Peter glared at her. 'We ain't thugs.'

'You look like one.' He had been so proud to show off his new black uniform, but the sight of it made her feel sick 'And what else do you call people who beat up anyone who disagrees with them? Or who go around smashing up shops?'

'We're only doing what's right.'

'So it's right to terrorise a poor old man in the middle of the night, like they did when they broke into poor Mr Solomon's pawnshop?'

'Old Solomon's a crook. It's about time he got what's coming to him.' Peter's lip curled. 'And you want to watch what you're saying,' he warned Dora. 'You don't want anyone thinking you're on their side.'

'Why? Will you come round and throw a brick through my window in the middle of the night too?'

They faced each other angrily across the steamy kitchen. Dora barely recognised her own brother any more. Peter used to be so full of fun and laughter, but since he'd lost his job and fallen in with Mosley's fascists he'd become a snarling bully.

'Why don't you like the Jews?' Bea piped up.

'Because they've got what's rightfully ours,' Peter told her, his gaze still fixed balefully on Dora. 'They own all the businesses around here, and they make all the money. They get rich and us honest British men don't get a penny.'

'But I don't understand,' Bea said, frowning. 'If they make all the money, why shouldn't they be allowed to keep it?'

'Listen to her,' Nanna said. 'Out of the mouths of babes.'

The sharp knock on the back door made them all look round.

'I'll get it,' Bea said eagerly, already on her feet and halfway across the kitchen.

'You'll be thanking me one day, for what I've

done,' Peter hissed to Dora.

'And you'll be behind bars, if you carry on doing it.'

'No chance. I'm a hero.'

'Stop it, all of you,' Rose shushed them. 'Haven't we got enough trouble in this house without you lot bickering all the time?' She looked up as Bea closed the back door. 'Who was it?'

'Mrs Peterson. She gave me this.'

They all stared at the cooking pot in her arms. 'Why did she give you that?' Rose asked.

'Dunno. She didn't say.'

'Has it got anything in it?'

Bea lifted the lid and peered inside. 'It's empty.'

Nanna and Rose looked at each other. 'Well, that's a bit rum, ain't it?' Nanna frowned.

They were interrupted by another knock. This time Dora went to answer it.

It was Tom Turnbull, a neighbour's son. He was carrying a battered old nightstand.

'Dad says to bring you this,' he said, dumping it down in front of her.

'Why?' Dora started to ask, but Tom had already bolted back over the fence.

Rose came up behind her. They both stared, mystified, at the nightstand in front of them.

'Do you know what's going on?' Rose said. 'Because I'm sure I don't.'

'Maybe we should ask her?' Dora nodded to where Mrs Prosser was heading towards them across the yard, staggering under the weight of a pile of clothes.

'Just a few bits and pieces my lot have grown out of,' she said, dumping them into Rose's arms.

221

'I thought they might do for your little ones.' She smiled sympathetically. 'I'm so sorry for your troubles, Rosie, I really am.'

Dora glanced at her mother's face. She could tell all kinds of emotions were going on behind that rigid mask.

Her pride finally surfaced. 'I can't take these—' She started to hand back the clothes, but Mrs Prosser put up her hand.

'It's not charity, Rose. We're just helping each other out, that's all. God knows, you've done the same for us enough times over the years. It's about time we were all able to do something in return.' She glanced uncertainly at Dora. 'I feel proper ashamed of myself when I think about how we just stood there gawping the other day. We should have done something about it then.'

She stood to one side as two of their neighbours staggered across the yard under the weight of a chest of drawers.

'I – I don't know what to say,' Rose murmured.

'You don't have to say anything.' Mrs Prosser patted her hand. 'Just call it a thank-you from everyone in Griffin Street.'

They kept coming throughout the afternoon. Every neighbour seemed to have something to donate, whether it was a spare chair or some old bedlinen. Rose thanked each visitor stiffly, but Dora could see her emotions were all over the place, moving swiftly between gratitude and agony that she had been reduced to accepting charity.

The last to arrive was Nick Riley. Nanna gave a cry of joy when she saw what he'd brought with him.

'My old rocking chair!' She watched him set it down in its usual place close to the fire. 'Where did you find it?'

'A mate of mine at the hospital told me where they sell off all the stuff they repossess, so I went and bought it back.' He stood there, looking embarrassed by his own act of generosity.

Nanna Winnie's hard little eyes brimmed with tears. She sank down in it with a sigh. But being Nanna, she couldn't let the moment pass without a gripe.

'This cushion's a bit damp,' she complained, wriggling her ample backside around.

'Give it here, we'll dry it out in front of the fire.' Rose lifted her eyes heavenwards.

'Thank you,' Dora whispered as she showed Nick out of the back door. 'She'd never admit it, but she's been lost without that chair.'

'Don't thank me, it wasn't my idea.' He nodded across the yard, to where Ruby stood on the other side of the fence. 'She organised it all. Roped in the neighbours and everything.'

'All I did was knock on a few doors and remind them all what your mum had done for them,' Ruby shrugged, her eyes cast down modestly.

'Thanks, Ruby.'

''S all right.' She lifted her gaze to meet Dora's. 'We're mates, ain't we? And mates don't do the dirty on each other. They stick together, no matter what. Don't they?'

Dora frowned at the meaningful look in her friend's blue eyes. She had the feeling that Ruby was trying to tell her something.

'Of course,' she replied. 'No matter what.'

They closed the door on the last of their visitors, then sat down among their new collection of possessions and looked at each other.

'Well.' Nanna was the first to speak for them. 'This is a bit of a turn-up for the books, isn't it? I must say, I didn't expect this when I put my teeth in this morning!'

'What do you think, Mum?' Dora asked.

Rose gazed around her. 'Everyone has been very kind,' she said. But from the bleak look in her eyes Dora guessed she was still trying to come to terms with it all.

'You don't look well, Rosie,' Nanna observed. 'You ought to go and have a little lie down. I reckon all this has been a bit too much for you.'

'I reckon you're right.' Rose got to her feet. 'I think I will have five minutes' kip.'

'Good idea. I'll bring you a nice cup of tea, shall I?' Dora said bracingly.

'Thanks, love.' Rose gave her a wan smile.

Nanna shook her head. 'Poor girl, this has all hit her hard,' she said, when Rose had gone upstairs.

'I don't see why,' Bea protested. 'We've got lots of lovely new stuff now.'

'Shut up, Bea!' they all chorused.

Dora was in the scullery making tea when there was another knock on the back door.

'Blimey, not again!' she heard Nanna cry. 'Answer it, Josie. It might be June Riley with a grand piano!'

Dora smiled to herself as she warmed the pot. But her smile vanished when she heard a man's voice saying, 'Is this where Alf Doyle lives?'

224

She froze, nearly dropping the teapot from her hands. She knew that voice. It belonged to Joe Armstrong.

'Why do you want to know?' she heard Nanna ask.

'Never mind that. Does he live here or not?'

He's dead, she thought. That was the only reason a policeman would turn up on their doorstep. They must have dragged Alf's body out of the river.

Forcing herself to stay calm, she emerged from the scullery. 'Joe?' she said.

He swung round. He wasn't in uniform, but rough work clothes. 'Dora? What are you doing here?'

'I live here. You've met my family, remember?'

Joe looked around, registering the faces for the first time. His broad shoulders slumped.

'Oh, no.' He pulled off his cap and ran his hand through his fair hair. He looked more pole-axed than angry now. 'So Alf Doyle is your–'

'He's my stepfather,' Dora told him.

'And he's my husband.' Rose's voice came from the doorway. Dora could see her holding herself rigid, braced for bad news. 'And this is my house, so if you've got anything to say you can say it to me.'

'He's dead, isn't he?' Nanna murmured. Bea burst into noisy tears. Josie's face was stony and expressionless.

Joe turned to Rose. 'I'm sorry, Missus,' he said. 'But I've got reason to think your husband got my little sister pregnant.'

Chapter Twenty-Two

It was as if all the air had been sucked out of the room. For a moment, no one moved. Then Rose said calmly, 'Josie, take Bea and Little Alfie upstairs.'

Bea started to whine. 'But I don't want to go–'

'You'll do as you're told!' Rose snapped, so fiercely that Bea fled without another word.

They listened to the sound of the children's feet thundering up the stairs, then Nanna turned to Joe. 'What's all this about?'

He glanced at Dora. 'The reason Joe's sister was in hospital was because she'd – lost a baby,' she explained for him.

'Got rid of it, you mean,' Joe finished for her savagely. 'Ended up at a backstreet butcher who ripped her apart and left her for dead.'

'And you think Alf was responsible?' Nanna said.

'I know he was. Jennie told me.'

Nanna shook her head. 'Dirty little sod. Well, that explains a lot, doesn't it?'

'You don't mean to say you believe him?' Peter turned to Joe. 'I don't care what your little tart of a sister says, you can't come in here making that kind of accusation about my family! My stepfather–'

'My sister is not a tart.' Joe's voice was a low growl, full of threat.

226

'She got herself pregnant, didn't she?'

'Only because your bastard stepfather took advantage of her.'

Peter started to square up to him, but Dora held him back. 'Don't, Pete. He's a copper,' she warned.

'I'm also pretty handy with my fists,' Joe said. The two young men went eyeball to eyeball for a moment, then Peter reluctantly backed down.

'Just get out,' he growled.

'Not till I say what I've come to say to Alf Doyle.'

'You'll wait a long time,' Nanna muttered. 'He's long gone.'

Joe's gaze flicked towards Dora. She nodded. 'We haven't seen him for more than five months.'

He frowned. 'That was the last time Jennie saw him too.' He looked straight at Dora. 'And you've not heard from him since?'

'Not a word.'

'And it's not for want of trying either,' Nanna said. 'My Rose has been down to the railway yard looking for him every day since he disappeared. She's been worrying herself into the ground wondering where he's got to. And all the time he's been carrying on behind her back!' Her toothless mouth was pinched with anger. 'I s'pose he took fright when he found out your sister was pregnant?'

Joe shook his head. 'That's the mystery. As far as I can make out from Jennie, he disappeared before she even knew herself.'

'Maybe she wasn't the only one he was messing about with?' Nanna suggested.

'Right, that's it.' Peter stepped in, taking charge. 'I've heard enough. Alf wasn't messing about with anyone. You know he'd never do that to Mum, don't you, Dora?' His gaze moved from Nanna to his sister. She could only stare blankly back at him.

'Why would she lie, Pete?' she said softly.

'I don't know, do I?' An angry flush spread up his face. 'But I know Alf didn't do anything. He's a decent bloke, one of the best–'

'Your brother's right,' Rose Doyle said. 'I'm ashamed of you all, thinking such a thing of Alf.'

They all turned to face her. She had been standing so silently in the doorway, Dora had forgotten she was there, listening. Her face was a frozen mask. Only the whiteness of her fingers clutching the doorframe gave any clue to her inner turmoil.

'Look, Missus, I'm sorry,' Joe started to say. 'I know this has all been a shock for you, but I need to know–'

'Get out.' The words came from between Rose's clenched teeth.

'Jennie didn't know he was married or she would never have gone near him. I know my sister, she wouldn't do something like that. She only found out when he'd disappeared and she started asking my dad about him. He was a friend of his, see. That's how they met–'

'I said, get out!'

'Not until I've had my say.' Joe stood his ground, his hands by his sides clenched into fists. 'Whether you like it or not, your old man got my little sister in the family way. She tried to get rid of it, and it nearly killed her.' He was breathing hard, his jaw rigid with anger. 'Our Jennie nearly died because of that bastard Alf Doyle. And I ain't going to rest till I make him pay.'

Dora looked across at her mother. Rose's face was pale and waxy, like a corpse's.

'You'd best go,' she said to Joe quietly.

'And don't come back!' Peter growled.

Joe shot him a belligerent look and for a moment Dora was worried they were going to start fighting. But then he barged out of the back door.

She followed him outside into the yard. It was a clear night, and the inky sky over Griffin Street was sprinkled with stars. Spring was on its way but the biting winter weather had yet to loosen its grip. Dora hugged herself, shivering.

Joe turned to face her. A patch of light spilled from the kitchen window, illuminating his face.

'I'm sorry,' he said. 'I should have realised when I heard the name ... but I just didn't think.'

'How did you find out it was him?' Dora asked.

'Jennie told me in the end. I suppose she thought it wouldn't matter as he wasn't around any more.'

'And you say he was a friend of your father?'

'He was a drinking pal of his.' Joe's face was grim. 'Used to come round to ours to play cards sometimes. I remember him myself. Big bloke, always laughing and joking around. Had plenty to say for himself.'

'That sounds like Alf,' Dora said.

'I'd have had plenty to say to him, too, if I'd known he was messing about with my sister!' A muscle flickered in Joe's jaw. 'Jesus, when I think about a man of his age ... what kind of an animal

229

would take advantage of a girl young enough to be his daughter?'

Dora closed her eyes, shutting out the memory that reared up in her mind. 'I don't know.'

'He promised her the world, from what I can make out. Told her he was going to marry her, give her a nice home of her own. Poor kid, he must have seemed like a bloody knight in shining armour!' He pressed his fists to his temples, as if he could force back his rage. 'If only I'd been there, if only I'd taken better care of her, she would never have looked at someone like him...'

'Shh, you mustn't blame yourself.' Dora reached up and laid her hand on his shoulder, trying to calm him.

Gradually she felt his iron-hard muscles relax under her fingers.

He sighed. 'Look, I know your mum's upset, but I've got to think about our Jennie. That bastard left her in a bad way and I want him to pay for it.'

'I know,' Dora sighed. 'And believe me, if I knew where he was I'd tell you.'

'Would you? Even though he's your stepfather?'

'Put it this way. There's no love lost between us,' she said.

She caught his searching look and dropped her gaze. 'I promise I'll tell you if we hear anything,' she said.

After Joe had gone, she went back inside the house to find Nanna and her mother in the middle of a heated argument. Josie had come back downstairs and was sitting on the rug by the fire, hugging her knees and staring unhappily into the flames while the argument raged around her.

'But you heard what he said, Rosie–'

'I don't care what he said. My Alf would never do something like that.' She turned on Dora as she closed the back door, angry and defiant. 'I don't want him anywhere near this house again, all right? I won't have him in here, spreading his lies.'

'We don't know if they are lies, Mum–'

'Not you, too!' Her mother's brown eyes flared. 'What's the matter with you all? Have you forgotten what a kind, loving man your dad was?' None of them answered. 'Look, I know my Alf better than anyone,' she insisted. 'And I'm telling you, he didn't touch that girl. I don't care what lies she tells, I know he'd never do that to his family.'

Dora and Josie glanced at each other, but neither of them said anything. They knew only too well what Alf Doyle could do to his family.

Chapter Twenty-Three

Oliver could hardly believe his eyes when Violet showed him their new home for the first time. He ran from room to room, looking out of all the windows.

'Look, a park!' He pointed out of his bedroom window to the lawns that lay beyond the sisters' block.

'It's not a park, darling. It's a garden.'

231

'Is it ours? Can I play there?'

'We'll see.'

'It's much nicer than our old house, isn't it, Mummy?'

'Yes, darling. It's perfect.' Violet looked around the room, so fresh and light, the spring sunshine streaming through the snowy white net curtains. It was almost too perfect.

She watched Oliver bouncing on his bed, his little face lit up with ecstasy, and wished she could feel the same joy. But her heart was filled with apprehension. She had been so lucky, first that Oliver had made such a complete and speedy recovery, and second that Miss Fox had offered them such a wonderful place to live, that she didn't quite trust it. Violet was so used to ill fortune, to going from one crisis to another, that she couldn't allow herself to relax.

It was in her nature to look for problems, and she hadn't had to look far. Although some of the sisters had welcomed her and Oliver, others had not been so happy about it. The Assistant Matron Miss Hanley had been the first to take her aside and make her feelings clear.

'A hospital is not a proper place for children,' she had warned Violet sternly. 'They cause far too much disruption.'

'Oliver won't cause any disruption. I'll make sure of that,' Violet had assured her. 'He is a very well-behaved child.'

'Yes, but he is still a child,' Miss Hanley insisted. 'And it is your responsibility to provide a home for him, not ours. I hope you don't intend for him to take his meals in the dining room?'

'Of course not. There is a kitchen in the flat. I will cook for him there.'

Miss Hanley's nostrils flared, as if this was the most outrageous idea she had ever heard.

'I do hope this means you won't neglect your duties?' she said.

'I'm sure you'll be there to remind me if I do.' Violet forced herself to smile tightly back at her.

Not surprisingly, Sister Wren was also against the idea. 'I always knew she was hiding something,' Violet overheard her telling Sister Holmes, shortly after they'd moved in. 'Fancy lying about having a child! If she can do that, it makes you wonder what else she can lie about. Nurses who live out always have something to hide, in my opinion.'

'I live out,' Sister Holmes reminded her with some asperity. 'I have to live at home to look after my elderly mother. Or do you think perhaps I'm leading some kind of exciting life, too?'

Sister Wren didn't reply, but Violet was sure she wouldn't stay silent on the matter for long.

'Take no notice of her,' Sister Blake had advised Violet. 'She's just piqued because Matron has given you her flat. She's obsessed with who has the best room in this hospital, and now you've beaten her hands down.'

'I didn't realise it was a competition,' Violet had said.

Sister Blake sent her a wise smile. 'Everything is a competition to Sister Wren.'

Violet was making some sandwiches for Oliver's lunch when Miss Fox arrived.

'Hello?' She tapped gently and then put her

head around the door. 'Do you mind if I come in?'

'Of course not, Matron.' Violet hurried out of the kitchen, wiping her hands, as instantly flustered as a student on a ward round.

'I'm sorry to interrupt. I won't make a habit of it, I assure you. I just wanted to make sure this young man is settling in all right?'

She smiled at Oliver, who came hurtling out of his bedroom, a toy aeroplane in his hands. He braked sharply at the sight of Matron standing in the hallway, formidable in her stiff black uniform.

His gaze travelled up the length of her body to rest on her elaborate white headdress. His dark eyes grew round with astonishment.

'Mummy,' he whispered loudly, his gaze still fixed on Matron, 'why does that lady have a bird on her head?'

Violet caught Miss Fox's eye and felt herself reddening. 'Matron, I'm so sorry–' she started to say. But Miss Fox just laughed and waved her apology aside.

'I suppose it does look rather absurd to a child, doesn't it?' Leaning down to Oliver, she replied, 'It's supposed to make me look important, young man. It's also there so that nurses can see me coming from a long way off and stop whatever naughty things they happen to be doing before I get there. And doctors too, sometimes,' she added.

'My daddy was a doctor,' Oliver announced, swooping his aeroplane through the air.

'Was he?' Miss Fox raised her eyebrows at Violet.

Oliver nodded. 'He saved lives, but then he died. Can I go and play in the garden, Mummy?'

Violet shot a nervous glance at Miss Fox. 'I don't know, Oliver. I don't want to you to be in the way–'

'Nonsense, the fresh air will do him good,' Miss Fox cut in briskly. 'He's been cooped up in a hospital bed for so long, he's bound to want to run about in the sunshine.'

'If you're sure, Matron?'

'Of course I'm sure.' Miss Fox beamed at Oliver. 'You go and have fun, young man. You deserve it.'

'But stay where I can see you,' Violet called after him, as he let himself out of the door. 'And don't touch anything, or get in anyone's way. And don't talk to anyone–' she added. But Oliver was already off, running across the grass as fast as his legs would carry him.

'He's looking a great deal better than he was the first time I saw him,' Miss Fox observed.

'Yes, he is.' Violet could hardly bear to think of that grim night when she'd been so sure she was going to lose him.

'And so are you.' Miss Fox turned to her. 'I trust the accommodation is to your liking?'

'Very much, Matron.'

'A little better than your last place, anyway.'

Violet thought about the dank, dark tenement, with its stale cooking smells and Mrs Bainbridge's scrawny cats screeching in the yard. Just remembering it made her shudder. How had she put up with it for so long?

'Yes, indeed. Thank you.'

235

'Oh, it's no trouble.' Miss Fox shrugged. 'As I said to you, this place was far too large for one person anyway.'

'I didn't mean for the flat. I meant for giving me a second chance.'

'You're a good nurse,' Miss Fox said. 'I didn't want to lose you.'

She turned her gaze towards the window. 'Your son appears to be settling in and making friends already, I see.'

Violet ran to the window and yanked back the curtain. Over on the far side of the garden, Oliver was watching Sister Sutton planting nasturtiums.

'I told him not to be a nuisance–' She started for the door, but Miss Fox stopped her.

'Leave him, he isn't doing any harm. Look.' She pointed.

As Violet watched them, she saw Sister Sutton's dog Sparky roll over obligingly to have his tummy scratched, while the Home Sister looked on approvingly.

'He's done well to win over such a difficult, ill-tempered creature,' Matron observed.

'Yes,' Violet agreed. 'I have heard Sister Sutton's dog can be rather disagreeable.'

Miss Fox gave her a sideways smile. 'I wasn't referring to the dog,' she said.

A moment later, Oliver came flying through the door, Sparky at his heels.

'Miss Sutton has asked me to have a picnic with her,' he announced breathlessly while Sparky yapped in unison. 'We're having pork pie.'

'But I've made sandwiches–' Once again Violet found herself addressing the empty air as Oliver dashed out, leaving the door swinging behind him.

'Oh dear,' Miss Fox said. 'It looks as if you've lost your lunch companion.'

'It does, doesn't it?' Violet hesitated for a moment, then said, 'I don't suppose you'd care for a sandwich, Matron?'

The moment she'd said it she worried she might have offended her. She might be approachable, but she was still Matron. But Miss Fox just smiled.

'That sounds like a delightful idea,' she said.

It felt odd to be sitting there together in what used to be Matron's sitting room, chatting away like old friends. Miss Fox was so easy to talk to, Violet decided. Perhaps a little too easy – she had to keep checking herself before she opened her mouth, just to make sure she wasn't giving too much away.

Miss Fox didn't give away too much, either. Somehow she managed to tread a fine line between warmth and decorum. She made Violet feel as if she was a good friend, while still commanding her respect.

'Well, that was delicious.' Miss Fox dabbed her mouth delicately with her napkin. 'But I really mustn't keep you any longer, Mrs Tanner. I have a meeting with the Board of Trustees about their forthcoming tour of the hospital.'

She rose to her feet. 'I'm glad you're settling in. I want you to feel that this is your home.'

'Thank you, Matron.'

But Violet felt nothing but guilt as she closed the door on Miss Fox. She liked her, and knew Matron had gone out on a limb to help them.

Violet really wished she could have been honest with her, and told her everything. Perhaps she would have understood? Perhaps she might even have tried to help them further?

Or perhaps she would have turned them away and told Violet never to darken the hospital's door again, she thought bleakly.

No, she couldn't tell anyone her story, no matter how good a friend they seemed to be. Because to put her trust in anyone would be to put herself and Oliver in grave danger.

Chapter Twenty-Four

It was the day of the Trustees' visit, and Sister Hyde was even more exacting than usual.

Straight after breakfast the nurses were set to work, pulling all the beds out into the middle of the ward, scattering tea leaves to settle the dust then sweeping them up. Floors were polished, bedsprings were dusted, lockers scrubbed inside and out, and the fluted-glass lampshades above every bed were taken down and washed.

The patients didn't escape, either. Those who could get out of bed were hauled off to the bathroom, while the rest were washed, powdered and put into fresh nightgowns. The air was filled with the smell of carbolic and freshly starched laundry.

Of course, there was no chance of anyone being allowed to take a break, much to Millie's frustration. It was Seb's birthday and she was desperate to telephone him to make up for not being with him.

Even then, Sister Hyde wasn't completely satisfied. She prowled the ward, running her fingers along bedrails and windowsills, her face rigid with disapproval.

'Look at her,' Maud Mortimer remarked, as Millie brushed her hair. 'Anyone would think we were getting a visit from royalty.'

Millie smiled. 'The Trustees *are* royalty, so far as this hospital is concerned.'

'I should imagine they are the same as any other committee – a collection of jumped up accountants, civil servants and busybodies, consumed by their own self-importance.'

Millie thought of Mrs Tremayne. 'You could well be right.'

'I am always right.' Maud peered over her spectacles at the newspaper in her lap. 'Seven across. "Press down". Second letter "e".'

'Decrease,' Millie replied without hesitation.

Maud glanced sideways at her. Millie tried to remain expressionless as Maud carefully double-checked it, counting the letters. 'You may be right,' she conceded with a sniff.

'I am always right,' Millie said.

'Please don't be clever with me, child.' Maud shoved the newspaper towards her with the back of her hand. 'You may fill it in.'

'Best not let Sister see me doing this,' Millie said, picking up the pencil. 'She'll send me off to clean the toilets again.'

'I won't tell if you don't.'

Millie dropped the pencil, swung round and found herself face to face with William Tremayne.

It had been so long since she'd seen him, the shock made her heart hammer against her ribs as if it was trying to fight its way out of her chest.

'What are you doing here?' she said.

'He's a doctor, you stupid girl. I would have thought this was the obvious place for him.' Maud looked William up and down. 'At least, I assume he is a doctor. He seems awfully young.' She peered at him closely. 'Where is Mr Forrest? Or that other one ... the unfortunate-looking man with the squint?'

'Mr Forrest is in theatre, and Dr Pascoe is unwell today.' William tried not to smile. 'My name is Dr Tremayne, and I'm the house officer on call. I understand you asked to see me?'

'A house officer?' Maud looked doubtful. 'Well, I suppose you'll have to do.' She fumbled to take off her spectacles with her limp hands. 'I need some sleeping pills.'

'Why?'

Maud gave Millie a long-suffering look. 'Really, is everyone in the hospital half-witted? Because I want to sleep, young man.'

William took the notes Millie handed to him. 'Are you in any pain?'

'Pain?' Maud regarded him incredulously. 'If you take a moment to read those notes, Doctor, you will realise that pain is the least of my worries. In fact, any sensation at all in my useless limbs would be very welcome indeed.' She sighed. 'I can't sleep because of all the constant hullabaloo that goes on in this ward. Listen to it.'

She paused for a moment. Millie listened too; she had become so used to the low moaning and whimpering that went on in the ward, she had ceased to notice it any more. 'It's far worse at night,' Maud continued. 'It's like trying to sleep in a cage full of mad owls. If you won't give me anything to help me sleep, then for God's sake, give it to them.'

William's dark eyes crinkled at Millie over the top of the notes. 'I'm sure that won't be necessary, Mrs Mortimer.' He flicked through the notes. 'I see you've had electrical and massage therapy?'

'A ridiculous waste of time,' Maud dismissed. 'As if shooting hundreds of volts through my legs is going to bring them back to life.'

'It worked for Frankenstein's monster,' Millie said, under her breath. Maud shot her a narrow look.

'Don't be impertinent. My limbs may be failing me, child, but my hearing is still intact.'

'I notice we have yet to try strychnine injections,' William observed, pulling a pen out of the pocket of his white coat. 'Perhaps they would be worth a try?'

'Will they cure me?'

'No,' he admitted, scribbling on her notes. 'But they will slow down the progress of your illness.'

'Then we will not be trying them,' she said.

William looked up at her and frowned, his pen poised. 'I don't understand? Surely anything that would halt–' He caught Millie's eye. She shook her head warningly.

'Very well.' He wrote a few words on the notes

and handed them back to Millie. 'I've prescribed you sleeping pills,' he told Maud.

'Thank you. Now you may go.' She closed her eyes and rested back against her pillows.

William stared at her nonplussed for a moment. Millie touched his sleeve. 'That's her signal for you to leave,' she whispered.

'She's rather a character, isn't she?' he commented as they both stepped away from the bed, out of earshot of Maud.

'You get used to her.'

'I'm not used to patients expressing opinions on their treatment.' He looked so shaken, Millie felt sorry for him.

'Mrs Mortimer has lots of opinions. Most of them at odds with the rest of the world, I'm afraid.'

He gazed around the ward. 'And are they all like that here?'

'Most of them aren't as lively as Mrs Mortimer. Many of them aren't even aware of what's happening to them.'

'Then it must be a very depressing place to work.'

'I used to believe it was, but I've come to think differently. We can't save these patients, but we can at least make their last days as comfortable as possible. And, you know, some of these women haven't had any comfort or care from anyone for years.' Millie glanced sideways at him. 'What? Why are you looking at me like that?'

'You've changed,' William said admiringly. 'You've grown up a lot since I last saw you.'

She felt hot colour scalding her face. 'I hope so.

242

But I still do idiotic things sometimes.'

'I'm glad to hear it. I'd hate to think you werc getting too serious.' He gazed deep into her eyes. 'How are you?' he said.

'I'm very well, thank you.'

'It's so long since I've seen you. Have you been avoiding me?'

'Of course not, why should I?'

'I just wondered if things were awkward between us?'

'I see no reason why they should be awkward,' Millie hissed out of the corner of her mouth, aware of Sister Hyde close by.

'I'm glad to hear it. I'd like to think we could still be friends. Even if you have forsaken me for another man,' he added teasingly.

Before Millie could respond, Sister Hyde came over to ask William to take a look at another patient, Mrs Little. As she hustled him off, she turned back to Millie and said, 'Benedict, please make absolutely sure Mrs Church has had a bedpan. I do not want any unfortunate mishaps when the Board of Trustees visit. Is that clear?'

The Trustees were almost an hour late. They arrived in the middle of the afternoon, by which time Sister Hyde was in an even more irritable mood.

'This is perfectly ridiculous,' Millie heard her whisper furiously to Staff Nurse Willis as they stood waiting in line to greet the visitors outside the ward. 'We have work to do and patients to care for. We can't wait about out here for the circus to arrive.'

243

'I'm worried about Mrs Little,' Staff Nurse Willis whispered back fearfully. 'Dr Tremayne doesn't think she has much longer. What if she dies while they're here?'

Sister Hyde sent her a withering look. 'What do you suggest we do about it? We can hardly tell the poor woman to hang on until they've gone, can we?'

While they waited, Sister Hyde walked up and down the line, inspecting her nurses like a sergeant major reviewing his troops. She picked out a crooked cap here, unpolished shoes and holes in stockings there. Only Helen escaped without a word of criticism, as usual.

Finally, the Trustees arrived, led by Matron. Half a dozen well-fed and very self-satisfied-looking men in suits, a very old lady with an ear trumpet, and Mrs Tremayne.

One look at Constance Tremayne and Millie understood immediately why Helen had been so afraid of her. Everything about her was stiff and self-righteous, from her tightly drawn bun to her buttoned up suit. She wasn't the head of the Trustees but she certainly acted as if she was, bestowing regal smiles all round.

Matron introduced her to Sister Hyde, who then introduced her to all the nurses. Millie felt her palms break into a sweat as Mrs Tremayne approached, and prayed she wouldn't want to shake her hand.

'I haven't felt this nervous since I was presented at court!' she whispered to Helen, who stood quaking beside her.

'How do you think I feel? She's my mother!'

Helen hissed back.

Mrs Tremayne whisked past Millie with barely a glance, and moved straight on to Helen. Millie felt for her friend as her mother greeted her coolly, her critical gaze moving slowly up and down, looking for faults.

Millie was shocked. She had never had a mother so she could hardly make comparisons, but she treated her maid at home with more warmth than Mrs Tremayne did her own daughter.

As they moved into the ward, Sister Hyde hissed to Millie, 'Now you're sure you offered Mrs Church a bedpan?'

'Yes, Sister.' No need to tell her Bessie had refused it, she thought. Sister Hyde looked worried enough.

Mrs Tremayne led the way around the ward, while the other Trustees straggled in her wake. She paused at every bed, offering words of comfort to each patient. Sometimes she would reach out a gloved hand and gently touch a shoulder or a fevered brow. She reminded Millie of pictures she'd seen of Florence Nightingale, passing calmly among the war-wounded at Scutari.

And then she reached Maud Mortimer's bed.

'And how are you today?' she asked, her voice dripping with condescension.

'Dying,' Maud snapped back. 'Slowly.'

'Oh.' Mrs Tremayne looked confused. 'But they're looking after you well?' she said, recovering her composure.

'Oh, yes, it's simply marvellous. We have endless larks in here, as you can probably imagine. In fact, we're all going out to play a spot of croquet

245

in the courtyard later. Perhaps you'd like to join us?' She looked up at Mrs Tremayne, her expression bland.

Constance Tremayne stared back at Maud for a moment, speechless. Then, gathering her dignity, she turned and stalked off to the next bed. Millie and Helen glanced at each other and tried not to laugh. Even Sister Hyde's mouth was twitching as she followed the party.

They were halfway across the ward when Helen whispered, 'Can you smell something?'

Millie sniffed. 'No, what?'

Helen shook her head. 'It doesn't matter. Probably nothing.'

'And who have we here?' Constance Tremayne said, approaching the next bed.

'Mrs Church, Madam. Pleased to meet you.'

Millie let out a sigh of relief. Thank goodness Bessie was in one of her lucid moods. Mrs Tremayne looked gratified to find someone who treated her with due deference.

'Do you know who I am, my dear?' She spoke very slowly.

Mrs Church looked up at her with glazed eyes. 'Someone important, I'm sure.'

'Well, yes, I am,' Mrs Tremayne acknowledged graciously. 'I am Constance Tremayne. I run this hospital.'

Millie stifled a snort of laughter. Sister Hyde scowled at her.

'I can definitely smell something,' Helen hissed out of the corner of her mouth. 'You don't think...'

Millie drew in a deep breath, and her eyes widened with horror. 'Oh, God. No!'

'Nurses, please!' Sister Hyde whipped round to reprimand them, then froze as she, too, realised what had happened.

'In that case, let me shake your hand, Madam.'

'Let's move on, shall we?' Sister Hyde stepped in swiftly.

'Just a moment.' Mrs Tremayne pulled off her glove and held her hand out. 'It's a pleasure to meet you, Mrs Church.'

'Please.' She reached her hand out from under the bedclothes and grasped Mrs Tremayne's as they all watched in silent horror. 'Call me Bessie.'

It was one of the longest days Millie had ever had to endure. The hours seemed to crawl past, and she began to despair of nine o'clock ever coming.

Sister Hyde blamed her completely, of course.

'I thought I told you to give Mrs Church a bedpan?' she hissed furiously.

'I did, Sister.'

'Then why didn't you make sure she used it?'

Millie was condemned to the sluice to clean up her dreadful mistake. But that was the least of her punishment. As she stood up to her elbows in water, soaking and scrubbing, she could only replay the dreadful incident over and over again in her head, wondering if there was anything else she could have done, any way she could have averted the disaster. But every time she saw the image of Mrs Tremayne in her mind's eye, it got worse.

At least it had brought a rare smile to Maud Mortimer's face.

'It serves her right, the patronising witch,' she'd said. 'Personally, I think Mrs Church spoke for all of us. I only wish I'd thought of making such a bold statement.'

Finally nine o'clock came, the night staff took over, and Millie could escape. She was hurrying back to the nurses' home, already thinking of getting into bed, pulling the covers over her head and never coming out, when she met William coming towards her.

'I don't see you for weeks, and then I bump into you twice in one day,' he greeted her with a smile. 'I hear the Trustees' visit was – eventful?'

She groaned. 'Who told you?'

'Actually, I've heard the story three times so far. The last time was from a porter in the mortuary.'

'Bad news travels fast.' She looked up at him. 'How is your mother? Is she very angry?'

'Her pride is a little dented, but I think she'll survive.' He grinned. 'I just wish I'd been there to see the look on her face.'

'Don't.' Millie closed her eyes briefly. 'It was horrible.'

'Look on the bright side.' He grinned. 'I don't think you'll have to endure another visit from the Trustees in a hurry.'

'Poor Mrs Tremayne. If it's any consolation to her, Sister Hyde has made me suffer for my mistake.'

'Think of it as a lesson to both of you,' William said gravely. 'You have learnt to ignore Mrs Church when she tells you she doesn't need a bedpan. And my mother has learnt never to remove her gloves when near a patient.'

Millie laughed. 'How do you always manage to

248

make me smile, even at moments like this?' she asked.

He shrugged. 'I'm a natural clown.'

'I think that makes two of us,' she said ruefully.

'Then we make a good pair.'

'Excuse me.' They turned as a figure stepped out of the shadows. 'I hope I'm not interrupting anything?' a familiar voice said.

Chapter Twenty-Five

'Seb!' Millie broke away from William and rushed into her fiancé's arms, full of excitement. 'What are you doing here?'

'I wanted to see you on my birthday. And I knew you were working, so I thought I'd come for a quick visit.' His gaze was fixed on William as he spoke.

'What a wonderful surprise! You can't imagine how pleased I am to see you.' Millie hugged him fiercely.

'Are you really?'

'Of course. Why wouldn't I be?' She pulled away from him, still smiling. 'You know William, don't you?'

'Indeed we have met.' William held out his hand in greeting. 'Nice to meet you again. Happy birthday, by the way.'

'Thanks.' Seb seemed rather cool as he shook hands.

'I'd better be on my way,' William said. 'I'm

supposed to be meeting some friends at the Café de Paris.'

'Gosh, that sounds like fun.'

'Why don't you join us? If you have no other plans, that is?'

Millie turned to Seb, her weariness forgotten. 'Shall we? I'm off duty now and it would be marvellous to spend some time with you on your birthday.'

He looked at his watch. 'Don't you have to be in bed for lights out in an hour?'

'Since when has that ever stopped me?' Millie grinned.

'I think what your fiancé is hinting is that he'd rather be alone with you,' William suggested tactfully.

'Nonsense, he loves the Café de Paris. You do, don't you, Seb?' Millie seized his hand. 'Please? I could do with having a good time, after the beastly day I've had. Oh, do let's! It will be fun.'

Seb's smile was tight. 'Why not?'

The Café de Paris was like an opulent sultan's palace, resplendent in gilt and red velvet, with its double sweeping staircases and sensuously curved balcony. It was hot and crowded with people all drinking, eating, dancing and generally enjoying themselves.

Millie breathed in the overheated air, scented with cigars, alcohol and French perfume. She could feel the atmosphere, charged with excitement, tingling through her veins as the maître d' showed them to their table.

'Isn't it wonderful?' She smiled over her shoulder at Seb, but her words were lost amidst the sounds of laughter, music and clinking glasses.

William's new girlfriend was waiting for them with another group of people. She was as tall as him, and dressed dramatically in flowing black silk evening pyjamas. She had made no effort with her hair, letting it fall in wild waves around her face. In one hand she held a glass, and in the other a long cigarette holder.

'She looks as if she's ready for bed,' Seb whispered close to Millie's ear.

William introduced her as Philippa Wilde. 'But everyone calls me Phil,' she added. Her voice was as firm and full of confidence as her handshake.

Her brows rose a fraction when William introduced Millie and Seb. 'So you're the famous Millie, are you? I'm pleased to meet you at last.' Her bronze eyes assessed her. Millie didn't understand why, and she wasn't sure she liked it.

They sat down and ordered cocktails. They drank and chatted for a while, their voices battling over the sound of the music and laughter around them.

'Will tells me you're training to be a nurse?' Phil said to Millie. 'Why didn't you want to be a doctor?'

She blushed. 'I don't think I'm clever enough for that.'

'Nonsense! You don't have to be clever. Look at William.' She pinched his cheek affectionately. He laughed, and kissed her hand.

Millie frowned. Will obviously found his girlfriend's directness charming, but Millie thought it plain rude.

Then, suddenly, Phil leant across to Seb and

251

said, 'I suppose you know William has a huge crush on your fiancée?'

'Phil!' William protested.

'What? It's true, isn't it?' She turned back to face Seb. 'You should see him when he talks about her. He gets terribly tongue-tied.'

'I'm sure that's not true,' Millie mumbled, mortified.

'I wouldn't be at all surprised,' Seb replied smoothly. 'Who wouldn't be in love with Millie?'

She smiled at him gratefully, but he wasn't looking at her. His gaze was wandering around the busy restaurant, searching for the waiter to order more drinks.

'And what do you do, Sebastian?' Phil asked.

He stared down at his glass. 'Not much, really.'

'He's a writer,' Millie put in proudly.

'Really? How fascinating. Might I have read anything you've written?'

'Not unless you read the diary columns.'

'He's going to be very famous one day,' Millie said loyally.

'I wouldn't go that far,' he mumbled.

'It doesn't matter really, does it?' Phil shrugged. 'If your career doesn't amount to anything, surely your father must have a spare castle you can live in?'

'I'm sure he does.' Seb drained his glass and signalled to the waiter again.

'You must forgive Phil,' William apologised for her. 'She does tend to become rather socialist after a few drinks.' He took the glass out of her hand and put it down on the table. 'Come on, let's dance.'

'But I was talking to Sebastian!'

'I'm not sure he wants to talk to you. Come along.' He stood up, drawing her to her feet.

Millie watched him leading her between the tables towards the dance floor. 'What an awful girl,' she said. 'I can't think what William sees in her.'

'Don't worry. I'm sure he'll always prefer you.'

She swung round, frowning. 'You don't believe that nonsense, do you? She didn't know what she was talking about. William and I are just friends.'

'You seemed very close when I arrived earlier?'

Millie laughed, until she saw Seb's blue eyes regarding her seriously over the rim of his glass.

'He was only trying to cheer me up, that's all.'

'If you say so.'

They sat in silence, watching the dancers on the floor. Millie's eyes were drawn to William and Phil. She danced sensuously, winding herself around him, her body melting into his. He held on to her, laughing at her uninhibited display. Millie envied them their closeness. She was beginning to feel the distance between herself and Seb stretching like the frozen wastes of the Arctic.

It wasn't fair, she thought. She'd only suggested they join William because she wanted Seb to have some fun. But instead he was grimly downing drinks as if determined to blot out the whole evening.

Finally she bent closer to him and said, 'You're not enjoying this, are you?'

His mouth twisted. 'Whatever gave you that idea?'

'Shall we go somewhere else?'

'I'd rather go home.'

'That suits me.' She was beginning to feel tired again anyway, as the exhaustion of the day caught up with her.

They took a taxi back to the hospital. Seb dropped her just before the gates.

'It's past midnight,' he said. 'Will you be all right?'

'I'll hop over the wall and up the drainpipe as usual,' Millie said cheerfully.

She leant over to kiss him. For once his kiss was cool, almost offhand.

She drew away, puzzled. 'Happy birthday, Seb.'

He looked at her bleakly. 'If you say so.'

In the early hours of the morning, Violet Tanner made another round of the hospital, then headed to Hyde ward. She had been told in the ward report that one of the patients was unlikely to survive the night.

The nurse in charge was sitting at the central desk, writing her report by the dim light of the shaded green lamp. She looked up as Violet approached.

'I've come to check on the Parkinson's patient. I was told her condition was deteriorating?'

'Mrs Little? She's in bed seven. Sister is with her now.'

'Sister Hyde is with her?' Violet crept down the ward, her soft-soled shoes barely making a sound on the polished floor. Sure enough, Sister Hyde was sitting beside the patient's bed, her tall, fleshless form bent towards her. As she drew closer,

Violet saw that she was holding the old woman's hand.

Sister Hyde looked up, smiling wearily. 'Miss Tanner.' She was in her uniform, as stiff and starched as ever despite it being four in the morning.

'What are you doing here, Sister?' Violet whispered.

'I couldn't sleep for thinking about poor Mrs Little.' Sister Hyde looked down at the elderly woman, fast asleep against the snowy pillows. 'I wasn't sure if she would make it through the night, and I didn't want her to die alone.'

Violet moved to the other side of the bed. 'How is she?'

'She has rallied a little. But they always do, just before the end. I don't think it will be long now.' She looked up at Violet. The dim light of the heavily shaded lamps threw deep shadows on her gaunt face. 'I suppose you think it's odd of me to want to be here?' she said. 'But when a patient is on this ward for so long, you grow to know them. And when you lose one of them ... well, I suppose it's almost like losing a member of your own family.'

Mrs Little stirred, her lips moving soundlessly. Sister Hyde grasped her hand. 'There, my dear. You're quite safe,' she said softly.

Violet stared at her. She knew Sister Hyde had a fearsome reputation, even among the other sisters. She felt as if she was being allowed to glimpse a side of her character she kept well hidden. A side that perhaps only the patients were ever allowed to see.

'Won't you sit down for a moment?' Sister Hyde invited. 'I would welcome some company, if I'm not keeping you from your duties?'

Violet was about to excuse herself then she saw the beseeching look on the older sister's face. 'I'm sure a few minutes won't hurt,' she said.

'Thank you. It can be a lonely business, sitting here waiting.'

Violet fetched another chair and they sat facing each other across the bed. Sister Hyde's attention was still fixed on Mrs Little's frail form, stroking her hand to let her know she was not alone.

'I take it she has no family?' Violet said.

Sister Hyde shook her head. 'Her husband and both her sons were killed in the war.' Her hand, resting on the bedcover, looked almost as old and wrinkled as Mrs Little's. 'She is quite alone, just like the rest of us.'

Her remark startled Violet. But before she could ask what she'd meant by it, Sister Hyde smiled and said pleasantly, 'How are you settling into your new home, Sister?'

'Very well, thank you.'

'I often see your little boy running about the garden – Oliver, isn't it?'

Violet was instantly on edge. 'I hope he isn't making a nuisance of himself? I do try to keep him quiet...'

'Oh, no, not at all,' Sister Hyde assured her. 'On the contrary, it's very pleasant to have the little chap about the place. It's not often we hear a child's laughter in our secluded community. I gather he has become a particularly firm favourite of Sister Sutton's?'

Violet nodded. 'He's been helping her in the garden. Although I suspect he is probably more of a hindrance than a help!' she added ruefully.

'Indeed?' Sister Hyde's brows rose. 'Then she must like him very much indeed. Sister Sutton guards those flower beds of hers jealously!'

'Everyone has been very kind to us,' Violet said.

That wasn't strictly true. Miss Hanley was still disgruntled about the whole situation, and Sister Wren was openly hostile. But Violet didn't mind too much. She had faced much worse over the years, and she knew how to deal with them.

No, it was the ones who were friendly to her that she found hardest to cope with. After so long on her own, she was wary about allowing anyone too close.

'Yes, we are generally a nice group of women,' Sister Hyde agreed. 'Although, of course, we have our little foibles and our fallings-out, like any family.'

'You think of them as family, then?' Violet said.

'They are the only family I have known for many years.' There was a trace of sadness in her smile. 'I came here to work the year Queen Victoria died, and I've been here ever since. My family, such as it was, are all dead now. If it weren't for the Nightingale, I would be as alone as poor Mrs Little here.' She looked up at Violet. 'Do you have any family? Apart from your son, I mean?'

Violet tensed. 'No,' she said.

'Then perhaps the Nightingale will become your family too?'

She shook her head. 'I don't like to become too attached.'

257

'Is that why you move from place to place so often?'

Violet looked up at her sharply. 'How did you know that?'

Sister Hyde's mouth curved. 'A guess, my dear. But an accurate one, from the expression on your face.' She looked at her assessingly. 'Why are you so disturbed by the idea of putting down roots?'

Violet opened her mouth to tell her that it was none of her business, then changed her mind. 'It's easier that way.'

'How can it be preferable to go through life without anyone to care for you?'

Her words cut Violet deeply. It isn't, she wanted to say. There were times when she yearned for a friend, someone to share her burdens with. But sharing her burden meant putting her trust in someone.

'I didn't say it was preferable,' she said shortly. 'I said it was easier.'

'It's never easy to go through life alone, my dear. Perhaps if you gave us a chance–'

Mrs Little stirred again, distracting them. Sister Hyde bent over her, studying her face in the darkness. 'It won't be long now,' she said.

'How can you tell?'

'You get a feeling for these things, after so many years nursing these women.'

'Do you need me to stay?' Violet was already on her feet, keen to escape Sister Hyde with her searching looks and even more searching questions.

Once again, the other woman seemed to read her thoughts. 'No, my dear, it's quite all right. I've already kept you from your duties for too long. I'm sure you have other things to get on with.'

But as Violet went to remove her chair, she added, 'You'll remember what I said, though, won't you? Give the Nightingale a chance. You never know, we may surprise you.'

Chapter Twenty-Six

'...And then take the catheter in the right hand, holding it away from the eye, and run the perchloride lotion over and through it – Doyle, are you listening? I'm doing this for your benefit, you know.'

'Yes, Staff. I'm sorry.' Dora dragged her attention back to the bedside, where Staff Nurse Cuthbert was demonstrating how to use a glass catheter. But she was still aware of Lettie Pike whispering to the new patient at the other end of the ward. From the way they both glanced her way, she had a good idea what they were talking about.

Cuthbert seemed to understand. 'It's five o'clock, Doyle. Go and have your tea, I'll finish this,' she sighed.

'Thank you, Staff.'

'And Doyle?'

'Yes, Staff?'

Cuthbert glanced down the ward. 'Don't let it upset you too much. They'll have something else to gossip about in a few days.'

'Yes, Staff. Thank you.' Dora forced a grateful smile, but deep down she knew this piece of gossip was too good for Lettie to let go. It had already been a week and she still hadn't found anything else to talk about.

It had been too much to hope that news of Joe's visit wouldn't get out. The walls of Griffin Street were too paper-thin, and Lettie Pike's ears far too sharp for that. The morning after it had happened she had sidled up to Dora and said, 'So what's all this I hear about your dad carrying on with another woman?'

The gossip had just blossomed from there, until Dora heard whispers everywhere she went.

Her stepfather had got another woman pregnant. Not just any woman, but a girl young enough to be his daughter.

And the fact that Jennie Armstrong had been a patient on the ward only added to the drama.

'The poor girl, you should have seen the state she was in,' Dora had heard Lettie telling one of the patients. 'Butchered, she was. She lost so much blood, it was a miracle she didn't die. 'Course, she can't ever have kids now. I know, it's a terrible shame, isn't it? Poor lamb.' She'd shaken her head, conveniently forgetting that she hadn't had a good word to say about Jennie when she'd been on the ward.

She was drinking her tea in the kitchen later when Lettie come scurrying in. She stopped dead when she saw Dora.

'What are you doing in here?' she demanded.

'Having my tea break, what does it look like?'

'Does Sister know?'

Dora put down her cup. 'Haven't you got anything better to do than stick your nose into my business?'

'I'm not sticking my nose into anything!' Lettie picked up her basket from behind the door and took out her outdoor shoes. Then, in the next breath, she added, 'Has that girl's brother been round again?'

'I daresay you'd know that better than me, wouldn't you?'

'He's not going to let it lie, you know. I don't reckon he'll be happy till he's found Alf.'

Dora said nothing as she watched the woman change out of her slippers.

'I expect your mum's in a right two and eight,' Lettie went on, her eyes gleaming. 'Can't be nice, can it, knowing your old man's been putting it about? But as I always say, if a man's happy at home he doesn't go out looking elsewhere.'

'Is that why your Len's always propping up the bar at the Rose and Crown?' Dora asked.

Lettie glared at her. 'And with a young girl, too,' she went on, ignoring the comment. 'That's not right, is it? Makes you wonder what kind of man he is.'

A chill ran through Dora. She watched Lettie stuffing her slippers into her basket and willed her to hurry up and go.

'You know what?' the woman continued. 'If I was your mum, I reckon I'd be asking a few questions about what else he'd been up to. I'd be worried about my own kids.' She looked closely at Dora, a thought occurring to her. 'You don't suppose he had a go at your Josie, do you? I mean, you hear of these things...'

'Let me help you with that bag.' Dora got to her feet, unable to stand it any longer, and went to pick up the basket.

'I can manage.' In her agitation to wrestle it back, Lettie's slippers fell out. As Dora went to pick them up for her, she noticed something nestling in the bottom of the basket.

'What's that?' she asked.

'Nothing.' Lettie gathered up the slippers and stuffed them back in hastily.

'Let me have a look.'

'No! It's none of your business what I've got.'

'It's those eggs, isn't it?' Another box of eggs had gone missing from the ward larder that morning. Sister Wren had once again had them turning out all the cupboards and lockers, looking for it.

'Did you take all those other things that went missing, too?' Dora asked her.

'I dunno what you mean.' Lettie tried to front it out, but the beads of perspiration on her upper lip gave her away.

'Oh, Lettie.' Dora shook her head, savouring the moment. 'What have you been up to?'

Lettie folded her arms in a last gesture of defiance. 'I suppose you're going to tell Sister?'

'Why not? It's what you'd do, isn't it?'

No sooner had the words left her lips than the door flew open and Sister Wren bustled in, her copy of *The Times* stuffed under one arm.

She looked askance at Dora. 'What are you doing here?'

'Staff Nurse Cuthbert sent me on my break, Sister.'

262

Sister Wren tutted. 'It's nothing but breaks for you young nurses, isn't it?' She turned to Lettie. 'I'm going to my sitting room to catch up on some private correspondence,' she said. 'I don't suppose you'd be a dear and make me a pot of tea before you go, would you, Lettie?'

Lettie didn't reply but stood rooted to the spot, staring at Dora.

'Lettie?' Sister Wren raised her voice.

'I–I–' Lettie opened and closed her mouth, still looking at Dora. Dora gazed back blandly.

Sister Wren peered at her. 'You've gone very pale all of a sudden. Is something wrong?'

'No, Sister.' Lettie found her voice at last. She set down her basket and picked up the teapot.

'I'd like a fresh pot, please, Lettie. And make sure it's not stewed. I can't abide stewed tea.' Sister Wren turned to Dora. 'What are you still doing here? Your break is over now, surely?'

'Yes, Sister.' Dora picked up her cup and took it over to the sink.

As she washed it, she cast Lettie a sidelong glance. Her hands were shaking so much she could barely spoon the tea into the pot.

Dora smiled to herself. She didn't have to say anything to Sister Wren about Lettie's crime. It was enough that she knew.

Chapter Twenty-Seven

The new London home of the Marquess and Marchioness of Trent was a tall, elegant Georgian house in Smith Square, just north of the Thames in Westminster.

Sophia, Lady Trent, received her guests in the drawing room, defiantly resplendent in a burnt orange Fortuny gown of fine pleated silk that clung lovingly to her eight-month bump, topped off by a sweeping shawl embroidered with a Chinese dragon.

'You make every other woman in this room invisible!' Millie laughed as she greeted her. Sophia certainly made her feel pale and insipid in her blossom-pink crêpe dress.

'Only if she stands in front of them!' Seb teased.

'Oh, do be quiet!' Sophia poked her brother playfully. 'I did it to shock,' she admitted to Millie. 'This is going to be my last public foray before I finally do as Mother says and retire from public life to await my happy event. So I wanted to make it a memorable one.'

'Well, it's worked. You look glorious,' Millie said.

'I wish I felt it.' Sophia grimaced. 'Carrying this huge weight around is giving me the most awful backache.'

'You should rest.'

'Don't! You sound just like David. He's completely changed his mind about our having this party. He agrees with Mother, thinks I should be lying in a darkened room or something, just because I've been having a few silly aches and pains.'

'What kind of aches and pains?' Millie asked.

'Oh, nothing to worry about,' Sophia said dismissively. 'Sir Charles Ingham came to see me this morning – on David's insistence, not mine – and he seems to think I've got ages yet. Anyway, I get so terribly bored doing nothing. I'd far rather be having fun. And it's not as if a house-warming party is exactly strenuous, is it?' She glanced past them and switched on a smile. 'Ah, look, there's Gordon. You must meet him, Seb. He's a publisher, frightfully well connected. I'm sure he'd be useful to you.'

There were a lot of well-connected people at the party. Ever the perfect hostess, Sophia had made sure she'd invited an interesting mix of the rich and powerful, with a judicious splash of the avant-garde. Politicians rubbed shoulders with writers, industrialists with minor royals. Over in the corner, a French artist, who'd just caused a stir in London with his rather shocking surrealist exhibition, was flirting with a well-known actress, who'd recently caused an even bigger stir by having an affair with her sister's husband. And, of course, there was the usual smattering of achingly fashionable Americans, without whom no social gathering seemed to be complete these days.

'I don't know how she does it.' Millie gave a despairing sigh. 'I really wouldn't have the foggiest idea where to start organising a party like this.'

'It's in her blood,' Seb said. 'Mother has been

training her for this from the moment she was old enough to word an invitation.'

Millie sipped her Martini and wondered if perhaps she should have listened to her grandmother more when she'd tried to educate her in such matters, instead of always looking out of the window and planning her escape.

'You do realise we probably won't have parties like this when we're married?' she told Seb.

'I'm glad to hear it. I can't imagine anything worse than filling our house with these dreadful people.'

'But we'll be social outcasts!'

'Good.' He smiled at her, his blue eyes full of warmth. 'Then I won't have to think of anything to say to that French chap who rolls himself in yellow paint and calls it art.'

They smiled at each other. Millie was glad the tension over his birthday had been forgotten, and they were back to the way they used to be.

'You sound like my grandmother. She's always saying my Aunt Victoria can't really be an artist because she's never been able to paint a passable bowl of fruit... Seb?' She frowned, aware he was no longer listening to her, but staring over her shoulder.

Millie turned to see why, and her heart sank. There, on the other side of the room, was William Tremayne.

'What is he doing here?' Seb muttered, his smile disappearing.

'Heaven knows. I didn't realise he and Sophia mixed in the same circles ... oh, he's coming over. Be nice, won't you?' begged Millie.

'I'll be utterly charming,' he replied, his jaw clenched.

Millie glanced at him worriedly as William approached.

'Hello again,' he said. 'We have to stop meeting like this.'

'I completely agree,' Seb said. Millie shot him a warning look, but luckily William didn't seem to notice.

'What are you doing here?' she asked.

'I was supposed to be meeting Phil. I believe she is acquainted with your brother-in-law's family in some way?' he said to Seb. 'But she isn't here. I fear she may have stood me up,' he sighed.

'Oh, dear, how dreadful. Perhaps she's been delayed?'

'Or had a better offer.' He smiled tolerantly. 'Philippa is a creature of impulse,' he explained.

She sounds extremely tiresome, Millie thought. But as William was clearly so besotted, she thought it better not to say anything.

Seb drained his drink. 'Excuse me,' he said. 'I must go and introduce myself to that publisher, otherwise my sister will despair of me. It was nice meeting you again,' he said to William.

They both stared after him as he pushed his way through the crowd. 'Why do I get the impression your fiancé dislikes me?' William asked.

Millie was about to tell him about Seb's silly jealousy, but stopped herself. It was all too absurd for words, and she didn't want to create even more tension and ruin the evening.

But the spell had still been broken. She and Seb did their best, mingling with the other guests,

267

laughing and chatting and trying to enjoy themselves. But everything seemed such a strain, and Millie didn't know why. It was as if William's presence had a depressing effect on Seb, dampening his spirits.

It was almost a relief when the end of the evening came, and it was time for them to leave.

'We must say goodbye to Sophia,' Millie said, looking around. 'Where is she?'

'David said she was upstairs, having a rest. I think the party has been more taxing for her than she thought,' Seb replied.

'I'm not surprised. I'll go up and see her.'

Millie made her way up the stairs to the second floor. 'Sophia?' she called out softly.

'In here,' came a feeble voice.

Millie opened the door and found herself in a grand bedroom, straight out of a Hollywood film, luxurious in shades of white and ivory. The ivory satin cover on the wide gilt-trimmed bed was ruffled, but there was no sign of Sophia.

Millie called to her again.

A door opened and Sophia stood in the doorway of her dressing room, clutching the frame for support. She'd changed into a dove-grey silk peignoir that perfectly matched the colour of her face.

'What is it?' Millie flew to her side. 'Sophia, what's the matter?'

But one look at her friend's stricken expression and she already knew the answer.

'Oh, God, Millie!' Sophia whispered, her voice hoarse with pain. 'I think... I think the baby's coming!'

Chapter Twenty-Eight

'But it can't be,' Millie said. 'It's not due for at least another month, surely?'

'I know!' Sophia wailed. 'Do something!'

She fought down her feeling of panic and forced herself to think. 'Should we call for Sir Charles?'

'I don't think there's time for that–' Sophia stopped talking and caught her breath for a moment. 'The pains are coming quite often now,' she gasped.

'How often?'

'All the ... time.' She looked at Millie anxiously. 'That's bad, isn't it?' She grabbed her arm. 'The baby can't come now, it can't! Oh, God, this is all my fault!'

'I'll fetch help–' Millie started for the door, but Sophia held on to her arm, fingers biting into her flesh.

'Nooo! Don't leave me! You're a nurse, you can help me.'

'I can't deliver a baby on my own. I haven't had any obstetrics training. I'll be back in one minute, I promise. Just hold on.'

'How am I supposed to do that – oh, God!' She doubled up as another wave of pain hit her. 'Hurry up!' she urged through clenched teeth.

Seb was waiting in the hall, Millie's velvet evening cape draped over his arm.

He turned to look up at her as she came down

the stairs. 'Did you find–' His smile disappeared. 'Millie, what is it? What's wrong?'

'I've got to find William.' She hurried into the drawing room, Seb following, and scanned the crowd. William was over by the window, charming a rather inebriated actress. Millie rushed over and grabbed his arm, pulling him aside.

'You've got to come,' she whispered. 'Sophia's gone into early labour.'

'Are you sure? Pregnant woman can have false pains for several weeks...'

'These are not false pains, believe me!' She tugged at his sleeve. 'Come on, William, or I'm worried she'll give birth before we get back!'

William stared at her tense face. 'I'll get my bag from the car.'

'Is there anything I can do?' Seb asked.

'Warn her husband what's going on, and get him to telephone this specialist of hers,' William said. 'And for heaven's sake, get rid of all these people!'

Seb's face clouded at the curtness of his order. But then he turned on his heel and hurried off.

Millie made to follow him, but William caught her by the sleeve.

'You're coming upstairs with me.'

'But I can't do anything! I've never delivered a baby in my life.'

'Let's hope Sir Charles Ingham gets here before it comes to that,' William said grimly.

Sophia had managed to get herself on to the bed by the time they reached her. 'Oh, thank God!' she wept when she saw them. 'It's definitely coming, I can feel it. Mother will kill me, I

270

know she will!'

That's the least of your worries, Millie thought, as William put down his bag, took off his jacket and rolled up his sleeves. As he moved around, he was already issuing instructions.

'We're going to need plenty of hot water, bowls and jugs, nail brushes, towels, perchloride of mercury lotion – you'll find it in my bag,' he added, as Millie looked blank, 'carbolic soap, towels, antiseptic gauze, wool and some cold sterilised water.' He muttered in a rapid undertone, 'You'll also need to sterilise a catheter ready for use, clean and shave the patient and give her an enema.'

Millie's head was spinning as she hurried around, trying to get everything together while William scrubbed up in the bathroom.

He returned, his worried frown replaced by the reassuring, professional smile she had seen so many times. 'Right, your ladyship,' he said briskly. 'Let's take a look, shall we?'

He drew back the coverlet and examined her as Millie mixed up the soap solution for the enema. When he looked back at her, his face was as white as the satin bedspread.

'What?' Sophia cried, seeing his expression. 'What is it?'

'I wouldn't bother doing that, Nurse,' he said, keeping his voice steady with an effort. 'I don't think there's going to be time.'

No sooner had he said the words than Sophia drew up her knees and let out an ear-splitting scream that seemed to go on for ever, echoing around the house and bouncing off the walls.

A second later, a fist crashed against the bedroom door and David shouted, 'What's going on in there?'

Millie slipped outside. David and Seb stood on the landing, both looking lost and worried.

'Seb said the baby's coming?' David's face was tense. 'I called Sir Charles, but he's attending a birth in Berkshire. What should I do? Shall I call an ambulance?'

'There isn't time.'

His face lost what little colour it had. 'What? You mean – it's happening now?' He glanced towards the door and back at her. 'Oh God, will Sophia be all right?'

'She'll be fine–' Another ear-splitting scream gave the lie to Millie's words.

David swallowed hard, his face pale. 'Just save her, please,' he begged.

'Millie!' William shouted from the other side of the door. 'I need you in here.'

She looked at Seb, who put his arm around his brother-in-law's shoulders. 'Come on, old man, let's go downstairs and have a brandy.'

With a last, pleading glance at Millie, David turned and allowed himself to be guided away. Seb looked over his shoulder at Millie.

'Please do what you can for her,' he mouthed.

'We will,' Millie nodded.

She returned as Sophia was recovering from another contraction. As the pain released her from its grip, she collapsed back against the pillows, sweating and exhausted.

'Not long now, I think,' William said encouragingly. 'You're doing very well, your ladyship. Try to rest between the contractions as much as you can.'

Sophia shot him a stony look. 'Given the situation we find ourselves in, I think you might call me by my name.'

Mercifully for all of them, it was a very quick delivery. Millie barely had time to finish sterilising all the instruments before the tiny, limp body slithered into the world.

'It's a boy,' William said.

As he clamped the cord, he caught Millie's eye. One look at his solemn face, and her heart plummeted.

'Is he ... is he all right?' Sophia looked from one to the other of them. 'He isn't crying ... why isn't he crying? I thought babies always cried?'

She struggled to sit up but Millie came to her side and held her gently by the shoulders, easing her back against the pillows. Sophia's peignoir clung to her, damp with sweat. 'He just needs a little bit of help to get his breathing started, I expect. Just try to rest.'

But Sophia fought her off. 'I want to see him,' she insisted. 'I want to see my son!'

Millie shot a look over her shoulder at William, who was briskly rubbing at the baby's tiny chest with the flat of his hand. His hair flopped over his eyes and he pushed it back with one wrist before carrying on.

'He's dead, isn't he?' Sophia murmured through dry, grey lips. 'My baby is dead–'

Just at that moment a thin, reedy cry drifted across the room. William turned to look at them, his dark eyes blazing triumphantly in his pale, sweating face.

'You have a healthy son, Lady Trent,' he said, his voice trembling with emotion.

Sophia burst into tears, as did Millie. Still sniffing them back, she quickly washed the baby and wrapped him in one of the new blankets monogrammed with the family crest that Sophia had ordered especially.

'You're a lucky little boy,' whispered Millie.

She carried the baby across the room and laid him in his mother's waiting arms. Sophia stared down at him, speechless with emotion.

'We'll clean up a bit, then let the proud father in, shall we?' William said.

When Millie opened the door a few minutes later, David was already standing breathless on the landing.

'I heard a baby crying,' he said. 'Is it–'

Millie smiled. 'It's a boy.'

'Good God! Really?' The expression of joy on his face made her want to cry again. 'Can I see him?' asked David, his voice thick with emotion.

He already had tears streaming down his face by the time he laid eyes on his son for the first time.

'I don't know how to thank you,' he said, over and over again.

'I'm just relieved we were here and able to help,' William replied. He gathered up his bag and he and Millie crept out of the room, leaving the new parents alone together.

It wasn't until they were out on the landing and the bedroom door had closed behind them that he let out a deep, shuddering sigh.

'Thank God,' he said, rubbing his brow. 'I was so scared–'

'Me too.' Her limbs were shaking as if she'd just run up a mountain. 'But we did it,' she said.

'So we did.' They looked at each other. Then, at exactly the same moment, they let out a shout of joy and relief.

They were still grinning foolishly at each other when Seb appeared at the foot of the stairs. 'Sorry to interrupt,' he called, 'but my mother is on the telephone. She wants to know if there's any news?'

'Tell her she has a grandson,' William called back. He turned to Millie. 'Seriously, I couldn't have done it without you.'

'Was it really your first delivery?'

'I've only helped out in the hospital, with the consultant looking on. You were a marvel at keeping everyone calm. Including me.'

'Now you can tick "Delivering a baby" on my training record!'

'Maybe you should tick it on mine, too?'

'You can't imagine how nerve-racking it was, Seb. I really thought we were–' Millie turned round to him, but he had gone.

Chapter Twenty-Nine

'Have you seen my newspaper?'

Sister Wren was pacing the passageway of the Sisters' block in her dressing gown when Violet returned from night duty. Most of the nurses looked better out of uniform, but Sister Wren's sparse, ashy curls did nothing to soften the sharp angles of her little face.

'I'm sorry, I haven't.'

Sister Wren tutted. 'That wretched newspaper boy must be late. Typical!' Without another word she flounced off, slamming the door of her room behind her so hard the frame rattled.

Good morning to you, too, Violet thought, letting herself into her own flat.

'Oliver?' There was no reply. He must still be asleep, she thought. 'Come on, sleepyhead, it's time to get–'

The room was empty.

Every nerve, muscle and sinew sprang instantly to life. 'Oliver!' She ran around the flat, throwing open doors and calling his name, over and over again. 'Oliver, where are you?'

She rushed out into the passageway, still calling to him. All the time her mind was racing, knowing her worst nightmare had come true.

'Violet, what is it?' Sister Blake emerged from her room, tying the strings of her cap under her chin.

'Oliver's been taken!'

'Taken? What on earth do you mean?'

'I mean he's gone ... missing,' she amended quickly.

'Calm yourself, my dear, he can't have gone far.'

'But you don't understand–' Panic gripped Violet's throat so tightly she could hardly get the words out.

Other doors opened down the passageway, and heads in various states of dishevelment popped out.

'What's going on?'

'Violet's son is missing.'

'Missing? Surely not?'

'He can't have gone far.'

The sisters congregated in the corridor. Sister Wren emerged from her room, her sharp-featured face indignant.

'Well! I didn't see all this fuss when I said my newspaper had gone missing,' she snapped.

Violet pushed past them and out through the doors into the garden. She was aware of Sister Blake following as she ran across the grass, frantically calling Oliver's name.

'When was the last time you saw him?' Sister Blake asked, catching up with her.

'Last night, when I put him to bed.' Violet's breath was coming in shallow gasps, making her head spin. 'I said goodnight, and told him–'

She told him what she always told him. *Don't go off with anyone, no matter what they might tell you.*

'He'll be here somewhere.'

No, he won't. The thought went round and round in her head. He's gone. They've found us, and they've taken him.

They heard the sound of a dog yapping. Sparky hurtled round the corner, nearly knocking them off their feet. 'Sparky! Come back, you bad dog.'

Violet started running towards the voice, Sister Blake hard on her heels, and almost collided with Oliver, barefoot and still in his pyjamas, running in the opposite direction.

He froze when he saw her, his face stricken with guilt. 'Mummy!'

'Oliver!' She grabbed him by the shoulders and

277

shook him. 'What have I told you about going out on your own?'

'I didn't mean to, but Sparky was barking outside my window. I only meant to go out and play for a minute...' His brown eyes brimmed with tears. 'S-Sorry, Mummy.'

Relief flooded through Violet, melting her bones. She sank to her knees, clutching him to her, tears streaming down her face. 'Oh, Oliver!' she sobbed. 'Please don't ever do that to me again.'

'No, Mummy.'

'There, I told you he wouldn't have gone far.'

She'd forgotten all about Sister Blake standing behind her. Violet dashed her tears away and stood up, one arm still fixed around Oliver's narrow shoulders, clamping him to her as if she would never let him go.

'Thank you for helping me look for him,' she said stiffly. Now the panic was over, she felt ashamed of her loss of control.

'Not just me.' Sister Blake looked over her shoulder. The other sisters were all picking their way in different directions across the lawn, searching under bushes, calling Oliver's name.

Seeing them, Violet felt a jolt of emotion. Sister Hyde was right, she thought; they did care.

'And as for you, young man...' Sister Blake looked down at Oliver, her expression mock-severe. 'You mustn't give your mummy a shock like that again, do you hear?'

Oliver nodded his head solemnly, his brown eyes shining with unshed tears.

'He won't,' Violet said. 'I'll make sure of that.'

'I'm sure you will.' Sister Blake smiled at her.

Then she turned and headed off across the grass, back towards the sisters' block, calling to the other nurses to give them the good news.

The rest of the day passed by uneventfully. Violet took Oliver to school, then came home and slept for a few hours. Afterwards, she busied herself with errands until it was time to collect her son from school again.

'Please may we go to the park?' he begged, as he always did when they walked past the tall wrought-iron gates of Victoria Park, with their stone dogs on either side, ears cocked, ever alert.

'After what you did this morning? I don't think you deserve a treat, do you?' Violet said severely.

'No,' Oliver agreed in a small voice. 'But you never let me go to the park, even when I'm not naughty,' he complained.

Violet felt guilty. He was right, she always managed to make some excuse. Either it was too cold, or too wet, or he was wearing his good clothes. But the truth was, the park was a big place and she was too afraid to let him out of her sight.

Even now, just the thought of it made her tighten her grip on his hand.

'Another day,' she said.

'Promise?'

'I promise.'

They entered the gates of the Nightingale, and skirted the main buildings towards the sisters' block at the back. As they headed down the gravel path that crossed the gardens, Violet heard her name being called.

She turned around to see Sister Wren hurrying

down the path towards them. She must have been watching for them from the window of her ward.

Violet sighed. 'Oh, dear, what does she want now?' she muttered under her breath.

Whatever it was, it wasn't good news. Sister Wren's narrow face was twisted with fury.

'Have you seen this?' She thrust the shredded remains of a newspaper into Violet's face.

She frowned at it. 'What is it?'

'My copy of *The Times*. The maid found it stuffed in the broom cupboard. Like this!' She waved it under Violet's nose.

'And what does that have to do with me?' she asked calmly.

'Don't take that tone with me!' Sister Wren spluttered with rage. 'You know as well as I do it was your child who hid it there!'

'Now just a minute...' Violet struggled to hold on to her temper. 'You can't go around accusing my son.'

'Who else could it be? He was skulking around this morning when the newspaper was delivered. It didn't rip itself up and stuff itself in a cupboard, did it?' Her tiny eyes glittered with malice. 'Someone must be punished!'

Violet turned to Oliver. 'Do you know anything about this?'

As soon as she looked at him she knew. Two bright spots of guilty colour flared in his cheeks. 'Remember what I've always told you, Oliver,' she coaxed gently. 'No one will be cross if you tell the truth. Do you know what happened to this newspaper?'

He stared up at her, his eyes dark brown pools of misery. Then, slowly, he nodded.

'I knew it!' Sister Wren hissed. 'You're a nasty, destructive little boy, and you deserve a good thrashing–'

She took a step towards Oliver but Violet barred her way. 'Lay one finger on my son and, by God, I will make you sorry!' she snapped.

They faced each other like spitting cats in an alleyway. Sister Wren quivered with fury, but even she seemed to know better than to take on an angry mother protecting her child.

'What is going on here, sisters?'

Miss Hanley bore down on them. 'What is this?' She towered over them, her broad masculine shape like a prize fighter's under her starched uniform. 'Nurses brawling in public?' Her glacial gaze swept from one to the other. 'You had better have a very good reason for this shameful display!'

'I'll tell you, shall I? This ... malicious little monster,' Sister Wren pointed a shaking finger at Oliver, 'has deliberately ripped up my newspaper and hidden the evidence!'

Miss Hanley's face darkened. 'Is this true?' she demanded.

'He admitted it himself!' Sister Wren squeaked. 'Bold as brass, he was. Didn't even try to lie about it.'

'I will pay for the damage,' Violet said calmly. 'And believe me, Miss Hanley, my son will be punished.'

'That's not good enough! Something should be done about this,' Sister Wren appealed to Miss Hanley. 'Matron must be told. We cannot have children running around, destroying other people's property.'

'I agree, Sister. I will speak to her about it. I have always believed a child's presence here was a bad idea, and this incident proves it.'

'I don't want to go!' Oliver burst into tears. 'Mummy, don't let them send us away!'

'It's all right, darling.' Violet bent to put her arms around him, hugging him to her. 'For pity's sake, must you discuss this in front of my son?' She glared at the two women over his shoulder.

At least Miss Hanley had the grace to look shame-faced, while Sister Wren said huffily, 'You've brought it on yourself, I'm sure. We simply can't have this kind of deliberate trouble-making here.'

'You've made your point, Sister,' Miss Hanley silenced her. She shot an uncomfortable glance at Oliver, still sobbing on his mother's shoulder.

'I didn't do it on purpose,' he wept. 'It was an accident. I only put it behind the cupboard to stop anyone being cross with him...' He stopped talking abruptly.

Violet shifted to hold him at arms' length. 'What are you talking about, sweetheart? Cross with who?'

Oliver looked warily at Miss Hanley and Sister Wren, then back to his mother. He shook his head, his mouth a stubbornly silent line.

'You must tell me, Oliver. It's very important.'

He hesitated for a moment, then leant forward and whispered. 'It was Sparky.'

'Sister Sutton's dog? You mean, he ripped the newspaper?'

Oliver nodded. 'He grabbed it off the paperboy this morning. I saw him out of the window. But before I could get it off him, he'd eaten it.'

'A likely story!' Sister Wren huffed.

'It's true!' Oliver turned to her, his brown eyes wide in his earnest little face. 'I've been trying to teach him to fetch the newspaper for Sister Sutton every morning, to save her legs, but he hasn't managed it yet. He nearly managed it last week with Sister Parker's *Daily Telegraph*, but then he ate it so Sister Sutton hid it in her coal scuttle and told her the paperboy hadn't been.' His cheeks flared red again as he realised he'd given away another guilty secret.

Violet looked up at Miss Hanley who was trying her hardest not to smile.

'Well, Sister, I think we've found the real culprit,' she said.

'I'm still not happy about this,' Sister Wren muttered furiously.

'In that case, I suggest you take it up with Sister Sutton,' Miss Hanley suggested.

Violet saw the look of angry disappointment on Sister Wren's face and felt almost sorry for her. 'I do feel my son was partly responsible. If you let me know how much I owe you—' she offered, but Sister Wren cut her off.

'Forget it,' she bit out.

As she stomped off, her shredded newspaper stuffed under her arm, Oliver looked at his mother. 'She won't punish Sparky or Sister Sutton, will she?' he whispered anxiously.

Miss Hanley smiled thinly. 'I'd like to see her try, young man.'

Sister Wren sat at the table in her sitting room, the tattered pieces of *The Times*' back page arranged in front of her like a jigsaw. It was so frustrating, trying to patch all those tiny shreds of print together. Every time she found an interesting advertisement, she had to search high and low for the post-office box address that went with it. And half the time she wasn't even sure she'd got the right side of the page, either.

She sat back and stared at the mess in front of her, seething quietly. She had already spent a fruitless half-hour and felt like throwing the whole lot away. But somewhere in the back of her mind she had the lingering fear that today was the day her dream man would finally appear in the Personal Column, and she wouldn't see the advertisement.

It was all the fault of that wretched Violet Tanner, she thought. Her ridiculously winsome child had even managed to soften the hard heart of Veronica Hanley. Next thing, she would be petting and fussing over him like silly Sister Sutton.

'Sister?'

She jumped as Staff Nurse Cuthbert stuck her head around the door. 'For heaven's sake, Staff, can't you knock?' she snapped. 'What is it?'

'There's a new admission on their way up. Uterine haemorrhage.' Cuthbert eyed the newspaper fragments laid out on the table, though Sister Wren was trying to shield them from view.

'Can't you deal with it?' she snapped.

'Yes, Sister. Sorry, Sister.' The staff nurse disappeared. As she closed the door, the draught wafted fragments of newspaper like confetti about the room.

'Damn and blast!' Sister Wren sighed, and began gathering them up again. As she did, three words, printed in bold, caught her eye.

Dangerfield, *née* Tanner.

She wasn't sure what made her pick it up. It was a common enough name, after all. But she felt a prickle of sensation.

The rest of the line was obliterated. But underneath there was another half-line with the words 'contact immediately', followed by a telephone number.

Sister Wren sat back and stared at the tiny shred of newsprint between her fingers. What did it mean? She'd often seen those advertisements, asking for a long-lost friend or relative to contact a solicitor's office 'to hear something to their advantage'. But this was different, more abrupt, less promising of good things. Just looking at those brusque words 'contact immediately' made the hairs on the back of her neck stand up.

'Sister?' Staff Nurse Cuthbert's voice came from the other side of the door. 'I thought you might like to know, Mr Cooper is on his way up to see the new patient.'

'I'll be there straight away.' Sister Wren stood up, straightening her cap. She looked down at the telephone number on the scrap of paper in her hand, then, on impulse, slipped it into her pocket.

Chapter Thirty

Sophia's room at the nursing home was be-decked with flowers. Every available space was so crammed with overflowing vases, Millie and Seb didn't dare move in case they knocked one over.

Sophia sat in the middle of it all, radiant in white lace, her face suffused with love as she gazed down at her baby son in her arms.

'Isn't he utterly perfect? I could look at him all day,' she sighed.

'Motherhood suits you,' Millie said.

'Doesn't it?' Sophia looked up, her face full of joy. 'I thought it would be rather tedious, but it isn't at all. Of course, it helps that everyone is spoiling me madly,' she added.

'So I see.' Millie gazed around at the flowers. 'It's like a florist's shop in here.'

'I know!' Sophia pointed across the room at a very tasteful arrangement of spring blooms. 'Guess who sent those?' Millie looked blank. 'Your Dr Tremayne!' She grinned.

Millie sent Seb a quick sidelong glance. 'He's not my Dr Tremayne,' she said quietly.

'I know, but he is rather dashing, isn't he? Far more glamorous than dull old Sir Charles Ingham. I've already told David I'm a little bit in love with him. How could anyone not be?'

'How indeed?' Seb's voice dripped sarcasm.

Millie felt the heat rising in her face. 'It was

nice of William to send flowers,' she commented carefully.

'Absolutely. If anything, I should be the one sending flowers to him,' Sophia agreed. 'When I think about what he did for me – and you, of course,' she added quickly. 'You were both absolutely marvellous, coming to my rescue like that.'

'You did all the hard work!'

'I was utterly hopeless, and you know it,' Sophia dismissed the comment. 'I would have been a gibbering fool if you hadn't been there to keep me calm. And when poor little Billy didn't make a peep for such a long time...' She suppressed a shudder. 'The consultant said he didn't know what would have happened if Dr Tremayne hadn't got him breathing the way he did.'

'Billy?' Seb said coldly.

'Oh, dear, I've let the secret out, haven't I? I promised Mother I wouldn't tell anyone until it was announced in *The Times*.' Sophia stroked her baby's cheek with one finger. 'David and I were both so grateful to Dr Tremayne, we asked if he would mind us naming the baby after him. And he's agreed to be a godfather, isn't that wonderful? Of course, you'll be his other godfather, Seb.' She smiled at her brother. 'Don't you think that's a marvellous idea, having a doctor for a godfather?' she said. 'Perhaps Dr Tremayne will inspire Billy to a career in medicine?'

'If Seb doesn't inspire him to a career in writing,' Millie added loyally. The frosty look Seb shot her silenced her instantly.

Sophia noticed, glancing from one to the other of them. 'Is everything all right?' She frowned.

287

'Everything is fine,' Millie assured her. 'So has your mother been to see her first grandchild yet?' she swiftly changed the subject.

'Of course!' Sophia rolled her eyes. 'She simply won't stay away.'

They talked about how besotted the duchess was with the baby, and how she and David's mother were locked in bitter rivalry over him already. Meanwhile Seb stood at the window, hands thrust into his pockets, staring moodily down at the street.

'Did you have to be in such a foul mood?' Millie scolded him as they left the nursing home half an hour later and made their way along Marylebone Road.

'I'm sorry, were you disappointed I didn't join you and my sister in your adoration of Dr Tremayne?'

'I'm disappointed you behaved like a sulky little boy,' Millie said. 'Anyway, what have you got against William? He saved your nephew's life, remember?'

'How could I ever forget that?' Seb said bitterly. 'I'm constantly being told what a hero he is.' He saw Millie's reproachful expression and his shoulders slumped. 'I am thankful to him for saving the baby's life, of course I am. I just wish I could have done more that night. Do you have any idea how utterly useless I felt while you and he were in there, delivering Sophia's baby?'

'You did your bit.'

'I called an ambulance, then plied David with brandy while he chewed his nails down to the elbows. It's hardly heroic, is it? Not the same as

288

saving a baby's life, at any rate.' His mouth twisted. 'Let's face it, I can't compete with Tremayne.'

Millie frowned. 'Why should you want to compete with him?'

'Isn't it obvious?' Seb laughed bitterly. 'I'm jealous as hell, Mil. And I can't stop asking myself why you would want someone like me when you could have him?'

She reached for his hand. 'But I don't want him.'

'Don't you?'

He started to cross the road but Millie held him back. 'Seb, you're not making any sense. I love you, you know that.'

'I'm not sure I do know that any more, Mil.' His blue eyes were full of sorrow. 'I feel as if we're spinning off in different directions, and I'm losing you. You belong to that world now, a world full of hospitals and doctors, seeing and dealing with things I couldn't imagine. And then there's me, stuck in my world full of shooting parties and social engagements, and the same people talking endlessly about the same things all the time.'

'That's my world too,' Millie protested.

Seb shook his head. 'It used to be, when we first met. But you despise it now. No, don't deny it. I saw it in your face that weekend we went to Lyford. You couldn't wait to escape.'

'Only because of that idiot Jumbo Jameson!'

'But don't you see? I'm just like Jumbo Jameson. We went to the same school, the same college, we have the same friends, go to the same parties. We're both rich, idle fellows, chasing the latest fad and fancy, pretending our lives have some kind of

289

meaning. But really we're both just treading water.'

'You're nothing like him, Seb. You have a career!'

'Oh, that! I've hardly set Fleet Street on fire so far, have I? A couple of diary pieces and a report on my cousin's wedding for the society pages.'

'Everyone has to start somewhere.'

'All I've really done is drink port with the other hacks in The Cheshire Cheese. I'll probably develop gout before I make it on to the front page.'

'I have great faith in you.'

'Do you, Mil? I'm not sure I do.'

She stared at him. She'd never seen Seb so depressed, it wasn't like him at all. She longed for him to smile, to make her laugh again.

'I don't care anyway,' she declared. 'I don't care if you give up journalism and spend the rest of your life shooting grouse with Jumbo Jameson. I'll still want to be with you.'

'Prove it,' he said.

'How?'

'Marry me.'

She smiled uncertainly. 'I will.'

'I don't mean in two years' time. I mean now.'

At first she thought he was joking. But the look in his eyes was deadly serious. 'We can be married in the summer,' he said. 'We could live at Billinghurst, at least until we found a place of our own nearby. You'd like that, wouldn't you? To be back in the country, living with your family? We could go riding every day, and I'm sure your father could find some useful work for me to do on the estate. I don't think I made too poor a job of it, last time I helped out!' He smiled self-deprecatingly.

'And what about me?' Millie said, her voice tinged with ice. 'Would he find something useful for me to do, too? Or would I be expected to produce a baby straight away, like Sophia?'

Seb's mouth turned down. 'That would be enough for some girls.'

'Not for me,' Millie said firmly. Then, seeing his disappointed expression, she added, 'I'm not saying I won't be as thrilled as Sophia to have a baby one day. But I want to get my State Registration first, and then–'

'Why?' he cut her off bluntly. 'Why do you have to finish your training when you know you're going to give it up anyway? It just seems like a complete waste of everyone's time.'

His words struck a painful chord with Millie, reminding her of the harsh comments Sister Hyde had previously made. It was even more painful because she couldn't find an answer for him. All she knew was that she dreamt of being able to write the letters 'SRN' after her name.

'I want to be able to say I've done something worthwhile with my life,' was all she could say.

'And marrying me wouldn't be worthwhile, is that it?'

She stared at him helplessly. 'Why are you doing this, Seb?' she pleaded. 'Why are you making me choose?'

'If you loved me there wouldn't even be a choice.' His voice was flat.

'And if you loved me you wouldn't ask,' she said.

They stood on the pavement, staring at each other. People streamed past, jostling them this way and that, but they barely noticed.

She waited for him to tell her he was joking, that he didn't mean what he'd said. Anything at all that would help her breathe again. But he was ominously, depressingly silent. Somewhere in the distance, she could almost hear her world crashing down.

'So that's it then,' Seb said finally. 'I suppose we both know where we stand.'

Millie looked at his stubborn expression, and felt something inside her begin to grow cold and harden like ice. Her gaze still locked on his, she slowly pulled her engagement ring off her finger and handed it to him.

'I suppose we do,' she said.

On duty the following morning, Millie threw herself into her work. For once she was grateful that Sister Hyde gave her the bathrooms to clean, because it gave her the chance to work off some of her pent-up energy and frustration. She mopped floors, polished taps until she could see her unhappy face reflected in the chrome, and scrubbed toilets as if she could somehow scrub out all the memories of last night too.

But all the time she couldn't help wondering if Seb was right. What was the point? she thought. Why struggle on through another two years of training, when everyone knew she was going to give it up anyway? No one would miss her, especially not Sister Hyde. She could go back to Billinghurst and marry Sebastian, and everyone would be happy.

Except me, she thought, grimacing at her reflection in the bath taps.

There were deep shadows etched under her eyes from a night without sleep. She hadn't told Dora or Helen about her broken engagement yet. Even though she knew they wouldn't spread gossip, she didn't want anyone knowing about it. It was as if saying it out loud would somehow make it true. And she wasn't ready to admit it yet.

She missed Seb already. Even though she hadn't been able to see him very often, he'd always been there, a reassuring presence in the back of her mind. His absence was almost physical, like a lost tooth. She had to keep going back and probing the spot where he had been, even though she knew it would cause her pain.

She worked so hard that even Sister Hyde seemed grudgingly impressed with her efforts. So Millie was confused when she was summoned by Sister while they were serving the midday meal to the patients.

'Yes, Sister?' She steeled herself for another reprimand.

'Benedict, I'm afraid Mrs Mortimer is having more problems with her hands. She can't manage her cup at all now, even with the dressing wrapped around it. She needs feeding, and has requested that you do it.'

'Me, Sister?'

'You, Benedict.' Sister Hyde's raised eyebrows told her she was as surprised by the request as Millie was. 'Usually, I would not allow patients to dictate such things, but Mrs Mortimer is being particularly trying, and I simply don't have the time or the patience to argue with her today. So you'll have to get on with it.'

She thrust the tray with the cup on it into Millie's hands. Good luck, her look said.

Millie carried the tray carefully down the ward, aware of the pitying looks of the other nurses as she went. She understood why; if Maud Mortimer's failing body had let her down again, she would want to vent her frustration on someone. Millie felt as if she was entering the lion's den.

She pasted a breezy smile on her face as she placed the tray down on Maud's bed table.

'Good afternoon, Mrs Mortimer,' she greeted her brightly. 'Are you ready for your dinner?'

'Of course I am, what else is there to do in this place but eat and sleep?' Maud snapped. 'And do stop beaming at me, girl,' she added. 'I chose you because I find you the least irritating nurse here, so don't flatter yourself. What is this anyway?' She stared at the cup, her lip curling.

'Broth, Mrs Mortimer.'

'Broth again? Goodness, how imaginative. That cook has the flair of Escoffier.' She settled back against the pillows with a martyred expression. 'Very well,' she sighed. 'You'd better get on with it. And I don't want any of your simpering or sympathy either,' she warned. 'My fingers have let me down, and that's the end of it. But my brain is still functioning perfectly.'

'Yes, Mrs Mortimer.'

Millie supported her carefully with her left arm while she held the cup to her lips with her right hand. There was silence as Millie concentrated on not spilling anything on to the cloth she'd placed around Maud's neck. But after about a minute, the old woman batted the cup away with

294

her wrist and said crossly, 'What is the matter with you today? You're usually chattering like a parakeet.'

'I'm sorry, Mrs Mortimer. I didn't think you'd want me to talk.'

'Since when has that ever stopped you? Goodness, if I didn't know better I would have sworn you were actually upset about something.' She turned her head to look at Millie, her eyes narrowed. 'You are, aren't you? What on earth is wrong with you? It must be something of cataclysmic proportions to upset your sickeningly sunny disposition.'

Millie lowered her gaze to the cup. 'Sister Hyde doesn't like us discussing our personal lives with the patients.'

Maud tutted. 'This ordeal is bad enough, without having to endure it in silence. Now you can either fill the time with the mindless chatter that passes for conversation in this place. Or you can talk to me properly.' She looked sideways at Millie. 'I assume there is a man involved?' Millie nodded. 'There always is, at your age. So you have had a disagreement with a boyfriend, is that it?'

'I have to get on with feeding you—' Millie lifted the cup to her lips again, but Maud jerked her head away.

'Not until you tell me what is wrong with you.'

'Very well.' Millie lowered the cup. 'If you must know, I've broken off my engagement.'

'Ah.' Maud was silent for a moment. 'And may I ask why?'

It was obvious she wasn't going to touch another drop of her meal until she'd found out everything, so Millie told her. Maud proved to be an un-expectedly good listener.

'So what do you think?' Millie asked, when she'd finished telling her tale. She half expected Maud to tell her she'd done the right thing, that no man had the right to dictate how she lived her life. She had been a suffragette, after all.

But she didn't say anything of the sort. 'Why does it matter what I think?' She seemed genu-inely surprised by the question.

Millie looked at her, crestfallen. 'I thought you might give me some advice,' she said in a small voice.

'It's rather late for that, don't you think?'

Millie stared down at the cup. 'Do you think I've done the right thing?' she asked again.

Maud sent her a wise look. 'My dear, if you have to ask me that, then I wonder if you have.'

Chapter Thirty-One

Violet hadn't meant to join the choir. But, as with everything else about the Nightingale, she found herself gradually drawn in, almost without rea-lising it.

It began just after nine on a fine March even-ing. It was one of the three nights a month Violet was allowed to take off, and after putting Oliver to bed she had planned to spend the time read-ing. But no sooner had she opened her book than the electric light above her head flickered, and the next moment she was plunged into darkness.

Violet put down her book with a sigh. She went round trying all the lights in the flat, but none of them worked.

Almost immediately, she heard voices in the passageway outside.

'What on earth has happened?'

'Is the rest of the hospital in darkness?'

'Where are the candles?'

'I'm just looking for them now...'

'Well, hurry up!'

'Don't fret, I've found them. Now I just need to find a match...'

Violet was more used to the dark than most. She quickly found the box of matches she kept on top of the kitchen cupboard and hurried out into the passageway, just in time to see a beam of torchlight at the other end.

'Ah, Sister Tanner.' Matron's voice greeted her calmly. 'This is quite a drama, isn't it?'

'What's happened?'

'That's what I'm trying to find out. I suspect it's simply a problem with the fuses. Fortunately it only seems to have affected this building, but I'm going to have a word with Mr Hopkins and see what's happening in the rest of the hospital.'

'Shall I come with you?'

She caught Matron's smile in the beam of the torch. 'Bless you, but that won't be necessary. I can see there are lights on in the other buildings, so I'm sure it's all a fuss over nothing. I just need to make certain everyone is all right, and get some matches from Mr Hopkins for our candles.'

'I have some here.' Violet held up the box.

297

'Then perhaps you could help the other sisters?' Matron nodded towards the sitting room from whence she had come. Piano music drifted softly through the half-open door. 'They're currently cursing each other for the fact that none of them smokes!'

Matron glided off towards the main buildings, and Violet pushed open the door to the sitting room. Half a dozen faces turned towards her in the gloom.

'Who's there?' a voice hissed. 'Is that you, Matron?'

'It's me ... Violet Tanner,' she called back. 'I've brought you some matches.'

'Thank God! Give them to me.' A hand snatched them from her in the darkness. A moment later there was the rasp of a match, and a flickering candle flame illuminated Sister Wren's pinched face.

She looked even more small-boned and diminutive out of her uniform, her little face surrounded by limp brown curls. She barely came up to Violet's shoulder.

As more candles were lit and handed around, Violet made out the faces of half a dozen sisters in the large sitting room. Sister Hyde was squeezed on to the end of the sofa on one side of Sister Sutton's spreading bulk, with the Sister Tutor, Sister Parker, squeezed on to the other, like a pair of narrow bookends. Sister Parry lit the candles in a candelabra on top of the piano, where Sister Blake sat.

'I quite like playing in this light. It's rather evocative, don't you think?' Her fingers ran lightly

298

and expertly over the keys. 'I imagine Chopin composed his piano concertos by candlelight like this.'

She looked up at Violet and smiled. 'Ah, I see you've discovered our little choir. Won't you sit and listen for a moment? We so rarely have an audience.'

'Which is probably just as well!' Sister Parry put in.

Violet was about to refuse, when she caught the look of challenge in Sister Hyde's eyes. 'Well, all right ... perhaps for a moment,' she said. She perched herself on the edge of the armchair nearest to the door.

'You'll have to forgive us if we're dreadful,' Sister Blake continued. 'We've only just started practising "Blow the Wind Southerly" so we're still getting a feel for it.'

As it happened, they weren't too dreadful at all. Although Sister Wren's reedy soprano was no match for the booming alto voices of Sister Hyde, Sister Parry and Sister Sutton. Sister Parker wasn't much help, since her spectacles kept slipping down her nose, making her lose her place in the sheet music.

Sister Blake stopped playing abruptly halfway through the second chorus.

'This won't do at all,' she said. 'The altos are drowning you out, Miriam. We really need another soprano.'

'Then we will have to wait until Miss Fox comes back,' Sister Wren said, putting down her music.

'Unless Violet would like to join in?'

'Oh, no!' She and Sister Wren both spoke at the same time, both in agreement for once.

'She doesn't know the piece,' Sister Wren argued.

'Neither do we,' Sister Parker pointed out in her soft Scottish voice, the candlelight glinting off her pebble glasses. 'We only started on the music an hour ago. I'm sure Sister Tanner can pick it up.' She beamed at Violet, who shook her head.

'No, really, I'm a hopeless singer,' she protested.

'Come along, my dear. I'm sure you can't be any worse than the rest of us,' said Sister Hyde.

'But Matron sings the soprano part with me,' Sister Wren insisted stubbornly.

'Yes, but Matron isn't here, is she? And heaven knows how long she'll be. Besides, we're going to need a solo soprano for this piece, too. Perhaps Violet would like to take that part?'

'I hardly think so!' Sister Wren broke in before Violet could refuse. 'If anyone sings solo, it should be me. I have been here the longest, after all.'

Even in the dim candlelight, Violet could see the stricken faces of the other sisters as they exchanged horrified looks.

'But we need you where you are,' Sister Blake stepped in smoothly. 'You are a vital piece of the puzzle, Miriam. The glue that holds us together.'

'If you were to sing solo, we would fall to pieces completely,' Sister Parker agreed solemnly.

'Well, I can see that,' Sister Wren agreed, mollified. 'But I think if I can't do it, then Matron should sing the solo part,' she added, with a glare at Violet.

'Then that's settled,' Sister Blake said. 'Violet can sing soprano.'

Violet was about to refuse again, but looking round at the other nurses' faces, she realised defeatedly that it would be quicker just to agree and get it over with than to argue about it.

'Very well,' she sighed. 'But I warn you, I'm rather out of practice.'

'Aren't we all?' Sister Parry murmured to her with a smile as she took her place beside her.

Violet was so nervous she could hardly keep her sheet music still. But once she'd managed to get through the first few bars, it all began to come back to her. It had been so long since she'd sung, she had forgotten the sheer joy of letting the music flow out of her.

She was so carried away by it, she lost track of where she was until Sister Blake finished playing and she saw them all looking at her.

'I'm sorry.' Violet dropped her music and bent to pick it up, suddenly flustered by their attention. 'I did warn you I was out of practice...'

'Not at all. That was beautiful,' Sister Blake said admiringly.

'It was indeed.' Miss Fox stood in the doorway, her torch in her hand. How long had she been there? Violet wondered. 'Why didn't you tell us you had such a fine voice?'

Violet stared at the floor, her face burning, as the others murmured their appreciation. All the while she kept asking herself why she'd ever got herself into this situation. The last thing she'd wanted was to be singled out in any way, good or bad.

'I was just filling in for you, Matron,' she said. 'Now I'd best be going...'

'Surely you can stay a bit longer?' Miss Fox urged her, against a chorus of protests. 'We can't lose our star singer already, not when we've just found her!'

At that moment the lights flicked back on. The first thing Violet saw was Sister Wren's face, taut with resentment. 'No, really, I have a lot to do,' she muttered. 'I'm sorry...' Putting down the sheet music, she fled before they had a chance to try and change her mind.

Chapter Thirty-Two

'Here, let me help you with that.'

Dora, bending over the bathtub to scrub a mackintosh sheet, looked around in surprise at Lettie Pike, standing behind her with a brush in her hand.

'It'll be quicker with two of us,' she said.

'Thanks.'

'You don't want to be here all night, do you? Not when you're supposed to be getting off at five.'

Dora straightened up and massaged the cramped muscles in her back as Lettie set to work, scrubbing enthusiastically. If anyone had told her a week ago that Lettie Pike would even be giving her the time of day, let alone lifting a finger to help her, she would have laughed.

But a lot had changed since she'd found that box of eggs in Lettie's shopping basket. Dora had never intended to tell Sister Wren about her stealing – for all her faults, Lettie Pike was still a neighbour, and people in Griffin Street stuck by each other – but she had been so grateful she had been falling over herself to be nice to Dora ever since.

Dora wasn't sure what made her smile more: the fact that Lettie had stopped spreading gossip about her family, or watching her making such a painful effort to be pleasant.

Working together, they finished scrubbing the sheet then wiped it dry and Lettie helped drape it over a roller to finish drying. Thanks to her, Dora managed to get off duty just half an hour after she was supposed to go – a record for her, since Sister Wren inevitably managed to find her 'just one more thing' to do before she would finally release her. But luck was on her side, as Sister Parker, the Sister Tutor, was visiting the ward to check up on her students, and Sister Wren clearly didn't feel she could be her usual merciless self in front of her.

It was a fine spring evening, and the London plane trees in the centre of the courtyard were a fresh acid green in the early evening sunshine. Dora was smiling to herself as she crossed the courtyard, heading for the nurses' home to get changed. But her smile disappeared as she saw her brother Peter emerging from the Porters' Lodge, followed by Nick Riley.

Her heart jolted. Only one thing would bring Peter to the Nightingale, and that was trouble.

'Pete?' Ignoring the risk of being caught and sent to Matron, Dora hurried over to him.

He turned to face her, his freckled face splitting into a broad smile. He was only a little taller than her, strong and stocky, with the muddy green eyes and bright ginger hair they had both inherited from their father. Somehow they suited him better.

'All right, Dor? I wasn't sure if I'd see you. Nick thought you might still be on duty.' He looked her up and down. 'Look at you, in your uniform. Don't you look a picture?'

But Dora hardly heard his compliment. 'What is it, what's wrong?' The words came out in a rush, tripping over each other. 'Has something happened to Mum or Nanna?' All kinds of dreadful fears crowded into her mind. 'Oh, God, it's one of the kids, isn't it?'

'Don't get in a flap, everyone's all right. Blimey, and I thought you nurses were meant to be calm in a crisis!' He put his hands on her arms, steadying her. 'It's good news, Dor. I've got a job!'

It took a moment for his words to sink in. She stared at him uncomprehendingly. 'What? But how? Where?'

'Right here. Nick heard there was a porter's job going and put in a good word for me. I've just been to see Mr Hopkins, and he gave me the job on the spot.' Peter grinned at her.

'Oh, Pete, that's smashing news.' Dora put her hand to her racing heart. 'I'm so glad for you.'

'It means I'll be able to start paying my way again, help Mum out a bit more,' he said proudly.

Dora looked past him to where Nick stood behind them, hands thrust into his pockets, kicking at a loose cobble with the toe of his boot.

'Thank you,' she said quietly.

'I didn't do anything,' he said. 'They needed someone, that's all.' Their eyes met and held for a moment. Then he dragged his gaze away and said, 'But you'll have to keep your nose clean, Pete. Mr Hopkins don't stand for no messing about.'

'I will, don't you worry.'

'And I hope this means we won't hear any more nonsense about the Blackshirts?' Dora added.

Her brother's face darkened. 'It's not non-sense,' he muttered.

Dora caught Nick's eye. He lifted his broad shoulders in a slight shrug.

'It's good news, anyway,' she said, determined not to let anything spoil the moment.

They left Nick at the Porters' Lodge and walked as far as the gates together, being careful to stay out of sight of anyone who might report her.

'How's Mum?' Dora asked the question that had been troubling her ever since she'd last been home.

'Oh, Dor, she's not right.' Peter shook his head. 'Hasn't been the same since that bloke Joe Armstrong came round. It's proper upset her, but she won't talk about it. Just tries to act like it didn't happen. And she went mad the other day when Nanna mentioned it.'

'I don't blame her. Poor Mum.'

'I know. I should have punched that sod when I had the chance, coming round upsetting every-one with his lies like that.' Peter ground his fist into the palm of his hand.

Dora couldn't look at him. 'You really think they're lies?' she said cautiously.

'Don't you?' He frowned. 'Come off it, Dora, you know Alf as well as I do. He's a diamond, and he was devoted to Mum. Do you honestly believe a decent bloke like him would do something like that?'

The blood sang angrily in her ears, and for a split second, Dora was tempted to tell her brother exactly what kind of a 'decent' bloke Alf was. But she knew she could never burden him with that knowledge.

'If he's such a diamond, why did he walk out on us?' was all she could say.

'I don't know, do I?' Peter shrugged his shoulders. Then he added in an undertone, 'If you ask me, he's had an accident and they haven't found him yet. But don't tell Mum that, will you? I don't want her any more upset than she is already.'

'I won't.' Dora shook her head. At least she and her brother could agree on something.

She was still in a good mood when she went for supper later that evening. Even the fact that the only space left on the second years' table was between Sister Sutton at its head and her least favourite student Lucy Lane didn't dampen Dora's spirits. Neither did the heap of grey, congealed mince that was served up on her plate.

As usual, she was so hungry she ate it all, barely stopping to speak until the plate was half-empty. Across the table, Katie O'Hara did the same. Only Lucy Lane picked fastidiously at her food, her upturned nose pointed even further skyward.

'I don't understand how you can bear to eat

306

this filth.' She shuddered delicately. 'But I suppose it's a case of what you're used to,' she added, with a sly sideways glance at Dora.

Dora paused, her fork halfway to her mouth. Lucy Lane never missed a single chance to have a dig at her and where she came from. She made no secret of the fact that as far as she was concerned, only girls from well-to-do families should ever be allowed to train as nurses.

And they didn't come much more well-to-do than Lucy Lane. Her father had made a fortune with a factory making lightbulbs, and he and Lucy's mother lived in fine style somewhere in town. As their only daughter, Lucy was spoilt rotten. She was forever bragging about the latest gift her father had bought her, or the fantastic parties she had been to.

Quite why she had decided to become a nurse Dora had no idea, since she also made it clear she was quite the most brilliant student at her boarding school, with a glittering academic career at Oxford ahead of her.

Across the table, Katie O'Hara rolled her blue eyes heavenwards and went on shovelling in food. Dora smiled. At least she didn't have to share a room with Lucy, unlike poor Katie.

They really couldn't have been a more ill-matched pair, she decided. While Lucy Lane was petite and precise, Katie was all softness, with her billowing dark hair, plump figure and lilting Irish voice.

'I was mentioned in Sister Parry's ward report today,' Lucy announced loudly, to no one in particular. No one responded. They all allowed her showing off to wash over them these days. 'I had to take the children down for tonsil surgery.'

'I've done that,' O'Hara said, through a mouth full of food. 'It's horrible, isn't it? The way those poor little mites scream when they're taken in. And you're left with the others all lined up outside, waiting for their turn. It's heartbreaking, it really is.'

'You're too soft, that's your trouble,' Lucy dismissed. 'You have to take a firm hand with children. It's for their own good. Sister Parry says so.'

Dora wasn't listening. She was watching Millie further along the table. For once, she didn't seem to be interested in joining in their conversation. And she was picking at her food with even less enthusiasm than Lucy.

'Are you all right?' Dora mouthed to her.

Millie looked up and gave her a sad little smile. 'I'm fine.' But Dora knew she wasn't. She had heard her the night before, weeping quietly into her pillow in the early hours. She longed to ask her why, but sensed Millie wasn't ready to talk about it. Dora didn't like to pry.

After dinner, Katie asked Dora to come to her room to revise.

'Please,' she begged, as they filed out of the dining room. 'Otherwise I'll only be stuck with that know-all Lane, telling me how stupid I am.'

The idea didn't appeal much to Dora either. But then neither did the prospect of going back to her own room. Helen was out with Charlie, and she had the feeling Millie wanted to be by herself.

'All right,' she agreed. 'As long as she doesn't

start telling me how stupid *I* am.'

'She wouldn't dare,' Katie laughed. 'You're the only one who ever stands up to her.'

But that still didn't stop Lucy from picking on both of them as they tried to study in the bedroom.

'What are the main complications you should watch for after a mastoid operation?' Katie sat cross-legged on the floor with her heavy copy of The Complete System of Nursing open on her knees. Dora sat on the bed opposite, staring at the ceiling as she tried to think.

'Let me see ... erratic temperature or sudden fall in temperature ... abnormally slow pulse ... squint or double vision ... drowsiness, pain, facial paralysis, rigors – and delirium,' she finished triumphantly.

'Very good.'

'You forgot vomiting,' drawled Lucy Lane. She was sitting on her bed, pretending to look out of the window. 'Vomiting not associated with the administration of food,' she added, with a smug smile at Dora.

'Why don't you revise with us?' Katie suggested.

'No, thanks. I already know all this.'

'You could help us?' Dora said.

'Why should I?'

They eyed each other coldly across the room. It rankled with Lucy that Dora regularly did better than her in tests, and had been mentioned favourably in ward reports too. Dora was only concerned with doing her best, but Lucy saw everything in her life as a competition.

'I'm too tired to study anyway.' Katie stifled a yawn.

'We have to carry on,' Dora said. 'Mr Wittard the ENT consultant is doing the lecture tomorrow. We need to know all this stuff before then.'

'You should have started revising a lot earlier then, shouldn't you?' Lucy pointed out primly. They both glared at her. The fact that she was right didn't make her any less obnoxious.

'They can't expect us to pick up our books after fourteen hours on the ward,' Katie complained. 'It's inhuman, that's what it is.'

'And we have to give up our one free afternoon to go to this lecture,' Dora reminded her.

'Why did I ever want to be a nurse?' Katie groaned.

'Because you didn't have any choice?'

'True. My ma would have disowned me in shame if I hadn't.' Katie was the second youngest of five sisters. The three eldest had all come over from their little village in the west of Ireland to train at the Nightingale, and Katie had been expected to do the same.

Suddenly Lucy sat up straighter and pressed her nose to the glass. 'I say, there's a man outside.'

'Where?' Katie scrambled on to Lucy's bed to get a better look. 'I can't see him. Where is he?'

'He was standing right by the steps a moment ago, but now he's disappeared into the shadow of the hedge. He'll pop out again in a minute ... oh, do stop shoving, O'Hara, you'll be through the window in a minute... There, look! Now do you see him?'

'Ooh, yes.' Katie gave a little squeal of excitement. 'I wonder what he wants?'

'He keeps looking up at the windows. I bet he's waiting for someone.'

'Maybe they're planning to elope?'

'Don't be ridiculous,' Lucy dismissed this. 'Why does everything have to be so dramatic with you? You've been reading those silly romances in *Peg's Paper* again, haven't you?'

'Well, he's definitely waiting for something,' Katie defended herself. 'And it must be important if he's prepared to risk coming here. If Sister Sutton catches him...'

'I don't suppose he has any idea he's stepped into the lair of a fire-breathing dragon!'

'Let's have a look.' Dora put down her books and went over to the window. She saw the tall broad-shouldered figure sheltering under the lamp post, caught the glint of fair hair in the lamplight, and felt a jolt of recognition.

'Joe?' She said his name without thinking. Katie and Lucy both swung round to face her at the same time, one excited, the other incredulous.

'You know him?' Lucy snapped.

Katie looked impressed. 'Is he your boyfriend?'

'No, he's just – someone I know,' said Dora.

'What's he doing out there?'

'Maybe he's come to declare his undying love?' Katie suggested.

Lucy's lip curled. 'Don't be stupid!'

'I'd better go and find out, hadn't I?'

'At this time of night?'

As if to prove the point, Sister Sutton's voice suddenly boomed out from the passageway,

'Lights out in fifteen minutes, Nurses.'

'She's right,' Katie said breathlessly. 'Sister Sutton will have your guts for garters if she catches you sneaking out to meet a man.'

'For heaven's sake, you make it sound like a lovers' tryst. I'll only be five minutes.' Dora opened the door a fraction and peered out. 'Sister Sutton's going upstairs. I'll slip out now, before she comes back down.'

'You'll be in trouble if you get caught.'

'Then I'll just have to make sure she doesn't catch me. Cover for me, won't you?'

'Don't worry, we won't say anything. Will we, Lucy?' Katie sent her a meaningful look. Lucy stayed silent, tight-lipped with disapproval.

Dora paused in the hall, listening for the sound of Sister Sutton's heavy tread on the landing above her head. Then she scurried down the passageway and let herself quietly out of the front door.

By the time she'd reached the stone steps of the nurses' home, there was no sign of him. She began to think she was imagining things as she scanned the darkness.

'Joe?' she whispered. 'Are you there?'

He stepped out of the dense shadow of an over-grown hedge. In the dim lamplight, she could see the relief written all over his face. 'Thank God it's you. I wasn't sure what to do ... I was going to knock but then I saw this big woman coming towards me and I just hid.'

'Just as well. If Sister Sutton had found you, we would both have been for it.' Dora shivered in the cool evening air. 'What are you doing here anyway? Look, if it's about Alf, I told you I'd let you know if I heard...'

'It isn't. I came because I need your help. It's our Jennie.'

'What's wrong with her?'

Joe's expression was grim. 'You'd better come and see for yourself. But I warn you, it's bad.'

Chapter Thirty-Three

Jennie sat huddled on a bench outside Victoria Park. As they approached, she turned her head to look at them. Dora caught her first glimpse of the girl's face, and let out a cry of shock.

'You see? I told you it was bad,' Joe said grimly.

She was barely recognisable. Under the harsh greenish lamplight, her face was a distorted, bloated mass of livid bruises. Congealed blood was crusted around her puffy lips, and tears oozed slowly from swollen, purple eyes.

Dora felt sick just looking at her. 'Who did this?'

'Dad found out about the baby.' Joe's voice was flat. 'I came home an hour ago and she was like this.'

'Poor lamb.' Dora crouched down in front of the girl and reached up to stroke a lock of hair off her face. It was matted with dried blood. Jennie was so badly beaten it was hard to know where the blood had come from. 'We need to get her to the hospital.'

'No!' Jennie managed to say the word through stiff, swollen lips. She clutched at Dora's hand.

'We thought maybe you could clean her up?' Joe asked quietly.

'But she could have broken bones, a cracked rib, or anything.' Dora stared at them helplessly. 'She needs proper medical treatment, more than I can give her.'

Jennie squeezed hard on Dora's hand. 'No hospital... Dad...' Her eyes were barely more than slits in her puffy face, but Dora could still read the panic in them.

'She doesn't want to get him into trouble,' Joe translated for her.

'He deserves it, after what he's done.' Dora took out her handkerchief and dabbed gently at a spot of blood oozing from the girl's temple. 'So if I can't get her to hospital, what do you expect me to do?' she asked. 'I can't tend to her here in the middle of the street, can I?'

'I – don't know,' Joe admitted. 'When I found her like this, all I could think about was getting her to you. I don't know what I expected, I just thought you could help...'

Dora read the appeal in his face, and made up her mind.

'I know somewhere we can take her,' she said.

It was well after ten and there was no one about in Griffin Street when Dora unlatched the tall wooden gate that led into the backyard of number twenty-eight.

The lights were on downstairs, casting a welcome glow across the cracked flagstones as they crept across the yard. Inside the kitchen, Dora could see Nanna Winnie rocking in her chair to one side of the fire, while her mother had her head down over her mending on the other. Josie sat reading at the kitchen table, elbows propped up, lost in a book as usual.

'Are you sure this is all right?' Joe whispered. He stood behind her, Jennie leaning heavily against him.

'I don't know.' Dora looked back at him, then at Jennie. 'But what choice do we have?'

Her family looked up as she walked in.

'Dora?' Her mother put down her mending and stood up, smiling but confused. 'Are you all right, love? Why–' She froze when she saw Joe standing in the doorway. 'What's he doing here?' she said in a stone-cold voice.

'We need your help, Mum.' Dora nodded to Joe, who carried Jennie into the kitchen. As he released her to close the door behind him, the girl's legs crumpled from under her.

Dora went to catch her, but her mother got there first.

'Help me get her into a chair,' she ordered Joe. He stepped forward and scooped his sister up into his arms like a child, carrying her over to the fireside. Rose cleared the mending from her chair and Joe placed his sister down in it carefully.

'Josie, go and put the kettle on. Mum, do we still have any brandy? She looks like she could do with a nip.'

When they'd both gone off on their respective errands, Rose turned to Dora. 'Are you going to tell me what's going on?'

She glanced at Joe. 'Jennie's dad found out

about the baby.'

'And he did this to her?' Rose stared back at the girl.

Dora saw her mother's faraway expression, and suddenly realised how hard it must be for her to face Alf's other woman. 'I'm sorry, Mum,' she said. 'I shouldn't have come here, but I just panicked. We had nowhere else to take her. She was too frightened to go to hospital, and she couldn't stay at home—'

'You did the right thing,' her mother said firmly. She turned back to face Dora, her smile fixed in place. 'We'd better set about cleaning her up, hadn't we?'

'Take her into my room,' Nanna said.

Together, they helped Jennie into the front parlour where Nanna slept, and carefully took off her clothes. Her body was as badly bruised as her face, with livid purplish-black blotches covering her back, stomach and legs. But, amazingly, Dora couldn't find any broken bones.

'He really put the boot in, didn't he, love?' she said sympathetically, as she wrung out a cloth in the basin of warm water Josie had brought her. 'Not to worry, we'll soon have you feeling better.' She glanced at her mother. Rose was standing by the bed, one hand to her mouth, her whole face creased with anxiety.

It took a long time to wash off all the dried blood. Dora cleaned Jennie's wounds as best she could, then put her into one of Josie's old nightgowns and got her into bed. The girl fell into a deep sleep almost immediately.

'I'm not surprised, after what she's been

through,' Rose said. 'Nanna can sleep in with me tonight, let her have this room to herself.' She stared down at Jennie. Even cleaned up, she still looked a mess, her face a distorted patchwork of purple, red and indigo. 'How could anyone do that to their own child?' she said wonderingly.

'I dunno, Mum.'

Rose was silent for a long time, her eyes fixed on the sleeping girl. 'So this is her, is it?' she said at last. 'She looks so young.'

'She's seventeen.'

'Is that all?' Rose's brow creased. 'That's only a couple of years older than our Josie.' She put her hands up to her face. 'Imagine if that was your little sister lying there, going through everything she's gone through. It doesn't bear thinking about, does it?'

'No, it doesn't.' It might have been, Dora thought. It was only by the grace of God that neither she nor Josie had fallen pregnant by Alf. She shuddered to think about what would have happened then.

'And she got rid of it ... the baby?' Rose asked.

Dora nodded. 'Left her in a right mess, it did. She nearly died. The doctors had to perform a hysterectomy to save her life.'

Rose frowned, trying to understand. 'So she won't have any more babies?' She bit her lip. 'That's so cruel. Poor, poor kid. It makes you wonder what they're thinking, doesn't it? Going to places like that.'

'She was desperate, Mum. You saw what her dad did to her. God only knows what he would have done if she'd still been pregnant. And with

Alf – I mean, the father – doing a runner like that, what choice did she have?'

She waited for her mother to respond, but Rose was silent. Dora glanced across at her, trying to read the thoughts behind her impassive expression, but it was impossible.

They left Jennie sleeping and went back downstairs. Joe, who had been standing uncertainly by the back door, stepped forward eagerly.

'How is she?'

'She'll be all right. No bones broken, just a lot of bad bruising.'

Joe let out a sigh of relief. 'Thank God.'

'She'll need plenty of rest, though.'

'She can stay here,' Rose said. 'We'll make room for her somewhere.'

'Thank you,' Joe said humbly.

Rose shot him a sharp look. 'That doesn't mean I believe a word she says. I still think she's lying about my Alf. I know he wouldn't do anything like that. But she's a child, and she needs help. I don't turn my back on anyone.'

Joe nodded. 'I understand. Thank you, anyway.'

It had started to rain as Dora headed back to the hospital. Joe insisted on walking with her, even though she'd told him there was no need.

'I want to,' he said. 'It's the least I can do, after everything you've done for Jennie.' He took off his jacket and draped it around Dora's shoulders. The warmth of his body seeped into her chilled bones.

'I thought your mum was going to slam the door in our faces,' he admitted, as they trudged back along the darkened streets past Victoria

Park. The shadowy shapes of trees loomed up at them on the other side of the railings.

'You don't know my mum,' Dora told him. 'She'd never turn away anyone in trouble.'

'You must take after her, then?' Joe smiled at her. Dora felt herself blushing in the darkness.

'I don't know about that,' she mumbled.

'I do. You didn't have to help us. You risked getting yourself into trouble, and I'm grateful for that. More than grateful.'

She felt him reach for her hand in the darkness and panicked, stuffing them both in her pockets on the pretence of keeping them warm.

'It's a shame Jennie doesn't have a mum looking out for her,' she said, changing the subject.

'I know, I've often thought that myself. I wonder if Dad might not have been so – over-protective.'

'You call that over-protective?' Dora couldn't keep the scorn out of her voice. 'I don't call half killing someone being over-protective. I call it being a brute!'

'So do I, after what he did to her tonight,' Joe said heavily. 'He's always led Jennie a dog's life. When she hasn't been working all hours, she's been stuck in the house, looking after us. And God help her if she tried to get out and make friends, have a bit of fun.' His mouth was a taut line. 'I wish I'd done more to help her,' he said. 'Maybe if I'd taken an interest, persuaded Dad to let her have a bit of freedom, she wouldn't have fallen for the first bloke to pay her some attention.'

'You mustn't blame yourself.'

'Who else is to blame? I should have been there, protected her from my dad–'

'And Alf Doyle,' Dora reminded him.

He looked at her carefully. 'You don't think much of your stepdad, do you?'

'Not really.'

'Why? Was he a bully too?'

'No, he was cleverer than that. Everyone thought he was the salt of the earth. A really good bloke,' she said bitterly.

'So why didn't you like him?'

'Let's just say, I could see right through him.'

'I wish I could get hold of him now,' Joe muttered.

So do I, Dora thought.

They stopped a few yards short of the hospital gates, and Dora handed him his jacket back. 'Best not come any further than this, someone might see you,' she said.

'How will you get in?'

'Never you mind!' She smiled, tapping the side of her nose.

As she walked away, he called after her, 'What shall I do about Jennie? Would it be all right to call on her tomorrow, do you think?'

'Of course. Call whenever you like.'

'Will you be there?'

She grinned. 'What's the matter? Don't tell me you're scared of my mum?'

'I dunno about your mum, but I wouldn't reckon my chances against that nan of yours!' He looked at her appealingly. 'Please? It's easier when you're there.'

'I don't know when I'll be allowed to go off duty tomorrow, but I'll visit as soon as I can,' she promised.

As she tiptoed through the gates, he called after her, 'I'll see you tomorrow, then?'

'Shh! You'll get me caught.' Dora held a warning finger to her lips. But as she turned around again, she saw a figure watching her from the window of the Porters' Lodge. Her heart leapt into her mouth, until she realised it was only Nick.

Thank heavens for that, she thought, giving him a little wave as she crept past. If it had been Mr Hopkins she would have been in real trouble.

Sister Wren woke up in a bad mood.

Not even the spring sunshine outside, nor the cheery greeting of the maid bringing her breakfast in bed, could make her feel any better about what had happened at their second choir practice the previous night. Even her dreams had been tormented by Violet Tanner's perfect soprano solo to 'Blow the Wind Southerly'.

It wasn't that Sister Wren was jealous. As she would tell anyone who listened, she didn't have a jealous bone in her body. But it was rather much to find oneself so utterly usurped. And by someone whose vocal range was limited, to say the least.

Not that the other sisters saw it that way. In the space of a week, Violet Tanner had become a firm favourite in the choir, with everyone wondering how they'd ever managed without her.

And then last night... It wasn't that Sister Wren wanted to push herself forward, not at all. But if Matron were suddenly going to decide that she didn't want to sing solo any more, then surely it would have been fair to offer the chance to the person who had been there the longest? Especially since she knew the part back to front.

But no, the minute Miss Fox had stepped aside, they had all clamoured around Violet Tanner, practically begging her to take the part.

Violet had made a big pretence of being modest, saying she didn't want to do it. But Sister Wren wasn't fooled for a moment.

'And how is she going to attend rehearsals, when she is on duty every evening?' she'd pointed out.

'Oh, well, that's easy. We'll just have to squeeze other rehearsals in during the day, when some of us are free,' Sister Blake had replied, in that breezy way of hers. And then they'd planned their next rehearsal for the following Tuesday, knowing full well that Sister Wren would be busy with Mr Cooper's ward round that day.

'Lovely morning, Sister.'

Sister Wren flinched as the maid yanked the curtains wide. 'Must you make so much noise?' she snapped. 'I have a headache.'

She massaged her temples delicately. Her resentment of Violet Tanner was like a tight hatband, constricting her head until she felt it would explode.

And of course, Violet had to be the first person she met when she arrived on duty that morning. She almost bumped into Sister Wren as she emerged from a side room, fastening her cuffs back in place. Doyle followed her out, pushing a trolley laden with towels, soap, and a basin of water.

'Good morning, Sister.' Violet smiled a greeting. Sister Wren didn't smile back.

'What were you doing in there?' she demanded.

'One of Mr Cooper's private patients was admitted early this morning. He is operating later and she needed to be prepared. And since your staff nurse was busy, I offered to help supervise the student.'

Sister Wren stiffened, sensing a criticism. 'Might I remind you, Sister, that this is my ward?' she said, drawing herself upright.

'Yes, of course, but–'

'Surely, then, you shouldn't be interfering unless I ask you to do so?'

'Actually, *I* asked her.'

James Cooper came out of the private room, shrugging on his jacket.

'Mr Cooper! I didn't realise you were there.' Flustered, Sister Wren put up her hand to primp her hair.

'I asked Miss Tanner to stay and assist me, and she very kindly agreed. I hope you don't mind?' He raised an eyebrow.

'No, not at all.' Sister Wren felt the heat rising in her face and struggled to compose herself. 'I'm very pleased Miss Tanner was able to step in,' she added, with a tight smile in Violet's direction.

'So am I.' The smile Mr Cooper gave Violet was a lot warmer than the one he'd given her, Sister Wren noticed.

Mr Cooper left the ward, and Sister Wren expected Violet to do the same. But she lingered, hesitating, as if trying to make up her mind whether to speak.

'Was there something else you wanted?' Sister Wren asked.

'Yes, there was.' She took a deep breath and said, 'It's about last night. That business with the solo...'

Sister Wren sent her a chilly look. 'What about it?'

'I just wanted you to understand it was nothing to do with me. I don't even want to do it. I would be glad to step aside for you.' Her face pleaded for understanding, but Sister Wren knew it was all pretence. Just like everything else about her.

'Oh, no, it's quite all right. I'm sure the other sisters wouldn't hear of it,' she dismissed this with a taut little laugh.

'Yes, but–'

'I assure you, I am not in the least upset about it.' She could hear her own voice growing shrill. 'I'm hardly going to throw myself into a sulk over a silly little choral piece, am I?'

Violet sent her a long, doubting look. 'Well, if you're certain?'

'Please don't give it another thought. I'm sure I shan't.'

She watched Violet walk away down the passage-way. As she reached the doors, James Cooper stepped out and opened them for her. Had he been waiting for her? Sister Wren wondered. She strained her ears to try to catch what they were saying, but all she heard was Violet Tanner's deep, husky laugh. The sound made her shudder, like nails drawn down a blackboard.

Sister Wren burnt with inner rage. Mr Cooper had never laughed like that with her, or inclined

324

his head so close to hers.

She fumed her way through the morning's duties, checking patients, linens, kitchen cutlery, and everything else that needed counting and ticking off. She handed out work lists and medicines, supervised cleaning and re-cleaning, and criticised the students' efforts at changing dressings, taking pulses and making beds.

And all the time a plan was fermenting in her head. A plan that she was sure would put a stop to Violet Tanner's reign at the Nightingale for ever.

Sister Wren couldn't make such a personal call from the telephone on her desk in the middle of the ward so she had to wait until the middle of the morning, when she could escape to the pay telephone in the main hall of the hospital.

Frustratingly, there was someone using it when she got there. A tearful young man was giving someone a blow by blow account of his wife's tedious labour and delivery. Sister Wren tapped her foot on the mosaic-tiled floor and ostentatiously checked her watch as the hustle and bustle of hospital life went on around them. But all the time, her thoughts were in turmoil. Was this such a good idea? she wondered. Yes, she was angry, but she had the feeling that once she made this call she would be letting a genie out of the bottle that might destroy someone's life.

You don't know that, she told herself impatiently, as the young man explained in a choked voice how he'd held his son for the first time. The solicitor's message could bring good news. Perhaps someone had died and left Violet a lot of money. She might even be thankful for the intervention if she turned out to be heiress to a secret fortune.

But deep down Sister Wren knew that there would be no fortune, no mysterious benefactor. There was something deep, dark and shadowy about that message, and all the others that had followed it in the newspaper every day since: 'Would Violet Dangerfield, née Tanner, please contact immediately the office of Burrows, Burrows & Edgerton, Solicitors, 59 High Holborn, London WC2. Telephone Kingsway 4773'. It wasn't a request. It was a demand.

She felt her nerve failing, and was just about to walk away when a voice behind her said, 'Excuse me? Miss?'

Sister Wren turned around. The young man had ended his call and was holding the receiver out to her.

'Do you want to make a call?' he asked.

Sister Wren looked from the telephone to him and back again. Then she thought about Violet, her perfect soprano voice and her husky laugh.

'Yes,' she said. 'Yes, I think I do.'

Chapter Thirty-Four

Being given the afternoon duty wasn't a favourite with the students. They still had to get up and report to the ward by seven o'clock, only to be told by Sister at nine to go away, change out of

326

their uniform and not report back until midday. And then they had to face nine hours on their feet without a break.

But for once Dora was hoping for the afternoon shift so she could get back to Griffin Street first thing and make sure Jennie was all right. She stood with the other nurses, trying not to catch Sister Wren's eye in case she read the desperation in her face and changed her duty out of spite. Luckily, Sister Wren seemed to have her mind on other things that morning, and handed out the off duty times in a quick, random fashion. As the other nurses went back to work, Dora rushed back to the nurses' home, changed out of her uniform, slung on her old brown coat and beret, and made her way to Griffin Street, breaking into a run as soon as she was out of the hospital gates.

In spite of what she'd said to Joe, she was worried. She knew her mother was a good, caring woman, but surely Dora had pushed her too far by bringing Jennie into the house? Last night she had been panicking too much to think of anything else, but now, in the cold light of a March morning, she realised she'd made a dreadful mistake.

Nanna Winnie was sweeping the yard when Dora came bursting through the gate. Little Alfie was with her, pulling up the weeds that grew between the cracks in the paving slabs.

'All right, love. Where's the fire?' she said, as Dora fought to get her breath back.

'Where's Mum?'

'Inside.' Nanna jerked her head in the direction of the house. 'With *her*.'

Dora felt her blood drain to her boots. 'What

are they doing?'

'Having a chat, so Rose says. Although I'm not allowed a listen, even though it's still my house.' Nanna's face was sullen as she pushed the broom viciously into the privy.

Dora glanced up at the window, as if she almost expected to see fists flying. 'I'd better go and see what's going on.'

'I wouldn't bother, you won't be welcome. Why do you think I'm out here, even though this cold weather is playing merry hell with my lumbago?' Nanna banged the privy door shut so hard it rattled on its rusty hinges. 'I dunno why you brought that one here, Dora,' she called after her as she headed into the house. 'Don't you think we've had enough trouble lately?'

Dora reached the top of the stairs just as her mother burst out of Jennie's room. Dora took one look at her, white-faced and trembling, and her heart sank.

'Mum?' she ventured.

Rose stared at her, her dark eyes glittering in her ashen face. Then she pushed past her and stormed upstairs to her own room, slamming the door behind her.

Dora climbed the stairs and dithered on the landing for a moment, looking from Jennie's door to her mother's, then made up her mind.

'Mum?' She pushed open the door cautiously. Rose was standing in front of the chest of drawers, pulling things out and flinging them on to the bed. 'Mum, are you all right? Nanna said you'd talked to Jennie–'

'Oh, I've talked to her, all right.' Impatiently,

Rose yanked out one of the heavy drawers and, struggling under its weight, tipped it out on to the bed.

Dora looked at the pile of clothes. They were Alf's things, the clothes he'd left behind when he disappeared.

'Mum, what are you doing?' she asked faintly.

'Something I should have done a long time ago.' Rose swung round to look at her, a strange, half-mad grimace on her face. 'Help me get this lot downstairs, will you?'

Dora obeyed, sweeping up an armful of clothes. Alf's sickeningly familiar smell stopped her in her tracks. She paused for a moment, her head spinning, fighting the urge to retch.

By the time she got downstairs, her mother was out in the yard, pulling bits of wood from the pile behind the privy. Nanna leant on her broom by the back door, watching her. Even Little Alfie had stopped plucking weeds to stare.

'What's Mum doing?' he piped up.

'God knows, mate.' Nanna sighed and shook her head. 'But I do know it's taken us weeks to collect that scrap wood.'

'She's building a bonfire,' Dora realised. 'Of Alf's things.'

Nanna stared at her, then at Rose. 'Is that right, Rosie? What's happened?'

'I'll tell you what's happened, shall I?' Rose hauled a piece of rotted railway sleeper on to the heap. 'I've come to my senses, that's what. Finally realised what a mug I've been all these years.' She straightened up, wiping her face. 'Since he went I've been waiting for him to come home, worrying about him, thinking all kinds of terrible things had happened… The sleepless nights I've had, wondering what's happened to my poor Alf!'

She looked up at them, her eyes glittering dangerously. There was a streak of dirt across her nose. 'And do you know what? He wasn't even worth worrying about. All these years we've been so-called happily married, he's been lying to me.'

Dora glanced back at the house. 'You believe Jennie's story, then?'

'Oh, I believe her, all right! Everything she told me was the God's honest truth – unlike that worthless good-for-nothing I was married to!'

Dora and Nanna exchanged a worried look as Rose bent down and hauled the wood into place.

'When I think of how much I trusted him,' Rose went on, her chest heaving. 'And all the time he was taking advantage of a young girl like that! I don't even want to think about what else he might have been getting up to behind my back.'

'Me neither.' Dora suppressed a shudder.

'Anyway, I've had enough,' her mother went on, bending to pick up another piece of wood. 'I'm finally getting rid of him, saying goodbye to that lying, conniving sod for ever. And good riddance to him!' She tossed a broken chair leg defiantly on to the pile.

Nanna looked horrified. 'You can't be serious?'

'I've never been more serious in my life, believe me. I want rid of him, Mum. I don't want to see anything of his in this house ever again.'

'Oh, I'm not arguing with that, love,' Nanna said. 'But you can't burn it.' She looked at the pile of clothes Dora was holding in her arms. 'The rag and bone man will give you a few bob for that lot.'

Dora glanced at her mother. Rose stood there, hands on her hips, her mouth set in a hard, determined line.

And then Dora saw the warmth slowly kindling in her dark eyes, followed by a reluctant smile. 'Oh, Mum!' she said, shaking her head. 'Trust you!'

'What?' Nanna looked from one to the other, genuinely bewildered. 'It's only common sense, ain't it? I mean, after all that rotten sod's done to this family, we might as well get a fish supper out of him. He's not worth wasting all that wood on either,' she added grumpily.

Dora and her mother looked at each other. A moment later, the backyards of Griffin Street rang with their laughter.

Chapter Thirty-Five

The offices of Burrows, Burrows & Edgerton smelt of old books and polished leather. Sister Wren felt most important as she sipped tea from a bone china cup, while the portraits of esteemed old lawyers in wing collars gazed down at her approvingly.

'I understand you have some information for us, Miss Trott?'

It was Mr Edgerton himself, no less, who sat on

the other side of the heavy mahogany desk. Sister Wren was gratified that it was a senior partner interviewing her, and not some lowly junior clerk. Clearly what she had to say was of greater importance than she'd imagined.

She paused, savouring the moment. She was enjoying the fact that the lawyer was paying her such attention, listening avidly to her every word. She could have told him what he wanted to know on the telephone, but it was so much more exciting to be here, to feel part of all the intrigue.

Because there *was* intrigue, she was certain of that. And Sister Wren wasn't going to leave until she found out all the details.

'Well, yes,' she said, toying demurely with the fingertip of her glove. 'But first I have a question for you. Why do you want to know about Violet Tanner?'

Mr Edgerton's smile grew chilly. 'I am afraid I am not at liberty to discuss it, Miss Trott,' he said stiffly. 'That is a confidential matter between my client and – the person in question.'

Sister Wren pursed her lips. She might have known he would make some difficulty. Solicitors were always so annoyingly discreet.

'Then I am not at liberty to give you the information you need.' She stood up. 'I am sorry to have wasted your time.'

'Wait.' Mr Edgerton regarded her thoughtfully over steepled fingers. 'Perhaps it would help overcome your – qualms – if you met my client?' he suggested.

Sister Wren almost squeaked with excitement. 'Indeed it would,' she said eagerly, glancing at the door. 'Is he here?'

'She is due here shortly.'

A woman! Sister Wren was even more intrigued as Mr Edgerton went outside to speak to his secretary. Who would it be? she wondered. An estranged mother or sister? A wronged friend, perhaps?

All kinds of theories were still crossing her mind five minutes later when the door opened and Mr Edgerton ushered his client in.

She was in her fifties, tall, grey-haired and severe-looking. Sister Wren did her usual critical glance, noting the cut of her black coat, good quality but at least twenty years out of date, and the polished leather of her shoes. Under the veil of the hat, she could make out a long face, with a pinched mouth, hooked nose and pale, prominent eyes.

'May I introduce my client, Mrs Sherman,' said Mr Edgerton in a hushed, respectful voice, ushering her to a seat. 'Mrs Sherman, this is Miss Trott. She has information about Violet.'

Sister Wren was instantly impressed, but Mrs Sherman barely acknowledged her as she arranged herself in her chair.

'Well?' she addressed Mr Edgerton bluntly. 'Do you know where she is?'

The solicitor looked discomfited. 'Mrs Sherman, I am afraid Miss Trott has some questions first.'

Mrs Sherman snapped round to look at Sister Wren for the first time. She felt her confidence wilting under the force of the pale, penetrating stare. But she forced herself to stay resolved. 'You must understand, Violet is a friend of mine,' she said with a simper. 'I could not think of doing anything that might put her at any risk.'

'If she's such a friend, I wonder why you would even come here in the first place?' Mrs Sherman retorted. 'Unless you thought there might be some financial reward in it for you?'

'I – the thought never occurred to me!' Sister Wren spluttered in outrage. 'I merely wanted to satisfy myself that nothing untoward would happen to Violet–'

'Really?' Mrs Sherman's mouth curled. 'Your concern is touching. And completely misplaced, I'm afraid. Violet hardly merits anyone's concern.'

'Really? And why would you say that?'

'Because I know her!' Mrs Sherman shook with the vehemence of her reply. 'I have had the misfortune of her acquaintance for some years, and I must tell you that she is quite the most heartless, dishonest and calculating woman I have ever met.'

She saw Sister Wren's expression of dismay, and seemed to collect herself. 'You must excuse me,' she said quietly. 'It is simply that I have seen the havoc that woman has wrought over the years, the cruelty she has shown to people close to her.'

Sister Wren frowned at her. 'Who are you?'

Mrs Sherman met her gaze steadily. 'I represent Victor Dangerfield. Violet's husband.'

'You mean, her deceased husband?'

'Is that what she told you?' Mrs Sherman smiled faintly. 'Then I have to inform you, Mr Dangerfield is very much alive.'

A thrill ran through Sister Wren. This had been

worth the bus fare from Bethnal Green after all. 'She is still married then?'

Mrs Sherman nodded. 'As far as he is concerned, certainly. He has never given up hope of her returning to him, despite the fact that she abandoned him five years ago, taking his only son with her.' Her mouth firmed. 'How that man could possibly go on loving her after the pain she has put him through, I simply do not know. But there you are. Such are the ways of the heart, I suppose.'

'She told us all she was a widow,' Sister Wren said.

'You see how she deceives? All the poor man has ever done is love her, and this is how she treats him.' The woman shook her head. 'Even now, he only wants her to be happy. If she wishes to live apart from him, that is for her to decide. All he wants is to be allowed to see his son.'

She looked hard at Sister Wren, trapping her in the full force of her stare. 'That's why I'm appealing to you, for his sake,' she said, her voice hoarse. 'If you know where Violet is, you must tell me. For Oliver's sake, if nothing else. A boy needs his father, don't you think?'

Sister Wren looked into her pale, strange eyes. She couldn't warm to Mrs Sherman, but she wasn't surprised by anything she had said. Violet struck her as the selfish, unfeeling type. Hadn't she tried to warn the other sisters, right from the start? But none of them had listened to her.

Well, they would listen to her now, she thought.

'I don't care what anyone says. She's not going

335

back to that house.'

Defiance flashed in Rose Doyle's dark eyes as she hauled a sheet out of the dolly tub. Dora had been given another afternoon shift, so she'd gone to visit and help with the Monday morning wash.

'Are you sure about this, Mum?' Dora chewed her lip worriedly. As Nanna Winnie would say, it was a rum state of affairs. Who would ever have imagined that Rose Doyle would become so protective over the girl who had got pregnant by her own husband?

'Sure as I've ever been about anything.' Rose fed the sheet through the rollers of the mangle. 'The poor kid's terrified, and no wonder. No, I've made up my mind. She's staying with us.'

Dora rested her weight against the handle of the mangle until it started to turn. 'But after what happened with her and Alf...'

'I don't blame Jennie for that,' Rose dismissed. 'How could I? She was just a kid. She didn't even know he was married. No, she did nothing wrong, in my eyes. If anyone's to blame, it's that swine.'

Dora stared at her mother, lost in admiration. Rose Doyle's big, forgiving heart never ceased to amaze her.

'What does Jennie have to say about it?' she asked, as she helped her mother haul the sheet clear of the mangle and over to the washing line.

'She doesn't want to go back, why would she? She's happy here. She's settled in nicely in the past week, and the kids all love her. She pays her way, too, so it's not like we have an extra mouth to feed. It feels as if she's part of the family already.'

Dora felt a slight stab of jealousy at the thought of Jennie Armstrong taking her place, being a big sister to Josie, Bea and Little Alfie, and helping Nanna Winnie around the house. But at the same time, she couldn't resent her for it. The girl had had a hard enough life, growing up without a mum and with her brute of a father. She deserved a chance.

Besides, she'd brought a lot of happiness back to the Doyle family. It was as if finding out the ghastly truth about her husband had liberated Rose. Now she could see Alf for what he really was, she no longer pined for him. There was no longer a place set for him at the dinner table – in fact, his name was never even mentioned.

And with Peter working as a porter at the hospital, and Jennie bringing in an extra wage, the family was finally finding its feet financially as well.

'What about the neighbours? I expect Lettie Pike will have something to say about it.'

'Lettie Pike can go to hell.'

As if on cue, there was a rustling from next door's yard. Rose winked at Dora.

'Did you hear that, Lettie?' she called out.

A moment later Lettie Pike appeared sheepishly from the privy. 'I can't help it if I had to go, could I?' she said huffily. 'I've got better things to do than listen to you, Rose Doyle!'

Rose watched her go back into her house and slam the back door. 'She's been in there for half an hour.'

'Maybe I should offer her an enema?' Dora suggested.

'I'd like to see that!'

They were still laughing as they wrestled the wet sheet over the line to peg it in place. The March wind caught it, lifting it like a sail and flapping it wetly back in Dora's face.

She spluttered, still laughing, and pushed it to one side – then let out a scream when she saw a man standing in front of her.

'Sorry, did I give you a shock?' Joe Armstrong grinned at her. He was dressed in his uniform, all polished shoes and shiny gilt buttons. His helmet was tucked under his arm.

'Just a bit.' Dora pushed her curls back off her face, suddenly conscious of what a mess she must look in her scruffy old wash-day clothes.

'I just thought I'd call round to see how our Jennie was doing.' He glanced at the house. 'Although I suppose she must be at work?'

'You suppose right.' Rose came round from the other side of the sheet to confront him, her hands on her hips. Even Joe, towering policeman that he was, regarded her warily.

'How is she?' he asked.

'She's doing all right, thank you,' Dora said. 'Now the cuts have healed and the swellings have gone down.'

'That's a relief.' Joe stared at the ground. 'Sorry I haven't been round more often this week, but I've been working overtime.'

'That's all right, son,' Rose replied, her voice losing some of its sharpness. 'But your sister's not safe to be left with your brute of a father, and that's a fact. That's why I want her to stay here, with us.'

He looked at her and for a moment Dora was worried he was going to argue, but then she saw the hope that lit up his green eyes.

'Really? You'd do that for Jen?' he said.

'We'd love to have her, we really would.'

He smiled. 'It would be a weight off my mind if I knew she was safe.'

'Then that's settled.' Rose beamed at him. 'And I reckon I owe you an apology too, son,' she added. 'I know I haven't been too welcoming in the past.'

'That's all right.' Joe looked sheepish. 'You get used to not being welcome, in my job.'

'I should think you do.' Rose dried her hands on her apron. 'Can I offer you a cup of tea, just to show there's no hard feelings?'

'Sorry, Missus, I can't stop. I'd be for it if my sergeant caught me supping tea when I'm meant to be on the beat.'

'Maybe next time then. You'll have to call round and see your sister again.'

'I will.'

He was staring at Dora as he said it. Rose looked from one to the other, then gave a funny little smile and said, 'Right, I'll leave you to it.'

Joe waited until the back door had closed behind her before he spoke to Dora. 'As a matter of fact, it wasn't just Jennie I came to see. I was hoping you'd be here.'

'Why?' She felt the colour drain from her face and knew she'd gone as white as the sheet she was pegging out. 'Don't tell me you've found Alf?'

'What? No,' he dismissed. 'I'm still looking, but I don't imagine he'll turn up any day soon.'

339

Then, just as she was letting out a sigh of relief, he added, 'No, I came to ask if you'd like these?'

He reached into his pocket and pulled out a handful of tickets. 'The lads at the station and the local fire brigade are having a dance at the Town Hall on Saturday. As you can imagine, we could do with a few girls coming along, or we'll end up tripping the light fantastic with each other. I wondered if a few of your nurse pals would like to come? And you, of course,' he added, a blush spreading up from under the stiff collar of his tunic.

'I'm sure they'd love to, if they can get the time off.' Dora took the tickets from him. 'I'll see what I can do.'

'Thanks.'

There was an awkward pause. Dora glanced around, and saw her mum and Nanna Winnie with their noses pressed against the kitchen window. She glared at them, but they paid no attention.

'Anyway, I'd best go,' Joe said. 'So I'll – um – see you on Saturday, shall I?'

'If I can make it.'

'I hope you can.' He paused for a moment, as if he was about to say something else. Then he turned and marched off through the back gate.

Dora turned back to the window. Her mum and Nanna Winnie had gone, with only the trembling net curtain to show that they'd ever been there.

Chapter Thirty-Six

'Go on, it'll be a laugh.'

Millie looked across the breakfast table at her friend's face, full of eager appeal. Dora had been pestering her about the police dance at the Town Hall all week. Even though Millie had told her several times she couldn't go, Dora didn't seem to want to take no for an answer.

'How did you get all those spare tickets anyway?' Lucy Lane asked.

Colour rose in Dora's face, clashing with the curls of fiery red hair that poked out from under her cap. 'A friend gave them to me.'

'A friend, eh?' Katie O'Hara cackled, nudging her. 'That wouldn't be a boyfriend, would it?'

'No!' Dora denied, a bit too quickly. Millie and Katie O'Hara glanced at each other across the table, both trying not to smile.

'As if!' Lucy smirked, poking at her porridge with her spoon.

Millie ignored her, turning back to Dora. 'I would love to come, but I've got to catch the early train down to Sussex for the christening tomorrow.'

'We won't be late back, I promise. We only have to go for an hour.' Dora looked appealingly at her. 'Please, Benedict? It's not often we get the same night off. Especially a Saturday night?'

Millie wished she could have gone, if only to

341

make her friend happy. Dora so rarely asked for any favours. But she knew she would be rotten company.

She was so nervous about seeing Seb at the christening. She hadn't seen or heard from him at all in the two weeks since they'd called off their engagement.

For the first few days, she had expected him to turn up at the nurses' home, or at least to write to her. But as the days passed and her hopes began to fade, she'd had to face the fact that it really was over between them as far as Seb was concerned.

Now she had to go down to Lyford for the christening, and she wasn't looking forward to it at all. But she was the baby's godmother, and just to make things even more awkward, Seb and William were both godfathers.

She caught Dora's quizzical glance across the table, and forced herself to smile back. She didn't know why she couldn't bring herself to tell the other girls about her broken engagement. Perhaps it was because if she said the words out loud it would make them seem too real.

She hadn't even told her family yet. She just hoped Seb wouldn't decide to announce it to everyone at the christening, and humiliate her.

'Why don't you invite Tremayne?' Millie suggested.

'She's already going out with Charlie tonight. Love's young dream!' Dora rolled her eyes. 'Please, Benedict,' she begged. 'The friend who gave me these invitations – Joe – well, I think he might have the wrong idea about me.' She blushed again, lowering her eyes demurely to her empty porridge bowl. 'If I go on my own, he might think – you know?'

'I'll go with you, if a miracle happens and Sister Wren lets me off at five,' Katie offered. 'I don't want to miss out on the chance of all those young policemen, do I?' Her round blue eyes gleamed in anticipation.

'We'll be home early, so you can catch your train in the morning,' Dora pleaded with Millie again. 'I promise we'll be tucked up in bed well before midnight.'

'Speak for yourself!' Katie laughed.

'I can't think of anything worse,' Lucy said with a delicate shudder. She leant across the table at Millie. 'I don't know about you, but I wouldn't be seen dead in a dump like that!'

The way she said it set Millie's teeth on edge. Lucy was always trying to make out that she and Millie were somehow a cut above the rest of them, just because Millie had a title and Lucy's father had made millions manufacturing light-bulbs. But she knew her own father would be utterly horrified by such petty snobbery.

It was the superior sneer on Lucy's face that changed Millie's mind. Before she knew what she was doing, she had turned to Dora and said, 'Oh, what the hell. You're right, we don't often get a night out together, do we? Count me in.'

'Smashing!' Relief was written all over her friend's kind, plain face. 'You'll enjoy it, I promise.'

But after a long, hard day on the ward, Millie began to regret her change of heart. The last thing she felt like doing was dancing. Her feet ached, her head was throbbing with tension from avoiding yet another stinging reprimand from Sister Hyde, and all she really wanted to do was to sink her aching limbs into a deep, albeit tepid, bath.

She was already daydreaming about easing off her shoes as she pushed the trolley out of the sluice, ready to start on the teatime beds and backs round ... and crashed straight into Dr Tremayne.

Bowls, flannels and tins of powder went everywhere. William dived to catch the bottle of meths with one hand before it crashed to the ground.

'Howzat?' He grinned, and handed it back to her. 'And to think they wouldn't let me bowl in the inter-hospital cricket match last summer.'

'Thanks.' She took it from him and bent to pick up the bowl, already steeling herself as she heard Sister Hyde's brisk footsteps bearing down on them.

'Really, Benedict! Why don't you watch where you're going?' she snapped. 'Are you all right, Dr Tremayne?'

'Quite all right, thank you, Sister. And it's I who should have been looking where I was going.'

He stooped to help reload the trolley, but Sister Hyde stepped in.

'No, Doctor, leave Benedict to do it. I need you to take a look at Miss Wallis. I think she may need an adjustment in her medication. And mind you mop all that up,' she instructed Millie over her shoulder as she ushered him away. 'I don't want anyone slipping and breaking their neck because of your carelessness.'

As he followed Sister Hyde down the ward, William turned back and gave Millie an apologetic shrug.

'You're late,' Maud observed a few minutes later, as Millie pulled the screens around her bed.

'I'm sorry.' Millie prayed Maud wouldn't be in one of her difficult moods. She was too tired to deal with it. All she wanted to do was go off duty.

'It doesn't matter, I suppose. I hardly have any pressing evening engagements planned.'

Millie smiled, in spite of her weariness. 'Let's get you turned over, shall we?'

'You're wasting your time, you know,' Maud complained, as Millie dabbed methylated spirits onto her jutting shoulder blades. 'I don't even know why you're bothering.'

'We've got to make you comfortable, haven't we?' Millie said soothingly, her mind elsewhere. 'We don't want you getting any nasty pressure sores.'

'It would be a fine thing if I did feel uncomfortable,' Maud replied tartly. 'It would be a fine thing if I felt anything at all!'

Millie lifted her head at the sound of William's voice, coming from the other side of the screen. He was talking to a patient, his voice warm and reassuring.

'Did I ever tell you I used to play tennis?' Maud said suddenly.

'No, I don't think you ever mentioned it.'

'Well, I did. And I swam. I was an excellent swimmer. My family had a house in Deal and I adored the sea. I was completely fearless, even as a young child. I used to tell everyone I would swim

345

the English Channel one day – are you listening to me?' she said sharply, jerking Millie out of her reverie.

'I'm sorry, Mrs Mortimer. I was miles away.'

'I should think you were!' Maud looked out-raged. 'Good gracious, I've had to listen to your ceaseless nonsensical chatter for weeks. You'd think you'd have the decency to listen when I finally want to speak!'

'You're right, it was thoughtless of me.' Millie dredged up a smile from the depths of her stout shoes. 'What was it you were saying?'

'It doesn't matter.' Maud's thin mouth turned down sulkily. 'It really isn't important, not now.'

She followed Millie's gaze as it strayed back across towards William's voice on the other side of the screen.

'You rather like him, don't you?' she remarked.

'Who?'

'You know perfectly well who. That young man. The one who calls himself a doctor. On the other side of the screens. The one you've been listening to when you should have been listening to me. What's his name? Ah, yes! Tremayne.'

'Mrs Mortimer, please!' Millie shot an anguished look towards the screens as Maud's voice rang out.

'Please what? Do you honestly think he hasn't noticed you watching his every move?' Maud sniffed.

'There. You're all finished.' Millie changed the subject hastily straightening Maud's nightgown and refastening it. 'I'll make your bed comfort-able now.'

'Is he the reason for your broken engagement?'

Maud's gaze was as sharp and penetrating as a scalpel. Millie looked away. 'Of course not,' she muttered, bending to tuck in the sheet.

'Very well, don't tell me the truth,' Maud said huffily. 'As long as you're not lying to yourself.'

'I really don't know what you're talking about.'

'I think you do.' Maud sent her a long, considering look. 'You know,' she said after a long pause, 'there are times when I wish I had swum the English Channel.'

'I beg your pardon?' Millie blinked at her.

'I told you, I wanted to do it when I was a girl,' Maud explained impatiently. 'When we lived in Deal I used to stand and look out to sea all the time. I'd tell myself that one day I would take the plunge, so to speak, and swim the Channel. I thought I might be the first person to do it, but of course Captain Webb beat me to it,' she smiled. 'Then I thought I might be the first woman to do it. I used to swim out to sea, wondering if I'd ever be brave enough to go all the way to France.'

'Why didn't you?'

Maud gave a little shrug. 'A thousand and one reasons. I went to school, then to university, then I was married... I told myself I still had time, but somehow I never did it.' She smiled wistfully. 'Oh, I'm not saying I didn't lead a very full life, or that I didn't achieve a great deal. But somewhere in the back of my mind I've always had this nagging little regret that I wasn't brave enough to strike out and make that swim.' She looked down at her hands, her fingers curling in towards her palms like the edges of a dying leaf. 'But of course it's too late now, isn't it? Too late for regrets.'

She looked up at Millie. 'Do you understand what I'm saying to you?' she said. 'Regret is a terrible thing, child. You must never reach my age knowing there are paths in life you wish you had taken.'

Millie was too flustered to speak for a moment. She didn't want to hear this; her life was already in a mess without a stranger trying to confuse her even more about her feelings.

'As I said, I don't know what you're talking about.' She finished straightening the bed hastily, desperate to escape.

'Where are you going?' Maud asked, as Millie pushed the screens back from around the bed. 'Aren't you going to stay and help me with my crossword?'

'I can't, I'm too busy.'

'But I've been looking at it all day. I've worked out most of the clues, I just need you to fill them in for me...'

Maud suddenly seemed very small and vulnerable. Her sharp blue eyes were usually so clear and incisive, but looking into them now Millie could see the milky veil of old age over them.

'Please,' she whispered

Her plea touched Millie's heart. Any other day she would gladly have spent time with her. But today she was tired and upset, and the last thing she needed was to suffer a vicious tongue lashing from Maud Mortimer. She'd had enough criticism from Sister Hyde that day.

'I'm sorry,' she said, glancing at her watch. 'I don't have time this evening. I'm supposed to be going off duty soon. Perhaps one of the other nurses could help?'

'It doesn't matter,' Maud said, turning her face away.

Her sulkiness rankled with Millie. She was a nurse, she reminded herself, not Mrs Mortimer's personal servant.

But then she told herself not to be so selfish. Maud was an old, sick lady, she was bound to be demanding. 'I've got tomorrow off, but I'll be back on Monday,' Millie said. 'Perhaps we could do the crossword together then?'

Maud turned her head to look at her. 'I'll have to check my diary,' she said.

Millie smiled, in spite of herself. 'You do that, Mrs Mortimer.'

As Millie left, she called after her, 'You'll remember what I said, won't you? No regrets.'

Millie turned to look back at her. 'What on earth would I have to regret?'

Dora had never been to a dance before. She stood in the doorway, gazing in awe at the cavernous room, alive with noise and colour. At the far end, on the small stage, a dance band in evening dress was already playing a lively number, their brass instruments catching the light, while the floor was filled with dancers swinging each other around. Dora had never seen anything like it. It was as if her Nanna's wireless had suddenly burst into vivid, noisy life in front of her.

'What a dump,' Lucy Lane said. In spite of her dismissive attitude earlier, as soon as she found out Millie was going she had decided to invite

herself along anyway. Now she stood in the doorway, looking around as if there was a bad smell
under her turned-up nose.

'Well, I think it's smashing,' Katie O'Hara said
loyally. 'It's better than sitting in our room studying, anyway. And it's a good excuse to get dressed
up.'

'You call that dressed up?' Lucy gave her outfit
a scathing glance. Dora caught Katie's blushing
face and felt for her. It wasn't Katie's fault that
her best dress was one of her Irish mother's
home-made creations, a flouncy style in black and
white that did little to flatter her plump figure.

Dora thanked her stars that her own mother was
more skilled with a needle, although her faded
blue flowery dress had seen better days. Lucy, by
contrast, was done up to the nines in fashionable
dark green crêpe, with a string of real pearls
around her throat.

Dora glanced at Millie. She looked lovely as ever
in a pale yellow dress, her blonde curls catching
the light from the lanterns strung overhead. But
her downcast expression made her look like a sad
angel.

'What do we do now?' Dora asked, looking
around. There was no sign of Joe, although it was
difficult to recognise anyone in the swirling crowd.

'Wait to be asked to dance, I suppose.' Katie
flashed an encouraging smile at a group of young
men who were loitering by a pillar on the other
side of the room.

'O'Hara! Do you have to be so shameless?' Lucy
hissed at her.

Dora wasn't sure she wanted to be asked. She

didn't think she would ever be able to move herself around the dance floor as fast as the other dancers, especially after so many hours on her feet on the ward.

Millie seemed to feel the same. 'I'm going to sit down,' she said.

'No one will see us over there!' Katie wailed, but Millie was already heading determinedly for the corner table. 'It's all right for her, she's engaged,' Katie hissed furiously to Dora. 'She should give the rest of us a chance!'

Dora smiled, but secretly she was relieved to be hidden away. She was beginning to wonder if coming to the dance had been such a good idea. She had come for Joe's sake, but there was no sign of him.

Lucy wouldn't let her forget that either. 'Looks like your young man has stood you up,' she remarked.

'I told you, he's not my young man,' Dora replied through gritted teeth.

'Obviously,' Lucy smirked.

Dora scanned the dance floor, torn between disappointment that he wasn't there, and relief that she didn't have to dance or make awkward conversation. She had been so worried that by turning up tonight she might give him the idea that she was interested in him. Now she realised with a pang that he wasn't remotely interested in her.

'Well, this is ridiculous!' Katie declared, standing up. 'If someone doesn't ask me to dance in the next minute, I'm going to ask them.'

'You can't do that!' Lucy looked scandalised.

'Why not? I used to do it all the time at the village dances at home.'

'This is different. You're in London now, not some little Irish village in the middle of nowhere. You can't act like a clod-hopping hoyden here. You have to be sophisticated.'

'I'd rather be a clod-hopping hoyden who gets to dance than a sophisticated wallflower!'

With a last defiant look at them, she plunged determinedly into the seething mass of dancers, searching for a partner.

'Look at her.' Lucy shook her head in despair.

'Leave her alone. At least she knows how to enjoy herself,' Dora said. 'Anyway, it looks as if her plan's worked.' She nodded towards the dance floor, where Katie was dragging a very handsome but rather surprised-looking young man on to the dance floor. 'Maybe we should try it?' She smiled at Millie, who seemed to be a million miles away. 'What do you reckon, Benedict?'

'Sorry?' Millie looked up vaguely. Dora moved closer to her.

'We don't have to stay, you know?' she said, over the blaring of the music. 'We can go home.'

'Nonsense, I'm enjoying myself,' Millie said, although her smile was strained.

'Are you sure? I know I nagged you into coming–'

'I would only have sat moping in my room if you hadn't.' Dora frowned. 'Why? Is something wrong?'

Millie's smile brightened a fraction. 'Of course not. I'm just tired, that's all. Anyway, we have to stay,' she added. 'You never know, your young man might be looking for you.'

'I doubt it,' Dora said. 'If he was here he would have–' And then she saw Joe, pushing through the crowd towards her.

'There you are!' he said. 'I've been looking everywhere for you. I was beginning to think you hadn't come. But then my mate Tom got collared by your friend, who told him there were a bunch of nurses sitting over here.' Joe smiled around at her friends. Dora had forgotten how handsome he was, dressed in his best suit, his fair hair neatly combed.

'This is Joe,' she introduced him, feeling suddenly proud. It gave her a little lift to see the look of utter disbelief on Lucy's pinched face.

'Would you like to dance?' he asked.

'Oh, no, I can't...' Dora was about to refuse until she caught Millie's encouraging nod. 'Well, all right then,' she said. 'But I'm warning you, I'm not very good.'

'That makes two of us,' he said, offering her his arm.

The first dance was a lively swing number. Dora was hopeless at first, tripping over and colliding with other couples. But Joe was a better dancer than he'd let on, and with his firm guidance she soon found her feet.

'You see?' he grinned. 'It's not as hard as it looks, is it?'

She was completely out of breath after two more dances. When the band slowed to a more sedate tempo, she went to leave the dance floor, but Joe pulled her back.

'Don't go yet,' he said.

'But my friends…'

'They're fine.' He nodded across the room, to where Katie was still whirling around in the arms of Tom. She might have taken him by surprise at first, but he seemed to be enjoying her company now. Even Lucy had found a partner to dance with, while Millie seemed quite happy chatting with some other girls who had joined their table.

'You see?' he said, drawing Dora in to him, his hand circling her waist. 'There's nothing to stop you dancing with me.'

She held herself rigid at first, scared by the unfamiliar feeling of his arms around her. But gradually, as the music took over, she found herself relaxing.

'I'm glad you came,' Joe said, his face so close to hers she could feel his warm breath fanning her cheek. 'I wasn't sure if you would, or if you'd just carry on playing hard to get.'

Dora pulled away slightly to look at him. 'I'm not playing at anything,' she said.

He smiled. 'I'm glad to hear it.'

She wondered if she should set him straight, tell him outright she wasn't interested, that they could never be more than friends. But she was enjoying the moment, and she didn't want to spoil it.

Joe was very attentive to her all evening, fetching drinks, making sure her friends were kept entertained, and dancing her off her feet. Dora was astonished at how often she took to the dance floor, and how much she enjoyed being in Joe's arms.

She caught the admiring glances some of the

other girls were giving him, and wondered why he had ever asked her to come to the dance. In spite of the way he acted, she couldn't believe he was really interested in her. Perhaps he was just being kind because of what she'd done for Jennie, she thought.

'Are you having a nice time?' he asked, when they were dancing again.

'Smashing, thanks. It makes a change to be out of uniform, anyway!'

'You look lovely.'

She looked away so he wouldn't see her blushing face. 'You don't have to say that.'

'I mean it.' He glanced down at her, his green eyes crinkling. 'Why don't you like it when anyone pays you a compliment?'

'I dunno.' She shrugged, embarrassed. 'I'm probably not used to it, I suppose.'

'Are you trying to tell me I'm the first man to fancy you?'

An image of Alf flashed into her mind. Suddenly Joe's arm felt like iron around her waist, pinning her against him. Panicking, she wrenched herself free from his grasp and stumbled off the dance floor away from him. The room seemed too hot, too crowded, she couldn't breathe...

And then her heartbeat slowed again, and she felt like an idiot. She couldn't even look at Joe as he followed her, shouldering his way through the dancing couples to get to her.

'Dora?' He caught up with her as she headed for the door. 'Where are you going?'

'Home. I – I shouldn't have come.'

'But we were having such a nice time.' He went

to grasp her arm, and frowned. 'You're shaking,' he said. 'What's going on? Is it something I said?'

'It's nothing. I just felt a bit dizzy, that's all.'

'I'm not surprised, after all that dancing. Shall we sit down? I'll get you a drink–'

'I'd rather go home.'

'Then I'll walk you.'

'No. It's fine, honestly.' Suddenly the room seemed hot and oppressive. She could feel perspiration trickling down the back of her neck.

'Dora, look at me.' He put his hand under her chin, guiding her face up to meet his. The gentleness in his amber-flecked eyes surprised her. 'Please stay,' he said. 'We don't have to dance any more, if you don't want to. We don't have to do anything you don't want. But I'd just like to be with you, if that's all right?'

She managed a shaky smile. 'I suppose so,' she agreed.

For the rest of the evening Joe didn't leave her side. He was good company, making her laugh and listening attentively when she talked about her family, and life at the Nightingale. He talked too, telling her funny stories about some of the characters he'd met while pounding the beat.

He was nice to her friends, buying them drinks and dancing with them so they didn't feel left out. Even Lucy Lane looked grudgingly impressed by the end of the evening.

When the dance was over, he offered to walk her home, but Dora refused. 'I'll walk back with the others,' she said, as they stood shivering outside the Town Hall.

'I'm sure they'd understand?' he said meaningfully, reaching for her hand.

'All the same, I'd like to walk back with them.'

'If that's what you want.' Even in the dim lamp-light, she could see the disappointment in his eyes.

She paused awkwardly, not quite sure what to do next. He was still holding her hand, unwilling to let go. 'Well ... thanks for inviting me,' she said.

'Can I see you again?'

She stared at him, genuinely surprised. She had meant to say no, to tell him there was no point, that he was wasting his time with her. But the words wouldn't come out.

He moved towards her, closing in for a kiss, and panic washed over her. But instead of going for her mouth, he planted his lips gently on her fore-head.

'I will see you again,' he said, smiling down at her in the darkness. 'You can bet on that, Dora Doyle.'

Chapter Thirty-Seven

Lyford's modest parish church was transformed for the baptism of William David Frederick Arbuthnot, son and heir of the Marquess of Trent. The altar overflowed with white and yellow spring flowers, the brasswork gleamed, and even the ancient organ was in fine tune, thanks to a gener-ous last-minute donation towards its restoration made by the baby's grandparents Duke and

Duchess of Claremont.

Millie stood with the rest of the christening party around the font, mouthing the words to 'Dear Lord and Father of Mankind' while trying desperately to stop her hymn book from shaking. On one side of her stood William, endearingly scruffy as ever, his tie crooked, dark hair flopping into his eyes as he bent his head to read the words. On the other was Seb, blond, sleek and self-possessed. The tension crackling between them was almost palpable.

As the hymn finished, she sneaked a sideways glance at Seb, bathed in beams of jewel-coloured sunlight streaming through the stained-glass window. His handsome, aquiline profile was very familiar to her, and yet it was like looking at a stranger.

She had been so looking forward to seeing him again, certain that once they came face to face they would both realise how foolish they had been. But Seb's cool reserve had shocked her. He had been polite but distant. Millie, ready to rush into his arms, was left feeling stunned and embarrassed.

Now, as she stood looking out over the crowded pews, she wondered if anyone had noticed his lack of warmth to her. Surely someone must have guessed what was going on? He could barely conceal his contempt for her. She felt exposed, her ignominy on show for everyone to see.

Finally, after what seemed like a lifetime, the service came to an end and she could escape. As the congregation began to stream out of the church, Millie went to join her father and grandmother to travel back to the house, but Seb's mother waylaid her.

'Where are you going? Surely Sebastian is driving you?'

Millie pointed towards her father's Daimler. 'I thought I'd go with my family...'

'Nonsense, they are already taking the vicar and my aunt.' Before Millie could protest, she called her son over. 'You're taking Millie back to Lyford, aren't you?'

'Well, yes, I suppose...' He looked at her doubtfully.

'Of course you are.' The duchess gave Millie a little shove towards him. 'Off you go. And don't be late,' she added. 'Luncheon is being served promptly at noon. I know what you young people are like.'

The arch look she gave them sent scalding colour flooding into Millie's face. Once they might have laughed about it together, but now she could hardly look at Seb as he flung open the door of his car for her to get in.

He didn't speak as he manoeuvred carefully out between the church gates and on to the lane. Then he said stiffly, 'How are you?'

'I'm well, thank you. And you?'

'Can't complain.' He swung the car on to the verge to avoid a passing tractor. 'How's – um – life at the hospital?'

Why do you care? she wanted to snap at him. But he was making an effort to be civil, and the least she could do was to do the same.

'Just the same as ever.'

'Ah.' He nodded. They drove on for a while,

making stilted small talk like strangers. Millie stared at the passing landscape of fields and trees, and thought how wretchedly she missed their old closeness. A few weeks ago they would have been roaring with laughter by now, chuckling together over the vicar's tedious speech or someone's absurd hat. How had that disappeared so completely, she wondered.

As Lyford came into view in the valley below them, she said, 'I take it you haven't told your family about our broken engagement yet?'

He shook his head. 'I thought it was for the best. I didn't want anything to ruin Sophia's day,' he said, his face grim.

'I agree.'

Seb glanced across at her. 'I take it you haven't either, judging by the fact that your grandmother didn't arrive at the church with a shotgun this morning?'

Millie smiled reluctantly. 'I'm not quite sure who she would have been pointing it at, if she had.' She dreaded breaking the bad news. She wasn't sure which would be worse: her grandmother's frustrated rage or her abject disappointment.

As if he could read her mind, Seb said, 'I could tell her for you, if that would make it easier? Or we could do it together?'

'Thank you, but it's better if I do it.' Millie picked at the seam on her glove. 'As Sister Hyde would say, this is my mess and I have to be the one to clean it up.' She smiled wryly.

She felt Seb turn towards her. 'Millie–' he started to say.

'Anyway, we don't have to tell anyone today, do

we?' she cut him off, desperate not to hear what he had to say. She had the feeling his words would be too final. 'I think we can bear to be civil to each other for a few hours, don't you?'

'Yes,' he said, turning his gaze back to the road. 'Yes, I think I could pretend for a few more hours.'

On Sundays, most of the sisters held their own kind of observance on their wards, whether it was simple prayers, hymn singing, or, in the case of the jazz-loving and somewhat eccentric Sister Everett on Female Medical, a selection of spirituals played on her harmonica.

Those nurses who were not on duty were expected to attend the local parish church of St Luke's, either for morning service or Evensong. And it was the duty of Miss Hanley and Sister Sutton to make sure they got there.

Just after noon, they led a straggling crocodile of tired-looking girls up the gravel path back to the nurses' home. Sister Parker had come with them as usual. And, as usual, her views were at odds with everyone else's.

'All I'm saying, Veronica, is that the sermon went on too long,' she said, her soft Scottish accent making her sound far more mild-mannered than she actually was.

'You can't say that!' Miss Hanley protested. 'The subject of the Atonement is complex and subtle. You can't explain it in five minutes!'

'You don't have to take four hours to do it, either,' Sister Sutton said shortly. 'I was quite numb with cold. Wiseman!' she addressed one of the nurses sharply. 'Pick your feet up, it sounds as if you're dragging a sack of coal. And do keep up, Pritchard, for heaven's sake!'

'A criticism of God's anointed messenger is a criticism of God,' Miss Hanley said primly.

'Really, Veronica!' Sister Parker's blue eyes gleamed with amusement. 'I don't think God would mind my saying the Reverend Jennings is an old windbag. He'd probably agree with me!'

Miss Hanley was still spluttering in outrage when Sister Sutton said, 'Who on earth is that?'

A woman was standing outside the Home Sister's ground-floor window, shading her eyes to peer in through the glass.

'The impertinence of her!' Sister Sutton trundled across the grass towards her. 'You there! What do you think you're doing?'

The woman turned around and regarded them calmly. She didn't seem in the least bit perturbed at being caught spying. 'I'm looking for Violet Tanner.'

'And you are?' Miss Hanley said.

The woman looked her up and down before replying. 'My name is Mrs Sherman. I am – an old acquaintance of Violet's.'

Miss Hanley regarded her suspiciously. Outwardly, there was nothing untoward about her appearance – she was a well-dressed woman in her fifties, tall and straight-spined, with an almost military bearing the Assistant Matron recognised as similar to her own. But there was something about her cold, pale eyes that sent a warning chill down the back of Miss Hanley's neck.

'Is she expecting you?'

Her smile lacked any warmth. 'I thought I would surprise her.'

Out of the corner of her eye, Miss Hanley caught Sister Parker's small shake of her head.

'You should speak to Matron,' she said. 'Come back tomorrow morning.'

'I don't have time for that!' Mrs Sherman bit out. Then, seeing Miss Hanley's frown, she recollected herself and said, 'Forgive me, I have come a long way and I'm rather tired. I have to catch a train back to Bristol tomorrow, and had hoped to be able to spend a little longer with Violet. We have a lot of catching up to do.'

'Nevertheless, I think it would be best if...' Miss Hanley didn't have time to finish her words before Sister Sutton broke in impatiently.

'Oh, for heaven's sake, Veronica! Violet's taken her little boy to the park,' she told Mrs Sherman. 'It's just across the road.'

'Thank you. I'm most grateful to you.' There was a glint of something like triumph in the look she shot Miss Hanley.

'What did you have to tell her that for?' Sister Parker hissed as they watched Mrs Sherman picking her way back down the path.

'Why shouldn't I?' Sister Sutton looked at them blankly, her chins wobbling in indignation. 'You heard her. She's a friend of Violet's.'

'She didn't seem very friendly to me.' Miss Hanley looked at Sister Parker.

'We must inform Matron,' they said together.

Chapter Thirty-Eight

Millie thought it would be easier with Seb being nice to her. But actually it made the pain in her heart much worse than if he'd just gone on being beastly. It was so hard, standing next to him, having him be so utterly charming to her in front of everyone, while knowing he was no longer hers.

It was even worse sitting across the table at luncheon, watching Georgina Farsley flirting with him. She might be with Jumbo Jameson now, but how long before she made a play for Seb once she knew he was free, Millie wondered with a stab of jealousy.

As soon as luncheon was over, she escaped on to the terrace to smoke a cigarette. She sat on the stone steps, careless of the damp seeping through her dress, and stared out over the immaculately manicured grounds and the trees tinted with pink and white spring blossom

She hadn't been sitting there long before Sophia came out to join her.

'Are you escaping too?' she asked, sitting down beside her and helping herself to a cigarette from Millie's packet. 'Billy's having a nap, thank God. I had to get some fresh air, or I'd simply faint.' She lit her cigarette with a click of Millie's lighter and took a deep drag, letting a thin plume of smoke stream out from between her lips.

'Have you heard the news?' she said.

Millie's mind flew to her own broken engagement, until she saw Sophia's smile. 'What news?'

'Lucinda is making an honest man out of my brother.' Sophia's grin widened. 'Isn't it too funny? All that planning and scheming finally worked. I'm not surprised ... she hasn't let poor Richard breathe by himself for the past two months.'

'That's – good news,' Millie said faintly.

'Good news for Lulu, certainly – she's walking around in there with a smile you could practically see from the moon, as are her parents. But not such good news for my brother. Or for you, darling,' she added. 'You do realise that now everyone will be expecting you to set a date for your wedding?'

She gazed at Millie through the curling smoke. 'Are you all right, Mil? You've gone rather pale.'

'I'm fine,' she lied. 'Just a bit shivery that's all.'

'It's probably all this talk of marriage that's done it to you,' Sophia laughed. 'Don't worry, it's not nearly as bad as all that. And I'm sure being married to Seb would be a lot more fun than being married to an old bore like Richard!' She looked up at Millie in surprise as she got to her feet. 'Where are you going?'

'Back inside. I'm getting a bit chilly out here.'

'Don't tell anyone about the engagement, will you?' Sophia called after her. 'They haven't announced it officially yet.'

There was no sign of Seb when she went back inside. Millie searched for him, but no one had seen him.

'I think he gave Georgina a lift to the station,' Lucinda Carnforth told her finally. She was

365

firmly clinging to Richard's arm, basking in the triumphant glow of a woman who had landed her prize. 'She had a row with Jumbo, who was monumentally smashed, and decided to go back to London.'

'I'm not surprised. Did you see the state of him?' Richard said. 'Mother has had him put to bed. One of the servants caught him being sick in the boot cupboard. He really is an utter disgrace.'

But Millie didn't care about Jumbo's fall from grace. She was too worried by the idea of Seb and Georgina heading off together.

A scenario formed in her mind. Seb had confided in Georgina about the broken engagement, and she had instantly ditched Jumbo. He'd gone off to drown his sorrows, leaving Georgina with a convenient excuse to ask Seb for a lift to the station. And, kind as he was, he would be only too willing to act as her knight-in-shining-armour, unaware that she was planning to seduce him.

Or perhaps he was aware, she thought with a stab of pain. Perhaps even now they were scheming together about how long it would be before they could decently be seen in public together.

She felt sick just thinking about it.

But now she was faced with an even more awkward dilemma. There was only one train back to London that afternoon. She needed to get to the station, but she couldn't face the thought of seeing Georgina and Seb.

It was William who came to her rescue. 'I can drive you back to London, if you like?' he offered. 'It seems silly for you to catch the train when I can take you right to your doorstep.'

It was the perfect solution, although typically her grandmother had something to say about it.

'Are you sure this is quite seemly?' she queried, when Millie said goodbye to her. 'I'm not sure it's proper for an engaged girl to be gallivanting off unchaperoned with another man. What does Sebastian say about it?'

Sebastian doesn't care because he's already gallivanting off with someone else, Millie wanted to blurt out. But she couldn't bring herself to utter the words.

'It seems like a very practical solution to me,' her father answered for her. 'Really, Mother, I'm sure Amelia won't be cast out from decent society for travelling alone in a car with someone.'

She felt too sick with misery to speak as they left Lyford and headed back to London, but forced herself to be sociable after a while, for William's sake.

'How is Phil?' she asked.

'I have no idea,' he replied frankly. 'I haven't seen her in weeks.'

She looked across at him sharply. 'Aren't you together any more?'

He shrugged. 'It's hard to tell with Phil. She's a bit of a free spirit, you might say.' His smile had a taut edge to it.

'She sounds like you?'

'True,' he agreed wryly. 'I'm just getting a taste of my own medicine. Rather appropriate, I suppose, for a doctor.' He glanced at her. 'I must say, although I find Phil endlessly fascinating, I do sometimes wish I had someone more devoted. Like your fiancé, for instance.'

Millie was sure he hadn't meant it as a barb, but it pierced through her fragile defences and straight into her heart.

'He's not that devoted,' she mumbled.

'Are you serious? He adores you.'

She turned her head to look out of the window, but it was too much to hope William wouldn't see the tears that rolled down her cheek.

He took his eyes from the road, craning round to look at her. 'Wait ... are you crying?' he asked, bewildered.

Millie shook her head, not trusting herself to speak.

'You are!' He pulled the car over to the side of the road, narrowly missing a horse and cart coming around the bend in the opposite direction.

'Careful! You'll get us killed.' Millie covered her eyes.

'Never mind that.' William twisted round in his seat to look at her. 'Are you going to tell me what all this is about?'

She was going to make up some excuse, the way she had with Sophia. But the kindness in William's dark eyes made her want to unburden herself.

'We've called off the engagement,' she murmured.

'What? Why?'

She shrugged. 'We wanted different things, I suppose.'

'But Seb worships you.'

'Then why is he playing fast and loose with Georgina Farsley?' she blurted out.

William frowned. 'How do you know that? Did

Seb tell you?'

Millie looked down at her hands, feeling suddenly foolish. 'He gave her a lift to the station,' she mumbled.

'And I'm giving *you* a lift back to London, but that doesn't mean there's anything going on between us!'

She raised her eyes to look at him. 'That's not what Seb thinks.'

'Ah.' He sat back in his seat, realisation dawning. 'So that's it. He's jealous.' He raked his dark hair back off his face. 'I know he's never been a great admirer of mine, and now I understand why.'

'It's not just you,' Millie said. 'He doesn't want me to be a nurse any more. He wants us to get married as soon as possible.'

'That doesn't sound like Sebastian. He's always struck me as a very fair-minded chap, not the kind to lay down the law. Although...' William stopped speaking.

'What?' Millie asked.

He looked at her. 'I suppose if I were Seb, I wouldn't want to be away from you a moment longer than was necessary either.'

It was as if all the air had been sucked out of the car. Suddenly Millie couldn't seem to breathe.

'What are you saying?' she whispered.

'I'm saying perhaps he has a point?' William's dark gaze moved from her eyes to her lips and back again. 'I know I've always had feelings for you, no matter how hard I've tried to pretend I don't. Perhaps I didn't pretend hard enough? Or perhaps neither of us did?'

369

As he moved in to kiss her, Millie knew in her heart she should be pushing him away. But a sudden rush of heat through her body melted her resistance, making it impossible for her to move.

William was right, she had been fighting this attraction for over a year now. It had been there, a voice whispering to her, ever since that first evening when he'd walked her home along the river. He hadn't kissed her then, but she badly wanted him to do it now.

When it came, the kiss was every bit as sweet and wonderful as she'd known it would be. William Tremayne had kissed enough girls to know exactly what he was doing. As his mouth moved against hers, at first gently, then with more urgency, Millie felt herself tingling from the roots of her hair to the tips of her toes.

They finally broke away from each other. William looked into her eyes, his dark gaze searching hers. Then he gave a sad, twisted smile.

'This is the point where you're supposed to fall into my arms and we live happily ever after,' he said. 'But that's not going to happen, is it?' She shook her head. 'Because you still love him.'

'I'm sorry,' Millie said wretchedly. She meant it, too. Deep down, she had so wanted William's kiss to spark the kind of fire deep inside her that Seb's did. But even though she felt herself to be expertly, thoroughly kissed, more so than she might ever be again in her whole life, it did nothing for her. It didn't give her the same thrill as being in Seb's arms, knowing he loved her beyond everything.

William moved back in his seat and started up

the engine. 'Typical,' he sighed. 'Why is it that when I find a girl I actually care about, she's already fallen for someone else?'

'I'm sorry.' And she meant it, too. In a way it would have been much simpler if she could just forget Seb and be with William.

'Don't be,' he said. 'Seb is a lucky man.'

Millie looked downcast. 'Except I've made a complete mess of everything.'

'No, you haven't.' William patted her arm. 'He'll come to his senses, you'll see. He'd be a fool if he didn't.'

'I hope you're right.'

'I am,' he said. 'And when he does, you can tell him how he almost lost you to the Nightingale Hospital's arch seducer.'

Millie gave him a watery smile. 'I don't think I'd dare!'

They drove back to the Nightingale in companionable silence. It felt a lot easier to be with William now she knew for sure she wasn't in love with him. He was good company, he made her laugh. But despite his best efforts to cheer her up, her unhappiness over Seb was still there, a permanent ache in her heart.

But she was determined not to let her low mood affect anyone else, so had managed to paste her brightest smile on her face by the time she'd climbed the stairs to the shared attic room.

Helen was lying on her bed, still in uniform. She was so tired she hadn't even taken her shoes off.

'Hard day?' Millie smiled, unpinning her hat.

'You could say that.' Helen stared up at the

ceiling. 'How was the christening?'

'It was...' Millie paused, trying to find the right word. 'Interesting,' she finished.

'Why? Did my brother manage to drop his new godson in the font?'

'Not quite!' Millie shrugged off her coat. 'How about you? How was Sister Hyde today? In a good mood, I hope?'

'Not really.'

'Why? Don't tell me she missed me?' Millie turned to smile at her, but the sadness in Helen's dark eyes gave her a jolt. 'Tremayne, what is it? What's happened?'

'I don't know how to tell you this.' Helen took a deep breath. 'Maud Mortimer died last night.'

Chapter Thirty-Nine

'Careful, Oliver. Don't go too near the edge!'

Violet called out to her son as he stood on the path looking over the boating lake of Victoria Park, watching the flat-bottomed boat ferrying passengers across the water. He paid no attention, too transfixed by the sight of the boat moving slowly across the water.

'He won't be happy until you've set sail, will he?' Sister Blake commented with a smile as she poured their tea.

'It doesn't look like it,' Violet agreed ruefully. She had promised him a trip on the lake, after she had fortified herself with cup of tea in the refreshment lodge. Oliver had sat still for all of two minutes until excitement overcame him and he'd begged to be allowed to go and watch the boats.

The energy of seven year olds never ceased to amaze her. They had already explored the bridges and the model village, and Oliver had run around the park several times, his little legs never failing him although hers were aching with the effort of keeping up.

'I wonder you haven't brought him here before?' Sister Blake said, passing her cup over.

Violet didn't reply as she added a spoonful of sugar to her tea and stirred it. Seeing the radiant joy on her son's face, she felt guilty that she hadn't kept her promise to take him to the park earlier. He had been longing to go for ages, but fear had always kept her away.

She might have made yet another excuse today had Sister Blake not convinced her to relent as they walked home from church.

'Where's the harm in it?' she'd reasoned, and for once Violet decided it might be worth taking a risk.

She'd taken quite a few recently. She had joined the choir, and made friends with several of the sisters. It was early days, but Violet could feel her frozen heart starting to thaw.

But she still had to be careful. She couldn't afford to relax too much, or to give away anything about her past.

She peered out of the window. Oliver waved back at her happily.

'What a joy he must be to you,' Sister Blake commented.

'He is my life,' Violet replied simply.

'Such a handsome little chap, too. And with your dark colouring. Does he take after his father at all?'

It was an innocent question but Violet stiffened, all her senses instantly on alert. 'A little,' she replied cautiously.

'That must be quite difficult for you, seeing him in your son?'

Violet's head went back at once. 'Why do you say that?'

'Only that it must remind you of the pain of losing him.' Sister Blake frowned quizzically. 'Why? What did you think I meant?'

Fortunately she was saved from answering as Oliver came in, pestering yet again to know when they could go on the boat.

'In a minute,' Violet said.

'But you said that a minute ago!' he whined.

'Then you must be patient.'

'Tell you what.' Sister Blake reached into her pocket and handed him a coin. 'Why don't you go and buy yourself a toffee apple from the kiosk while you're waiting?'

Oliver looked down wide-eyed at the coin in his palm and then up at Violet. 'May I, Mummy?'

'Very well. But stay where I can see you,' she called after him as he sped from the café.

'I think between you, Sister Sutton and the other sisters, my son is in danger of becoming very spoilt,' she scolded Sister Blake.

'He's become quite the little pet, hasn't he?' she said. 'Even Miss Hanley has a soft spot for him, although she would never admit it.' She smiled.

'I'm sure some people think we must be stuffy old maids, all living together as we do. But most of us love children. I daresay some of us would have liked to have had a family of our own, if things had been different.'

'Would you?' Violet asked.

Sister Blake nodded. 'Very much.'

'But you decided to stay a nurse instead?'

Sister Blake looked wistful. 'I would love to say I did it out of dedication to the nursing profession, like Sister Hyde and some of the others. But the fact is, my choice was made for me.' She twirled her teaspoon slowly in her empty cup. 'The man I loved died during the war.'

'Oh, I'm sorry.' How many times had Violet heard the same story? Almost every woman she knew had lost a father, brother, husband or son in the war. Her own beloved father had been killed at Arras, and her brother a year later. 'Where was he killed?'

'He wasn't. He was badly injured at Passchendaele. A mortar shell blasted his spine. He lay drowning in the mud of the battlefield until one of his unit found him and brought him home.' Her mouth twisted. 'I sometimes wonder if it wouldn't have been kinder to have left him to die,' she said bleakly.

'Surely not?' Violet was shocked.

'You didn't know Matthew.' Sister Blake shook her head. 'That mortar blast did more than break his spine. It broke his spirit, too. He couldn't face being confined to a wheelchair. He tried to break off our engagement, told me to go and find a whole man, someone who could be the husband

I deserved. As if I'd ever want anyone else!'

'So what happened?'

'I refused, of course.' Sister Blake shrugged. 'I had finished my nursing training by then, so I got myself transferred to the specialist orthopaedic hospital where he was being treated, down on the south coast. It meant being away from my home and family, giving up everything I'd ever known. But I would have gone to the ends of the earth for Matthew, I truly would.' Her eyes grew misty. 'Perhaps if I'd realised what it would do to him emotionally, having me see him like that, I wouldn't have been so hasty.' She looked down at her ringless hands, lacing and unlacing them on the table in front of her. 'He killed himself, you see. On the very day peace was declared.'

'I'm so sorry.'

'It was a long time ago now. And I try not to dwell on it too much.' She looked up at Violet, forcing a smile. 'I'm not the only woman who lost a loved one, am I? You know what it's like.'

Violet was stung by guilt as she picked up her teacup and glanced out of the window. Poor Sister Blake, what would she say if she knew that Violet was spinning yet more lies? The more she got to know her and the other sisters, the more wretched Violet felt about deceiving them. They liked her, they had taken her and Oliver to their hearts, and she repaid them with deception. She hated herself for it, and yet she had to go on with it, for Oliver's sake.

And then she saw Mrs Sherman.

Even through the crowds of people enjoying the spring sunshine, Violet's gaze picked her out immediately. She stood on the far side of the lake, tall and ramrod straight, staring across the water.

Violet had had countless nightmares about this moment, from which she would wake up bathed in panicky sweat. But this time there was no such escape.

The world spun, and she dropped her teacup with a crash.

'Violet? Are you all right? You've gone terribly pale...' Sister Blake's voice sounded faint and distant, as if it was coming from the bottom of a well. But Violet was already on her feet, pushing past her and out into the sunshine.

There was no sign of her son.

'Oliver!' She screamed his name, looking wildly around her. Several blank, startled faces stared back at her.

'Violet?' She jumped as Sister Blake came up behind her, putting a hand on her shoulder. 'Violet, what is it?'

'I've got to find Oliver.' She started pushing her way through the throng of people, still screaming out his name. 'Oh, God, where is he? Oliver!'

'Mummy?' She whirled around. He was standing behind her, clutching his toffee apple.

'Oh, thank God!' She rushed to him and grabbed his hand, looking around her wildly, expecting Mrs Sherman to appear at any moment like an avenging angel. 'Come on, we have to go.'

'But the boats—'

'Another time.'

'You promised!' He dug his heels in, nearly pulling her off balance. 'You promised we could go on the boats!'

'Oliver, do as you're told!' Panic and fear made Violet scream at him. She saw his face crumple slowly into tears but had no time to comfort him. All she could think of was getting away, finding somewhere safe to hide as she half carried and half dragged him, sobbing, through the throng of people.

She could hear Sister Blake behind her, calling out her name. But Violet didn't heed her as she ran, her lungs bursting, gripping Oliver's hand so tightly she could feel his fragile bones being crushed in her grasp. She was too afraid to loosen her hold on him in case he ran away from her, straight to Mrs Sherman.

Car horns blared as she bolted across the road and through the hospital gates. Still she didn't stop running, through the archway and across the courtyard, then beyond the hospital buildings to the sisters' block.

Oliver's outraged sobbing echoed off the walls as she fumbled with her key in the lock. She opened the door, shoved him inside, then locked it behind her. Her heart pounding, she yanked the curtains closed, plunging them into shadowy darkness.

She peered through a crack in the curtains. Suddenly the beautiful garden, bathed in spring sunshine, seemed alive with all kinds of dark, nameless horrors. She needed to escape, but she was cornered like helpless prey. Fear overwhelmed her, rising up in her throat, almost choking her.

She dragged Oliver into the bedroom and closed the door. Pulling the suitcase off the top of

378

her wardrobe, she began to throw clothes in it.

He stopped sobbing and regarded her curiously. 'What are you doing?'

'We have to go, sweetheart.'

'But I want to stay!' His lower lip jutted obstinately. 'I like it here. I helped Sister Sutton plant some seeds, and I want to see them grow.'

'I know, darling, but we have to leave. The bad people have found us. It's not safe for us here.'

Oliver's brown eyes widened with fear. Then he folded his arms defiantly. 'I'm tired of running away from the bad people. I don't want to run any more,' he declared.

Violet looked at her son, her panic subsiding. She put down the clothes and went over to him.

'Neither do I, sweetheart,' she sighed sadly, stroking his face. 'But we can't stay.'

There was a knock on the door, and Violet froze.

'Miss Tanner?' She heard Matron's voice on the other side of the door and allowed herself to breathe again.

'Stay here,' she warned Oliver. 'Keep as quiet as a mouse, and don't move. Can you do that for me?' He nodded solemnly.

'Is Matron one of the bad people?' he whispered.

Violet stared grimly at the door.

'Let's find out, shall we?' she said.

Chapter Forty

It was Sunday afternoon, but Matron was in her full black uniform, her expression solemn under her elaborate head-dress. Miss Hanley stood behind her, grim-faced as a gaoler.

'I think we need to have a talk, don't you?' Matron said.

Violet let out a deep, shuddering sigh. The time had come to be honest at last and it felt strangely like a relief.

'Not here,' she said glancing over her shoulder. 'I don't want Oliver to hear.'

'Very well. We will talk in my office. Miss Hanley will look after your son. Don't worry,' Matron said. 'She will not let any harm come to him. Will you, Miss Hanley?'

Violet glanced at the Assistant Matron. They might not have seen eye to eye on everything, but she had a feeling Miss Hanley was a woman to be trusted. Oliver would be safer with her than with anyone, Violet decided.

In Matron's office, Violet went to sit down in the chair on the visitor's side of the heavy mahogany desk, but Matron directed her to one of the polished leather armchairs that flanked the fireplace. It was the same place she had sat the day Matron had invited her to stay at the Nightingale. At the time, it had all seemed too good to be true, and now she knew it was. Miss Fox asked the maid to bring them some tea, and seated herself in the armchair opposite.

'I'm leaving,' Violet blurted out.

'Very well.' Matron regarded her with calm grey eyes. 'If that's what you wish, I wouldn't dream of trying to change your mind. But first I would like an explanation. I feel you owe me that, at least.'

Violet floundered, unsure of where to start. Until Matron said, 'Miss Hanley tells me you had a visitor?'

Panic raced through her. 'Mrs Sherman was *here*?'

Matron looked at her consideringly. 'I take it she's the reason for your sudden desire to depart?' Violet nodded. 'Who is she, may I ask?'

'My husband's housekeeper.'

'Don't you mean his former housekeeper? Your husband is dead, surely?' Violet shook her head. 'So you're not a widow after all?'

'I only wish I were,' she murmured. She saw Matron's look of surprise, but no longer cared. 'My husband is a monster,' she declared, lifting her chin. 'He made my life a misery from the day I married him.'

'Then why did you?'

'Because I was young, stupid and naïve. Stupid enough to allow myself to be flattered when a consultant showed an interest in me. And naïve enough to believe my mother when she told me that marrying a man old enough to be my father would be the making of me.'

But she couldn't blame anyone else for what she'd done. Her mother had only wanted the best for her; it had been Violet's decision alone to

381

marry Victor.

Mr Victor Dangerfield. One of the country's top neurosurgeons. The medical journals called him a genius, a pioneering surgeon capable of making the blind see and bringing the dead back to life. With power like that at his fingertips, was it really any wonder he had turned out to be an arrogant, narcissistic bully?

There was a knock on the door, and the maid entered with the tea tray. Violet paused, collecting her thoughts, while Matron busied herself pouring them both a cup. Then she settled back in her chair and looked at Violet expectantly.

'Start at the beginning,' she said. 'And I want you to tell me everything.'

And so Violet told her. It was the first time she had ever told her story to anyone who really wanted to listen. She had tried to tell her mother once, but Dorothy Tanner refused to hear anything against her perfect son-in-law. Now, at last, Violet had someone who was ready to hear what she had to say, and it was such a relief to let it all out.

She was twenty-two years old when Victor Dangerfield had swept her off her feet and married her.

Looking back, she wondered how it had ever happened. Victor Dangerfield was wealthy, powerful and charismatic. He could have had any woman he wanted. And yet he had chosen a shy mouse like her, picked her out as she hid away at the end of a line of nurses when he arrived on the ward to do his round. She wondered if that had been part of the attraction for him. Victor was the kind of man who needed a wife who would worship and revere him at home the way the nurses did at the hospital.

Whatever his motives, once he had decided she was the one he wanted, she had had very little say in the matter. He didn't court her so much as overwhelm her: so forceful was his personality that they were engaged to be married almost before she had realised what had happened.

But there was a moment when she tried to voice her doubts. As the wedding approached, she had confided her fears to her mother. Victor was in his forties, twice her age, and she felt she barely knew him. He was charming and attentive, but she knew nothing of what lay beneath the surface. She didn't know his background, his friends, his family. She couldn't remember having a single serious conversation with him.

But her mother had just laughed off her fears, told her how lucky she was that someone like Victor Dangerfield had ever looked her way. Dorothy Tanner had struggled to cope since her own husband died, and she knew the value of finding a good man to take care and provide.

And so Violet had pushed her doubts to one side and married him. But they had only been married a matter of weeks before she realised what kind of man she had taken for a husband.

She stared down at her teacup, unable to meet Matron's eye as she told her story. Even now, she still felt embarrassed and ashamed, as if it were somehow her fault.

'We had been married less than a month the first time he beat me,' she said flatly. 'I remember, it was all to do with a set of curtains.' She smiled faintly at the memory. It seemed so petty and ridiculous now. 'I'd moved into his house, you see, and it was full of heavy, dark furnishings and fabrics that looked as if they had been there since Victorian times. Of course, being a young bride, I was keen to make my mark on the place. So I ordered some new curtains. I didn't tell him, I thought they would be a nice surprise.' Her mouth twisted bitterly.

'And he was angry about it?'

'Oh, no, he was never angry.' That was what was so terrifying about him. Anger would have been preferable to the chilling, calculating punishments he meted out to her. At least she could have predicted anger. But his blows could come out of nowhere. 'He was very calm as always. He instructed me to take them down and throw them on the fire. Then he hit me around the head, so hard it burst my eardrum.'

She saw Matron wince.

'You didn't go to the police?'

Violet shook her head. 'Who would have believed me? You have to remember, my husband was a prominent surgeon – a man of status. Men like that don't beat their wives, do they? It's only working-class men coming home drunk from the pub who set about women. Even if I'd tried to tell anyone, Victor would have made sure they didn't believe me. My husband can be highly persuasive when he wants to be. He managed to persuade me often enough. For a long time, I was convinced everything was my fault. That I'd deserved my punishments through my own foolishness. I thought if only I could be a better person, less of a disappointment–'

'You poor child.'

Tears stung the back of Violet's eyes. It was the first time anyone had ever taken pity on her, she realised.

'The beatings weren't the worst of it,' she said. 'I know it sounds hard to believe, but I think I could have put up with the physical pain of a cracked rib or a few bruises But it was what he did to me here.' She tapped her temple. 'That was what really hurt. He made me feel as if everything was my fault. Every criticism he gave me, every time he punished me, I had to apologise for offending him. And if I didn't, he would make me suffer more. He would burn my clothes, or forbid the servants to feed me, or lock me in my room. Sometimes he would simply ignore me for days on end. I was like a dog he had to bring to heel. And, of course, I always came in the end.'

'But why, my dear? I simply don't understand it.' Matron looked perplexed.

'Neither do I,' Violet admitted. 'It's so hard to explain. It's different when you're there, in the middle of it all. It's as if you can no longer tell right from wrong, or up from down.'

'But wasn't there someone who could have guided you? Your mother, perhaps?'

'My mother wasn't allowed anywhere near us after we were married.'

It was ironic, she reflected. Dorothy Tanner had been so mad keen for her daughter to marry well, to increase her own social standing. And yet Victor despised her. He ridiculed her pretensions to Violet, and wouldn't allow her to visit.

But such was the power he exerted over people, Dorothy still adored him. She had refused to countenance Violet's desperate pleas to return home after the way her husband treated her, and even now remained firmly loyal to her son-in-law.

Of course, there had been one woman closer to hand to whom Violet might have turned: Mrs Sherman, Victor's devoted housekeeper. Violet had to struggle to keep the venom out of her voice as she spoke the name.

'I think she was secretly besotted with my husband. She had been his housekeeper for many years before I came along. I don't know if she was jealous of me, or if she couldn't accept the idea of Victor bringing a new bride into the house, but she treated me with nothing but unkindness and contempt from the day I arrived.'

'Did she know about your husband's violence towards you?'

'She not only knew, she took pleasure in seeing me suffer.' Violet's voice shook with anger at the memory. 'There were many times when she could have stepped in and saved me from humiliation. But she didn't. And the few times I appealed directly to her for help, she brushed me off as if she didn't know what I was talking about. Sometimes I genuinely wondered if she even allowed herself to acknowledge how cruel Victor was. Surely no human being could have allowed it to go on otherwise.'

Violet drained her cup, and Matron refilled it immediately.

'I'm surprised you wanted to have a child with

him,' she remarked, passing it back to her.

'Like everything else, that wasn't my decision.' Violet's gaze drifted towards the window. The sun was going down outside. She began to feel nervous at the idea of the descending twilight, knowing Mrs Sherman was lurking nearby. 'Victor was obsessed with the idea of being a father. He desperately wanted a son to continue the Dangerfield name. I think that's one of the main reasons he married a young girl like me.' She stirred her tea slowly. The sound of the spoon rattling in the teacup seemed to echo in the silence of the room. 'He was extremely – frustrated – that I didn't conceive immediately.'

Frustrated. It was such a small word for the world of pain that he had inflicted on her for her failure.

'Then, finally, two years into our marriage, it happened. And my life changed overnight.' She smiled, remembering. The nine months of her pregnancy were the most peaceful of her whole marriage. 'Victor stopped beating me, and treated me as if I was the most precious thing in the world to him. He simply couldn't do enough for me. But even though I tried to be happy, I couldn't help dreading what might happen after the baby was born. I started to have nightmares that I'd given birth to a daughter. I just couldn't imagine what Victor would do if I didn't give him the son he expected.'

She tugged at her thumbnail between her teeth, a habit she had developed during her pregnancy and had not been able to shake off since.

'But you had a boy?'

'Yes, I did. But it was a horrible, difficult labour, and I was confined to bed for a month afterwards to recover my strength. By the time I was well enough to get up and start looking after my son, I found it was too late. Mrs Sherman had already taken over.'

The housekeeper looked after every aspect of the baby's care, directing the nanny and nursery maids as if she were his mother. Only reluctantly did she give him up to be fed, and even then she would watch Violet jealously from the doorway of the nursery, itching to snatch him away from her as soon as she could.

'I tried to fight back, but with her and Victor ranged against me, it was almost impossible,' Violet explained helplessly. 'I was utterly wretched and miserable. The only pleasure I had were the moments I managed to steal with my son. But even those were denied me when Oliver started to get older. I began to realise that if I didn't want my boy to turn into a monster like his father, I had to get away.'

And so she had planned her escape. She secretly applied for another job, arranging for letters to be delivered to a post-office box in Bristol so Victor wouldn't know what she was doing.

'I didn't apply to hospitals but to private individuals instead,' she said. 'I applied under my maiden name, and claimed I was a widow. I felt wicked writing the words, but then I began to wish they were true.

'At first I was turned down because of Oliver. But finally I found a job looking after an elderly lady in the Midlands. Even then, I wasn't sure I would be able to get away.'

The memory of that day still haunted her. She'd planned her escape for Mrs Sherman's day off, knowing the housekeeper was due to visit a friend. But at the last moment, Oliver had gone down with yet another chest infection, and Mrs Sherman had decided to stay and nurse her little angel.

'I panicked, told her there was no need, but she insisted. I'd ordered a taxi to pick us up. I could see the time drawing nearer and nearer – I knew if it arrived while Mrs Sherman was there then the game would be up for ever. I would probably end up dead,' Violet said flatly.

She had told Mrs Sherman to go out to the chemist for some Friar's Balsam. Mrs Sherman argued. For once panic had made Violet fearless. She stood up to her, pointed out that she was the nurse and Mrs Sherman should do as she was told, for Oliver's sake. Or would she rather Mr Dangerfield was told that she had left the child to suffer? Mrs Sherman rather huffily set off into town on her bicycle, assuring Oliver she would only be gone for a few minutes.

As soon as she left, Violet hastily dressed Oliver and gathered up her few belongings in a couple of cases. The taxi was late, and she was terrified Mrs Sherman would reappear over the hill before she could get away.

'But you managed it?' Matron was on the edge of her seat, her expression tense.

'By the skin of our teeth, yes. I spotted her cycling back up the hill as we were heading down to the village. If that train had been delayed by just a minute, I dread to think what would have happened.'

Violet looked down at her wedding ring. She had sold her original one soon after she'd run away, not realising how much she might need the badge of respectability in the years to come. The one she wore now was a cheap ring she had found in a pawnshop in Wolverhampton. 'But even after we'd escaped, I was terrified that Victor would track down the taxi driver and somehow find out where I'd gone. I knew he would never stop looking for us.'

From then on her life had become a game of cat and mouse all across the country, using different names, different stories, to try to throw her husband off the scent. She had lived so many different lives in the space of the last five years she could hardly remember who she was supposed to be from one day to the next.

'But I knew it would only be a matter of time before he found us. And now he has.' She turned unhappy eyes to meet Matron's. 'Now do you see why I can't stay?' she pleaded.

Matron stared back at her. 'I see why you can't go,' she said.

'But Mrs Sherman knows I'm here. It's only a matter of time before she brings Victor here, and then–'

'And then we will deal with him,' Matron said firmly.

Violet laughed. 'Oh, Miss Fox,' she said, almost pityingly. 'Do you really think you will be equal to my husband?' She shook her head.

'I know that you will stand a better chance

against him here than if you run off on your own.'

'And why should that be?'

Matron frowned at her. 'Because here you are amongst friends.' She rose to her feet. 'It's your choice, of course. If you want to leave, I can't stop you. But I urge you to reconsider.' She smiled. 'Don't underestimate us, Violet.'

Chapter Forty-One

Suicide.

Millie seemed to hear the word wherever she went on that cold, grey morning.

'Sleeping pills,' the ward maid whispered as she made up the fire. 'They reckon she saved them up to finish herself off. Must have been planning it for a long time.'

'I don't understand it.' Millie heard two first years discussing it in whispers outside the sluice door as she tested the rack of early-morning urine samples. 'How could it even have happened? The patients are always supervised taking their medicines, aren't they?'

'There's nothing to stop them sticking a pill under their tongue and then spitting it out when the nurses have gone, is there? I bet that's what she did, the cunning old cow.'

'Don't talk like that! It's wrong to speak ill of the dead. I don't know how she even managed it with her hands the way they were. It must have taken a lot of effort.'

'Maybe someone did it for her? I would have shoved a few pills down her throat if I'd known.'

'Don't say that!'

'Why not? Don't forget how she used to torment us and call us names. I'm not sorry she's gone!'

Unable to stand it any longer, Millie burst out of the sluice and confronted them. 'Haven't you two got anything better to do than gossip?' she snapped. They both stared at her; Millie was known to be the most easy-going of the seniors and never one to pull rank. But today she wasn't feeling sunny-natured.

'You,' she addressed the second girl, 'have you finished with those bedpans?'

'Not yet.'

'Then you'd better get on with it, hadn't you? Go on!' They both glared sullenly at her but knew better than to argue. Easy-going or not, Millie was still senior to them, and answering her back could earn them a trip to Matron's office.

Millie closed the sluice door and leant against the counter top, fighting the urge to be sick. She could hardly bear to be on the ward this morning. Maud's empty bed was like a silent reproach to her. The place seemed depressingly silent without her imperious voice ringing out, summoning a nurse to complain about something or other. When the porter brought up the newspapers, Millie had found herself searching through it for Maud's copy of *The Times,* ready to start on the crossword when she had a spare moment.

She had pulled herself together with effort and forced herself to start testing the samples, determined to get on with her work. But grief still ached in her chest, making it hard for her to breathe.

She felt totally alone in her sadness. No one else seemed to mourn Maud's passing. They gossiped about it, but only because they had precious little else to talk about and a suicide on Female Chronics was such a novelty. Sister Hyde went about her business, handing out work lists and giving orders, as if there was nothing wrong at all.

No one seemed to care that it was Maud who had died. Irascible, infuriating Maud, with her sharp tongue and even sharper intelligence, who had a lifetime of stories to tell and no one to listen to them.

She had tried to tell Millie, though. On Saturday night – was it really only thirty-six hours ago? It felt like a lifetime. Millie remembered Maud's strange mood, how she had wanted to talk about her childhood hopes, her dreams. She must have known she was going to end her life that night.

Why hadn't Millie realised what was happening? A good nurse would have known, she felt sure of that. A good nurse would have spotted the warning signs.

That night Maud had wanted Millie to stay with her. It was odd for her to ask for anything, and yet she had begged her to stay. Would it have made any difference if she had, Millie wondered. If she hadn't been in such a hurry to leave, perhaps Maud would have known there was someone who cared about her, and it would have given her the strength she needed to carry on...

But she hadn't. She had been selfish, too keen

to get off duty. Desperate to go to a silly dance she hadn't even enjoyed.

What was the last thing Maud had told her? Not to have any regrets.

Too late, Maud, she thought bitterly. Because she knew she would regret walking out of that ward for the rest of her life.

Helen came in as she was washing up the specimen glasses.

'Have you finished the testing?'

'All done.'

Helen looked around. 'Where's Mrs Weaver's sample? You haven't thrown it away?'

'Of course. Why?'

'Didn't you check her notes? It's a twenty-four-hour sample. You were supposed to put it with what we collected yesterday.'

'I didn't know, did I?' Sweat broke out on Millie's brow. 'Maybe no one will notice?'

'Benedict, this is a patient we're talking about. It doesn't matter if no one notices, the results will still be wrong.'

'What am I going to do?'

'Only one thing for it, I'm afraid – you're going to have to come clean to Sister.'

Sister Hyde's brow was already furrowed with irritation, even before they explained what had happened.

'I suppose this is your doing, Benedict?' Millie stared at the polished floor, her hands knotting behind her back. 'I might have known. Why is it that disaster always seems to follow you around, Nurse?'

'I don't know, Sister,' she mumbled.

'I do. It's because you are thoughtless. You spend far too much time daydreaming about engagement rings and nights out, and do not pay nearly enough attention to the task in hand—'

Millie didn't hear the rest of what she was saying. A strange buzzing sound filled her ears, like a swarm of angry bees inside her head. She stared at Sister Hyde's face, saw her thin lips moving as she listed Millie's failings yet again. She didn't need to hear them, she already knew them all off by heart. She was thoughtless, muddle-headed, untidy, completely incompetent. She would never, ever make a good nurse as long as she lived.

But she didn't need Sister Hyde to tell her that. It was staring her in the face, every time she looked at Maud's empty bed.

The angry buzz still filled Millie's head. She could feel pressure building up, as if her brain would burst. Before she knew what she was doing, she was pulling off her apron.

Sister Hyde stared at her. 'What do you think you're doing, Benedict?'

'Something I should have done a long time ago, Sister.' She yanked the grips from her cap, tore it off her head and stuffed it into Sister Hyde's hands.

Then she walked down the length of the ward, letting the doors swing shut behind her.

The air in the Porters' Lodge crackled with tension as the two men squared up to each other.

'What did you just call me?' Harry Fishman muttered. He was big and solid, brown eyes scowling from under a shock of blue-black curls.

Five minutes ago he had been laughing and joking with the others as he waited for the kettle to boil.

'Fancy a cuppa, new boy?' he'd called out to Peter, who was playing cards with Nick.

'No, thanks, I'll make my own.'

Nick stiffened, instantly alert to the tension in the room. The other men felt it too. They stopped talking and looked from one to the other, waiting.

'Oh, yes? And why's that, then?'

Nick flashed a warning glance at Peter. Harry was a good bloke, ready to have a laugh with anyone. But he had fists like ham hocks, and even Nick would have thought twice about taking him on.

'Because I don't take anything from dirty Jews.'

The hatred in Pete's eyes shocked Nick. He had grown up with Peter Doyle, and had never seen him so full of malice. His broad, freckled face burnt with it, his stocky body rigid with tension.

Harry Fishman scowled. 'Come over here and say that!'

'Pete–' Nick put out his hand to stop him but Peter had dropped his cards and was already on his feet.

'What did you just call me?' Harry repeated his question.

Peter barely came up to his shoulder, but he looked the other man squarely in the eye.

'You're a dirty Jew,' he snarled.

Nick saw Harry's hand go back. He sprang like a panther, getting in between the men and trapping Harry's fist in mid-air.

'You don't want to do that,' he said softly.

Harry glared at him, his jaw tightening. 'Stay out of this, Nick. It ain't your fight. Stop protecting him.'

'I'm protecting you, mate,' Nick said quietly. 'What do you think old Hopkins is going to say about porters scrapping on duty?'

Harry hesitated for a moment, then slowly lowered his fist. 'You're right,' he said. 'That little runt's not worth losing my job over.'

As he turned away, Peter jeered from behind Nick's shoulder, 'That's right. Run away, you coward!'

Harry swung round, but Nick beat him to it. Grabbing Peter under the chin, he rammed him up against the wall.

'And you!' he said. 'Just shut it, all right? Do you want to get yourself sacked, you silly sod?'

Mr Hopkins already had his eye on Peter. He'd warned Nick to keep Doyle out of trouble.

'He's getting under a lot of people's skin,' he'd said. 'I only took him on because you vouched for him. Now it's up to you to make sure he stays on the straight and narrow.'

Peter's eyes bulged, showing wide circles of white around the startled green. 'N-No,' he managed.

'Then behave yourself.' Nick released him. 'Come on, you can help me with the linen delivery.'

As they left, Harry Fishman sidled over and whispered, 'You want to keep a muzzle on that dog of yours, Nick. Before he bites the wrong person.'

He glanced across at the other porters, watching in hostile silence. He knew that unless he had been there, not one of them would have stood up to defend Peter if Harry Fishman had decided to throw that punch.

He didn't blame them either. If it hadn't been for Dora, he would have belted Peter himself.

'You've got to keep your nose clean,' he warned as they headed towards the hospital laundry. 'Mr Hopkins won't put up with any of your Blackshirt rubbish in here.'

'It's not rubbish,' Peter muttered defensively. 'What Mr Mosley says is right. There's going to be trouble in the East End, you see if there ain't.'

'And there's going to be trouble in here, if you don't learn to keep your trap shut.' Nick looked sideways at him. 'I mean it. You don't want to make any enemies in this place. Not if you want to keep your job.'

Peter said nothing. His mouth was a set, stubborn line. Nick remembered that expression from when they were kids. Peter had always been in trouble then, standing up to the bigger kids like a little mongrel terrier, growling and snapping and refusing to admit he was in the wrong.

The laundry was warm and welcoming after the brisk chill outside. The thick, steamy air smelt of freshly starched linen. Women with their sleeves rolled up and scarves wrapped around their heads were busy folding and feeding sheets into hissing pressing machines, while others tended the bank of giant tubs that rumbled at the far end of the laundry.

Nick showed Peter where to find the finished

bundles of linen and towels, and how to load up a trolley with the separate orders for each ward.

'They should already be bundled up, but be sure to count them and double check against the list for each ward before you take them up,' he said, showing him the piece of paper with every item marked. 'The sisters play merry hell if you forget something and they have to send down for it.'

With their trolleys loaded up, they made their way to the service lift. Nick pulled the doors closed, shut the grille and pressed the button. At first Peter was sulkily silent, but as they made their way around the wards, delivering bundles of linen, his frostiness started to thaw.

Their final call was to Wren. 'Watch the Sister here, she's a right snappy cow,' Nick hissed as he pushed the trolley through the double doors.

'Blimey, look at all these women in their nighties!' Peter snorted with laughter. Then he caught sight of his sister, at the far end of the ward. 'There's Dora, look. Cooeee! Dor!'

He started to wave, but Nick dug him sharply in the ribs. 'Shhh! Nurses ain't allowed to talk to men while they're in uniform.'

'But she's my sister!'

'You could be the Pearly King of Bethnal Green and she still wouldn't be able to talk to you!'

It took all his self-control for Nick not to look at Dora himself as he handed the list to the staff nurse to check. Thankfully the bitch of a Sister was nowhere in sight, otherwise she was bound to give him trouble over something.

'Thank you.' The nurse signed her name and handed the piece of paper back to him. 'Put it in the linen cupboard, will you?'

'I can never get over how different Dora looks in her uniform,' Peter remarked, as they unpacked the bundles on to the shelves. 'Sort of grown-up.'

'She is.' Finally, Nick allowed himself a glance sideways at her. She was taking a patient's pulse, her head bent as she held the woman's wrist. He caught a glimpse of her profile, her blob of a nose, her wide, smiling mouth. The patient said something to her and she laughed, a merry, husky sound that made Nick's heart race uncomfortably in his chest.

'You know she's courting now?'

It was a casual comment, but it hit him like a blow. Nick spun round. Peter was lifting another bundle of linen into the cupboard, apparently unaware that he had just thrown his friend's world into chaos.

'Who's she courting?'

'That policeman – Joe Armstrong? The one whose sister's lodging at our place.' Peter grinned. 'He seems very keen. He's always dropping round on the off chance Dora might be there. He took her dancing the other night. Can you imagine that? Our Dora dancing!' He laughed. 'Anyway, Mum and Nanna are convinced it's all serious. I can't imagine anyone wanting to go out with my sister though, can you?'

Nick glanced over his shoulder at Dora. She scribbled a figure on the patient's chart then hung it back in place. As she did, she spotted Nick and gave him a warm smile.

'No,' he muttered. 'I can't imagine that at all.'

Chapter Forty-Two

By the time Millie got back to her room, Sister Sutton had upended her bed again. Seeing the sheets, pillows, blankets and mattress tipped in an untidy heap was too much for her. Sinking down in the middle of the wreckage, Millie cried her heart out.

This was it. It was over. She could never go back to the ward, never set foot inside the hospital again. Matron would send for her, and she would be instantly dismissed. And good riddance.

But even as shame and misery washed over her, she felt relieved. She was so tired of trying every day, and failing every time. Of knowing that all the other nurses, even the first years, were better and cleverer than her, more competent, more everything. Finally she accepted what Sister Hyde, Matron and everyone else had known for ages: she was a terrible nurse.

Perhaps if Maud Mortimer's care had been left to someone who knew what they were doing, she would still be alive now.

'I might have known your room would be a mess, Benedict.'

Sobbing noisily into her pillow, she hadn't heard the creaking tread on the attic stairs. Now Sister Hyde stood in the doorway looking down at her, Millie's crumpled cap still clasped in her hands.

Millie instantly stumbled to her feet, wiping her

puffy, tear-ravaged face.

Sister Hyde's brows rose. 'I'm pleased to see you have remembered your manners, at least.' She looked down her long, aquiline nose at the girl. 'Now, perhaps you would care to explain what that ridiculous outburst on the ward was all about?'

Millie felt her nerve failing under Sister's severe gaze, but held it together long enough to say, 'I'm leaving, Sister.'

'And why, may I ask?'

Millie stared at her. Wasn't it obvious? 'With respect, Sister, you've told me yourself. I am thoughtless, untidy, incompetent, I daydream constantly–'

'Yes, yes, I'm aware of all that,' Sister Hyde cut her off impatiently. 'But I've told you all that before and you've never decided to leave. Why now, girl?'

Millie braced herself. There was no point in lying about it. Fixing her gaze on the spotted mirror behind Sister Hyde's shoulder, she said flatly, 'Please, Sister, it's my fault Maud – Mrs Mortimer – died.'

Sister Hyde went very still for a moment. 'Explain yourself,' she said.

Millie opened her mouth, and everything came out in a rush. About Saturday night, how she had neglected Maud, refused to stay and talk to her when she needed her most.

'And you think Mrs Mortimer decided to kill herself because you didn't help her with *The Times* crossword?' Sister Hyde said slowly.

'There's more to it than that, Sister. I didn't

listen to her. Looking back on it now, I'm sure she was trying to tell me something. The clues were there, just like a crossword. The way she talked about not having regrets... If only I'd listened to her, perhaps she wouldn't have felt so alone...' Millie swallowed hard. Tears were beginning to roll down her cheeks again but with Sister Hyde staring so hard at her she didn't dare wipe them away on her sleeve.

Sister Hyde pulled her gaze away and looked around for somewhere to sit down, finally selecting the rickety chair in the corner. Millie prayed silently it wouldn't collapse under her; none of them had ever dared sit on it before.

She took a few moments to compose herself before she began to speak. 'Listen to me, child,' she said finally. 'Mrs Mortimer decided to end her life a long time ago, and there is nothing anyone could have done to stop her.' Millie opened her mouth to speak, but Sister held up a silencing hand. 'Yes, you could have stayed with her. You could have sat up with her all night, and she would merely have done it another night instead. There is nothing anyone could have done,' she said firmly, her gaze holding Millie's. 'Do you understand that?'

Millie nodded dumbly. She desperately wanted to believe it.

'As you know, Mrs Mortimer was a woman of great dignity, and she was facing a most undignified death. She knew that, so she decided to take matters into her own hands while she still could. It had nothing to do with her being unhappy, Benedict. It was the last act of a fiercely independent woman, making her own decision to die rather than subjecting herself to a slow, cruel death.'

Millie sniffed back her tears. 'I know she wanted to die, but I wanted her to want to live,' she blurted out. 'I tried so hard to cheer her up and make her happy, to show her she had something to live for. But in the end I failed her...'

'You didn't fail her at all, child. Don't you see that?' The shadow of a smile crossed Sister Hyde's gaunt face. 'On the contrary, you are probably the reason she didn't kill herself a long time ago.'

Seeing Millie's puzzled expression, she explained, 'When Mrs Mortimer first came to us, she was withdrawn, wretched and unhappy. She was like an angry snake, striking out at anyone who came near her. But you managed to win her trust. Not only that, you actually made her smile. Mrs Mortimer would have ended her life sooner or later, but you made the last few weeks of it far brighter than they might have been.' She looked up at her. 'You have a gift for that. A gift for understanding people, bringing out the best in them. It's a rare gift indeed. Not many people have it, but all good nurses do.'

It took a moment for Millie to reply. 'But I'm not a good nurse,' she said finally.

'Not yet,' Sister Hyde agreed crisply. 'Indeed, you have a great many faults and failings. I give you the simplest of tasks and yet still you manage to get them wrong. You are an accident waiting to happen. Every day I despair of you.' Millie cringed, but then Sister Hyde went on, 'However, these are all faults that can be overcome with proper training and self-discipline.' She fixed Millie with a severe look. 'Why exactly do you think I am so hard on you?'

'Because I'm hopeless?' Millie ventured.

'Because I see in you the potential to be an excellent nurse. Why else would I waste my breath on you? If I seem frustrated at times, it is only because I know that potential is going to be wasted by your rushing off to get married.'

'I might not be getting married now,' Millie admitted unhappily.

Sister Hyde looked uncomfortable. Like Sister Sutton, discussing personal matters didn't seem to come easily to her. 'That is – regrettable for you, and I am sorry to hear it,' she said shortly. 'But if you do decide to stay, then I will endeavour to start training you properly for the rest of your time on Hyde.'

'That's only two weeks,' Millie said.

Sister Hyde gave a weary sigh. 'Then we will just have to do the best we can, won't we?'

She got to her feet and handed over the cap. 'Will you come back? I warn you, you might regret it if you do. You must be prepared to put all your silliness behind you, and buckle down to some very hard work. Are you ready for that?'

Millie hesitated for a moment. Now her initial relief at walking out had worn off, she realised how much she would miss nursing. She took the cap from her. 'I'm ready,' she said.

'I'm pleased to hear it. I'll expect you to report for duty at seven o'clock tomorrow morning. Not a minute later, is that understood?'

'Yes, Sister.'

As Sister Hyde turned to leave, Millie plucked up the courage to voice the thought that had been troubling her since that morning.

'Please, Sister, may I ask a question?'

Sister Hyde's eyes narrowed at her impertinence. 'Go on,' she said.

'They said ... Mrs Mortimer saved up her sleeping pills?'

'That is correct.'

'But where did she keep them? We change the patients' beds and clean out the lockers so often, surely it wouldn't be possible to hide anything?'

Sister Hyde paused for a moment, then said, 'I believe she may have hidden the pills in her spectacles case.'

'But surely no one would know...' Millie caught sight of Sister Hyde's forbidding expression and stopped speaking. She didn't ask how Sister knew where Maud had hidden her pills.

'I believe that's enough questions, Benedict, don't you?' Sister Hyde said. 'Suffice it to say, Mrs Mortimer is where she wants to be, and that is at peace. Let's leave it at that, shall we?'

Millie looked into her wise, surprisingly kind eyes, and realised Sister Hyde was right. She still had much to learn.

Chapter Forty-Three

Violet lurked in the shadows by the school gates. Her eyes were fixed on the doors, but still aware of everything around her. Every movement, every passer-by, made her twitch.

She checked her watch again. She hadn't wanted to send Oliver to school, but Miss Fox had advised her to maintain some semblance of normality, for his sake. At the time it had seemed like a wise decision but now, out in the open, she felt exposed. She couldn't allow herself to breathe until she saw him safe again.

'Excuse me?'

At the sound of the man's voice behind her, Violet's legs turned to jelly. She felt a hand on her shoulder and let out a scream. Seconds later, Miss Hanley appeared, bearing down on them like one of the Furies, her furled umbrella raised like a weapon.

'Unhand her at once!' she boomed.

'P-Pardon me,' the man stuttered, stepping away from her. 'I only wanted to tell you you'd dropped this.' He held out Violet's purse to her in a trembling hand.

She took it from him, embarrassed colour flooding her face. 'Thank you. I'm sorry, I thought you were someone else...' she called after him, but he was already hurrying away, looking nervously back over his shoulder at her.

Miss Hanley lowered her umbrella. 'I take it that wasn't him? He didn't look like a cad.'

'I feel so foolish.' Violet bit her lip. 'It's quite ridiculous to be jumping at shadows like this.'

'Anyone would act the same way, in your position.'

'All the same, it's not fair to involve everyone here in my situation.'

Matron had been as good as her word, mustering the sisters to come to Violet's aid. She and Oliver never went anywhere unescorted. When she was working on the wards, the other sisters took it in turns to sleep in her flat and watch over her son.

Violet was touched by the way they had rallied round her. She knew she had done little to earn such generosity, keeping them at arms' length for so long.

Even Sister Wren had come to her aid. Violet had been angry at first when she'd confessed all about answering the advertisement in the newspaper, but after she had calmed down she realised that this confrontation had been inevitable. If it hadn't been Sister Wren, then it would have been someone else eventually. And besides, Sister Wren felt so wretchedly guilty about it, Violet couldn't be angry with her for too long.

'Nonsense,' Miss Hanley dismissed her comment. 'We are like the Three Musketeers. "All for one, and one for all". And I must say, I am rather looking forward to coming face to face with that ghastly Sherman woman again. I will certainly be giving her what-for, I can tell you!' She gave her umbrella a firm shake, as if to emphasise her point. 'Although,' she continued, 'it has been three days since she last showed her face. Do you think perhaps she has decided to go home?'

'Perhaps,' Violet agreed. 'But I know she'll be back. And I daresay she will bring my husband with her next time.'

She shuddered. The thought of coming face to face with Victor again frightened her more than she could ever admit.

The doors opened, and the children began to stream out. Violet gripped the wrought-iron gate, craning her neck to peer at their faces, every muscle in her body tense until Oliver came into view. Then, finally, she could breathe again.

They walked back to the hospital quickly, Miss Hanley's long manly strides setting the pace. As Violet listened to Oliver's chatter, she was aware that the older woman was deep in thought.

As they approached the hospital gates, she finally spoke.

'I wonder, Miss Tanner, are you familiar with the Battle of Narva?'

'I beg your pardon?'

'The Battle of Narva. Swedes against the Russians? In the year seventeen hundred?' Miss Hanley shook her head. 'There's no reason why you should have heard of it, I suppose. It is a rather obscure battle in the Great Northern War, not something you'd necessarily find in our history books.' She smiled apologetically. 'You must forgive me, I'm rather a military history buff. It's what comes of following one's father's regiment halfway round the world, I suppose.' She caught Violet's blank look and continued, 'The Battle of

Narva was significant to military historians because it was such an outstanding example of how surprise and initiative can turn the tables and overwhelm far superior numbers. Let me explain...'

Violet listened, still bewildered, as Miss Hanley went into great detail about how the Russians had outnumbered the Swedish troops, but how, by using the element of surprise and with the weather on their side, the Swedish army somehow managed to outwit an enemy five times their own size.

'And all in under two hours, can you imagine that?' Miss Hanley said, her square, plain face flushed with rare excitement.

'It sounds very impressive,' Violet agreed. 'But I'm afraid I don't really understand what it has to do with me?'

'Don't you see? It's a question of strategy. The Russians hugely outnumbered the Swedish army. They were far more powerful. The last thing they expected was for the Swedes to bring the fight to them. Which is why they were so hopelessly routed.'

Slowly, her meaning began to dawn on Violet. 'So what you're saying is, you think I should take the battle to Victor? That I should go and see him, rather than wait for him to find me?'

'Exactly. That way you will have the element of surprise.'

'It would take more than surprise for me to get the better of my husband.' Violet was frightened enough at the thought of seeing him again. The idea of getting on a train and going back to

Bristol, of actually walking up to his front door, made her feel physically sick.

She was almost certain she wouldn't be able to do it. And if she did, she was just as certain she wouldn't live to tell the tale.

'It's either that, or run away from your enemy,' Miss Hanley pointed out. 'But then it's no longer a battle, is it? And it's certainly not one you can ever win.'

They passed through the courtyard and the sisters' block came into view. At last Violet felt her tense muscles begin to relax. She was safe here. Like a rabbit scurrying back into its hole.

She looked at Miss Hanley. For all her baffling talk of military strategy, she had a point. It wasn't a battle between Violet and Victor. It was a hunt. And she was the one being hunted.

Miss Hanley seemed to guess the thoughts racing through her mind. 'I can't tell you what to do,' she said. 'But I certainly know what I would do.' She regarded Violet steadily. 'It's up to you. Do you want to meet your opponent face to face, as equals on the battlefield, or do you want to spend the rest of your life as someone's helpless prey?'

'We'll miss half the feature if we don't hurry up!'

Ruby caught Nick's impatient look in the reflection of her powder compact. He was restless, but she refused to be hurried. It was good to keep a man waiting.

'One more minute.' She unscrewed her lipstick and started to apply it.

'I've never known anyone take as long to get

411

ready as you,' he grumbled.

'I've got to look my best, ain't I?'

'You're going to be sitting in the dark!'

'Don't you want everyone to think you're stepping out with the best-looking girl in Bethnal Green?'

'I'd rather see the start of this film!'

'Keep your hair on.' She pressed her lips together, then snapped her compact shut. 'All done. See? Wasn't I worth waiting for?' She blew him a scarlet-painted kiss. Nick shook his head, his smile reluctant. No matter what mood he was in, she knew he couldn't resist her flirting for long.

Dora was in next door's backyard when they left the house. And she wasn't alone.

'Look,' Ruby whispered. 'That's the bloke who's courting Dora. Let's go and say hello–'

She started towards them, but Nick held her back. 'No,' he said. 'Leave them be.'

'But we've got to be polite.'

'We're late enough as it is.' He took her arm and steered her firmly past them, so she could only give her friend a little wave and a smile as they hurried out of the back gate.

Once out in the street, he lengthened his stride until Ruby had to trot to keep up with him.

'Not so fast, I can't keep up with you in these shoes,' she complained. He slowed down a fraction, long enough for her to fasten herself to his arm. 'What's up with you?' she said.

'I told you, I don't want to miss the film,' he muttered back.

'We never watch it anyway.' Most of the time

neither of them cared what was happening on the screen, it was just an excuse to be alone together in the dark on the back row.

But tonight Nick kept his eyes fixed on *The Demon Barber of Fleet Street*. It was a gruesome film, and Ruby used every excuse it gave her to cuddle up to Nick and bury her face in his shoulder. But even though he put his arm around her, he never turned his head to kiss her. From the blank look on his face as he stared at the screen, Ruby wondered if he was even watching it himself.

Later, they walked home through the darkened streets, Ruby clinging to him.

'I'm never watching another horror film again as long as I live,' she declared, tightening her hold. 'I doubt if I'll sleep soundly in my bed again.'

She tried to keep up a conversation as they walked home, chattering on about this and that. But when he didn't answer one of her questions for the umpteenth time, frustration overcame her.

'Are you even listening to me?' she demanded, pulling away from him.

Nick stared at her blankly. 'Sorry?'

'I knew it! You haven't heard a word I've said, have you? I may as well be talking to a flaming brick wall for all the notice you're taking!'

'I've got a lot on my mind,' he said.

She gazed at his profile in the darkness. 'Like what?' He was silent. 'Go on, you can tell me.'

He turned his head slowly to look at her. His face was expressionless. 'It doesn't matter,' he said.

He put his arm around her, but for once the steel of his muscles failed to reassure her.

She had seen the look in his eyes, and she knew that whoever he was thinking about, it certainly wasn't her.

They got back to Griffin Street and Nick went to lift the latch on the back gate, but Ruby stopped him.

'Not yet,' she murmured, winding her arms around his neck and moving in for a kiss.

She might not have been much good at anything else, but Ruby Pike was a good kisser. All the boys she'd ever allowed that far had said so. She knew just what to do, how to start softly, then gradually get hungrier, more urgent, letting her tongue flicker into their mouths just enough to get them going, to make them want her.

Not that she needed to use any expertise with Nick. Just being with him aroused her so much she could barely contain her own desperate need. And he always responded to her. No matter what mood he was in, she could coax and tempt him with her hands and lips and tongue, until he was just as desperate for release as she was.

But not tonight. He barely kissed her in return, his body as rigid as a wall of granite. Finally he caught her wrists and eased her gently away from him. 'No,' he said.

She looked up at him, hurt. 'Why not?'

'I've got an early start in the morning. And Mum's probably gone out. I don't want to leave Danny on his own too long...'

He bent forward and kissed her again, but there was no passion in it. It was as if he was just going through the motions, his mind elsewhere.

Ruby could hardly look at him as he let them in through the back door and she watched him climb the stairs. His broad shoulders looked as if they had the weight of the world on them.

Fear began to uncurl in her stomach as it dawned on her that this time she might really be losing him. And there wasn't a damn thing she could do about it.

Chapter Forty-Four

Curlew House was just as Violet remembered it. It stood alone amid the Mendip Hills, a gaunt Gothic building, proud, isolated and forbidding.

She held her breath as the taxi rounded the bend and she saw the dark, jagged silhouette on the skyline.

'Drop me off here,' she told the taxi driver. 'I will walk the rest of the way.'

'Are you sure, Miss? The weather's taking a nasty turn.'

He was right. The sky had turned the colour of pewter, and a tearing wind drove sheets of rain across the moor. Appropriate weather, Violet thought. There must have been fine days when she lived here, but looking back on it, she couldn't remember a single day when the sun had shone on Curlew House.

Birds wheeled screaming overhead as she made her way through the wrought-iron gates and up the winding drive. She kept her head down, her face averted from the tall, narrow windows, afraid that if she looked up she might see eyes watching her.

Her nerve almost failed her as she forced herself up the wide stone steps to the front door. She hesitated, her hand on the bell pull. This was it, she realised. Once she rang that bell, there was no going back.

She took a deep breath, and pulled on the chain. The dull sonorous clang that echoed within the house sounded like a death knell.

It was some moments before she heard the slow, stately tread in the hall. Then Mrs Sherman opened the door.

Violet saw the look of shock on her face, and instantly knew Miss Hanley was right. She certainly had caught her off guard.

The housekeeper stared at her speechless for a moment. 'You!'

'Hello, Mrs Sherman.' Violet forced herself to stay calm, just as she'd practised. 'May I come in?'

Nothing had changed. The house seemed to close in on her, with its oppressive dark walls and heavy aged furniture. She found herself tiptoeing across the black-and-white-tiled floor out of habit, her whole body tense lest she accidentally say or do something to incur Victor's wrath.

She was aware of Mrs Sherman following her into the drawing room, keys jingling on her belt like a gaoler. Barely a night went by when Violet didn't wake up, bathed in sweat, after hearing those jingling keys in her nightmares.

'What do you want?' the housekeeper demanded.

Violet forced herself to stand straight, to stay calm. She knew Mrs Sherman could smell fear, that she thrived on it. She was determined not to give her the satisfaction. Not any more.

'I'm hardly going to tell *you*, am I?' She pulled off her gloves with studied casualness and gazed around the room. Her eye went to the ornate black marble fireplace. Once, when Victor had thrown her across the room in a fit of rage, she had cracked her skull against it and bled so profusely that even he was concerned. Mrs Sherman had covered the dark stains on the polished wooden floor with a Chinese rug. It was still there to this day.

Violet suppressed the tremor that went through her and turned to face the other woman with a forced smile. 'Aren't you going to offer me any tea? That's what servants do isn't it?'

The older woman's mouth curled in contempt. 'I wouldn't serve the likes of you!'

Violet sighed. 'That's probably for the best, since I couldn't trust you not to poison me.'

An angry muscle worked in Mrs Sherman's rigid jaw. 'You have a nerve, coming here like this!'

Violet raised her eyebrows. 'But I understand you have been looking for me?'

'Not you. The boy. Where is he?'

'You don't really think I'd bring him here, do you?' Violet smiled pityingly. 'He's quite safe, back in London. Being well looked after.'

'By those old maids at that hospital?' Mrs

417

Sherman's face was scornful. 'That's no place to bring up a child.'

'Really, Mrs Sherman!' Violet forced herself to smile. 'You're an old maid too, don't forget.' The title 'Mrs' was a courtesy one, conferred on all high-ranking female household staff. 'Unless my husband has committed bigamy and married you?' she added. 'Oh, don't look so mortified, Mrs Sherman. I'm well aware that you've loved Victor from afar for years. What a pity he couldn't bring himself to marry so far beneath him. It might have saved us all a lot of heartache, don't you think?'

Mrs Sherman gasped with outrage. 'You're the one that was beneath him!' she shot back. 'Nasty, ill-bred little creature, trying to claw your way up the social ladder like that revolting mother of yours. I wonder what he ever saw in you–'

Violet stood and stared as the other woman's rage and spite rained down on her like a shower of sparks. She had never seen Mrs Sherman lose her icy control before. For the first time she felt as if she had the upper hand.

'Your jealousy does you no credit, Mrs Sherman,' she said, silencing her. 'Now, I haven't come here to waste my time arguing with you. I wish to see my husband.'

'You can't. He doesn't want to see you.'

'We both know that isn't true, don't we? Or why would he spend so much time and effort putting advertisements in the newspapers and sending you to look for me?'

'I told you, it wasn't you he was looking for. It was the boy. He wanted to see his son.' Mrs Sherman recovered some of her old froideur, her back straightening. 'You were nothing to him. You never were. Only a means to an end,' she said coldly.

Violet ignored the insult. 'Nevertheless, I intend to see him.' She sat down on the polished leather Chesterfield and arranged the folds of her coat around her.

Mrs Sherman's chin lifted. 'He won't take you back, if that's what you've come for.'

Violet laughed. 'Oh, Mrs Sherman, can you really be so deluded?' She shook her head. 'I haven't come to beg for a reconciliation. That is the furthest thing from my mind. I've come to tell him to leave me alone.'

'And I'm sure he will be only too happy to do so – if you hand over the boy.'

'So he can be brought up by you? In this prison?' Violet looked around in disdain. Victor Dangerfield's ancestors glared frostily from the walls. While she'd lived here their constant disapproval had cowed her almost as much as her husband's violent outbursts.

'This is Oliver's home,' Mrs Sherman said stiffly. 'He belongs here, with his father.'

Violet shook her head. 'He belongs with me. What kind of life would he have here? With a father who knows only how to hate, to bully, to be cruel?'

'He loves the boy.'

'He doesn't know the first thing about love, and neither do you!' Violet reined in her temper, determined to stay calm. 'If I have anything to do with it, Oliver will never even know this place exists,' she said levelly.

'We'll see about that, won't we?' The house-keeper's voice was heavy with meaning.

Violet looked up at her. 'Is that a threat, Mrs Sherman? Because I'm afraid you don't frighten me any more. And neither does my husband.'

It was true, she realised. For five years, Curlew House, Mrs Sherman and Victor had been the stuff of her nightmares, taking on monstrous, almost supernatural qualities of fear and terror.

But now, coming here again, she realised that it was just an old, decaying house. And Mrs Sherman was just an old, very ordinary woman.

She glanced at her watch. 'I don't have much time before my taxi returns. Now, may I see my husband?'

'He is not at home,' Mrs Sherman said shortly.

'Where is he?' For a panicky moment she worried he might have gone to London. Perhaps he was at the Nightingale even now.

'I can't tell you that.' Mrs Sherman's eyes slid away from hers. 'I will arrange for you to speak to his lawyers–'

'I want to know where he is!' Violet cut across her.

'He is – abroad. He no longer lives here for most of the year. He prefers the climate in the South of France.' She started to usher Violet back towards the door. 'Perhaps if you'd contacted the solicitors as he requested in the advertisement, it would have saved you a wasted journey. As it is–'

Footsteps creaked overhead.

Violet looked at the ceiling. 'Who is that?'

'No one. We are ... having the chimneys swept.'

'At this time of year?' She was through the door

and into the hall before Mrs Sherman could stop her.

'You can't go up there.' The housekeeper rushed after her, blocking the way at the foot of the sweeping staircase.

Violet glanced at her, saw the stricken look in her pale eyes. 'Why not? What are you hiding?'

'Me,' said a voice above them. 'She is hiding me.'

The voice stopped Violet in her tracks. She swung round as Victor emerged from the shadows at the top of the staircase.

'Hello, Violet,' he said. 'Welcome home.'

Chapter Forty-Five

Her first reaction was one of shock.

He came down the stairs, leaning heavily on the banisters. He was much thinner than she remembered him, his sharply drawn face softened only by a small pointed beard.

But the effect he had on her was still the same. She gripped the carved newel post to stop herself from running

'Hello, Victor,' she said.

'Violet, how unexpected,' he greeted her genially. 'You really should have told us you were coming. You know how Mrs Sherman loathes surprises.'

He reached the foot of the stairs and Mrs Sherman darted forward to help him, but he shook her off with a flash of impatience that reminded Violet of the man she'd once known.

'I can manage, Mrs Sherman, thank you.' He smiled tensely at Violet. 'She does like to fuss, after my recent illness.'

He picked up a walking cane from the foot of the stairs, and limped towards the drawing room. Violet could see his teeth clenched with effort. Just for a second, her heart went out to him.

'You'll have some tea.' It was more of a statement than a question.

'No, thank you.' In spite of her weariness after her journey, she had quickly made up her mind to take nothing from Victor.

He looked at her sharply, but didn't argue. 'Then perhaps, Mrs Sherman, you would be good enough to bring me some?' he requested.

He sat down in one of the armchairs, breathing hard from the effort. Violet chose the seat farthest away from him.

He looked at her for a long time. His skin had the yellowing translucence of wax, she noticed. 'It's good to see you again, Violet,' he said.

'I wish I could say the same about you,' she replied.

She saw a flash of irritation in his dark eyes, quickly masked. 'How is my son?' he asked.

'Very well.'

'Mrs Sherman tells me he has grown into a fine boy. You seem shocked?' He looked amused. 'Did you think she'd have left London without getting at least a glimpse of Oliver. She has been watching both of you,' he said. 'She is my eyes and ears.'

'She always was.' Violet fought to keep her voice neutral, but inside she felt angry and violated.

'Not that you made it very easy for her to find you,' he went on. 'You've been very clever, Violet, covering your tracks.' He sounded almost admiring. 'I didn't think you capable of such deceit.'

'Then you underestimated me, didn't you?'

'Obviously.' His eyes held hers, dark and compelling in his thin, drawn face.

Mrs Sherman came in, bringing the tea on a tray. She set it down on the table and was about to pour it when Victor dismissed her with a wave of his hand.

'You can leave that, Mrs Sherman. I'm sure my wife will see to it.' He didn't look at her as he said it. Violet felt a twinge of pity for the other woman as she stood awkwardly for a moment before hurrying out of the door.

Violet had been a victim of Victor's casual cruelty too often not to notice its effect on someone else.

'We still have your belongings upstairs,' he said. 'Mrs Sherman packed them up and stored them in the attic.'

'You should have burnt them.'

'Mrs Sherman wanted to, but I refused. I always knew you would be back – eventually.' He smiled thinly, pleased with himself.

'Why should I ever come back here?'

'Because this is your home.'

She stared at him in disbelief. 'You can't really think that!'

'Why not? Surely this house still holds memories for you. It was where I brought you as a bride, after all...'

'You want to talk about memories, Victor.' She

423

pointed to the fireplace. 'Remember how badly I bled the night you threw me against that? Even you were afraid, as I recall.'

He winced. 'It was an unfortunate accident. You stumbled–'

'Yes, I stumbled. Just like I stumbled in the bedroom, and cracked all my ribs. And in the dining room, and ended up with this.' She yanked up her sleeve to show the puckered line of pale skin where the wound had never healed cleanly. 'Or what about the bruises your fingertips left around my neck, time after time?' She saw his averted face and realised that he would never be able to confront the reality of what he had done.

But that didn't matter any more. She no longer cared.

'What do you want, Victor?' she asked.

'I want Oliver.'

'Never.' She shook her head.

'But he's my son. He must ask about me?'

'I've told him you're dead.'

Victor flinched. 'You told him that? That was very cruel of you.'

'You would know all about cruelty, wouldn't you?'

He paused for a moment. Reaching across, he picked up the teapot. It took both his hands to hold it, Violet noticed.

'Very well,' he said. 'I will instruct my lawyers to begin proceedings against you. And I'm warning you, there is not a court in the land that will grant custody to a woman who runs away from her husband.'

'And there isn't a court in the land that will

grant custody to a dying man, either.'

His cup rattled briefly in its saucer. 'I don't know what you mean.'

'Victor, please. I've been a nurse long enough to spot the signs of advanced cancer.'

When he finally looked up at her, the look in his eyes was grudgingly impressed.

'You're very observant.'

'How much time do you have left?'

'Weeks, possibly months. It's spreading so fast now it's difficult to tell.' She could see him stiffening against the pain, refusing to give in to it.

'You must be suffering a great deal?'

His mouth tightened. 'You'd like that, wouldn't you?'

'Actually, no.' Impossibly, she felt a surge of pity. She no longer had a shred of love left in her for him, but that didn't mean she couldn't feel some kind of human compassion. Even if he'd never shown any for her.

He must have seen the expression on her face because he pounced on it. 'That's why I want you to come home,' he said. 'You and Oliver. I want us to be a family again. Just for the time I have left.'

'No!'

'It would only be for a short while. A few weeks at most.' His voice faltered. 'I don't want to die alone.'

'You won't be alone. You have Mrs Sherman.'

'Ah, yes. Mrs Sherman.' His mouth twisted bitterly. 'Perhaps we get the companions we deserve in life.' He regarded her steadily. 'If you won't come back to live with me, at least allow me to see my son one more time. I want to say goodbye to him.'

She hesitated for a moment, then shook her head. 'It would only confuse him.'

'Please.'

It was the first time he'd said the word to her without it being edged with sarcasm or malice. Even then she regarded him warily, expecting the wounding remark, the physical blow, that would follow.

Victor stared at the Chinese rug in front of the fire. Violet wondered if the dark stain would still be there on the floorboards underneath. 'I realise I probably have no right to ask a favour of you,' he said. 'But nonetheless I am appealing to you, as a human being. And as someone who once loved me,' he added.

Violet looked at him, seeing the thin face, waxy skin stretched over prominent bones. He seemed such a pathetic figure, so frail, his bony hands grasping his stick. Hard to imagine that those hands had once dragged her from this room by the hair, yanking her head back so hard she thought her neck was going to snap.

But now the power had shifted. Now he was the one who was scared and isolated.

'I'll think about it,' she said shortly.

Chapter Forty-Six

'Now expel the air ... that's it. Keep the point of the needle upwards while pushing the piston ... oh, do stop shaking, Nurse Benedict. You're hardly inspiring confidence, are you?'

'Sorry, Sister.' Millie's hands were slick with sweat as she turned the screw on the piston, checking the dose on the rod. Aware of Sister Hyde's beady eyes on her, she checked the dosage on the patient's notes, rechecked the fluid in the syringe, then showed it to the Sister for her to check again.

Mrs Isles, the elderly victim who had been selected for Millie to practise on, eyed her apprehensively. 'You do know what you're doing, love, don't you?' she whispered.

'Oh, yes,' Millie assured her, smiling shakily. 'I've practised on lots of oranges in PTS.'

Sister Hyde shook her head. 'Swab the needle with alcohol,' she sighed. 'Now you're ready to proceed with the injection.'

That was easier said than done. The poor old dear didn't have a lot on her bones to start with, so finding a suitable area wasn't easy. But finally Millie pinched a portion of wrinkled flesh and poised the needle.

'Well? What are you waiting for? Do it, girl!'

Millie caught Mrs Isles' terrified eyes a second before she plunged the point of the needle in, releasing the skin as she did so. She was already picturing the patient howling in pain, blood everywhere, Sister Hyde yelling at her, telling her she was an idiot. So the silence that followed was almost deafening.

Unable to believe what she'd done, she withdrew the needle and held the swab over the pinprick of blood. Swallowing hard, she looked expectantly at Sister Hyde, awaiting her fate.

She gave a curt nod. 'Very good, Nurse,' she said. 'Bring your training record to me and I will sign it before you go off duty.'

It was as if the sun had come out and angelic choirs had filled the skies. But before she could enjoy the moment, Sister Hyde added, 'Don't stand there gawping like a fish, girl. Get this lot cleared up. And mind you do it properly.'

Millie stared after her as she strode back down the ward, her stout shoes squeaking on the polished floor. Mrs Isles grinned toothlessly at her.

'Bet you weren't expecting that, were you, love?'

'Not at all.' Millie had been working very hard over the past week, and doing her very best. True to her word, Sister Hyde had been spending as much time as she could demonstrating various techniques, and Millie had tried to take it all in. And her efforts seemed to be paying off; once or twice she had even caught Sister Hyde watching her with something like approval.

Millie grinned at the patient. 'Thanks for not screaming when I injected you.'

'Didn't feel a thing,' the old lady reassured her.

'Your first subcutaneous injection – well done!' Helen congratulated Millie as she sterilised the equipment in the sluice a few minutes later. 'Sister Hyde seemed pleased with you.'

'I know.'

'You don't seem too happy about it?' her friend said, watching her closely.

'I am, it's just–'

'You're still thinking about Seb, aren't you?'

Millie pressed her lips together. It had been a lot easier when no one knew about her and Seb breaking up. But she'd grown tired of trying to put a brave face on everything, and once she'd told William there didn't seem much point in keeping it from her friends.

But now she had to suffer their endless sympathy instead. She appreciated it, but it didn't help her to forget her dire predicament.

She nodded. 'I miss him,' she said simply.

'You should talk to him.'

'Oh, no, I couldn't!'

'Why not? You can't go on moping for ever, neither engaged nor disengaged. If nothing else, you've got to decide how to break the news to your families.'

'You're right.' Millie sighed miserably. 'We should talk about that, at least.'

But she dreaded the idea of seeing Sebastian again even more than she dreaded the thought of telling her grandmother she'd lost him.

Rumours of their broken engagement were already beginning to drift around London. It wouldn't be long, she was sure, before they reached the ears of Lady Rettingham in deepest Kent.

'And you never know,' Helen suggested brightly.

'You might see each other and fall madly in love again.'

'Or we might not,' Millie said dolefully. That was what she feared most. This strange, half-disengaged state might not be making her very happy, but it was a lot better than the thought of being apart from Seb for ever.

Dora hauled the sack of soiled dressings down the stone steps to the stoke hole. It was her last day on Wren, and Sister was making the most of her chance to give Dora all the worst jobs to do.

Not that she minded. Tomorrow she would be on Female Medical with Sister Everett, the eccentric woman who played hymns on her harmonica and kept a parrot in her room, but who was known to be very fair and kind to students.

Going down to the stoke hole was like descending into hell. The narrow flight of steps led down to a closed off area of the basement that was infernally hot, the darkness lit only by flickering tongues of flame. Acrid smoke belched from the gaping, fiery mouth of the furnace. Hellish as it was, it was popular with the nurses. They would gather around the stoke hole, dodging showers of sparks, frantically smoking cigarettes before their absence was noticed.

There were no nurses down here today. But there was Nick Riley.

He was shovelling coal into the furnace. He'd stripped off the top half of his overalls, and the hard muscles of his chest and arms glistened in the flickering firelight as he worked.

Dora hesitated at the bottom of the steps, not

sure what to do. She was still standing there when he stopped to wipe his brow with the back of his hand and saw her.

'Sorry! I didn't notice you there.' He grabbed his overall, shoving his arms into the sleeves.

'It's all right.' She moved past him stiffly and made to lift the sack, but he reached for it.

'Here, let me.' Their hands brushed as he took it from her, and they both jumped back from the contact.

Nick threw the sack in one-handed, and they stood awkwardly, watching the flames engulf it. He was so close she could smell the manly scent of his skin. Combined with the heat, it made her feel dizzy. She knew she should walk away, but her feet felt as if they were glued to the stone floor.

'Is it true about you and Joe Armstrong?' His voice was so low, she could barely hear it over the crackle of the flames.

Dora looked at his strong profile, illuminated by the firelight. His dark hair curled damply around his face, sticking to his neck.

'Who told you that?'

'Are you courting?'

'What if I am?'

Nick picked up a poker and jabbed at the fire, sending up a shower of sparks. 'He doesn't seem like your type,' he commented at last.

Dora flicked an angry look at him. How dare he! He didn't want her, not now he had Ruby. How dare he try to interfere in her life?

'What do you know about it?' she reacted scornfully. 'You don't even know what my type is.

You don't know anything about me.'

'Don't I?'

He turned to look at her, a scorching look that took her breath away. They weren't touching, but she could feel the heat from his body wrapping around her like a passionate embrace.

He was right, she thought. Without being told, he knew everything about her. And she knew everything about him, too. There was an elemental connection between them that neither of them could fight.

'I – like Joe,' she said quietly. 'He's kind, and he treats me well–'

'Is that why you chose him and not me?' Nick burst out. Reflected firelight burnt in his eyes.

It felt as if they were standing on the edge of a precipice. One word, one more step, and they would both be plunging headlong into the abyss, into something they couldn't control.

'Please, Nick,' she whispered. 'Why do you have to say this now?'

'Because I can't stop myself!' His voice was broken with emotion. 'God knows I've tried to fight it, to keep myself away from you. But I can't watch you with him, knowing how I feel about you.'

'And how do you think I feel?' Dora shot back. 'I've had to watch you with Ruby!'

His eyes narrowed. 'Don't blame this on me,' he said hoarsely. 'I came to you, remember? That night I tried to kiss you, to tell you how I felt. But you just pushed me away. That night's haunted me ever since.'

'It's haunted me too!'

Their eyes held, locked together in a conversation that needed no words.

Finally, he said softly, 'If I did it again, what would you do?'

Dora couldn't answer him. She was so desperate for him to kiss her she had to fight the urge to take hold of him and pull him to her. Just being this close to him was causing a ball of heat to build up deep inside her belly.

'Answer me.' His voice was ragged with longing, his gaze fixed on her mouth. 'If I came to you again, would you push me away?'

Slowly, she shook her head. 'You know I wouldn't. But we can't,' she said. 'We've got to think about Ruby.'

'Jesus!' He stepped away from her, running a hand through his dark, damp curls. 'What else do you suppose I'm thinking about? It's the only thing that's stopping me taking you in my arms and kissing you now.'

He turned back to the fire, attacking the coal with the poker. 'I have to finish with her,' he said bluntly.

Dora stared at him, appalled. 'You can't! She loves you, it would break her heart–'

'So what am I supposed to do? Stay with her when I'm in love with someone else? Don't you think that would hurt her more in the end?'

Dora was too nonplussed to speak for a moment. 'You ... love me?' she said slowly.

Nick glanced at her, the corners of his mouth lifting. 'Dora Doyle, I've always loved you,' he said gruffly. He dropped the poker with a clatter. 'So will you wait for me?' he asked.

Dora hesitated. Happiness was bursting out of her, but it was tempered with guilt. 'But poor Ruby–'

Nick took a step towards her, so close she could feel the heat from his body. 'Dora, I'm going to finish with her whatever happens. I care about Ruby. She's a good girl, and it's not fair to mess her about.' He looked at her, firelight flickering in his eyes under his mop of dark curls. 'So will you be waiting for me, or not?'

She smiled up at him. 'Yes,' she said. 'Yes, I'll be waiting for you.'

Chapter Forty-Seven

'Why are we here, Mummy?'

Oliver stared up, wide-eyed, at the tall gates of Curlew House, his hand tightening in hers.

Relief surged through Violet. She had been so afraid he might remember the house, and the people who lived there.

'We've come to visit someone, darling.'

'Who?'

'Someone Mummy used to know, a long time ago.'

She had decided not to tell him who Victor really was. As she had explained to her husband, she didn't want to confuse the boy. It was one of the conditions she had made before agreeing to this meeting, and Victor had conceded at once. Violet had sensed his desperation and was moved by it despite herself.

They set off up the drive but Oliver hung back, digging his heels into the gravel.

'I don't want to go,' he said. 'I don't like it here.'

Neither do I, Violet thought, gazing up at the dark, ivy-covered walls of the Gothic house. Even in the fresh spring sunshine the place seemed gloomy and forbidding. A chill of apprehension ran over her skin.

It had taken a lot of soul-searching before she'd agreed to return here. Her first reaction was to stay away, but much as she hated the idea of seeing Victor again, she couldn't find it in her heart to deny him the right to see his son one last time.

'We have to, sweetheart. The person we have come to see is very sick, and we need to cheer him up.'

'Is he dying?' Oliver asked, fascinated.

'Yes.'

He looked up apprehensively at the tall, narrow windows. 'Will we have to see his body?'

'No, we won't.' Violet squeezed his hand. 'It'll only be a short visit, and then we can catch the train back home.'

She brought herself up sharply, realising what she'd said. It was a long time since she'd said the word 'home' and really meant it.

Mrs Sherman must have been watching for them because she had the door open before they were halfway up the drive. She ran down the steps, holding out her arms.

'Oliver! My darling boy!' She made to embrace him but Oliver cringed behind Violet, hiding his face in her coat. Mrs Sherman's face fell. 'He doesn't remember me,' she said flatly.

'No,' Violet said. 'He doesn't.' She could spare her husband some compassion, but not Mrs Sherman. If the older woman had had her way, Oliver wouldn't have remembered his mother either. 'Oliver, this is Mrs Sherman. Say how do you do?'

'How do you do?' Oliver mumbled reluctantly, his face still hidden in her hip.

'How is Victor?' Violet asked.

'His health is failing fast.' Mrs Sherman kept her gaze locked on Oliver, devouring him with her pale, strange eyes. 'He should be confined to bed, but he insisted on coming downstairs to receive his–' She caught the warning flash in Violet's glance. 'His guests,' she amended, through tight lips.

Victor was waiting for them in the drawing room. One glance told Violet that he had deteriorated rapidly since their last meeting. He sat hunched forward in his wing-backed chair, both hands resting heavily on the point of his cane. But he was as immaculately dressed as ever, although his suit hung off his shockingly thin frame. Victor had always set great store by appearances.

His dull, yellowish eyes lit up at the sight of them. 'You came,' he said.

'I said I would.' Violet put her arm around her son, still clinging to her, and propelled him gently forward. 'Say hello to Mr Dangerfield, Oliver.'

'How do you do, Oliver? I'm pleased to meet you, young man.' Victor held out his hand, stiffly formal. But Violet could see his mouth trembling, as if he was fighting to keep in a great outburst of emotion.

He looked up at her. 'Will you leave us?' he asked.

'No.' Violet and Oliver spoke together. Behind them in the doorway, Mrs Sherman gave a tut of impatience.

Oliver gazed at Violet with fear-filled eyes. 'Please don't go, Mummy,' he begged.

'I won't.' She stroked her son's head, smoothing down his dark hair. 'He can sometimes be wary of strangers,' she said to Victor.

Not that she would have left him, in any case. Even now, she couldn't trust her husband not to break his promise and try some trick to take her son away from her.

Victor's mouth firmed. 'As you both wish,' he said. 'But I hope you will have tea with us this time?' He sent her a meaningful look. 'Mrs Sherman has taken a great deal of trouble to prepare it.'

He nodded to the housekeeper who sprang forward avidly. 'I have baked all your favourites,' she told Oliver, her pale eyes shining. 'Fairy cakes, angel cake, banana loaf–'

'I like chocolate cake best,' he announced. 'Sister Parker has chocolate cake for us sometimes, when I visit her and Sister Sutton for tea,' he added importantly.

Mrs Sherman's lips quivered. 'I'm afraid I don't have chocolate cake,' she faltered.

'It doesn't matter,' he told her kindly. 'I'm sure your cakes will be smashing. Won't they, Mummy?'

Victor's cruel laugh turned into a hacking

cough. 'The child knows his own mind,' he said.

Violet ignored him, noticing Mrs Sherman's stricken expression. Only the hardest and most unfeeling person would not have felt for the other woman's distress.

Mrs Sherman had prepared a magnificent spread for tea. As they took their places around the table she watched them with longing from the doorway, her gaze still fixed on Oliver. Violet sensed her reluctance to be out of his presence.

'Won't you join us, Mrs Sherman?' she invited her boldly. Mrs Sherman's gaze flicked from her to Victor, hope flaring in her eyes. 'I'm sure Mr Dangerfield won't mind, as this is a special occasion?' Violet stared at Victor, daring him to disagree.

She noted the look of quiet fury on his face, but all he could say was, 'Yes, please join us, Mrs Sherman.'

Sitting down to tea together reminded Violet of all the interminable meals she had taken in this house, sitting at the table with her eyes lowered, terrified that Victor would pick her up on some dreadful mistake she had made in her manners. Speaking only when spoken to, not daring to offer an opinion, fearful of a black look from beneath his bushy brows.

But Oliver's presence had transformed him. He talked to the child animatedly about his likes, dislikes and interests. Which were his best subjects at school? Which sports did he enjoy? Victor devoured the information with a keen interest Violet had never seen in him before, his face lighting up with pride as Oliver boasted about the prize he had won at school for his spelling, and the adventure stories he loved to read. She saw the way Victor looked at his son, and her heart ached for the family they might have been.

Gradually Oliver lost his shyness as he talked about his school, the hospital, and the garden he was planting with Sister Sutton.

'And I'm teaching Sparky to fetch a stick,' he told them proudly. 'Although he's not very good at it yet.'

'Would you like to play in our garden?' Victor suggested.

Oliver gazed longingly out of the window. 'May I?'

'I don't think so, darling...' Violet began to say, but Victor cut her off.

'I don't see why not,' he said.

'He's wearing his best clothes.'

'You wouldn't deny the child fresh air and fun for the sake of some mud, would you?' Victor's eyes glinted challengingly. 'What a spoilsport your mother is, Oliver.'

Violet was silent, staring at him with intense dislike. He couldn't help himself. He had to dominate her. Even now he was trying to twist her son against her.

'Mrs Sherman will help you with your coat.' Ignoring Violet's wishes Victor nodded to the housekeeper, who rose eagerly from the table and held out her hand to the boy.

Oliver hesitated. 'May I go, Mummy?' he asked.

Violet gave him a tight smile. 'Of course, darling. But stay where I can see you, won't you?'

'And don't go off with the bad people!' Oliver

439

finished for her, singing out the words merrily.

'Is that what I am to him? One of the bad people?' Victor asked in a low voice, as they watched him play from the window. She couldn't drag her eyes away, fearful that if she took her eyes off her son for even a second he would be spirited away.

'For a long time, yes.'

'And am I still one of the bad people?'

'You tell me.'

They stood in silence, watching their son running on the grass, his arms outstretched like an aeroplane in flight. The old grandfather clock measured the passing minutes with a steady, echoing tick.

'He's a fine boy,' Victor said at last, not looking at her. 'A credit to you.'

She steeled herself, waiting for the barb. It didn't come. 'Thank you,' she said.

He leant heavily against the stone sill, supporting himself with a thin, claw-like hand. 'I wish things had been different.'

'So do I.'

'It's not too late.' He turned his gaze on her. 'You could come back and live here?'

'So you can try and turn him against me?'

'So I can spend some time with my son before I die.'

She steeled herself. 'I've already told you, Victor, that's out of the question.'

'Why? The boy is a Dangerfield. I need him here.'

She looked at him, understanding. 'This is nothing to do with loving your son, is it? You're just a scared, sick man who doesn't want to die alone.'

'The child belongs with his family,' he bit out.

'Family!' Her mouth curled with contempt. 'We were never a family, Victor.'

'He is *my* flesh and blood!'

'Perhaps. But he is not your family.' She stared at him, unflinching. 'You have no family, Victor. You lost your family the day you first raised your hand to me.'

A muscle twitched in his jaw. 'Perhaps we should ask the boy if he wants to stay here?' he snapped.

'I decide what's best for him.'

'Running up and down the country, dragging him from hovel to hovel – is that what you call doing your best?' he sneered. 'I can give him more than you ever could.'

The steely hatred in his eyes wrenched Violet back into the past. She saw herself on the floor, cowering under his raised hand.

'I am his mother,' she whispered, her courage failing her.

'And I am his father.' Victor lifted his hand and Violet flinched before she realised he was gesturing to Mrs Sherman to bring Oliver inside again.

Panic filled her chest. 'What are you doing?'

Victor gave her a chilly smile. 'I am going to talk to my son.'

He turned slowly, shuffling around on his cane as Mrs Sherman ushered Oliver into the room. He was out of breath and pink-cheeked from running, his dark hair sticking up.

'Did you enjoy the garden, Oliver?' Victor smiled at him.

441

'Oh, yes, thank you, sir.' He turned to Violet. 'You should come and see it, Mummy. There's a little summerhouse, and a wood – and a lake with fish in it, just like the park!'

'I know, sweetheart,' she said quietly.

Victor addressed the child. 'How would you like to play in that garden every day?'

Violet stiffened. 'Victor–' she began, but he held up a hand to silence her.

'I have asked the boy a question,' he bit out.

Oliver frowned in confusion, looking from one to the other. 'I – I don't understand–'

'It's quite simple, Oliver. I am asking if you – and your mother, of course – would like to come and stay here. You could have the garden to play in, and you could choose which flowers to plant. Mrs Sherman could help you. Isn't that right, Mrs Sherman?'

'Yes, sir.' Violet saw the housekeeper's tight smile out of the corner of her eye.

'You could even have a dog, if you wished,' Victor promised.

'A dog?' Oliver's face lit up. 'You mean a puppy?'

'One of your very own. Think of the fun you could have, and all the tricks you could teach it.'

Violet's heart sank, and she tried to step in. 'Really, I don't think–' she started to say, but Victor cut her off.

'Let the child speak for himself,' he said curtly, eyes still fixed on Oliver. 'Well, boy? What do you say to that?'

Oliver considered it for a moment. 'It sounds very nice, sir,' he replied cautiously. 'But if you don't mind, I prefer the gardens at the hospital. I really don't think Sister Sutton could manage without me there. She finds it very hard to bend in her old age, you see. And there would be no one to throw sticks for Sparky. He's old too, but he's getting quite good at playing fetch.' Oliver glanced warily at his mother. 'If that's all right?' he said.

'Of course it is, sweetheart.' Violet smiled with pride in her son. She turned to Victor. 'I think you have your answer.'

They left soon afterwards. As Violet bundled Oliver into his coat in the hallway, Victor asked, 'Will you bring him again?'

She met his gaze, something she had rarely dared to do before. 'No,' she said. 'No, I don't think I will.'

His eyes narrowed, but he nodded briefly. Even her husband knew when he was beaten.

'I understand,' he said quietly.

'Who was that man, Mummy?' Oliver asked again, when they were in the taxi heading back to the station.

'I told you, darling. He's just someone Mummy used to know.'

'So he isn't my father?'

Ice trickled down her spine. 'What makes you say that?'

'That old lady whispered it to me, when we were in the garden. But I told her not to be silly, because my father was handsome and clever and he's dead.' Oliver pulled a face. 'And I didn't like that old lady. She kept trying to touch me, and she had hands like claws. Like a witch.' He twisted round to look out of the narrow strip of back window. 'Do you think there were ghosts in that old house, Mummy?'

Violet glanced back at Curlew House, receding into the distance. 'I think there probably were.'

'How horrible.' He flopped back in his seat. 'We don't have to go back there, do we?'

Violet stroked his head. 'No, Oliver.' She smiled. 'We don't have to go back there ever again.'

Chapter Forty-Eight

Ruby Pike had never looked so lovely. She was wearing a new pink dress that clung to her figure, her blonde hair falling in soft waves around her face.

'Do you like it? It's how Jean Harlow does hers,' she said, primping her curls with her fingers.

'It's – very nice.' Nick could hardly look into her eyes.

She went to kiss him, but he averted his face so she caught only the corner of his mouth. 'Shall we get going?' he said, moving towards the door.

'Where are you taking me tonight?' Ruby smiled up at him. 'There's a new film on at the Rialto.'

'I thought we'd just walk down to the café for pie and mash.'

Her painted mouth curved downwards in disappointment. Usually she would complain, say she was wearing the wrong shoes, or tell him in no uncertain terms she hadn't dressed up like a Hollywood starlet just to sit in some greasy Joe's.

But this time she nodded compliantly. She seemed very anxious to please, almost as if she knew what Nick was planning to do.

He'd lain awake all the previous night, trying to work out how to break the news. There was no easy way to tell her it was over, but it had to be done. He couldn't go on pretending, it wasn't fair on either of them.

He thought about Dora, seeing her smiling face in his mind's eye. He still couldn't believe that she actually loved him. Dreams didn't often come true for the likes of Nick Riley, but this one had.

Now he began to dream of other things, too. He saw them flying off to America together with Danny, to start their new life. He saw them arriving in New York, stepping off that aeroplane, hand in hand, their hearts full of hope. He'd talked about going often enough, but deep down he'd always doubted if he could take that final step. Now, with Dora by his side, he felt brave enough to take on the world.

'Nick?' Ruby's voice brought him up short. He started guiltily. He'd been so preoccupied with his own thoughts, he hadn't realised how far they'd walked. Now she was standing outside the pie and mash shop, both hands planted on her hips. 'Are we going in, or what?' she demanded.

Inside, the brightly lit café was warm and busy. The aroma of freshly baked pies mingling with the pungent tang of cooked eels was usually irresistible, but for once Nick didn't feel hungry as they slid into one of the wooden booths that ran down one side of the café. On the other side, a large

445

woman in a white overall served a line of customers from behind the marble-topped counter, ladling pie and mash and liquor on to plates and handing them over with one hand while deftly ringing up the till with the other.

'What are you having?' Nick offered, pulling out his wallet.

'Just a cup of tea for me.'

He frowned at Ruby. He was in no mood to eat, but it wasn't like her to miss out. 'You sure?'

'I know. I'm a cheap date, ain't I?' Ruby's smile didn't meet her eyes as she took off her hat and fluffed up her curls.

He watched her as he lined up at the counter for their order. She seemed miles away as she sat writing her name in the steamed-up window. He wondered with a jolt if she really did know what was coming. Perhaps she was preparing herself for it as much as he was?

Whatever troubled thoughts were in her mind seemed to be gone by the time he returned to the table with their tea. From having nothing to say, Ruby suddenly seemed anxious to fill the silence. Nick listened to her gossiping about the goings-on at the garment factory, and her brothers' latest brush with the law, letting her words wash over him as he struggled to work out what he was going to say.

Finally, as they drained the last of the tea in their cups, he knew he couldn't put it off any longer.

'Listen, Ruby–' he began.

'Ooh, look,' she said, pointing out of the window. 'You see that woman's coat? I was thinking of buying one just like it. What do you think?'

'Very nice. Ruby, I've been thinking '

'I'm not sure it would suit me, though. I think you have to be a lot taller to carry that fashion off.'

'Ruby–'

'And the colour is a bit dull, isn't it? I like something nice and bright myself–'

'Ruby!' He caught her hand, turning her towards him.

'Listen to me, please. I've got something to say to you.'

She sobered instantly, her smile disappearing. 'I've got something to say to you, too.'

Her sudden seriousness caught him unawares. 'What is it?'

'You go first.'

'No, you.'

'All right.' She looked down at their hands, still clasped together on the table, then back up at him. 'I'm pregnant,' she said.

Nick felt as if he'd had an unguarded blow to the stomach, knocking all the wind out of him. The smell of the greasy food suddenly made him feel sick.

'You what?'

'For gawd's sake, Nick, don't make me say it again. It's taken me all my nerve to say it once.'

He stared at her. She sat across the table from him, her blue eyes huge. She'd chewed off most of her lipstick 'Well, say something!' Her smile wobbled.

'But how–?'

Her eyebrows rose. 'Do you want me to draw

447

you a picture?'

'No, I mean – I thought we were careful?'

'Accidents happen.'

He ran his hand through his hair. It suddenly felt as if his ribs were squeezing the air out of him, making it impossible to breathe.

It couldn't be true, not now. How could he have been so stupid?

'Have you told anyone else?'

She shook her head. 'I thought you should be the first to know.'

He glanced down at her belly, flat under her pretty pink dress. 'And you're sure?'

'Sure as I can be.' Her smile faltered. 'Look, it's all right, you don't have to look so worried,' she said. 'I've asked around at the factory, pretending it was for a friend. They reckon there's a woman on the Mile End Road who helps out girls in trouble...'

'No!' Nick shook his head. 'You're not going to one of them butchers. I've wheeled too many girls down to the mortuary for that. I don't want to see that happen to you.'

'So what are we going to do?' Ruby licked her lips nervously.

Nick looked at her. He felt as if the bottom was dropping out of his world. Everything he wanted, everything he'd hoped for, was receding from him, and he couldn't stop it.

'Only one thing we can do, isn't there?' he said grimly.

Millie placed the bunch of daffodils on Maud Mortimer's grave. Father had chosen a nice spot for her in the churchyard, under blossom-laden cherry trees. Millie smiled to herself. She thought it was lovely here, but she could just imagine Maud complaining bitterly about the pink and white petals falling on her.

Her father had been very understanding when Millie had explained why she wanted Maud buried at Billinghurst. 'No one knows where the rest of her family is buried, and I don't want her to be alone. Does that sound very silly?'

'Not at all, my dear. I think it's very commendable of you to show such concern. I'll talk to Reverend Butler, and see if we can arrange a funeral for her here. We'll make sure she has a good send-off, don't you worry,' he reassured her.

Her grandmother, needless to say, didn't agree.

'What an extraordinary idea,' she'd declared. 'You'll be wanting strangers buried in the family vault next!'

But Millie would much rather have faced the dowager countess's despair over Maud's funeral arrangements than discuss the other subject she knew was playing on her mind.

She had been pressing Millie from the moment she'd arrived the previous evening.

'I assume you're here to see Sebastian?' she'd said at dinner. 'You do know he's staying at Lyford, don't you?' she added, with a searching look as Millie tried to hide her surprise.

'No, I didn't.'

'I am shocked. You are supposed to be his fiancée, after all.'

Millie helped herself to vegetables from the silver dish the footman was holding. She could feel her grandmother's eyes on her, and wondered if the rumours about her and Seb had reached Billinghurst yet.

'You must visit him, of course,' her grandmother said.

'No! I mean, I can't. I have to catch the lunchtime train back to London tomorrow. I'd rather spend the time I have with you and Daddy.'

She turned pleading eyes to her father, who shrugged helplessly. They both knew that once his mother had an idea in her head, there was no shaking it.

'Don't be silly, you have plenty of time. Unless there is a reason why you don't want to see him?' she added, narrowing her eyes across the table.

Millie stared down at her plate. Much as she'd tried to put it off, she knew it was inevitable that they would meet sometime.

'That's settled, then.' Her grandmother took her silence for assent. 'Benson will drive you over there in the morning.'

Millie tried to hide her wretchedness, but her father noticed.

'Really, Mother, must you interfere?' he rebuked her.

Lady Rettingham glared at him. 'Henry, if I didn't interfere, your daughter would still be a tomboy climbing trees and making rafts on the lake!' she replied with asperity.

Which was why, as Millie paid her respects to Maud in the churchyard on that fine April morning, Benson was waiting for her beyond the lychgate, standing patiently beside the Daimler, the brass buttons on his green coat glinting in the pale sunlight.

'Oh, Maud. What a mess.' Millie plucked a few petals off the neat patch of earth. 'What am I going to do when I see him? What am I going to say?'

Almost immediately she heard the old lady's voice in her head, and her final words.

No regrets.

It was too late for that, thought Millie. She was already bitterly regretting ending her engagement, but she couldn't see how that was ever going to change.

Benson sprang to attention as she came down the path out of the churchyard.

'Lyford, your ladyship?' he said, opening the door for her.

'I suppose so,' Millie sighed.

The duke and duchess were in London, so at least she was spared the awkwardness of meeting them. The butler informed her Lord Sebastian was out riding.

'He should return shortly, if you would like to wait?' he said, stepping back from the door.

'I'll wait for him in the stableyard.' Millie couldn't imagine anything worse than sitting in the drawing room, waiting for him to arrive. The sooner they got this awkward first meeting over with, the better. Her temples were already beginning to throb with pent-up tension.

At least in the yard she could relax for a moment. The duke was known for his ability to spot a good horse, and Millie enjoyed inspecting some of his latest acquisitions. The smell of leather and horseflesh and even the rotting smell of dung made her feel curiously reassured.

She was in the tack room chatting to one of the grooms when she heard the clatter of hooves on the cobbles. She went outside, shading her eyes from the sun, as Seb walked into the yard astride a magnificent grey stallion.

She had forgotten how handsome he was, his hair glinting golden in the sun. His fitted breeches and white shirt showed off his lean, hard-muscled body. She ached to run to him, but forced herself to stand rigidly in the shadows.

He didn't see her at first. She watched as the groom came out and caught the horse's bridle, then muttered something to Seb. He looked over and saw her, astonishment crossing his face.

'Millie? What are you doing here?'

'Hello, Seb.' She felt suddenly shy and tongue-tied.

He slipped from his horse, handed the reins to the groom and strode over to her. He stopped dead a few paces from her, as if there was an invisible fence keeping them apart.

'I didn't expect to see you here,' he said stiffly.

'I was visiting my family.'

'Ah. Of course.' He slapped his crop against his gleaming leather boots. The silence stretched between them.

'I was coming to see you,' he said finally, his gaze fixed on the muddy cobbles. 'I kept meaning to telephone or send a note. But then I put it off.'

'So did I.'

'I didn't really know what I was going to say.'

'Nor me,' she admitted.

'It's not easy, is it? Finding the right words.' His

452

smile was strained.

He was going to tell her it was over. She knew it, and she dreaded it, but she didn't know how to stop it. Her heart pounded in her ears, almost deafening her.

'I'm sorry,' Millie blurted out. 'I don't want us to be apart anymore. I hate not being engaged.'

He lifted his gaze to look at her, hope flashing in his blue eyes. 'I'm the one who should be apologising. I was a first-class idiot. I should have known better than to start laying down all those absurd rules and ultimatums.' His words came out in a rush of apology.

'No, no, it was my fault for being so stubborn, for thinking my nursing was so important–'

'It is important.'

'Not as important as you.'

They stared at each other for a moment, letting the meaning of their words sink in.

'You were quite right to throw my ring back at me – I think I would have done the same.' Seb looked rueful. 'Can you ever forgive me?'

'There's nothing to forgive.'

He held out his arms and Millie rushed into them, weeping with relief. They stood in the middle of the stable-yard, oblivious to everyone and everything around them, clinging to each other as if they would never let go.

'Oh, darling, I've missed you so much,' Seb murmured, pressing his lips into her hair. 'As soon as we walked away from each other that night, I knew I'd made the worst mistake of my life. But, stubborn idiot that I am, I couldn't bring myself to run after you. And then when I saw you at the christening...'

'But you were so cold to me.'

'I was doing my best to keep my distance!' he groaned. 'I thought it was what you wanted.'

'I looked for you,' Millie mumbled, against his chest. The smell of horses, sweat and leather mingled with the sharp lemony tang of his cologne. 'But Lucinda told me you'd gone off with Georgina Farsley. I thought you and she might be...' she trailed off, miserable at the memory.

'Georgina?' Seb laughed. 'How many more times do I have to tell you? I'm not remotely interested in that predator. She asked me to take her to the station because she wanted to make Jumbo jealous, that's all. Unfortunately for her, he was too drunk to notice she'd even gone!'

'They make a hopeless couple, don't they?' Millie smiled.

'They're not the only ones.' He held her closer, so she could feel the steady beat of his heart through his shirt. 'You don't know how close I've come to turning up at the nurses' home and battering the door down in search of you.'

'I wish you had.'

'I thought you'd just hate me more.'

'I could never hate you.' Millie pulled away from him. 'I've made up my mind,' she said. 'I want us to get married as soon as possible.'

He regarded her wanly. 'What's brought this on?'

'Just something someone said to me.' She told him about Maud Mortimer, and the last talk they'd had. 'It made me think about regrets, and I realised then I didn't want to regret losing you.'

'But you don't have to lose me,' he said. 'Don't

you see? I was a jealous fool, thinking I didn't want to share you with anything or anyone else. But I had no right to try to clip your wings like that. You love nursing, I realised that the night you took care of Sophia. And you're good at it, too. I suppose that was why I got so angry, because I realised how much you loved it.'

'But I love you more. And I can't wait to marry you.' She had expected him to take her in his arms and kiss her again, so the deep frown on his face disturbed her.

'I'm afraid you might have to,' he said. 'I'm leaving for Berlin next week.'

'Berlin!' She stared at him, shocked.

'The editor has offered me the chance to go over there and comment on the political situation. Just a few local colour pieces, but if I do well they might lead to a permanent job on the Foreign Desk. Isn't that marvellous?' he said.

Millie was barely listening. 'When were you going to tell me?' she asked numbly.

'That's why I was going to come and see you. But you rather beat me to it by coming here. Not that I'm complaining,' Seb added quickly. His blue eyes searched her face. 'Don't look like that, Mil. You should be pleased for me. This is my big chance. Just think, one day I could be the Chief Foreign Correspondent, rushing off to report on wars around the world!'

Millie shivered. 'Don't talk like that, Seb. We don't need any more wars. And you don't need to go all the way to Germany either. Why can't you go on being a journalist here?'

'Because I need to prove myself. Not just to the

editor – to myself.' His face was wistful. 'I think that's why I've been acting like such a fool lately. I felt – I don't know – as if I wasn't really any good at anything. You had your nursing, and I had nothing. I thought I needed you to give up your vocation for me, when really what I needed to do was to find a vocation of my own. Something to be proud of.'

'I'm proud of you,' Millie told him fiercely.

His smile was edged with sadness. 'That's not enough, Mil. I need to be proud of myself. You do understand that, don't you?'

How could she not understand? It was what had driven her from the ballrooms of Belgravia to a hospital in the backstreets of Bethnal Green.

'Of course I understand,' she said, suppressing a sudden rush of emotion. 'You mustn't take any notice of me, I'm just being silly and selfish because I know I'll miss you.'

'And I'll miss you. More than you could possibly imagine. Which is why I wondered if you wouldn't mind wearing this for me again?'

He reached into the pocket of his jacket. Millie saw the black velvet ring box and felt her eyes begin to sting with tears.

'My ring!'

'I've been carrying it around ever since you gave it back to me. I had it in my pocket on the day of the christening, but there didn't seem to be the right moment to ask you...' He flicked the box open, and she saw the diamonds and emeralds sparkling in its velvety depths. 'So I'm asking you now.' He sank down on to one knee.

'Seb!' Millie glanced around at the grooms who

were leaning over the stable doors, grinning. 'Get up! You'll be covered in mud.'

'Do be quiet, Millie, you're ruining the romance of the moment.' He held the ring up to her, his face solemn although there was a glint of amusement in his blue eyes. 'Amelia Benedict, will you do me the honour of agreeing to marry me? Again?'

Millie laughed. 'Put like that, I can't really say no, can I?'

Chapter Forty-Nine

'Engaged?'

Dora stared at June Riley as she sat at their kitchen table, drinking tea. It couldn't be true, it had to be a mistake. Not after all the promises he'd made.

'So they tell me.' June flicked the ash of her cigarette into her saucer. 'Reckon they're getting all the paperwork done this afternoon. *She* wants a proper church wedding.'

'Better get it done quick then.' Nanna Winnie sent them a knowing look as she sat in her rocking chair, shelling peas into her lap.

'That's what I thought.' June exhaled a thin stream of smoke from the corner of her mouth. 'She must be in the family way, that's all there is to it.'

'Hasn't your Nick said anything to you about it?'

457

'Me?' June laughed bitterly. 'I'm the last person he'd talk to about anything. But we all know he's a dirty little bastard. I'm surprised it's taken him this long to get caught.'

'At least he's doing the right thing by her.' Nanna tipped an apronful of peas into the bowl at her feet.

'Serves him right,' June muttered. 'That Ruby's a right little madam, she'll bring him down a peg or two. And as for her mother!' She stubbed out her cigarette in the saucer. 'If he thinks I'm bad, wait until he's got Lettie Pike bending his ear night and day.'

'They ain't going to be living with you, then?' Nanna said.

'Give over! Can you imagine that one living with us? We'd end up killing each other in a week!' June cackled. 'No, they're going to be moving in with the Pikes, God help 'em. Mind you, she's already got ideas about getting one of them fancy new flats the Corporation are putting up on Roman Road.'

'You wouldn't get me in one of those.'

'Nor me. But you know what these young 'uns are like.' June shook her head and delved into her packet for another cigarette. 'And that one's definitely set on going up in the world. Never mind about the rest of us. Who's going to keep an eye on our Danny if my Nick moves out, that's what I want to know?'

They both looked up as Dora got to her feet and grabbed her coat.

'Where are you going?' Nanna asked.

'I've got to get back to the hospital. I'm back on duty in an hour.'

'Ain't you going to stay to see your mum? She's only nipped out to take some mending back to the laundry.'

'Tell her I'll come round again in a couple of days.'

Dora left them gossiping and hurried outside. She waited until she was through the back gate and safely out of view in the alley before leaning against the wall to steady herself. The damp of the cold brickwork seeped through her thin coat but she hardly noticed as she stood there, eyes misted with tears, staring up at the narrow strip of grey, sunless sky between the crowded tenements.

Nick and Ruby were engaged. It made no sense. Just a few days ago he'd told Dora he loved her and had begged her to wait for him. She'd been floating on a cloud ever since, warmed by the knowledge that one day they would be together. She fell asleep at night, dreaming of his strong, protective arms around her, imagining the feel of his kiss...

But even then, in the back of her mind, she had wondered if it was all too good to be true. Now she knew that it was. Reality came crashing down, dropping her back on to the cold, wet cobbles of Griffin Street with shattered dreams and a heart made of lead.

She pulled herself together. She couldn't stand bawling her eyes out in the alleyway where her mum or one of the neighbours might come along at any moment. She was due back on the ward soon. And while Sister Everett was nowhere near as mean-spirited as Sister Wren, she still expected her nurses to be on time.

Dora's heart sank as she turned the corner towards the Nightingale and saw Nick and Ruby standing at the gates.

She was saying goodbye to him before he went to work. They looked very lovey-dovey, with Ruby's arms wound around his neck as she smiled up into his eyes, every inch the blushing bride-to-be.

Dora stopped in her tracks, panic washing over her. She couldn't bring herself to walk past them, but there was no other way in but through the big wrought-iron gates.

She was just about to retrace her steps around the corner and wait for them to go when Ruby spotted her.

'Dora! Over here!'

She saw Nick's head whip round, caught the stormy look on his face as she forced her feet to move towards them.

'I was hoping to see you.' Ruby clung to Nick. 'I s'pose you've heard our news?'

Dora nodded. She couldn't allow herself to look at him. 'It's the talk of Griffin Street. Congratulations.' Her throat was so dry she could barely croak out the word.

'Thanks, mate.' Ruby held out her left hand. 'What do you think?' She smiled, waggling her finger.

'It's – lovely.' Dora looked dutifully at the small diamond, but she couldn't take it in.

'We've just been to see the vicar, to get it all sorted out. He can't fit us in for a month, but it should be all right.' Ruby giggled and put a hand

460

over her flat belly. So Nanna and June were right, Dora thought. That explained it, but it didn't make it hurt any less.

'And I want you to be my bridesmaid, of course,' Ruby added.

Dora looked up sharply. 'Me?'

''Course. You're my best mate, silly. Who else would I have?'

Dora risked a quick glance at Nick. He looked as helpless and horrified as she did.

'Go on, say you'll do it?' Ruby begged her. 'I'll be so nervous on the big day, I'll need you with me to help me stay calm.'

All kinds of conflicting emotions battled inside Dora's head. Was it possible to hate and love someone at the same time? she wondered. She hated Ruby for taking away the man she loved. But looking into her smiling face, she realised none of this was her friend's fault. She was just a girl in love, planning her wedding and wanting everyone to share her happiness. How could Dora ever think of spoiling that for her?

If anything, she should hate Nick for raising her hopes and making her promises, and then crushing her dreams. But she couldn't do that either.

'I'd love to,' she said.

Ruby beamed. 'I'm glad,' she said. 'And you can help keep an eye on this one, make sure he doesn't go off with anyone else before the big day!'

Dora flashed Nick a guilty look. 'I'll do my best,' she muttered. She looked up at the clock tower. 'I must go, I'm due on duty soon.'

'I'll look at some patterns for dresses...' Ruby called after her as she hurried towards the main hospital buildings.

'Dora, wait!' She heard Nick's footsteps crunching on the gravel behind her and sped up.

'Can't stop, I'll be late,' she muttered, her gaze fixed straight ahead.

They passed the Porters' Lodge and she expected him to leave her alone, but he kept following her, through the archway of the main buildings and out into the cobbled courtyard.

'Dora, talk to me. Please!'

'I can't talk to you, I'll get into trouble. Anyway, there's nothing to talk about.'

'I'm sorry.' The desolation in his voice almost stopped her in her tracks, but she forced herself to keep walking. 'I tried to finish it with her, I really did.'

'But you ended up getting engaged instead?' She couldn't keep the bitterness out of her voice.

'She told me she was expecting. What else could I do?'

He was right, she thought. No matter how much she might want to scream and cry and rage at the unfairness of it all, he was right.

'There was nothing else you could do,' she said. 'There's nothing anyone can do now.'

The nurses' home was ahead of her. But before she could reach it, Nick suddenly grabbed her, pulling her around the side of the building to the overgrown patch where nurses went to hide from the Home Sister.

They crammed together in the narrow space between the brick wall and the tall hedge, so close she could see the rise and fall of his broad chest. It was torture, being so close to him and yet unable to touch him.

'Leave me alone,' she whispered. 'I have to get changed. Let me go.'

She made to move past him but he pushed her back against the wall, his body almost pinning hers. The male scent of him overwhelmed her.

'I can't let you go. That's the trouble. I love you.'

He tilted her chin, forcing her to stare into his navy-blue eyes, so full of pain and tenderness. There was something mesmerising about the harsh planes of his face, with its flattened boxer's nose and the sensuous curve of his mouth. Looking at him made her want to cry. 'I'll always love you, for the rest of my life. But you've got to understand, there's nothing I can do about it.' His voice was raw with emotion. 'I can't let Ruby go through this on her own. It's my responsibility and I have to face up to it. I'm trapped, Dora.'

'Why? Why did you have to do it?' She turned on him, anger coursing like molten metal through her veins. 'It didn't have to be like this, did it? This is *your* fault ... it's all your fault!'

'Don't you think I know that?' Tears glistened in his eyes. 'I wish I could turn the clock back. I'd do anything for none of this to have happened, for us to be together–'

'But we can't be, can we? We can't be together because of you!' Rage, frustration and pent-up pain burst inside her, and Dora beat him with her fists. 'I hate you!'

'You don't mean that.'

463

'I do! I hate you, Nick Riley.' Her fists pounded against the hard muscled wall of his chest. 'How could you do this, how could you–'

He reached up and grabbed her wrists, pinning them to her sides. Their eyes met and locked, and the next moment his mouth was on hers, kissing her passionately.

For a brief moment Dora surrendered to him, letting her body melt against his, giving in to the clamour of her own desperate longing. They kissed with the passionate urgency of two people who knew this would be the last time for both of them. She memorised every moment, the feel of his mouth exploring hers, the taste and smell of him, the rough stubble of his skin rasping against her...

She broke away from him. 'We can't,' she said.

'I know.' He sounded wretched. 'What do we do now?' he said gruffly.

'We walk away from each other. We walk away and never look back.'

His eyes met hers, dark and desolate with longing. 'I don't know if I can do that.'

'You must. You've got to do it, for Ruby and the baby. And you've got to do it for me, too.'

She looked down at their hands, still clinging to each other. 'You have to let me go. And I have to let you go. It's the only way.'

Her fingers curled around his hand. Part of her longed for him not to let go, to go on holding on to her for ever. But then, slowly, he pulled away, fingers slipping out of her grasp.

She took a deep, steadying breath. 'All the best, Nick,' she whispered. 'I hope you and Ruby will be very happy.'

Mustering every ounce of strength and courage she had, she turned and walked away, her legs shaking.

'Dora!' She heard him call her name, but she didn't look back. She couldn't look back. Not ever again.

Chapter Fifty

Millie woke up to a sea-scented breeze filtering through the faded curtains and the sound of sea-gulls screaming outside the window. She opened her eyes and looked across the pillow. Seb lay propped up on one elbow, watching her intently.

'Good morning, Mrs Smith,' he smiled.

Millie giggled, admiring the curtain ring on the third finger of her left hand. 'Do you think the landlady believed us?'

'Probably not. Especially when you started laughing as I was trying to sign the register.'

'You'll have to make an honest woman of me now.'

'I can't wait.' He leant over and planted a soft kiss on her brow. 'You don't regret this, do you?' he asked, his blue eyes suddenly serious.

'Why should I? It was my idea, remember?'

It was she who had suggested spending their last night together. And she had no doubt she had done the right thing. It might only have been a humble little bed and breakfast on the south coast and not the bridal suite of the Savoy, but last night couldn't have been more special or more perfect for Millie.

'No regrets.' She smiled up at him. 'How about you?'

His mouth curved. 'How can you even ask that, when I've been dreaming about this since the moment I met you?'

He kissed her, and she felt her body stirring with desire again. She had learnt the mechanics of sex while sitting in a draughty classroom, with Sister Parker scratching away in chalk on the blackboard, but the reality of lovemaking had been a revelation to her.

Seb pulled away and looked down at her again. He was so handsome first thing in the morning, his ruffled fair hair falling across his face, his lean muscled body glowing golden in the early sunlight. She put out her hand, marvelling at the warm, smooth feel of his skin.

He groaned at her touch. 'Don't!' He caught her hand and kissed the fingertips. 'We can't. I have to leave soon.'

Sadness swept over her. 'I wish you didn't have to go.'

'Right at this moment, so do I,' he admitted. 'But this is something I need to do. You understand that, don't you?'

Millie nodded. She knew he was excited at the prospect of flying out to Berlin, and the new adventure that awaited him there. Looking at his bright, eager face, she understood some of the heartache he must have felt while feeling she was slipping away from him.

'I don't want you to see me off at the airport,'

he said.

'Why not?'

'Because if you're there, I don't know if I'll be able to get on that plane.' He looked rueful.

'It's only for a few weeks,' she said. 'And I'll be here waiting for you when you get back.'

'Will you?'

She smiled. 'You know I will.'

She lay back, gazing at her makeshift wedding ring. 'Do you think we dare go down to breakfast?'

'Probably not.'

'I'm rather afraid of that landlady.'

'I've got a better idea anyway.' He rolled on top of her, pinning her down.

'Seb! I thought you said we didn't have time?' she laughed.

'I changed my mind,' he said, moving in for a long, lingering kiss.

There was already a queue outside the Queen's Theatre on Poplar High Street when they arrived.

Joe looked worried. 'I didn't think it would be this packed. The house doors aren't supposed to open up for another half an hour.'

'Don't fret, it'll be fine,' Dora reassured him.

'But you've been on your feet all day. You don't want to stand out here.' He frowned up at the sky. 'And it looks like it's going to rain.'

Dora smiled, in spite of her aching feet. It was true, she could have done with a sit down. But Joe had made such an effort, she didn't want him to think she didn't appreciate it.

'It'll be worth it,' she said.

467

'I hope so.' Bless him, he was so anxious to please. They'd been out twice in the past fortnight, and each time he had put so much effort into making sure she had a good time.

Last time they'd gone up west to a very fancy restaurant. 'Only the best for my girl,' he had said as he pulled out his wallet. Dora was grateful, but the truth was she had felt intimidated by her fancy surroundings. Instead of relaxing and enjoying herself, she'd spent the whole evening worrying in case she accidentally used the wrong fork or put her elbows on the table.

She looked at him, dressed up to the nines in his best suit. There weren't many young men who would go to so much trouble. But sometimes she wished he wouldn't try so hard to impress her.

Luckily there were several street entertainers to make the wait go quickly. Vendors walked up and down the queue, selling apples, oranges and hot roasted nuts. Joe bought them a bag of chestnuts which they shared while they watched the entertainment. First there were a couple of sand dancers in full Egyptian costume, followed by a fat middle-aged man with a bright red face and bushy sideburns. He stood at the front of the queue, belting out 'Danny Boy' at the top of his voice while his wife passed the hat around.

'Garn! Get off, you're rubbish!' Across the road, raggedly dressed children sat on the kerb eating chips out of newspaper and jeering at the free show.

'I hope the singers on the stage are better than he is,' Joe whispered to her.

'I hope he doesn't do himself an injury!' Dora

grimaced back.

No sooner had she said the words than some-thing very strange happened. The man stopped singing abruptly, his eyes went very wide and, with a strange choking sound, he sank to his knees.

'What's he doing now?' the children shouted from across the road.

'Is this part of the act?' someone behind them asked.

No one seemed very sure, until the man's wife let out a scream and sprinted back up the queue to her husband, scattering coins from her hat as she went.

Dora thrust the bag of nuts into Joe's hands and ran after her. He followed on her heels.

By the time they reached the man, he was lying on the pavement, his arms and legs jerking like a puppet on a string. A thin stream of froth was bubbling from between his lips.

'What is it, Bert? What's wrong?' His wife's voice was shrill with terror. Dora moved her gently aside and knelt down beside him.

'He's having a convulsion,' she explained, fingers already working frantically to loosen his collar studs. Flesh bulged over the edge of his tight collar.

'He's never had one before!' His wife looked outraged.

'Well, he's having one now.' She turned to Joe. 'Quick, give me something to put in his mouth to stop him biting his tongue.'

Joe patted his pockets. 'How about this?' he said, pulling a pencil out of his inside pocket.

Dora opened his mouth and wedged the pencil in between his teeth. She managed to snatch her hand out of the way before his jaws clamped shut. Then she pulled off her coat and put it over him.

'Take my jacket, too,' Joe shrugged it off and gave it to her. She bundled it up into a ball and put it under the man's head.

By the time the ambulance had arrived, the man had regained consciousness and was staring around in confusion.

'Don't try and move,' Dora advised. She looked at his wife, who seemed to be in a worse state than her husband. 'He'll be all right,' she said. 'He'll just need a warm drink and some time to recover quietly.'

The woman clutched Dora's hand. 'Thank you,' she whispered. 'I don't know what I would have done if you hadn't been here.'

'Looks like we've missed the show.' Joe nodded towards the doors, where the theatre manager was hanging up a sign saying 'House Full'. They'd been so involved with looking after the man they hadn't noticed the theatre doors opening and the queue starting to move.

'We couldn't very well leave him, could we?' Dora brushed herself down and put her coat back on.

'You did a good job, looking after him,' Joe said admiringly. 'You didn't even have to think about it.'

'If I'd thought about it, I probably wouldn't have done anything,' she admitted. 'We're not supposed to tend to emergencies on our own while we're training.'

They stood on the empty pavement, looking around them. 'What do we do now?' Joe said.

'I don't know. Go home, I suppose.' She shrugged.

Joe's frown deepened. 'But I wanted to give you a night to remember.'

'Oh, I don't think I'll forget tonight in a hurry, do you?' Dora said ruefully.

At that very moment, thunder cracked overhead and the heavens opened, emptying a deluge of rain that came so suddenly they didn't even have time to get to the nearest doorway before they were drenched.

They stood there staring at each other. Joe looked so comical, soaked from head to foot, fair hair dripping on to his outraged face, that Dora couldn't help laughing.

'It's not funny,' he grumbled.

'You're not standing where I am!'

'But everything's ruined. And I'd planned it so carefully. I wanted everything to be perfect. I wanted to give you the best night of your life–'

He looked at Dora, who was still laughing, and a reluctant smile started to tug at the corners of his mouth. Next minute he'd burst out laughing too.

'Look at us, a pair of drowned rats! Some evening this has turned out to be.' He shook his head. 'Now you'll never come out with me again.'

'I will ... as long as you stop trying so hard!'

He looked rueful. 'I just wanted to put the smile back on your face.'

'You've certainly done that!' Dora held on to

her aching sides.

It was true, she thought. It felt like such a long time since she'd really laughed at anything. What with her family's money problems, her mother's heartache over Alf, and her own sadness over Nick, there hadn't been much to smile about lately.

But now, with Joe, she felt her leaden heart begin to lighten. It was time to forget the past and to give him a chance to make her happy, she decided.

'You look lovely when you smile,' he said. 'You should do it more often.'

She looked up into his eyes, her eyes shining. 'Maybe I will,' she said.

'And to my wife Violet, I leave my full estate, where the context so admits the estate shall mean all my property of every kind wherever situate, and all my property of every kind wherever situate over which I have a general power of appointment, and the money, investments and property from time to time representing all such property...'

Violet watched the dust motes dancing in the sunlight as Mr Edgerton, the solicitor, talked. He had been talking for what seemed like hours, but all she could think about was escaping into the fresh air. The atmosphere in the office was stifling. The solicitor's droning voice and the musty smell of old books were beginning to make her head ache.

Mrs Sherman sat beside her, stiff and unmoving. Her face was rigid, but her fingers plucked at a loose thread on her coat.

Finally, Mr Edgerton finished speaking and laid down the thick parchment document. 'I believe that is everything,' he said. He peered over his spectacles at Violet. 'It seems your husband has left you a very wealthy woman, Mrs Dangerfield.'

Violet stared at him blankly.

'But they were estranged!' Mrs Sherman burst out, breaking the silence of the room. 'She hadn't lived with him for five years. That will is out of date!'

Mr Edgerton turned to look at her. 'I can assure you it isn't, Mrs Sherman.'

'And I can assure you it is!' Mrs Sherman's nostrils flared with anger. 'Mr Dangerfield told me himself he had rewritten his will so that everything went to his son. She got nothing!' She pointed a shaking finger at Violet. 'He told me everything was to be held in trust, and I was to administer it on Oliver's behalf until he came of age. He said–' Her voice quivered with emotion, and she fought for control. 'He said he would see to it that I always had a roof over my head.' She looked at the solicitor, her pale eyes wild and bulging. 'You came to the house yourself, Mr Edgerton. Just before he passed away.'

'You are correct, Mrs Sherman. Mr Dangerfield did amend his will, two weeks before he died.' Mr Edgerton picked up the piece of parchment. 'This is the amended will, I promise you. You may see the date and his signature, if you wish?' He offered it to her but she looked away, her mouth pressed into a thin, angry line. 'I'm afraid that perhaps your employer misled you as to his intentions...'

His voice was sympathetic.

Violet glanced across at Mrs Sherman's face, blank with shock.

'Very well,' the older woman said, her chin lifting. Without looking at Violet, she said, 'If Mrs Dangerfield will allow me some time to pack my belongings and find a new place to live, I will leave Curlew House as soon as possible.'

'You don't have to go.' Violet found her voice at last and turned to the solicitor. 'I don't want my husband's money, Mr Edgerton. Not a penny of it. I never did.' She cast a quick sideways glance at Mrs Sherman. 'I am content for the estate to be placed in trust for my son. And I would like Mrs Sherman to go on living in Curlew House. I know she will take care of it for Oliver.'

Mr Edgerton frowned. 'And you would be agreeable to this, Mrs Sherman?'

Mrs Sherman's lips parted but no sound came out. She gave the curtest of nods.

'Well, I suppose ... although this does seem most unusual.' He peered at Violet. 'If you're sure, Mrs Dangerfield? You might want to reconsider–'

'I won't,' she said firmly. 'And my name is Tanner. Violet Tanner,' she corrected him.

After the meeting, she and Mrs Sherman found themselves out in the street together.

'I suppose I should thank you,' the older woman said stiffly, as if each word pained her.

'There's no need, I assure you,' Violet replied, equally coldly.

'I will take good care of the house ... for Oliver.'

'I have no doubt of that.'

There was a tense silence. Violet was just about

to walk away, when Mrs Sherman suddenly said, 'I don't understand ... Mr Dangerfield told me he had changed the will. He promised he would take care of me.'

Violet looked at her lined, gaunt face. She looked so old and afraid, Violet wondered why she had ever been so terrified of her.

Poor Mrs Sherman. In a way, she had been as much a victim of Victor's sick, twisted cruelty as she had.

'He promised he would take care of me too, Mrs Sherman,' she said softly. 'Now perhaps you can see what kind of man he really was.' She pulled on her gloves. 'If you'll excuse me, I have to go to work.'

Oliver was already there, waiting for her. Miss Hanley had kindly volunteered to collect him from school, although Violet suspected it wouldn't be long before he was making his own way home. She watched him running around with Sparky on the lawn, watched fondly by Sister Sutton as she tended her garden. Later they would have tea together, and when it was her night off, Violet would join Sister Blake and the other sisters for choir practice.

She smiled to herself. Victor might have left her a house, but she had already found a home.

This Large Print Book for the partially sighted, who cannot read normal print, is published under the auspices of

THE ULVERSCROFT FOUNDATION

THE ULVERSCROFT FOUNDATION

... we hope that you have enjoyed this Large Print Book. Please think for a moment about those people who have worse eyesight problems than you ... and are unable to even read or enjoy Large Print, without great difficulty.

You can help them by sending a donation, large or small to:

**The Ulverscroft Foundation,
1, The Green, Bradgate Road,
Anstey, Leicestershire, LE7 7FU,
England.**
or request a copy of our brochure for more details.

The Foundation will use all your help to assist those people who are handicapped by various sight problems and need special attention.

Thank you very much for your help.